A

MARVELLOUS

LIGHT

TOR
DOT
COM

A TOM DOHERTY ASSOCIATES BOOK
NEW YORK

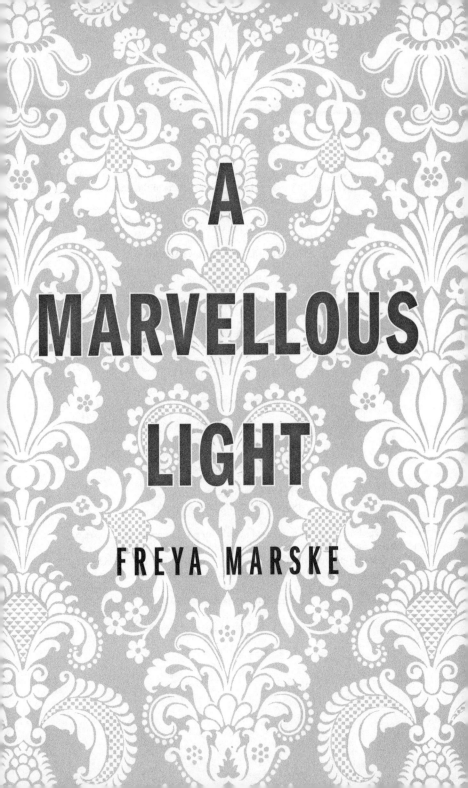

A MARVELLOUS LIGHT

FREYA MARSKE

A MARVELLOUS LIGHT

Copyright © 2021 by Freya Marske

Edited by Ruoxi Chen

A Tordotcom Book
Published by Tom Doherty Associates
120 Broadway
New York, NY 10271

www.tor.com

Tor® is a registered trademark of Macmillan Publishing Group, LLC.

The Library of Congress Cataloging-in-Publication Data
is available upon request.

ISBN 978-1-250-78887-0 (hardcover)
ISBN 978-1-250-78889-4 (ebook)

Our books may be purchased in bulk for promotional, educational, or business use. Please contact your local bookseller or the Macmillan Corporate and Premium Sales Department at 1-800-221-7945, extension 5442, or by email at MacmillanSpecialMarkets@macmillan.com.

First Edition: November 2021

Printed in the United States of America

0 9 8 7 6 5 4 3 2 1

*For the bar at the end of the universe
and everyone the devil met there.*

A

MARVELLOUS

LIGHT

1

Reginald Gatling's doom found him beneath an oak tree, on the last Sunday of a fast-fading summer.

He sat breathing rapidly and with needle-stabs at each breath, propped against the oak. His legs were unfelt and unmoving like lumps of wax that had somehow been affixed to the rest of him. Resting his hands on the numb bulk of them made him want to vomit, so he clutched weakly at grass instead. The tree's rough bark found skin through one of the tears in his bloodstained shirt. The tears were his own fault; he hadn't started to run in time, and so the best route of escape had appeared to be through a tangle of bramble-hedge that edged the lake here in St. James's Park. The brambles had torn his clothes.

The blood was from what had come after.

"Look at him panting," said one of the men, scorn thick in his voice. "Tongue out like a dog."

The best that could be said about this man at present was that he stood partly between Reggie and the glare of the sun, which was dipping slowly through the afternoon sky, cradled in a tree-fork of blue space like a burning rock pulled back in a slingshot. Hovering. Waiting. At any moment it could be released and come flying towards them, and they'd all be brightly obliterated.

Reggie coughed, trying to banish the nonsense simmering in his mind. His ribs spasmed with renewed pain.

"Now, now," said the other man. "Let's at least be civil."

This voice was not scornful. It was as calm and uncaring as the sky itself, and the last shreds of courage in Reggie shrivelled up to hear it.

"*George,*" Reggie said. An appeal.

The calm-voiced George was facing out into the park, presenting Reggie with a view of the silken back of his waistcoat and the white of his shirtsleeves: cuffs rolled up fastidiously, but still speckled with blood. He was surveying the open green space at the foot of the slight incline crowned by the oak tree. On this summer Sunday, St. James's was busy with humanity taking their last gulps of fine weather before autumn closed over their heads. Herds of children shrieked and ran, or fell out of trees, or tossed pebbles at the indignant ducks. Groups of friends picnicked, couples strolled with aimless leisure, ladies bumped parasols as they passed one another on the paths and used the excuse to adjust the fall of their lace sleeves. Men lay dozing with boaters tipped over their faces, or nibbled on grass blades as they reclined on an elbow and turned the pages of a book.

None of these people looked back at George, or at Reggie, or at the other man; and even if they did, their gazes passed on without focus or concern. None of them had so much as glanced over when the screaming had started. Nor when it continued.

Reggie could only just glimpse the pearly whisper of uneven air that signified the curtain-spell.

George turned, stepped closer, and hunkered down, careful with his trousers, brushing a speck of dirt from the polished toe of his shoe. Reggie's entire body, wax-legs and all, tried to flinch back from George's smile. His nerves remembered pain and wanted to press the body itself into the rough bark, through it—to dissolve somehow.

But the tree was unyielding, and George was too.

"Reggie, my dear boy." George sighed. "Shall we try this again? I know you found part of it on your own, and thought you could get away with hiding it from us."

Reggie stared at him. The sharp, surprised wail of a child who'd likely scraped his knee rose somewhere in the distance.

"What earthly good did you think it would do you?" George asked. "You, of all people?" He stood again—the question clearly rhetorical—and made a curt gesture to his companion, who took his place in front of Reggie.

Get on with it, thought Reggie, squinting at the uncovered ball of the sun. *Hurl yourself at us. Now would be ideal.*

"You found the thing. You snatched it. Now, tell us what it is," the man demanded.

"I can't," said Reggie, or tried to. His tongue spasmed.

The man brought his hands together. There was no finesse to his technique, but by God he was fast; his fingers flickered through the crude shapes of the cradles and came alive with the white glow of his spell before Reggie could so much as inhale. Then he took hold of Reggie's hands. His grip was inescapable. His heavy brows drew together and he frowned down at Reggie's palms as though he were about to read Reggie's fortune and tell him what his future would be.

Short, thought Reggie hysterically, and then the white crawled over his skin and he screamed again. By the time it ended, one of his fingers stood at an awful angle where it had twitched itself out of the man's grip.

"What is it?"

This time, the bind sensed Reggie's desperation to comply and answer the question. His tender, throbbing tongue now felt as it had when the spell had been laid in the first place: branded and sizzling. He whined around it, clutching at his face. The sound he made seemed to crawl in the air, and yet it affected the park-idyll not in the slightest. The people around them could have been figures in a painting, blissfully unaware of a small child throwing a tantrum on the gallery's marble floor, safe on the other side of the frame.

"Fucking hell," the man said. "You bloody little worm. M'lord. Look."

"Damn and blast" was George's comment, staring down at Reggie's tongue. The symbol of the bind must have been glowing there. It felt like it. "He didn't do that to himself. Still, there are limits to a secret-bind. Ways to wriggle around its edges." He frowned. "What is it, Reggie? Play a game of charades, if you must. Write it, draw it in the dirt. Find a way."

A scrap of hope rose in Reggie at the idea. When he tried to move his hands, they burned with a flash of reproving heat, then went as stubbornly unresponsive as his legs. No. It wasn't going to be that easy for any of them.

George's eyes were narrowed. "Very well. Where is it now?"

Reggie shrugged in complete honesty.

"Where did you last see it?"

The pain of the bind gave a wary pulse, and Reggie didn't dare test his voice. But this time his hands lifted when he told them to, and he waved them frantically.

"Ey," said the other man. "Now we're getting someplace."

"Indeed." George looked out over the park again. He shifted his gaze north, then kept turning, a slow circle like a man lost and seeking landmarks. When he had rotated fully on the spot, he began to build a spell of his own, with the elegant mastery of a jeweller laying minuscule cogs.

George flung his magic-brimming hands wide and a map appeared in the air in front of Reggie, as though a small tablecloth had been shaken out and hung over a line. Blue lines glowed in the air against a background of nothingness. The thickest line formed the familiar snake of the Thames, and the city spilled out around it.

Reggie jabbed at the approximate location of his office. Nothing palpable met his fingers, but the map changed at once, showing a much smaller portion of London. The river formed the eastern and southern borders, and it stretched out to Kensington in the west and followed the northern border of Hyde Park. It was a lovely spell. Reggie wondered what level of detail he would discover, if he kept jabbing and jabbing.

"Not where we are now, you imbecile."

This time, Reggie managed to indicate the building itself: ironically, yes, a bare stone's throw to the east from where they were, though Reggie's finger fell closer to Whitehall than the St. James's end.

"Your office?" For the first time George sounded surprised.

Reggie managed to nod before the dormant bind seared up in punishment. He barely noticed when the map flickered into nothing. He kept his tongue thrust out as though he could somehow shove the pain away, and tears ran down his face. The two men were looking across the park in the direction of the building.

"Do we—" the other man began.

"No," said George. "And that's all we'll get past the bind, I expect. It's enough. Finish up." George didn't look at Reggie. "We're done here."

Again, the man in the cap moved fast. The second-last thing that Reggie saw was the tide of white, cobwebbing up to cover his entire body. The last thing he saw, as he took his last breath, was the sun glinting off the top of George's walking stick as George strolled through the curtain of his own spell and down the hill, unhurried, a man with nowhere in particular to be.

2

Robin was definitely going to punch someone before the day was out.

Currently topping his list of ideal candidates were his family's estate steward and the chap who'd managed to stab Robin's foot with his umbrella on the front steps of the Home Office this morning. And although Robin would never hit a woman, the frayed edge of his mood was unravelling further with the incessant tapping of his typist's ring against her desk.

Robin gritted his teeth. He was not going to set himself up as a tyrant and snap at the girl over trifles, not on his very first day in this job. He would hold out for the prospect of going to his boxing club and venting his feelings with a willing opponent.

The ring-tapping halted as footsteps heralded someone entering the outer office. Robin sat up straighter behind his desk and moved one ragged pile of paperwork a few inches to the left in a doomed attempt to make the whole thing look less like a hurricane had blown through a library. This would be his nine o'clock meeting, then.

Hopefully the other person would have a bloody clue what they were meant to be meeting *about*.

"Mr. Courcey!" came Miss Morrissey's voice. "Good mor—"

"Is he in?"

"Yes, but—"

The footsteps didn't halt, and the speaker strode right into the room.

"What have you been doing, I was—" Silence snatched the man's words away as his eyes landed on Robin. He stopped dead a few steps inside the door, which was also a few steps from Robin's desk; it was a very small office.

Robin swallowed. For less than a second, there had been relief in the newcomer's voice and rather a charming smile on his face. They had vanished with such abrupt, chilling totality that Robin could almost convince himself he'd imagined them.

The man shifted a leather folder from one hand to the other. He was slim and pale, with fair, colourless hair and a face currently folded into an unpleasant expression that suggested he'd stepped in something on the street and its odours had only just reached his nose.

It was, Robin reflected wistfully, an eminently punchable face.

"What the bloody hell is this? Where's Reggie?"

"Who's Reggie?" It had already been a difficult morning. Robin was not above returning fire with rudeness where rudeness had been offered. "Who are you, come to that?"

A pair of blue eyes narrowed. They were the only mark of colour in the man's countenance—indeed, in his entire appearance. His clothes were neat, expensively tailored, but all in shades as unremarkable and drab as his dishwater hair.

"I'm the Queen of Denmark," he said, coldly sardonic.

Robin clasped his hands on the desk to prevent himself from clinging to the edge of it. He was the one who belonged here, much as he wished otherwise. "And I'm Leonardo da Vinci."

Miss Morrissey appeared in the doorway, possibly having sensed the likelihood of blood being drawn if the edges to their voices got any keener. Robin managed not to stare at her as he'd done when they'd first met, barely a quarter of an hour ago. He had met Indians before, of course—and even come across some lady civil servants, rare creatures though they were. But he'd never expected to have an example of both categories calmly introduce herself as Miss Adelaide Harita Morrissey, his sole subordinate, and fire a series of reproachful comments at him about how the Minister really could have found a replacement sooner, if Mr. Gatling had been moved into a new position, and she was sorry about the mess on the desk but maybe they could get a start on it after his first meeting, which was in—goodness, five minutes, go ahead and take a seat and should she fetch some tea?

Now Miss Morrissey laid a hand on the Queen of Denmark's arm. "Mr. Courcey," she said hurriedly. "This is Sir Robert Blyth. He's Mr. Gatling's replacement."

Robin winced, then cursed himself for it. He'd have to get used to hearing the damn honorific sooner or later.

"Sir Robert," she went on, "this is Mr. Edwin Courcey. He's the special liaison. You'll be working mostly with him."

"Replacement." Courcey looked sharply at her. "What happened to Reggie?"

Reggie, Robin had gathered by now, was Gatling. If he and Courcey had been on friendly terms, and Gatling hadn't bothered to tell his colleague that he'd moved on—or been moved on, His Majesty's Civil Service being what it occasionally was—then that would explain his surprise, if not his generally unpleasant demeanour.

Miss Morrissey didn't look pleased. "Nobody's told me anything. I did try to tell the Secretary's Office—*and* the Assembly—that vanishing without word for a fortnight is odd even for Reggie. And on Friday I received a curtly worded note, saying that a replacement would be here on Monday. And here he is."

Courcey directed his look at Robin. "*Sir* Robert. Who are you related to that I'd know?"

"Nobody in particular, I'm sure," said Robin through his teeth. Perhaps that wasn't entirely true; his parents had been well known. They'd made sure of that. But barefaced snobbery made Robin feel contrary.

"Oh, for God's—" Courcey cut himself off. "I don't suppose it matters. Thank you, Miss Morrissey."

The typist nodded and swept back to her own desk, closing the door behind her.

Robin shifted in his seat and tried not to feel trapped. It really was a cramped office, and dark to boot. The sole window lurked awkwardly near the ceiling as though to say it was there on sufferance and didn't intend to provide anything so pleasant as a view.

Courcey installed himself in the chair across the desk from Robin, opened his folder to a blank piece of paper, pulled a pen from a pocket of his waistcoat, and laid them both on the desk with the air of someone not prepared to have his time wasted.

"As she said, I'm the liaison for the Minister, which means—"

"Which Minister?"

"Hah," said Courcey sourly, as though Robin had made an unfunny joke instead of a desperate enquiry.

"No, I mean it," said Robin. "You're going to give me a straight answer. I can't sit here all day pretending I know what the blazes I'm meant to be doing, because I *don't*. It took me an hour to find this place this morning, and that was mostly by knocking on doors. *Assistant in the Office of Special Domestic Affairs and Complaints.* And this is it! The entire office! I don't know which department or commission it falls under! I don't even know who I report to!"

Courcey raised his eyebrows. "You report directly to Asquith."

"I—what?"

There was no way that could be right. This nothing position, so lowly that nobody had heard of it—and yet, muttered part of Robin's brain, he had his *own typist,* instead of access to a room of them—had been given to Robin because his parents had managed to make an enemy of the wrong person, and Robin was wearing the consequences. Healsmith wouldn't have looked so smug if he was handing Robin a job that reported directly to the Prime Minister.

Courcey's mouth looked lemon-ish now. "You really don't
even know what the job is."

Robin shrugged uncomfortably.

"Special affairs. Special liaison." Courcey did something with
his hands, moving his fingers together and apart. "Special. You
know."

"Are you some kind of . . . spy?" Robin hazarded.

Courcey opened his mouth. Closed his mouth. Opened it
again. "Miss Morrissey!"

The door opened. "Mr. Courcey, you—"

"*What*," said Robin, "*is your pen doing?*"

There was a long pause. The office door closed again. Robin
didn't look up to confirm that Miss Morrissey had prudently
kept herself on the other side of it. He was too busy gazing at
Courcey's pen, which was standing on one end. No—it was
moving, with its nib making swift loops against the uppermost
sheet of paper. The date had been written in the top-right corner: Monday 14th September, 1908. The ink—blue—was still
drying. As Robin watched, the pen slunk back to the left margin of the paper and hovered there like a footman who was
hoping nobody had seen him almost drop the saltcellar.

Courcey said, "It's a simple enough . . ." and then stopped.
Perhaps because he had realised he was applying the word *simple* to something that was anything but.

Perhaps not.

Robin's mind was oddly blank, as it had been sometimes at the
end of a particularly fiendish examination, as if he'd scooped
out its worthwhile contents with his fingers and smeared them
grimly onto the page. The last time he'd felt this way was when
he found out that his parents were dead. Instead of surprise,
this. An exhausted, wrung-out space.

Robin waved his hand between the pen and the ceiling.
Nothing. No wires. He didn't even know how wires would

have worked to create such a thing. But the action seemed necessary, a last gasp of practicality before acceptance flooded in.

He said, with what he could already tell was going to be a pathetic attempt at levity: "So when you said *special . . .*"

Courcey was now regarding Robin as though Robin were an unusual species of animal, encountered in the wild and possessing a large mouth full of larger teeth. He looked, in short, as though he were bracing himself to engage in a wrestling match, and was wondering why Robin hadn't pounced yet.

They stared at each other. The room's weak light caught on the pale tips of Courcey's lashes. He was not a handsome man, but Robin had never been inspected this closely by other men except as a prelude to fucking, and the sheer intimate intensity of it was sending confusing signals through Robin's body.

"You know," said Robin, "I'm beginning to suspect there's been a mistake."

"How astute of you," said Courcey, still with that lion-tamer tension.

"I might be lacking one or two vital qualifications for this position."

"Indeed."

"I suppose your pal Gatling could conjure pigeons from his desk drawers with a snap of his fingers too."

"No," said Courcey, the syllable drawn out like toffee. "This position's still part of the Home Office, it's not a magician's job. *I'm* the liaison to the Chief Minister of the Magical Assembly."

"Magical. Magician. Magic." Robin glanced at the pen again. It continued to hover, serene. He took a long breath. "All right."

"All right?" The humanising note of exasperation was matched by something flaring in Courcey's face. "Honestly? You expect me to believe this is the first time you've come across any kind of magic, and you're sitting there without so much as—and the best you can muster is *all right*?" The blue eyes searched him again. "Is this a joke? Did Reggie put you up to this?"

It seemed late in the day to be asking that question. Robin wanted to laugh. But Courcey hadn't asked it with anything so normal as hope. The light in his face had retreated, as though someone holding a candle up to glass had taken a few steps backwards. It was the resigned expression of someone on whom jokes were often played, and who knew he was expected to laugh afterwards even if they were more cruel than funny. Robin had seen the candle-flicker of this expression at his parents' sumptuous dinner parties, when the person making the joke was most often Lady Blyth herself.

"It's not a joke," he said firmly. "What else do you want me to say?"

"You aren't going to suggest that you must be going mad?"

"I don't feel mad." Robin reached out and touched the pen. He had expected it to be immovable in the air, but it allowed him to take hold of it and move it around. When released, it floated without urgency back to hover near the margin of the paper.

"How does it know what you want it to do?"

"It's not sentient," said Courcey. "It's an imbuement."

"A what?"

Courcey took a deep breath and clasped his hands together. Robin, who had suffered under long-winded tutors at Pembroke, recognised the symptoms and braced himself.

Sure enough, the words quickly stopped making sense. Apparently magic was as inherently fiddly as Latin grammar, and required the same sort of attention to detail even when constructing what Courcey described as a minor object imbuement.

The pen, apparently seized with the desire to be helpful, transcribed everything Courcey was saying in a neat, spiky hand. It didn't make any more sense written down. Robin's eye caught on the phrase *like a legal contract* as Courcey was explaining how British magicians used a shorthand of gesture called cradling in order to define the terms of any given spell, including those that rendered an innocent pen capable of darting fussily back and forth across the paper.

"Does the pen sign the contract itself?" said Robin, struggling to stay afloat. This won him another of the suspicious, flat-mouthed looks that meant Courcey thought he was trying to be funny. "Show me something else," Robin tried instead. "Anything."

A corner of Courcey's lip tucked between and drew out of his teeth. He pulled something from the same pocket that had housed the magical pen, and glanced over his shoulder as if to reassure himself that the door was closed.

Excitement crawled over Robin's scalp. He didn't think Courcey actually meant him any harm; the man was far too prickly. If he'd been trying for charm Robin might have been worried.

What Courcey had pulled from his pocket was a loop of plain brown string, which he wrapped around both of his hands. He then held them about a foot and a half apart, pulling the string taut.

"Like scratch-cradle," said Robin. And then *"Oh"* as the light dawned. "Cradling."

"Yes. Now be quiet." The lip did its disappearing act again. Courcey's fair brows drew together.

Scratch-cradle was an activity for pairs: one person to hold the strings, the other to pinch them and twist them into a new position. Courcey was doing it alone, and the complex pattern forming as he hooked his fingers, moving loops of string around with his thumbs, bore no resemblance to the soldier's bed or the manger or any of the other figures that Robin remembered from playing the game in nursery days.

Robin's own hands, resting on the desk, began to feel as though he were holding them over the cracked lid of an icebox. He could almost imagine that his breath was beginning to mist as it did in winter, and that Courcey's was doing the same.

It was.

The mist became a single dense cloud between them, a white clump the size of a walnut. Courcey's fingers kept moving like supple crochet hooks. After nearly a full minute, something emerged, glittering.

Robin had never been the sort to pore over the proceedings of the Royal Society, and had never personally applied his eye to a microscope. But he knew what this shape was. The snowflake was only the size of a penny, but the light caught on it, showing up tiny complexities and flashes of colour. It was still growing.

Something more than scorn was seeping into Courcey's expression now, like watercolour applied with the very tip of a brush to a wetly swept piece of paper. Concentration. Satisfaction. He kept his eyes on the growing snowflake and plucked at a single part of the tangled web of string with his forefinger, again, again, keeping up a steady rhythm.

When the snowflake had reached the size of a small apple, Courcey moved his fingers more quickly, and the snowflake sagged and dripped into a puddle of water on Robin's desk.

Some sort of reaction seemed expected. Robin didn't know what to say. He'd felt a pang when the snowflake, so carefully built, had melted. He was quietly, startlingly charmed that for all his curt, practical manner, Courcey had chosen such a pretty kind of magic to show Robin. He wanted to say that it reminded him of a snow painting by the Frenchman Monet, sold just last year at one of his parents' charity auctions, but he felt awkward about it.

"That was lovely," he said, in the end. "Can anyone do it? If it's just a matter of—making contracts, and learning what to do with your hands."

"No. You're either born with magic or you aren't."

Robin nodded in relief. The whole thing was still strange and fascinating and barely credible. But here he was, credulous, and nobody was going to expect him to make some sort of meticulous contract with an intangible force by waving his fingers around, so it seemed like something he could live with.

"But if this is a job for people who *aren't*," he said, "surely you've got to be used to explaining about the whole—special—nature of it."

"Usually the Chief Minister advises on the appointment. Someone's cousin. Someone with no magic, but who knows magic." Courcey frowned. "Secretary Lorne is a friend of the Minister's, he's always understood . . ."

"Oh," said Robin. "No, it wasn't Lorne. He's on a leave of absence. Something with his wife's health. It was Healsmith who gave me the job."

Courcey shook his head, frown deepening. "Don't know him. And if *he* doesn't know—devil take it, what a mess. And none of this explains where Reggie's gone and why the position's available to begin with." He stood, tucked both pen and string away, picked up his folder, and turned to leave.

"Wait," Robin blurted. "Aren't we meant to be . . . meeting?"

"Dealing with an unbusheling is enough for one day. I don't have time to walk you through the job as well. Ask Miss Morrissey—by the sounds of it, she's seized the reins anyway." He tapped the folder. "This can wait until tomorrow." The hints of emotion were gone again. This look said that Courcey wouldn't be unhappy if he returned to find that Robin had disappeared from this office with the same suddenness with which he'd appeared.

Courcey left. Robin drew his fingertip through the small pool of water on the desk, streaking it.

"Sir Robert?"

"Miss Morrissey." Robin pulled a smile onto his face. Simply having it there made his shoulders relax.

His typist closed the office door and leaned on it. "Mercy, what a mess."

"That's what Courcey said."

"I didn't know you didn't know." Miss Morrissey's version of the lion-tamer look was, alarmingly, more fearless than Courcey's. She looked as though she were calculating the going rate for lion skins. Robin was calculating the odds that she'd had a glass pressed to the door during the last few minutes. "I've never been part of an unbusheling before. What did he show you?"

"Unbusheling?"

"*We are man's marvellous light?* Oh, no, you wouldn't—the English slang's biblical, obviously, and the French say *déclipser.* Their idea of a pun. In Punjabi it's got nothing to do with light, it's either a snakeskin being shed or the tide going out, depending on where you are—"

"Stop," said Robin. This really was like being back at university. "I beg you, Miss Morrissey. Pretend I'm very stupid. Small words."

"Unbusheling. A revelation of magic." Miss Morrissey looked apologetic. "Perhaps I'll fetch that tea?"

"Tea," said Robin with relief. "Just the thing."

Fifteen minutes later they'd demolished the pot between them, as well as a plate of shortbread. Robin had learned that Adelaide Harita Morrissey had sat the competitive exam to work for the General Post Office, then was poached out of a junior supervisory role by Secretary Lorne himself, because her grandfather was a member of his club and had dropped her name right when Lorne was digging around for someone—"Like me," she finished, through biscuit crumbs. "Like Reggie—Mr. Gatling."

"You haven't any . . . magic?"

"Not a drop," she said cheerfully. "All went to my sister. Now, let's get you properly settled in."

The position of Assistant in the Office of Special Domestic Affairs and Complaints, Robin discovered, was a bewildering mixture of intelligence analysis, divination, and acting as a glorified messenger boy. He was to comb through complaints, letters, and hysterical newspaper stories, working out which of them might represent real magic. Anything suspicious he was to collate and pass on to the liaison. Courcey.

In exchange, Courcey would tell him of anything upcoming

that might be noticed by ordinary people, or that the magical bureaucracy thought it necessary for the Prime Minister to know. At two o'clock on a Wednesday, Robin would deliver a briefing.

To the PM. In person. It was quite mad.

One of the hurricane piles on the desk was mail; some was addressed to Gatling by name, and unopened. Those letters directed to the office itself had been gutted with a letter opener then conscientiously re-stuffed.

"I've been doing most of it for weeks, really," said Miss Morrissey, running her finger along the furred edge of an envelope. "Reggie rather dumped me in the midden, even before he disappeared. He's been running all over the country. Chasing reports, so he said. He was acting like he was on the track of something very important and mysterious, but I thought he was just bored." She turned the ring on her second finger, pensive. "He's never been very suited to sitting patiently behind a desk."

"You do realise this has all been an absurd mistake," said Robin. "How am I supposed to pick what's—your lot—and what's sheer nonsense? I've not grown up with this. I'll be stabbing in the dark."

Miss Morrissey's look may as well have accused Robin of tipping her back into the midden.

Robin weakened. "But I'll help as much as I can, of course. Until Courcey talks to his Minister and gets this all ironed out. Until someone suitable can take my place. I'm sure it'll only be a few days."

3

It was raining when Edwin left the Home Office. A smell of petrol fumes rose from the wet streets, cut with damp wool and something rich and startlingly organic, like a bed of soil freshly turned. Edwin noticed it with the part of his mind that held him back from stepping in the paths of carriages and motorcars. The rain tapped gently on his hat and coat, and beaded the leather of his briefcase.

He was on a street corner when he stopped, hand abrupt and white-knuckled on the wet metal of a lamppost, and took a few deep breaths with his eyes closed.

He should have stayed in the bloody room. Leaving a complete stranger alone in the wake of an unplanned unbusheling, even in the hands of a girl with as much common sense as Adelaide Morrissey, was foolish. And Edwin Courcey wasn't a fool. It was the one thing he had to pride himself on.

He certainly couldn't congratulate himself on his pluck. Given even a morsel of courage, he would have made an attempt to know Reggie better. He would have taken Reggie up on the offer to tag along on that useless ghost-chasing trip to North Yorkshire a month ago. Or even offered to meet Reggie for drinks, or a show, or whatever it was that thousands of young men did with their friends.

Maybe then Edwin would have some idea of the fellow's haunts, beyond his home address. Edwin hadn't been able to wrangle any details out of Reggie's landlady since the first day he'd been there. Mr. Gatling had not been home, as per the usual pattern. Mr. Gatling was going to find himself behind in the rent if he didn't show himself someday soon.

Which left Edwin with this. He'd been avoiding it, but today he didn't have much choice. The word *replacement* rattled inside his skull. This wasn't another of Reggie's irresponsible jaunts. If Reggie had been replaced, then someone had given up on expecting him to return.

The walk to Kensington took nearly an hour, and the rain neither vanished nor intensified to the point where Edwin would have surrendered and hailed a cab. His destination was a house in Cottesmore Gardens, a forbiddingly crisp concoction of gleaming windows and washed brick. The Gatlings' butler took Edwin's name and had barely vanished with it for a minute before Anne Gatling appeared. She beckoned Edwin into the front parlour and paused in the doorway to raise her voice down the hall, flicking a stream of raw red sparks from her fingers, clearly a private signal between sisters.

"Dora! It's Win Courcey!"

"Edwin," said Edwin.

Anne blew the last sparks from her fingertips and came fully into the room. She couldn't have been many years off thirty and was only recently affianced, despite sharing in her family's impeccable dark good looks. Having the unmagical Reggie as a brother was a count against the Gatling girls, in their circles; who knew if their own power could be trusted to breed true?

"Hullo, Win," she said amiably. Edwin thought about correcting her again. He discarded the idea before she took breath to add, "How's Bel? I haven't seen her in an age. The wedding? No, it must have been since then."

"Bel's doing fine. Anne, I'm here about Reggie."

"What's he done now?"

"Do you know where he is? He hasn't been to work in a fortnight."

"Work?" said Anne. "Oh, that's right. Not to worry. Someone once told me you have to stand on a table in frilly drawers spouting outright treason before anyone can be bothered to fire you from government service. I'm sure he'll get back to it when he's bored enough."

"So you haven't heard from him? He's not spent a single night in his rooms; I've checked." A band of dull pain was forming around Edwin's temples, and it tweaked itself tighter as a sudden muffled sound, like a ripple of music, intruded on the room from a nearby cabinet.

"That blasted clock," said Anne, following his gaze. "I thought Dora was going to put it in the linen cupboard. If it weren't a family heirloom I'd have tossed it out of an upstairs window by now." She went and fished a large object, bundled in cloth, from the cabinet. It had stopped emitting music by the time it was unwrapped, and proved to be a handsome standing clock, the boxy casing a deep reddish wood and the face a mosaic of coloured nacre.

Anne said, "It kept perfect time until last month, when it turned whimsical. Now it announces the hour three times in an afternoon, or else four times in ten minutes."

"Magical?" Edwin asked.

Anne nodded. "Doesn't need winding, supposed to last for centuries. But nothing runs forever, I suppose. I asked Saul to look at it, but he didn't want to prod for fear of breaking something. And there's only one thaumhorologist in London, so of course the man charges a prince's ransom." She gave the clock a rueful look. "We're hoping it runs out of power before we run out of things to wrap it in."

"May I?" Edwin brought it over to the low table where the light was good. The back panel was imbued to click neatly open with a finger-stroke down the seam. The clock's insides were still ticking; Edwin felt like a surgeon operating on a pair of breathing lungs. Cogs and gears were set around a polished sphere of what looked like more wood, held in a silver bracket. Hung on small hooks around the clock's inner walls, like coats in a dollhouse, were a series of objects: a twist of dried grass, a silver ring with a triangular dent in it, a red ribbon, a broken grey chain link. Edwin didn't touch anything. He watched the moving cogs for a little while, then replaced the back.

"I think it's an oak-heart mechanism," he said. "I've read about them. Properly treated oak will absorb a large amount of power and release it slowly, like wound-up springs. And you're right, it won't run forever. Someone needs to pour a lot more magic into the heart, that's all. Like watering a plant, if the plant only needed water every hundred years."

"That sounds simple."

"It is and it isn't. The imbuement still needs clear parameters. Most trained magicians with a certain level of power could do it. Do you have paper . . . ?"

What looked like household accounts emerged from one of Anne's skirt pockets, and she indicated the back of the page for his use.

"Saul's your fiancé? English-trained?"

Anne nodded and Edwin wrote down a rough sheet of instructions for the man, making the annotation for the cradles very clear. His pen's scribe imbuement responded only to voice. For the first time he wondered about how one would go about linking it to the actions of one's hands. Or sound—could it take down music on a stave, as played aloud? There'd be limitations on speed and complexity, but perhaps—

"Pity you can't do it for us yourself," said Anne.

Edwin's hand paused. "Yes." He finished the last lines: *Take care to avoid the device's other components when applying imbuement to the wood. This appears to be a delicately arranged system.*

"Oh, I didn't mean to be *rude*. But surely you—"

"Yes."

"In any case, this was easier than calling in some stuffy old expert!" said Anne. She looked at the paper. The annotations would mean as much to her as written Chinese, but any magician trained in the English system would be able to follow them. "What do we owe you for your services, Win?"

It was clearly a joke, but Edwin said, "Send me a note if you hear anything from Reggie. I've got rooms at the Cavendish."

For the first time, Anne appeared to actually focus on Edwin's face. She frowned. "Honestly, I'm sure it's nothing. But let me ask Dora and Mama."

She rang for a maid, who was dispatched to fetch the other members of Reggie's family to the parlour. Both confirmed that neither of them had heard from him for over a month. Transparently, they didn't find this unusual. Even more transparently, they were finding it an effort to dredge up any kind of real concern for his well-being.

The Gatlings were old magic—not as old as the Courceys, but old enough. The widowed Mrs. Gatling treated Edwin with the distant, pity-tainted politeness that one might use with ailing children, and the pity only thickened when she asked after Edwin's own mother. The pleasant distraction of the clock having faded, Edwin was itching to leave. He escaped after writing down his address and extracting a renewed promise from Anne that she'd send on any news of her absent brother.

The rain had thickened. Edwin turned up the collar of his coat and dashed as far as Knightsbridge Station, then took the Underground to Leicester Square. He was in the mood to not talk with anyone and, as sometimes happened, felt perversely like surrounding himself with people to not-talk to. As the train rattled along he worried at Reggie's absence some more, as though at a loose tooth. Having a counterpart as easy to deal with as Reggie had always been a stroke of good luck. Edwin didn't deal well with most people.

And now he had to *deal* with Sir Robert Blyth, who had the speech and the manner of every healthy, vigorous, half-witted boy that Edwin had spent his school and university years trying to ignore. A perfect specimen of incurious English manhood, from the thick brown wave of his hair to the firm jaw. Not enough wit to be sceptical. Not enough sense to be afraid.

What on Earth had possessed Edwin to show Blyth one of his own creations?

Come now, Edwin told himself, merciless. *You know the answer to that.*

The answer was that Blyth, fresh to magic as an apple emerging from a spiral of peel, knew just enough nothing to be a temptation. He didn't know to sneer at Edwin's use of the string to guide his cradling, like a child learning hand positions. Before Edwin showed him the snowflake spell, Blyth hadn't seen anything more impressive than a floating pen.

His face had lit up. Nobody had ever looked at any of Edwin's spells like that.

Lovely, Blyth had said.

Edwin hadn't considered the aesthetics of the thing before. It was an experiment in crystallisation technique that had taken Edwin half a year to develop. As far as he knew, he was the only magician in England who could do it. And he still couldn't manage the cradles without the crutch of string.

Aboveground, Edwin made his way up Charing Cross Road to one of the smallest bookshops, which sat between two larger and grander ones like a boy squashed between his parents on a bench.

"How d'you do, Mr. Courcey?" said Len Geiger as the bell hung by the door gave a rattling peal.

Edwin pulled off his hat and returned the greeting, forcing himself to stop and ask after Geiger's family even though his feet wanted to drag him straight past the register. The warmth of the shop and the damp of the rain gave the air a greenhouse feel, which vanished as Edwin moved between shelves to the back of the shop. Here the air was as it should be: dry, edged with dust and leather and paper.

The mirror hung on the wall in the shop's back corner was as tall as a man and spattered with tarnish, dimly reflecting the shadows and spines of books. Edwin touched the mirror's surface and the illusion winked out in response to what he was. Not much of a magician, but enough. He stepped through into the room beyond.

At first glance this looked like a smaller reflection of the room Edwin had just left. More books, on more shelves. It had the quiet of an unoccupied chapel or the stacks of a library. Edwin set briefcase, hat, and coat down near the mirror through which he had stepped, and exhaled. He came here as other men went to gaming-rooms or brothels, orchestral performances or opium dens. Everyone had their own vice of relaxation. Edwin's was just considered duller than most.

He browsed for a pleasant half hour, touching the spines of books with a reverent finger, occasionally pulling one from the shelf to check its table of contents. He resisted the urge to shove Manning's abysmal thesis on visual illusions back into the shadows of other, worthier books.

Midway through the shelf labelled NATURAL SCIENCES & MAGICS, Edwin spotted an indigo-blue cover with the title stamped in gold: *Working with Life: Kinoshita's Sympathies & Manipulations*. His breath caught, and he let it out in a low whistle.

Geiger's face creased around his smile when he saw the book in Edwin's hand, and he pulled out brown paper and string to wrap it. "Knew you'd appreciate that one, sir," he said. "Got it in a box of donations two days ago. Thought I'd leave you the pleasure of finding it your own self."

Edwin next ducked into another bookshop, this one even shabbier in appearance. Here he made an offhand comment about the weather, which was answered with a solemn nod and the slide of a much slimmer book, this one already brown-papered, across the counter.

The Cavendish was serving lunch in the dining room by the time Edwin returned home. He ate and took his purchases up to his rooms, which had been cleaned, with a fire lit in the largest grate. Fresh-laundered clothes hung in the wardrobe and lay folded neatly in the dresser. Edwin could have afforded his own valet, and his rented suite included a modest servant's quarters, but at university he'd fallen out of the habit of being so closely attended. What he'd fallen into instead was the habit of enclosed privacy and quiet, and he'd no intention of fishing himself out of it. The Cavendish was well staffed and accustomed to catering to the needs of bachelors.

He cracked the window of his sitting room. Rain-washed air refreshed his face. Along with it came the noise of the city, but this was distant and familiar enough that Edwin would stop hearing it within minutes. He made tea and burned his finger on the kettle, and begrudged the amount of magic it took him to heal it and avoid the annoyance of having his cradling string rub against the sore spot for the next week.

The smaller of his two book parcels, when unwrapped, held a thin purple volume that was closer to a glorified pamphlet. Edwin opened it to a random page and read enough for his lips and his cock to twitch in unison, then set it aside and took the book from Geiger's to his favourite velvet armchair in front of the fire.

Normally he'd have sunk into the dry, fascinating words as gratefully as he'd sunk into the atmosphere of the bookshop itself. He found it difficult today. The bruises from the visit to Reggie's family were starting to smart: the pity, the familiarity, the blatant mirroring of Edwin's own disgust at what he *was* compared to what he *should be*. Little wonder that the unmagical Reggie, like Edwin, had borne the expense of living outside his family home in London, and visited them so seldom.

And on top of that, tomorrow Edwin would have to go back to Whitehall and deal with Blyth again.

At least that would be a limited irritation. Edwin would explain the mistake to the Minister. Blyth would be given a cup of tea and sent back to his own life. Someone more suitable would be found in the interim. And eventually Reggie would reappear, and laugh at Edwin for worrying over nothing.

Edwin ran his eyes twice more over the page and then, when the words refused to line themselves up and be seen, replaced the sweep of his sight with that of a fingertip, finding pleasure in the tiny roughness of the paper. Edwin's collection of small enjoyments was carefully cultivated. When he exhaled his worry he imagined it going up in the snap of the fire. He thought about the meticulous cogs of the Gatlings' clock, and the particular hazel of Sir Robert Blyth's eyes.

In the gaps between small things, Edwin could feel his quiescent magic like a single drop of blood in a bucket of water: more obvious than it deserved to be, given its volume. He could breathe into the knots in the back of his neck. And he could feel out the edges of the aching, yearning space in his life that no amount of quiet and no number of words had yet been able to fill.

Edwin had no idea what he ached *for*, no real sense of the shape of his ideal future. He only knew that if every day he made himself a little bit better—if he worked harder, if he learned more, *more* than anyone else—he might find it.

4

The attack came while Robin was thinking about roast beef.

Charlotte Street was full of rattling wheels and scuffing feet as he walked home from his boxing club. The day's rain had cleared into a sullenly overcast sky. Robin's wrist ached from where he'd let annoyance and the brain-spinning impact of the day—*magic, magic*—distract him during his last bout against Lord Bromley. Scholz, the scowling German ex-champion who owned the boxing club, had treated Robin to a heavily accented diatribe on keeping his wrists and shoulders at the correct angle.

Roast beef. With potatoes crisped at the edges and fluffy on the inside, and golden Yorkshire pudding, and a savoury drape of gravy over the whole.

Robin sighed. No doubt the dinner at home would be fine, but the club only did that particular roast on Mondays. On a normal evening he'd have much preferred to join the group of his friends going directly from the boxing ring to the club's dining room, then head home late enough into the night that he could dodge whatever conversations were waiting for him.

This was not a normal evening. It had not been a normal day, even by the off-balance new standards for *normal* that had invaded Robin's life since his parents had died.

"Sir. Moment of your time, sir."

Robin wouldn't have looked up, but the rough voice was accompanied by a touch on the back of his hand, and he wondered if his pocket was being picked. He loosened his arms, ready to lash out, and slowed his steps.

That was a mistake. A loop of yarn slid over his hand and tightened on his wrist. Robin thought first and absurdly of the string that Courcey had used to make the snowflake.

"Look here," Robin said sharply, and would have gone on, but the loop tightened further and the words died in his mouth.

Perhaps his first thought hadn't been so absurd. The yarn was *glowing,* yellow-white where it cinched the dark sleeve of his coat. It looked hot, like it might burn the fabric—might burn *him*. Robin tried to flinch away.

His body refused to flinch just as his voice refused to raise itself and shout. A horrible, numbing warmth drenched him, like the stupor of cosy blankets in early winter mornings, but with none of the comfort. His body hung on him like rags. Unmoving.

Robin had once been knocked to the ground hard enough to drive the wind from his lungs. He remembered vividly the sheer animal fear of lying there in the long, long seconds before he recovered, unable to gasp, trying to force an action that should have been instinctual, his aching throat struggling against the dumb sluggishness of his rib cage.

He was still breathing now. But somehow it felt worse.

Without any guidance from his own will, Robin's chin lifted and he gazed straight ahead. At least now he was looking his attacker in the face, and—

Robin's gut lurched with a new horror. The man in front of him—or so he assumed; the voice had been that of a man, at least—had *no face*. He had a rough shirt and sun-browned hands that gripped the other end of the glowing yarn, and a matching sun-browned neck. At the top of that neck was a head-shaped nothingness: a queasily shifting fog.

"That's it," the man said. "Come nice and quiet."

It was less than an hour off sunset, hardly the inky midnight one thought of as playing host to ruffians. There was enough light for someone to notice if Robin frantically waved his arms. There were more than enough people on the streets to stop and ask questions if Robin yelled for help.

If, if. Robin could do nothing of the kind.

He followed the man, meek as a trusting child. Pulled on the end of a string. Viewed from behind, his captor had a head of remarkably normal fair hair. There was a clear line where the hair became not-hair—became the fog.

Robin's captor led him off the street and into an alley that smelled of rotting apples. Two more men were waiting for them. They, too, wore the fog masks, and were dressed like street workmen. One of them was heavyset; the other had a thick coating of dark hair on his knuckles. Robin's brain landed on detail after irrelevant detail as though he were trying to memorise a painting for an exam and expected to have the image snatched away at any moment. His heart was causing a hell of a ruckus against his ribs.

"Right, Mr. Whoever-You-Are. Blyth," said the man holding the string. "I'm taking this off your hand now. And you're going to keep nice and quiet, and answer my questions, all right? Because I reckon you can count, and I reckon even a man from Scholz's saloon knows he can't hold his end up against three, when we've got more than just fists on our side. And we've not been told to kill you, but we've not been told to *not*. If you catch my meaning."

Robin wondered if the man expected him to nod, and how he was meant to go about it. But the yarn was tugged off his wrist without any further ado, and he gasped in relief as his body came back under his own control. He shook out his hands and felt his knees tremble.

"Now—" said the man, and Robin hauled off and popped him in what he assumed was the jaw.

The next thing that Robin knew, he was blinking awake, propped against the wall of the alley. The rotten smell was abruptly a lot closer to his nose, and something damp was seeping through the seat of his trousers. It was not a comforting combination.

"That was a bloody stupid thing to be doing," said the man. Robin would have liked to see the blood on the man's split lip—he'd certainly *felt* his knuckles grind flesh against tooth— but the fog mask kept it obscured.

"Do the other two speak?" asked Robin, nodding at them. He was angry enough that it was keeping him afloat above the fear. "Or are they more in the looming silently line?"

He was ignored. "Mr. Blyth. You're in Mr. Gatling's shoes now. You're in Mr. Gatling's office."

"And Mr. Gatling is very displeased?" Robin demanded. "Is that it? He can damn well come back, then. His typist's upset." That was an exaggeration. Courcey had seemed upset. Miss Morrissey had seemed . . . miffed.

"Mr. Gatling hid something in his office that's very important, didn't he? But it's proving tough to locate. You're going to help us."

Robin found the words *Like hell I am* in his mouth and tasted them longingly. But he was wary now. These men had tailed him from the office, and then from his club. They knew his name. They weren't going to be put off easily.

"What is it? What did he hide? And how do you know it's there? If it's that important, he's probably taken it with him, wherever he's buggered off to."

The fog swirled a little. A chill chased across Robin's neck.

"No, the contract's there," the man said. "Had that from his own lips, and he weren't lying."

"There's a lot of paperwork in that office" was all Robin could think of to say.

An impatient sound. "Don't play foolish, Blyth. Gatling must've had someone muffle it for him. It doesn't have the feel of power to it anymore. But it'll be there."

"What?"

A pause. "He didn't tell you any more specifics than he told us, ey? Secret-binds'll do that. Something hidden, we reckon. Something that doesn't belong."

This was turning into one of those dreams where you turned over the Latin paper to find that it had been replaced with Ancient Egyptian instead.

"Not one word of this is making a single bloody ounce of sense," said Robin. "And—" He managed to bite that back too. Instinct told him that admitting he'd had his first glimpse of magic that very day was more likely to hurt him than help him at that precise moment.

When Robin didn't continue, his speaking captor gestured to one of the loomers, who knelt down and took hold of Robin's right arm at the wrist and just above the elbow. The fear flared urgently, but Robin recognised superior strength when he felt it. Trying to pull away would just wrench his shoulder for nothing. His fingers curled into a tight enough fist that he could feel the blunt edges of his fingernails.

It took Robin a second to recognise what the speaking man was doing as cradling: the same thing that Courcey had done, except that Courcey had used string, and had been much slower than this. Robin stared, because for a moment it seemed that there *was* string there, the same glowing yarn that had noosed him. But there wasn't. The glow clung only to the man's fingertips, then gathered in his palm as he upended his hand onto Robin's forearm and moved it as though smearing paint.

In the wake of the man's hand a pattern laid itself over Robin's sleeve. Something like geometry, or a foreign alphabet. Robin barely had time to notice its details before it seeped into the fabric, fading slowly. Gone.

Robin's arm was released. He cradled it to his chest, but there didn't seem anything wrong with it. Bones intact. Muscles working fine.

He said, "Whatever you—"

Sudden, excruciating pain captured his forearm as though a cage of red-hot wires had been clasped around it. The pain startled a frantically guttural sound from between his teeth. He'd broken bones in his time, as a boy and an adult. None of them had felt anything like this.

He couldn't have said how long it lasted. The wires tightened, and then they were gone, and Robin's throat felt like he'd been yelling for the Light Blues on three consecutive race days.

"There," said the man. "That'll give you something to mull over while you're shuffling all that paperwork in your new office. Keep those eyes peeled. Find the last contract. I wager you'll be a lot more happy to help the next time we come calling."

Robin emitted the wheezy opinion that every single one of their mothers had conceived them in congress with pox-ridden barnyard beasts. The knowledge that his parents would have been horrified if they'd heard their model firstborn spitting out words he might have licked up from the gutter slightly made up for the parting kick that was delivered to his stomach as the men walked out of the alley.

After a long count of ten, Robin held his ribs and struggled to his feet.

On Robin's arm, the strange symbols no longer glowed. Instead they were as black as any tattoo. Blacker, in fact, and crisper, than those examples of body art that Robin had seen— mostly on sailors in the street but once, memorably, on a fellow scholar who'd found someone prepared to ink a few lines of Horace into the delectable dip of his lower back.

There was no lingering pain. No redness of the surrounding skin. Just the shapes and almost-letters, stark against Robin's skin. When he stared too long at them they seemed almost to crawl.

Bowden knocked on the door to Robin's dressing room, and Robin hastily smoothed the shirtsleeve back down.

"Perhaps you didn't hear the dinner gong, sir," said Bowden reproachfully. Bowden had been the late Sir Robert's valet and was doing his respectful best to encroach upon Robin's own dressing habits. It was equal parts affection and an understandable anxiety to remain employed, even though Bowden's hair was as white as Robin's shirt.

Robin submitted to Bowden's arthritic fingers fumbling his cuff links and helping him into his dinner jacket, and made a mental note to talk to Gunning about a pension for the man.

Robin sat at the head of the dinner table and hated it. If it were left up to him and Maud then they'd have abandoned the whole thing in favour of an informal supper, but the mouths of the housekeeper and butler formed identical moues of disapproval whenever Robin hazarded the prospect of anything less than a proper family dinner, even when the family in question now numbered only two.

At least they were in the small dining room, cosy with wood and memory, instead of the sparkling cavernous room that had been the scene of the late Sir Robert and Lady Blyth's social triumphs.

"—the *entire* pond, ducks and all." Maud was coming to the end of a story about her friend Eliza's brother Paul, and some exploit involving a runaway bicycle. "And Paul and his friends are going to the Gaiety tomorrow night, and have promised to tell us all about it," she added, her voice gaining a provocative edge. "Liza says that Paul is arse-over-nose for a blonde in the chorus line."

"Sounds like fun," said Robin, taking a bite from a lamb cutlet.

The somewhat awkward silence was that of Maud realising that there was no point in needling the dinner table with unladylike talk, because Robin wasn't going to leap in and disapprove. It was an empty reflex now, Robin thought. Ingrained. It was all still too fresh for things like that to be unlearned.

Robin glanced up at the painting of their father that stared in benevolent solemnity down from the wall. Unwanted grief rose like acid in his throat.

"I have an announcement" was Maud's next sally.

Robin smiled. Maud had approximately three announcements per week. "What is it, Maudie?"

"I want to attend Newnham."

"No, you don't."

"I do! I shall die if I don't!"

"No, you shan't," said Robin. "Pass the mint jelly."

Maud deflated. "I dare say not, but you know what I mean."

"Why on Earth do you want to go to Cambridge?"

"Why'd you?"

"That's different and you know it," said Robin.

Maud lifted her chin and speared a carrot as though it had offended her, an annoyed little shadow in her black crepe-trimmed dress. She'd refused to buy jet jewellery, but hadn't dared pearls; her neck and ears were defiantly bare. Mourning dress was particularly unfair on eighteen-year-old girls, she'd told Robin. At length.

"Look, ask me again next week," Robin said.

"You always say that when you're trying to dodge something."

"You know what Gunning said yesterday," said Robin, grasping for a solid excuse. "We haven't enough money that we can toss it around."

Martin Gunning was his parents'—now his, although the possessive still felt slippery—primary man of business in London. Robin had guiltily rescheduled until he couldn't put the man off any further, and had marched into the study to meet with him with the vague feeling of climbing the gallows.

Gunning had stood with frustration painting his face as he reminded Robin about the wills of Sir Robert and Lady Blyth, which were as sparkling and selfless and attention-grabbing as any words they'd uttered in life. They committed the bulk of their liquid assets to various funds and orphanages and projects that would probably do them the favour of immortalising their names—and divided, as an afterthought, the rest between their children. In his more forgiving moments, Robin believed they were the wills of two people in the prime of their life who never honestly thought they could die. They were showpiece documents.

And Robin didn't even have the luxury of wholehearted resentment, because the irony was that those documents had probably done a lot of good. Orphans and nurses and starving families in the East End wouldn't care a whit about the *character* of their deceased benefactors. Charity done out of ruthless self-promotion was still charity.

It only mattered to Robin and Maud that *the rest,* once the loans had been repaid, fell dismally short of what would be necessary if the two surviving members of the Blyth family were to continue to live as they had always done.

Gunning had uttered a long, stultifying speech about death-duties and how Robin needed to let him take what was left of their family's capital and invest it sensibly, thinking of the future. Start putting some of it back into the Thornley Hill estate so that eventually it might pull its weight again.

And meanwhile, Robin was still a member of His Majesty's Civil Service, because his parents' delightful piece of career whimsy had somehow turned into their family's most reliable source of income.

From a magical liaison job. Robin stared at a white patch of plate between his creamed spinach and his lamb, and thought of snowflakes, and fog.

"Ten new gowns would be *tossing* money," said Maud, steely. "Newnham's different. The education of women is the promise of the future."

Robin sighed. "Has that Sinclair girl been dragging you to suffragette rallies again?"

The steely look strengthened; Robin weakened.

"I'll talk to Gunning again tomorrow," he said. "There are still plenty of things we can sell."

"Some of this boring art, to begin with," said Maud. "And in any case, you've got this new job—"

"Working at the Home Office again," said Robin hastily. "That's all I'll tell you about it for now."

Distracted, Maud turned a look of mingled admiration and hilarity onto him. She clearly thought he'd wrangled himself an intelligence job and was clamming up to protect national secrets. Robin's grip on his fork faltered with the memory of pain.

Mercifully their talk turned to sport after that, and the investigation into the deadly ballooning accident at the Franco-British Exhibition the previous month, and then the dessert course was done and Robin escaped to the smallest sitting room with a glass of port. He loved his sister, and normally wouldn't have minded spending the rest of the evening with her. But his thoughts were unspooling and his shoulders were high. He was, he realised, bracing himself constantly for another flare of that hot-wire sensation.

He removed his dinner jacket and settled in a comfortable chair, letting the warmth from the fire soften his tight muscles. His eyes wandered the familiar frames that crowded the walls.

A real curator might have found some rude things to say about the art that adorned this house. It was a cluttered collection with no unifying theme, full of pieces that Robin's parents had simply wanted to own for their value as objects. The best of the lot was in this sitting room: a John Singer Sargent painting of his mother, completed when Robin was still an infant. The famed portraitist had been freshly arrived in London from Paris, and Sir Robert Blyth had leapt at the chance to commission him just as public opinion began to drag Sargent into fashion.

The artist had captured Priscilla, Lady Blyth. The lightly arch look, and the smile, were exactly right. And as for the shadows encroaching on one side of the face, the hand tucked just behind the skirt, unseen—well. Of those few people who saw the true self of Robin's mother, only Sargent had dared to put it on display like that while she still lived. The painter must have known that neither she nor her husband would catch the irony, neither of them loving art for itself.

Lord Healsmith had been another of the few to see past the Blyths' sparkling facade. Sir Robert, usually so canny a judge of character, had made an error when calculating exactly how much flattery could be applied to his lordship before it began to ring false. A cold public snubbing had been revenged, over time, by one of Lady Blyth's most ice-blooded and sweet-mouthed campaigns of social poison, with the result that Lady Healsmith had fled to their Wiltshire estate to escape the glances that followed her in the street.

Robin had heard the way his father laughed when his mother proclaimed her victory.

Healsmith himself had accepted the warning, bottled up his anger, and let it ferment until it was safe to express his dislike. Robin couldn't entirely *blame* the man, but he did wish Healsmith had chosen some other form of expressing it. Buying up advertising space on a block of flats, for example, and papering it with a denunciation of the much-lauded Blyths.

But you didn't speak ill of the dead.

You punished their son, instead.

A soft knock on the door announced Maud, who crossed the room and perched herself on the arm of Robin's chair. She gnawed on her lower lip before looking Robin in the eye. "I didn't mean it, about the art."

"I know," said Robin.

"But I did mean it about Cambridge." His sister's heart-shaped face was uncharacteristically solemn. It was almost, but not quite, the look of their father in his dining-room portrait.

"You always mean it, Maudie," Robin said. "That's your charm. But you've never mentioned university before."

"I wasn't sure before. Now I am. Look here, Robin, I know what you think, but I'll still mean it next week. Next month."

Robin made himself consider the idea seriously. It was like trying to balance an egg on its point. "I thought you wanted a court presentation next year."

"Maybe I want both."

"Maudie—"

"Oh, the hell with it, Robin," Maud exploded, "they're *gone,*" and then shut her mouth and cast a stricken look at the half-open door.

Robin's mind filled in the unsaid words: *They're not here to object.* To insist that their only daughter follow the stepping-stones of the peerage, schoolroom to social season to marriage, and not soil her hands or her mind with the enlarging independence of the middle class.

Never mind that the baronetcy of Thornley Hill was the barest scrape of landed nobility. Nor that the daughter of a baronet who'd stripped his estates to finance his city life was hardly a gem of eligibility.

"I know," Robin said, feeling his resistance crumble at the lines between her eyes.

"You'll think about it?"

"I'll think about it."

Maud nodded, bent to kiss his cheek in an uncharacteristic display of softness, and left again.

I'll think about it. It wasn't a lie. No more than "working at the Home Office" had been a lie. Robin didn't lie to his sister.

On any other night he'd have cheerfully tried to smother himself with a pillow or recite Greek verbs in order to *escape* thinking about it, and about what the blazes he was going to do with the house—art and all—and how they were going to afford to pay their active servants, let alone pension off old ones. He had no idea about any of it. It would probably all work out, somehow, but in the meantime every conversation about the future felt like Robin's brain was being kicked, and he hated it.

Oh, look at yourself, murmured an irrepressible part of Robin. *Portrait of a sulky aristocrat in repose.* Someone should paint him, indeed: lounging here among his grand belongings, drink in hand, weighed down by the dreadful woes of having both a well-paying job and a baronetcy.

He let out a soft chuckle at the absurdity of it and ran a hand over his face, then found himself rubbing the base of his port glass restlessly up and down his arm, over the magical tattoo. Or whatever it was. The entire attack had taken on the form of a photograph in his mind: vividly captured, but bled dry of colour. When Robin fumbled after the memory of his own fear, it was elusive. The man's voice was not. He could hear its rough command.

The contract's there.

Something that doesn't belong.

Whatever Reggie Gatling had gotten himself involved in, it had closed itself over Robin as well, like a trap springing shut.

As he often did when fretting over something, Robin pulled his lighter from his pocket and turned it in his hand. He wasn't tempted to go in search of cigarettes. Half the time he forgot the thing had a useful purpose. It was just a squared lump of gold, a comfort when he ran his thumb over the engraved *R* on its surface.

It was unpleasantly warm in the sitting room. Robin felt flushed, and small sparks of light danced at the edge of his vision; he tucked the lighter away, then loosened his collar and unbuttoned his waistcoat, but it didn't settle. His next sip of port had an odd peppery edge to it and seemed to tingle at the edges of his tongue long after he swallowed.

Time stretched like rubber. Robin leaned forward in the chair, and frowned. And then—

It was not like looking at a book, or a canvas, or even like sitting in the front row of the theatre so that the performance stretched to the very edge of your gaze. There was no sense of having a gaze. Or eyes, or any kind of body. There was just the image.

An enormous terraced garden at night, alight with lanterns and alive with a heady profusion of flowers. The skies above had the gentle murkiness of clouds, fading out from the glow of a hidden moon. Statues dotted stone balconies and silhouetted themselves against that glow. A large golden pheasant with a coloured riot of a tail scuttled across manicured lawns and disappeared beneath the shadows of a bush.

The image changed. A cave of some kind, dimly lit. A blond woman in a beaded dress the colour of strawberry fool was crying, her hair tumbling in disarray around her face, her hands moving through the cradling motions of a spell even as tears spilled down her cheeks.

Change. An interior view, up through a ceiling made of clear glass set in intricate shapes within a lead frame, like a huge stained glass window had been bleached of all hue and wedged here on its side. Shoes and shapes of people moved across the glass, busy as the King's Cross main platform.

Change. A man sprawled across a bed, pale enough that the veins shone bluish through his bare skin, fair hair sticking to a sweat-slick brow and mouth forming unheard words or sounds of pleasure. He slurred one hand across his own face and grabbed vainly at a handful of sheets with the other. His back arched, lifting his chest. His eyes opened and his features cohered.

Edwin Courcey.

Robin jolted back to himself, half out of his chair and breathing like a man at the end of a ten-mile run. His glass of port had fallen to the ground; the rug had saved the glass, but the liquid had created a dark patch. His eyes smarted at the firelight for a few seconds before returning to normal.

He fumbled his cuff link off and his shirt to his elbow. The tattoo was unchanged. He'd half expected it to be moving, or changing colours. He didn't know anything about any of this.

Edwin Courcey.

Robin shook his head as though he could rid it of the things he'd seen, not to mention the tendril of unexpected arousal that had curled itself around that delirious vision of Courcey: that canvas of sweat and abandon and bare collarbones. Robin rescued his port glass and stumbled over to the decanter to pour himself another. Until the triple-punch of today, he'd managed to get through twenty-five years of life without magic revealing itself to him. Anyone from that world was obviously expert at hiding their real selves when they wanted to, and the *real* Courcey had made it very clear that he saw Robin as an outsider and an inconvenience; possibly even a danger. Robin didn't know him at all. He was Robin's best hope of answers, but he couldn't be trusted.

Robin drained the glass, hoping it would soothe the kicked-hard feeling of his brain. He would worry about that when he planned to worry about everything else. Tomorrow.

5

Edwin arrived at the liaison office the next morning and had to blink several times before he accepted that the scene in front of him was truly happening. The hem of Miss Morrissey's skirt disappeared in a snowbank of paper strewn over the office floor. She was sitting on a wooden box; after a moment Edwin recognised it as one of the three sturdy drawers that had made up the filing cabinet, which was now a hollow frame. Here and there amongst the chaos of paper lay the late contents of the bookshelf. Edwin's stomach squeezed at the sight of splayed pages and bent-back spines.

Sir Robert Blyth sat cross-legged on the desk. Around him was a battlefield of detritus that was probably the contents of the desk's drawers, and yet more paper. He had a pile of envelopes in his lap and was reading something.

"What have you done?" Edwin demanded.

Blyth looked up. "Come in, close the door," he said cheerfully. "Oh, wait, no—it doesn't do that anymore."

"What?"

"Close."

Edwin's fingers dipped through empty space. There was a scorched, splintered gap in the door where the knob had once been.

"Someone was in a temper," said Miss Morrissey. "There's no particular imbuement on the locks. A robust opening-spell would do it."

Edwin hung his hat and coat on the stand in the outer office and waded into the battlefield. "My apologies," he said stiffly. "I assumed . . ."

"That I tossed my own office?" said Blyth.

"It was like this when I let myself in, at eight o'clock," said Miss Morrissey.

Edwin looked around again. Viewed with that eye, it was obvious. "Someone was looking for something."

"Yes. Your friend Gatling has gotten himself muddled up in some sort of serious trouble," said Blyth. Belatedly, Edwin realised that the cheer in Blyth's voice was too high-pitched.

"What do you mean?" Edwin asked sharply. "What do you know about it?"

Blyth waited as Edwin picked his way into a patch of bare rug. Up close, Blyth didn't look like a man who had slept well. Those mild hazel eyes had pinches of tension at their corners. There was a stubbornness to his mouth.

"I mean," Blyth said, "that I was attacked last night by—magicians—who seemed to think that because I'd stepped into Gatling's position that very morning, I'd have known to search his office for secret documents and would be happy to hand them over."

"Documents?" Edwin found his hand drifting towards the pocket holding the small vial of lethe-mint he'd prepared that morning, and forced it back down by his side before the movement could become obvious.

Blyth unbuttoned one of his cuffs and pushed it up his arm. He proceeded to tell them a story that Edwin had to interrupt several times, including a forced pause where he scrambled for a piece of blank paper and set his pen to taking notes. Fog masks: that would be a simple illusion spell. Something that Reggie had hidden. And glowing shapes that became a tattoo. Blyth's voice halted when he talked about that.

Edwin frowned and made Blyth repeat the words that had

been exchanged between himself and his attackers. "Are you sure that they didn't say anything else about where Reggie might be now?"

"No, I'm not *sure*," said Blyth, looking at Edwin with dislike.

"Well, then—"

"I was *distracted*, due to being knocked out and tortured and tugged around on a piece of string."

A small index card flicked out of the stacks of Edwin's mind. There was a spell by the unfortunately fanciful name of the Goblin's Bridle, which could be used to calm frightened horses and make them biddable. The idea of it being used on a person made him feel ill.

"It hurt. And then when you looked, later, it was on your arm? Anything else you can remember? How the cradling—oh, this is *useless*, as if you could tell."

Another held gaze from Blyth, longer this time. That stubbornness had redoubled. "No. Nothing else."

"I'm so sorry, Sir Robert," said Miss Morrissey. "It does sound like you had an awful night."

"Thank you." The dislike melted away and Blyth smiled at her. "Didn't you say something about Gatling behaving oddly, before he vanished?"

"Yes. Ever since he got back from that trip to the North York Moors." She frowned. "It was some tiny mining town where the inhabitants were reporting ghosts walking through the streets."

"Ghosts?" Blyth's eyebrows shot up.

"He did say it'd all been a misunderstanding when he got back," said Miss Morrissey. "Nothing magical involved. But he was vague about it. That *was* when he started acting all mysterious."

"It was a fool's errand in the first place," snapped Edwin. "Visible ghosts? Nonsense. There's no such thing." But half of his annoyance was with himself. Nonsense or not, if he'd accepted the invitation to go along—if he'd even acted *interested* instead of telling Reggie not to waste his time—would Reggie have liked him more, trusted him more? Enough to confide in Edwin about this dangerous mess he'd become mixed up in?

"Well," said Blyth firmly. "I'm as keen as anyone to find Gatling, because I'd like to shake five kinds of hell out of him. He told them this thing was in the office. He's the one who sent them here. This is *his* fault." An irritated wave of his arm.

Edwin reached for Blyth's wrist, meaning to get a closer look; Blyth jerked it away, then firmed his lips, as if angry with himself for what had clearly been an instinctive reaction. He untucked his legs from their crossed position on the desk, letting them dangle like a barrier between the two of them, and shoved his arm defiantly forward. Blyth's forearm was corded with muscle and dotted with freckles and moles. His skin was warm.

Edwin looked over the symbols of what Blyth had called the tattoo, and which began at the wrist and stopped an inch from the crook of Blyth's elbow. They weren't any alphabet that Edwin was familiar with, but the arrangement of them— each symbol linked to the next by a dark tendril, creating a sort of cyclical sentence—made his stomach sink. He only realised when Blyth's fingers curled like dry leaves in a fire that he was tracing the symbols with his fingertip.

"It's a rune-curse of some kind," he said, releasing Blyth. "That's all I can tell without further research."

"A curse." Blyth took a deep breath. "The bounder did say he was giving me something to mull over. Seemed to think it'd make me more pliable." Fear flickered in his face. "Could it? Do that to me? Like—laudanum dropped into my drink?"

"Miss Morrissey?" inquired Edwin. "Can you make anything of it?"

She peered at the curse in turn, coming close enough that Edwin could smell the floral-chemical scent of her hair, pinned up in its usual nest of luxuriant black. "Alas," she said.

"I haven't a clue. And I'm hardly the best person you could be asking."

No. A continuance of the sinking sensation in Edwin's stomach signaled exactly whom he should be asking, and the very idea made him want to take a train to Dover and fling himself over the cliffs.

"Something hidden in the office," Edwin said instead, looking at the chaos around them.

"I'd assumed they'd have tossed the office first thing, if they knew it was here," said Blyth. "But no, they had to wait until *I* arrived."

"There are ways to look for magical items without resorting to this kind of petulance," said Edwin, bending to pick up the most egregiously wronged book within arm's reach. He smoothed the bent pages and set it on the desk.

"That's what confused me," said Miss Morrissey. "They could have searched the office five times for something that holds power, and we'd have never known."

"No, he said a contract." Blyth cast a meaningful glance around the mounds of paper. "I do remember that, because you'd been going on about how all of magic is—oh, blast. Is it *not* a piece of paper then?"

"If he meant a spell, he'd have said a spell," said Edwin, but he wasn't sure. He thought longingly of the sixteenth-century French magician who'd claimed to have found a method for reliving a person's memories alongside them. Having to rely on the firsthand account of an unmagical amateur who'd only stumbled into his unbusheling the previous day was galling.

"I haven't found anything with the slightest whiff of a legal flavour to it. Before you stormed in I was opening his letters. Not that it's helped much." Blyth sifted through a slim pile of unopened envelopes. "And these ones don't look awfully promising either. Three within the fortnight from someone who signs himself the Grimm of Gloucester—"

"Crackpot of the first order," said Miss Morrissey, and Edwin nodded in agreement. The Grimm had been writing his lurid, unreadably rambling letters to this office for decades now.

"And here's one from a Mrs. Flora Sutton, in an envelope that—ugh—smells like it's been doused in attar of roses. Was the chap having an affair with a dashing widow, do we think? Or perhaps . . . not even a widow?"

"She'd hardly have written to him at the office, if so," Edwin snapped. "Don't be foolish."

Blyth raised his eyebrows. "Calm down, old man. Only joking."

Only joking. The words reminded Edwin unpleasantly of the fellows who tended to be friends with his brother Walt: bullishly immune to sarcasm, and smirkingly aware of their power. Most of their jokes weren't the slightest bit funny.

Showing any kind of reaction just provided more ammunition. Edwin knew that. Still, he found himself glaring.

"You've been cursed, and you think this is a time to make jokes?"

Blyth shoved his sleeve down again. "*I've* been cursed, so *I'll* make all the jokes I please."

Edwin thought again, with a startling pinprick of guilt, of the small bottle of lethe-mint in his pocket. *Like laudanum dropped into my drink.* Blyth had come uncomfortably close there.

But dammit, Edwin couldn't let Blyth go stumbling back to his life under the power of an unidentified curse. Knowing or unknowing. Edwin didn't believe in that kind of cruelty. No matter what kind of person he was, Blyth deserved to be disentangled fully.

Which meant that Edwin wasn't going to go charging off to the Minister to demand a new Home Office counterpart. He was stuck with this one, at least until he could learn enough about that curse to remove it.

"As I said, I'll need to do some research. And"—damn, *damn,* no avoiding it—"there's someone who should take a look at that curse. His family's always had a knack for working in runes." *If he even let them in the front door.*

"Very well, if you think it's worth a try," said Blyth. "We'll be here. Sorting. You can go and fetch this someone."

"Fetch," Edwin said. "Of course. Is there anything else I can bring back for you, Sir Robert?"

That appeared to sail over Blyth's head. "Though really, I haven't the foggiest idea what I'm looking for here. Why don't you stay and help? It'll go faster with three."

There was no magic at all in Blyth's voice, in the note of casual command that rang golden in his vowels, but something about it tried to capture Edwin's feet anyway. Edwin swallowed a hot mouthful of resentment and fumbled for his watch. It was nearly ten o'clock. He could invent a pressing engagement and insist that they meet up later; Blyth wouldn't question it.

Miss Morrissey's contemptuous look, from her position on the floor, dared him to try. Besides, the likelihood of Hawthorn allowing himself to be *fetched* anywhere was about par with the likelihood that Edwin would spontaneously gain the ability to freeze a lake's surface with a wave of his hands. A feat that he had, in fact, seen Hawthorn accomplish when they were boys.

"Yes, very well." He knew he sounded ungracious. "At least putting all of this in order will familiarise you with some aspects of the position." *Reggie's* position. Still Reggie's.

"Crackpots and far too much paper," said Blyth. He directed the smile at Miss Morrissey, but he'd started it—perhaps by mistake—when he was looking at Edwin, and it was like being caught in the last rays of sunset. "Sounds like government work to me."

They left Miss Morrissey in a halfway tidied office. At a certain point in the re-filing process, she'd given up all pretence that she wasn't seizing the opportunity to impose order on what seemed to have previously been a rather slapdash approach to organisation. She'd all but shovelled them out of Whitehall with the calm promise that she'd have a briefing paper ready for Robin to deliver to the Prime Minister the next day.

Robin was beginning to get a sense for the way the Office of Special Domestic Affairs and Complaints had functioned under his predecessor. Or rather, adjacent to him. Possibly even despite him.

It was odd. Courcey didn't seem the type to have any patience for laziness or clutter, and nothing he'd said about Gatling had made the man seem extraordinarily likeable. Though the puzzle of Gatling's personality couldn't hold a candle to the puzzle of his disappearance, or of this mysterious contract—or, for that matter, the entire enormous mystery of magic, which Robin could feel sucking at the edges of his concentration even more strongly today as the buffer of shock began to wear away.

Today's rain barely counted as rain except that the air was more wet than otherwise. There was nothing worth raising an umbrella against as Courcey led Robin across Green Park in the direction of Mayfair. The lawns stretched away from them, dotted with ducks on the hunt for worms, and the paths were pearled with puddles.

Robin nearly fell in one when the pain started.

It came from nowhere, as sudden as it had been when the curse was laid—that same invisible cage of red-hot wires, so intense that his mind tried to scream the impossibility of it. He managed to catch the rather more audible scream behind his tongue, where it silently strained. No point making a fuss in the middle of a public park. But oh *God,* it hurt.

When it stopped he was bent over his own arm, breathing hard. A muscle in the back of his neck twinged as he straightened, as if he'd thrown a poor punch. Courcey's eyes were wide, the blue of them washed out by the sky.

"It hurt," Robin said, forestalling questions. "Like when they put the blasted thing on in the first place."

"It—looked like it." For a second Robin thought Courcey might reach for him, but the man curled his hand in an awkward fist. "Well. At least now we know what it does," he added. "Good. That may help. Can you walk?"

"I'm not a damned invalid," said Robin, nettled by the decisiveness of the word *good*—as though Robin were nothing more than the problem on his bloody arm.

He strode ahead to prove it, and Courcey didn't say anything else.

Despite himself, Robin could hear his mother's voice murmuring approvingly about the address that was their destination. A small house for the neighbourhood, but the *right* neighbourhood, oh yes. It took some time for the door to be answered by an imposing black man with a faintly harassed air that snapped, instantly, into the unflappable calm of the best butlers.

"Good morning, Mr. Makepeace," said Courcey. "We need to talk to Lord Hawthorn."

"Mr. Courcey." The butler gave Courcey a look that acknowledged familiarity while also not giving an inch on the subject of whether that familiarity would increase their chances of being allowed entry. "I'm afraid his lordship is extremely occupied—"

"It's important," said Courcey.

Makepeace paused. Clearly, a lot was happening in the unsaid parts of this negotiation. The butler dragged his impassive gaze over Robin. Robin tried to nod like someone who wasn't going to shove his shoe in the door if they were turned away without any chance of assistance.

The door, however, opened wider. The butler relieved them deftly of hats and coats and, to Robin's surprise, led the way up a wide set of polished stairs instead of depositing them in a parlour. The house was sparsely decorated, but the wall running alongside the stairs was done in an emerald-green patterned silk damask that deserved all the space it was being given.

"Who is this friend of yours?" Robin murmured as they

were ushered down an equally sumptuous corridor and towards an open door.

"John Alston, Baron Hawthorn," said Courcey. "Son of the Earl of Cheetham." His eyes cut sideways. "I . . . would not characterise us as friends."

Robin's first impression of John Alston, Baron Hawthorn, was that he looked like one of the knights in a book of illustrated tales that Robin had read as a boy. He was even taller than Makepeace, with dark hair and a brutally handsome profile, an uneven nose, and an unforgiving mouth. He gave off the distinct air that he needed only an illustrious steed and a lance to be ready to pose for a bronze statue.

Robin's second impression was that Lord Hawthorn had *also* been visited by disruptive thieves during the night, because the room into which they were led was a morass of belongings strewn over every surface.

The butler cleared his throat. Once the pause had been elongated enough to make a point about the rudeness afforded to the peerage, Hawthorn turned fully to look at them. He had a boot in one hand and a silver flask in the other.

Another pause. This one was even longer, and even ruder.

"You're a damned traitor, Makepeace," Hawthorn said finally. His voice was deep and bored. "I'm dismissing you from my service. Begone from this house."

"I'll pack my belongings immediately, my lord," said Makepeace.

"Hawthorn," said Courcey, as soon as the door closed behind the butler's unconcerned exit. "Are you going someplace?"

"Yes, I am." Hawthorn dropped the boot onto the floor and the flask into the nearest open trunk. "A sterling observation, Courcey. Quite up to your usual rigorous standard."

"I'd hoped you might have learned to carry on a civil conversation by now."

"How long has it been?" An expression too lupine to be a smile stalked across Hawthorn's face.

"Not long enough," said Courcey. He was as flat and cold as he'd ever been. Perhaps it was the fact that Robin had been thinking of knights that now gave that coldness a feeling of armour: a metal plate beaten smooth and held out for protection. "I wouldn't have come here if it wasn't important."

"I presume you didn't come to oversee my packing." Hawthorn leaned back against the dresser. "If I wanted a fretful pigeon to snap at me about the fact that folding socks is beneath my station, I'd have let Lovett pack my trunks instead of sending him off to pick up my new shirts."

"I need," said Courcey, each word arranged like a grudging chess piece, "your help."

"*We* need your help," said Robin, tired of playing invisible. He began to work on his cuff and sleeve again. At this rate he was going to have to invent a detachable sleeve that was held with buttons at the shoulder. Or perhaps Courcey had a spell that could unravel seams, and re-sew them in an instant.

Hawthorn ignored Robin. His eyes were still on Courcey. "Is that so."

"I know you're not—"

"I sincerely hope you mean you're looking for a tip in regards to the Derby races. Or perhaps you'd like the name of my tailor?"

Colour stained Courcey's cheeks. "If you'd just let me—"

"Because I really can't think how *I'm done with all of that* could leave any room for misunderstanding," said Hawthorn. The weight of authoritative dismissal in his tone was astounding. "Especially from you, Courcey, with your oh-so-clever mind."

"Lord Hawthorn," said Robin loudly. He took a step forward and raised his arm. Now, finally, Hawthorn's gaze fell onto the curse marks there.

Courcey said quickly, "Blyth here has been cursed. As you can see. It seems to be causing pain attacks, brutal ones. And Reggie Gatling's disappeared."

"I can't think why I should care."

"Just *look* at it," said Courcey. "Ten damned seconds of your precious time. Your family's always been strong with runes."

"Strong," said Hawthorn. "Is that what I am? Jealousy's an ugly emotion, Courcey."

"Jealous?" Courcey hissed. "I may not have much magic, but I've more than you."

"And I've lost more of it than you'll ever have, and doesn't that burn you up?"

"*Lord Hawthorn.*" Robin was clear out of patience. "I don't know you, you don't know me, and we're clearly intruding on your time. But Courcey seems to think you can help me. And I'm . . . asking for your help. Please."

Hawthorn inspected Robin as though looking for fault in a horse he was thinking of buying. Robin managed not to ruin the effect of his plea by asking if his lordship would like to inspect his teeth next.

"Pretty manners, this one," said Hawthorn, to Courcey. "Much prettier than yours."

Courcey seemed stunned into silence by the size of that particular hypocrisy, and Robin couldn't blame him.

Hawthorn continued, "You, whatever your name is—no, I don't care—you've been led here under false pretences. I am not a magician. I have no opinions on magical matters, and no interest in being dragged into them, even for ten seconds. A fact of which Mr. Courcey here is perfectly aware."

"You needn't worry that if you do me one favour I'm going to be knocking down your door at all hours, my lord," said Robin. "Especially as you're clearly about to depart for—where, exactly?"

"Lapland," drawled Hawthorn.

Courcey stirred. "Really? You know, I read that—"

"No, not really. New York," said Hawthorn repressively. "Get your pity project out of my sight, Courcey. I've packing to finish."

Courcey's eyes narrowed. "You could have been done help-ing us in the time it's taken you to explain exactly how unhelp-ful you delight in being."

Hawthorn's eyes narrowed in return. He pushed off the dresser, taking a few steps into their space. Courcey was no more a short man than Robin was, but his slightness made the inches that Hawthorn had on the both of them seem exaggerated.

"And you should have known better than to try to wriggle around me like this. If you were here for a fuck, that'd be dif-ferent. I suppose I might be willing to bend you over my bed for old times' sake."

Robin's blood froze. He *couldn't* have heard that correctly.

Beside him, Courcey had gone absolutely still. Robin looked at him, and knew instantly from the look on the man's face that he had, in fact, heard exactly those words emerge from Hawthorn's mouth. It was unthinkable. Nobody would con-fess offhandedly to that particular crime in front of a complete stranger. Unless Hawthorn had somehow guessed—somehow *recognised*—

A calmer, less terrified part of Robin pointed out that even if Robin had been the kind of person to clutch at the pearls of disgusted morality and run straight to the police, there was no real evidence. It would be the word of an impoverished baronet against the word of Baron Hawthorn, son of an earl. Based on a single lewd joke.

"Then again," Hawthorn went on, "perhaps I wouldn't. Pal-lid little librarians were never really to my taste."

Furious humiliation washed Courcey's expression like a pail of tossed water. Robin glanced away, and anger flared in his chest.

"Don't pay me any mind," Hawthorn added, directed at Robin now. "I'm just riling him up. Can you blame me? It's so easy to do."

"I rather think I *can* blame you, my lord," said Robin, "given you're being a complete arse for no reason at all."

After another frozen eternity—during which Robin's skin crawled with the knowledge that he'd likely just made an enemy of the one person Courcey thought could help them—Hawthorn gave a crack of rough but genuine laughter.

"Good luck with your curse, Mr. Nobody," he said. "Never fear: Courcey here just loves a good puzzle. He goes far wilder for figuring things out from books than he ever did for anything that I—"

"You bastard," said Courcey, a strained whisper. "You *fucking* bastard, Jack."

"The curse," said Robin, striking out desperately for a change of subject—and finding one. Looking anywhere but at Courcey had meant he'd looked more closely at the pattern on his own arm. "It's changed."

"How?" said Courcey. He frowned down at it. "Are you sure?"

"Yes. There's more of it," Robin said. "More lines—it's more intricate. And it's covering an inch more skin than it was last night." He swallowed against a new rise of trepidation. "What does that mean?"

"Nothing good," said Hawthorn. His shrug, when they both turned to him, was insouciant. But his eyes had sharpened.

"Jack," snapped Courcey.

A deep, put-upon sigh. "A rune-curse that replicates its own pattern in situ is a bad sign. Whatever its purpose is, it'll keep getting worse."

A spasm of icy dismay made Robin's shoulders twitch. "How do I get rid of it?"

"I don't know—no, Courcey, I don't." Hawthorn's sharpness now had an edge of—not pity, else Robin would have found himself throwing some more unwise punches. But a frank sympathy. "I do wish you luck with it. But I'm not whatever solution you're looking for." His gaze wandered to Courcey and Robin waited for another piece of off-colour humour to emerge from that smirking mouth. Instead his lordship gave a small bow.

"Good to see you, Edwin, old chap. Don't give my regards to your family. I never liked any of them."

Courcey turned on his heel without returning either bow or farewell. He was halfway down the corridor when Robin, still in the doorway, felt sickly heat spread beneath his collar. Blotches of light danced at the corners of his vision; he clutched at the doorframe. The peppery sensation on his tongue was the same as it had been last night. He could smell caramel on the edge of burning, and a sudden wild flare of salt and flowers, like a summer breeze distilled—

The ocean sliced the scene in half, an endless horizon of sea against blushing sky, the watercolours of sunset fading up to a darkening blue. Lord Hawthorn stood with one elbow leaned on a railing, looking outwards, nodding as though in response to speech. He turned suddenly and pulled a watch from his pocket by its chain, glancing down to check the time. He looked up and then gestured. Pointing to something.

Even as the image began to fade Robin was aware of a burning curiosity as to what was happening, as it were, just out of the frame. He tried to sink further into it, as one did with the waking dregs of a dream. His eyes stung. *Move,* he thought, *show me,* and the image lurched, and Robin could almost see—

He was, he was surprised to learn, still upright. His hand was a pale claw on the doorframe. His legs felt like damp feathers. Someone was supporting him with a grip on his other arm.

"—with us. There."

The support, Robin realised once his eyes focused, was Hawthorn. The man must have crossed the room at speed. Courcey was a few feet away, frowning.

"I'm fine," Robin said. "Sorry."

"Was that another attack?" asked Courcey. "The same pain as before?"

"No," Robin said, before he could muster his thoughts enough to say *yes,* and seize on the excuse. But the immersive image had involved no pain in his arm or anywhere else. One mercy at least. "No, I just felt faint. I'm—recovering from a flu."

A thick eyebrow arched. Robin waited for some sort of disparaging comment about swooning like a schoolgirl. Hawthorn had startling eyes, the sort of bright blue that might be called merry in a woman. Up close, he really was unfairly handsome, and his grip on Robin's arm was strong and careful. But that willingness to wound was visible in the curve of his mouth. Robin would have rather kissed a fresh-caught pike.

"Try not to faint onto anything breakable on your way out" was all Hawthorn said.

Makepeace, not looking at all like a man whose position was imperilled, showed them to the door and helped them into their coats. The butler and Courcey exchanged a rueful look.

"New York," said Courcey. "For how long?"

"Goodbye, Mr. Courcey."

"Yes, all right."

The door closed behind them with finality. *New York*, Robin thought. A trip across the ocean. He shivered a little as he followed Courcey back down into the street.

Courcey glanced at him. "Are you—"

"I'm fine," said Robin yet again.

He wondered if coming clean about the visions would have made a difference, back there in the house. Somehow he doubted it. If Hawthorn hadn't been prepared to even look at the physical evidence of the curse, there was no reason to think that hearing about effects beyond *pain* would have budged him further.

Courcey nodded and lapsed into a silence as brittle as the first freeze of a river. Robin could only guess at what he was thinking. A thawing comment of some kind was needed.

"What an utterly charming fellow," Robin said.

The sound Courcey made was small, a clearing of the throat. If it had started as laughter then he'd caught it early. "Yes. That's the way Hawthorn is. Can't get through the simplest conversation without taking the chance to insult everyone in the room."

Robin managed, narrowly, not to point out that Courcey hadn't been doing himself any favours by reacting in such an obvious way. Indeed, Robin had been surprised at how easily Hawthorn had dismantled Courcey's shell of competence and reserve.

Or perhaps it wasn't surprising. If Hawthorn's joke, which hadn't sounded much like a joke, had referred to a true—liaison? relationship?—between the two men.

Robin glanced sideways. The shell had certainly hardened again. Courcey's face was set and pale and unflinching, framed between collar and hat. When Robin overlaid that image with the one of Courcey sprawled bare and panting on a bed . . . it was preposterous. The man was like a porcelain figurine. There was the sense that if you tried to remove his clothes you'd find them painted on.

Robin shifted his jaw, uncomfortably aware of his own clothes. It had been—some time, that was all, since he'd been sexually intimate with another person. And he'd been accosted quite against his will by *lurid visions* of this one.

"I knew he'd be like that," Courcey muttered.

"Thank you," Robin said.

Another of those wary looks, bracing for mockery. "For what?"

"For trying anyway, I suppose. It can't have been pleasant."

"No worse than a handful of splinters when you're spinning an orchard from twigs."

"What does that mean?"

Courcey coloured. "Nothing. It's a saying. A kind of proverb."

"A magical proverb? Like the—marvellous light thing? Miss Morrissey told me, when she was explaining about unbusheling," Robin added when Courcey looked startled.

"*We are man's marvellous light / We hold the gifts of the dawn / From those now passed and gone / And carry them into the night.*" Courcey spoke coolly enough that it took a moment for the rhythm to emerge. "It's a verse from an old poem by a magician called Alfred Dufay. There's a spell-game set to it, that children learn. The other one is just—something you say." He sighed. "The poem's very long, and not very good. I can show you the whole thing. We've a book of Dufay's work in the family library at Penhallick."

"Thank . . . you?"

Courcey's mouth twisted. "We've one of the largest private collections in the country, including a handful of books that contain information on rune-curses. I'll go there this weekend, to try to find out more." After a moment he added, any reluctance smoothed so far into neutrality that Robin couldn't hear it: "And you should probably come along. I don't want to rely on a drawing of the curse, especially if it's changing, and I might need to do a few tests."

Robin swallowed both an unmanly squawk of *Tests?* and the instinctive groan of someone to whom research had always felt like pushing a lump of marble uphill. "All right. Books are at least somewhat less likely to hurl insults at one," he said.

"It is one of their major appeals," said Courcey, and Robin found himself unexpectedly smiling.

6

The station platforms were crowded on that Friday afternoon. It was the third weekend of autumn; the Season was over, the weather promised to be crisp but still eke out occasional scraps of sunshine, and half of London was fleeing to the country for either prolonged shooting jaunts or Saturday-to-Monday house parties. Edwin saw a cluster of young women laughing and waving from atop piles of luggage as a train pulled out, the moving air sending their hat-ribbons fluttering.

Blyth had acquired them first-class tickets from the office account, at Miss Morrissey's insistence. They were heading to Penhallick to investigate an intrusion of the magical world onto the unmagical, she'd pointed out, with a meaningful glance at Blyth's arm. That fell within the bounds of their job descriptions.

For the first stretch of the journey north they shared a compartment with a dignified couple who spoke in the shorthand murmurs of the long-married. Blyth read the *Times;* Edwin worked his way through two chapters of Kinoshita, not bothering to waste energy on disguising the cover. For the most part, people didn't see the unfamiliar unless it threw itself in their face.

Or emblazoned itself on their arm, he supposed, looking up from a deeply confusing paragraph about using fish to navigate by sea. The train was pulling in to Harlow and the couple were gathering their luggage. Blyth ducked to avoid a blow from a

hatbox, folded his paper, and met Edwin's eyes as the compartment door closed, leaving them alone.

"Come on, then," Blyth said. "Tell me about this estate we're
headed to."

Kinoshita nipped Edwin's finger as he reluctantly closed it.
"There isn't a lot to tell. I can't claim it's been in the family for
generations. My parents bought Penhallick just after my sister
was born, and to hear them talk it was ramshackle at best. I
think they liked having something they could splash their
own tastes over." Edwin brushed a fingertip up and down the
book's edge. "It's a large house, but there's plenty of room to
keep to yourself. If that's what you want."

"Why do you do this?" Blyth asked, abruptly. "The—liaison
thing?"

It wasn't difficult to follow his reasoning. Edwin's family
had money. *Edwin* had money, even if he lacked the precise
vowels of someone who hadn't needed to rely on a scholarship to get to Oxford. Edwin was not, to even the dimmest
observer, a man delighted by his post of employment.

"I was asked to do it. The Chief Minister's a friend of my
father's." And when Edwin had tried, uncharacteristically, to
dig in his heels and refuse, Clifford Courcey had made it a con-
dition of his youngest child's allowance. Edwin keenly remembered the humiliation of that discussion. The implication that
Edwin was never going to be good for anything else. "It's not
strenuous. I've plenty of time for my research." Edwin lobbed
the question back across the net. "Why are *you* doing this?"

Blyth shrugged. "I scraped my Second at Cambridge by the
skin of my teeth, and probably scraped my way through the civil
service exam even more narrowly. I was never going to get put
on anything grand. I did spend a few years as a junior in Glad-
stone's office. But—look, Lord Healsmith hated my parents. He
was looking for a way to take it out on me, and he had the
chance to shove me into a job that looked like a dead end."

"But you're titled," said Edwin. "I wouldn't have thought . . ."

"Baronet," said Blyth, which Edwin had already guessed; the man was hardly old enough to have nabbed himself a knighthood. Blyth looked glum about it. "Only inherited a month ago."

"I'm—sorry."

Another shrug.

Edwin gave up on politeness. "Why are you bothering with this sort of employment at all? Why aren't you off administering a country seat, or whatever it is that baronets do?"

A pause. "Idealism?"

"Civil servants don't get to choose their masters. It's Asquith and the Liberals now; it could be someone else in another few years."

Blyth's mouth twitched. He didn't look offended. "You don't think it's possible to want to serve your country?"

"Would you do it if you weren't paid to do it?" Edwin countered.

It was the wrong thing to say. The hints of humour vanished.

"No," Blyth said, and looked out the window.

Edwin put the pieces together. A few years directly under the Home Secretary; that sounded about right, for landed gentry of mediocre intelligence, despite the so-called egalitarianism of the entrance exam. And now Blyth had been shoved into a job that did, from the outside, have all the trappings of demotion. But he'd turned up anyway. Because he was being paid.

Edwin turned the picture in his mind a few times and then set it firmly aside.

He cleared his throat. A peace offering. He was woefully out of practice at making friendly overtures, but he could scrape together some small talk. "And your family, are—"

Between one word and the next, Blyth made a low, strangled noise and doubled over where he sat, his body clenching around his right forearm.

"Blyth." Edwin lunged across the compartment, stumbled over his own feet, and half fell onto the floor with a curse. His cheeks burned, though Blyth hadn't noticed. Blyth might not have noticed if the train had left the tracks and hurtled onto its side. *"Blyth,"* Edwin said again, laying a hand on the man's knee in order to haul himself up and sit next to him.

Blyth's whole body was shivering at a frequency finer than the vibration of the train carriage. Edwin snatched his hand back as Blyth, with what looked like real effort, uncurled his body and lifted his head. His chest rose and fell and his breath rasped through parted lips. He looked as though he was trying to drive the thumb of his left hand through his forearm. Then, as suddenly as he'd tensed, he slumped on the seat with a long, loud inhalation.

"The damned—*damn*," Blyth said.

"How many times has it happened since the park?" Edwin demanded.

"Just once, two days ago," Blyth said. "Lasted longer this time."

Two days ago. Wednesday. Hopefully not while Blyth was reporting to Asquith; *that* would have made an impression.

"A longer attack fits with what Hawthorn said about replication," Edwin said, reluctant. *Worsening.* Damned damn indeed. He should have dragged Blyth to Penhallick the day after it was laid. Who knew how quickly it would progress? "You should have told me it had happened again."

Blyth gave him an exceedingly stubborn look. God save Edwin from the idiotic flower of English manhood. "I've had worse in the boxing ring. And a cricket ball knocked my finger out of joint, my second year at Cambridge. That was no picnic either." He waggled the finger in question: browned, blunt, and strong.

Edwin became aware that his own fingers were clenched around his cradling string in his pocket. A useless and belated reflex. "Are you sure it's—finished? Gone?"

"Yes. Distract me. What were you saying, before it hit?"

It took Edwin a long second to scramble after the memory. His heart was pounding in his throat. He returned to his own side of the compartment.

"Family," he said. "Not your—I mean, you're the eldest? Inheriting the seat. The title."

"It's only me and my sister. Maud." The lines of pain were fading from Blyth's face. "You're doing me a favour, inviting me away for the weekend. I'm escaping at least three awkward conversations. Maudie's furious; I think she had her heart set on a roof-raising row. She likes having a head of the family she can actually argue with. 'Head of the family.'" Blyth echoed himself. "Honestly, it's an awful thought. I'm useless at it. Wish the last Sir Robert had had the sense to produce a couple more sons before he got around to me." He shook his head, a smile starting to hover at the edges of his mouth. "Sorry. I must stop doing this. Blathering on like some terrible doom's befallen me when there are chaps who'd cheerfully give their arm for a title."

A bubble of memory took the opportunity to burst in Edwin's mind. "Sir Robert Blyth," he said. "And Lady Blyth. I *do* know the names. I've heard them talked about."

"That would have pleased them." Blyth seemed a straightforward sort, but it was hard not to scent his ambivalence.

"Philanthropy? Charity works?"

"Yes."

The ambivalence was practically a miasma in the carriage now. Edwin didn't press further, and Blyth's shoulders dropped by an inch. Renowned parents and complicated feelings. Edwin could have some sympathy for that.

"You should start calling me Edwin," he said before he could lose the nerve.

"I'm sorry?"

"We're informal, at Penhallick. And you'll be swimming in Courceys."

"Is that what your family calls you? Just Edwin?"

Walt had called him *Eddie* for nearly a year, when Edwin was nine and Walt thirteen, simply because Edwin hated it so much. Their mother had begged their father to put a stop to it, after Edwin had wept ragingly into her skirts, and Walt had waited two weeks before retaliating. Carefully, where the bruises wouldn't show. And the burns on Edwin's hands had been Edwin's own fault, Walt pointed out; nobody had *forced* him to scramble among the embers for what remained of the notebook where he'd recorded a year's worth of fledgling experiments with new spells, and which he'd thought he'd hidden carefully enough.

No, he'd paid the price to bury *Eddie*. There was nothing he could do about *Win* except lie to delay the inevitable.

"Yes. Edwin. Why, what do your family call you?"

"Perils of being named for my father. Robin." Blyth's smile made him look barely out of school. "You should do the same, if we're to be friendly."

"We are *not*," Edwin began, but made himself stop. "Robin. All right."

Edwin settled himself back against the leather of the seat. It was real. The rattle of the window in its frame was real. Robert Blyth was not exactly imaginary—no, he was too solid, too broad-shouldered, his voice too loud and too warm: the voice of someone who'd never had cause to make himself smaller. But the urge Edwin had to creep closer to that warmth, to imagine that it might be for *him*, somehow . . . that was illusion. Robert, *Robin*, was exactly the kind of person that Edwin had learned to dislike, and who had never needed instruction to dislike him right back. If he sometimes seemed to care for what Edwin thought, that was illusion too. There were exactly two people in the world who gave the smallest damn for Edwin's opinion, and Len Geiger was only one of them because he might have gone out of business without the large chunk of Edwin's allowance that ended up in his till every month.

No. It was just that Edwin was the only magician Robin Blyth had met so far who wasn't actively wishing him harm.

Jack—Hawthorn—didn't count. Indeed, his lordship was determined not to be counted. Not that it had stopped him from reinforcing the point: Edwin was an annoyance at best, something to be brushed off one's coat and ejected from one's house. Edwin didn't care for this warm-voiced near-stranger's opinion either; he *didn't*, but surely he was allowed to hate that Hawthorn had made Edwin's inferiority so clear right in front of the man's face.

And now they were headed to a place where that inferiority would be made even more obvious.

Edwin tucked his hand into his pocket, tangled his fingertips in his string, and watched a row of poplars flick past the train window, rough yellow fingers reaching to the sky.

A vehicle that only escaped the label of dog-cart by the narrowest margin carried them from the tiny station through a two-pub village, along a road that meandered east, then deposited them and their luggage at the mouth of a narrower and better-kept road with a sign announcing PENHALLICK HOUSE.

It was an odd name for Cambridgeshire. Robin took an experimental breath, as though they might have somehow— magically?—ended up in Cornwall instead, but there was no sea edge to the air. He exhaled and felt foolish.

"It's an easy walk from here," said Courcey. Edwin. Edwin. The name suited him, in a fussy way. Apart from the straw of his hat, perched atop his pale hair, he still looked every inch the polished city man. He did not look like someone who had volunteered them to haul their luggage up a long, sloping drive simply for the joy of the stroll.

"I don't mind a walk," said Robin, mostly because Edwin seemed to be expecting him to argue.

The light was turning towards dusk and there was barely a breath of breeze to stir the leaves. Birds yelled from the hedges and bushes as they walked.

"So much for the quiet of the countryside," said Robin. "Looks like a pastoral scene by any artist from the past two centuries; sounds like a fish market."

"And people talk of country dirt as *clean* dirt as though that makes it any easier to remove from your trouser cuffs." Edwin wasn't smiling—in fact, he looked faintly disgusted—but they shared a look of more fellow-feeling than Robin might have hoped for.

Off administering a country seat, indeed. Robin had nothing at all against the country, but could never shake the impression that it would rather everyone buggered off to town and let it administer itself back into wilderness.

He was aware of the uselessness of this opinion when held by a baronet. No doubt Gunning would be thrilled if Robin were to remove himself to Thornley Hill and start tromping tweed-clad around its grounds with a gun slung over his forearm, discussing crop rotation with grizzled farmers.

Robin shook himself and caught up with Edwin, who was waiting at the crest of the gradual slope they'd been ascending.

Penhallick House sat cradled in the early dusk like a smug child in the crook of its mother's arm. A splash of lawn ended in the pale gravel of the driveway and melded into the lines of gardens, set here and there with trees that rivalled the house in height.

It was only as they drew closer to the house itself that Robin's mental classification hurtled abruptly from pastoral romance to outright religious fantasy as an angel floated into view from behind a thick chimney-stack.

Clad all in white and bathed in light, Robin thought stupidly. Or bathèd, rather.

"Dear *Lord*," he choked, when the thought settled home, and dropped his bags.

"And it begins," said Edwin, soft and resigned.

The angel made a highly non-ethereal whooping sound and waved in their direction. It was a young woman with a crown of blond hair, a thick plait tumbling unfashionably down over her shoulder. She was wearing a white dress that looked more like a classical robe, and she was inarguably . . . *floating*, as though seated on a wide swing that had become unmoored from its ropes at the height of its arc and simply failed to notice.

She was also holding a serious-looking bow and arrow. As Robin watched, she notched arrow to bowstring, tugged it back, and aimed directly at the two of them.

No. At Edwin.

"Wait—" Robin said, in real alarm.

She released the string. Robin shoved sideways, driving his shoulder into Edwin's, trying to force the both of them to the ground. He felt the dull pain of bodily impact, then the more immediate one of his hand making the close acquaintance of the gravel drive. He shook his head and rolled off Edwin and to his feet, and only then became aware of the bright new pain in his left leg.

"Ow," said Edwin, but he sounded more dry than hurt.

"Oh, you *dolt*, whatever did you do that for?" came an exasperated shout from above Robin's head. "You confused it."

Robin looked down at the stinging section of his leg, where his trousers now sported a frayed tear. When Robin touched the damaged part, his fingertips came away with a tiny smear of blood. It was such a small wound. Almost polite. *Welcome!* Robin thought, *enjoy your stay!* and let out a spurt of laughter. This place was incredible already.

"This place is incredible," he told Edwin. Goodwill was surging beneath his skin and he wanted to share. He knelt and helped Edwin up, and was surprised when Edwin grabbed at Robin's jaw, holding him still and staring into his eyes as though to read his fortune there. Edwin had a smudge of dirt on his cheek. The light was giving his hair fruit colours.

"Apricots!" said Robin.

"Fuck," Edwin muttered, dropping his hands.

Robin covered his own mouth. He realised a moment later that he'd meant to cover Edwin's, and laughed at his own mistake. Then he laughed more at the look on Edwin's face.

"Bel!" Edwin shouted. "Get down here and help me fix him." Edwin was doing that clever thing with his fingers again, making the string come alive. Robin watched in delight as the cradle filled with pale green light. Edwin knelt at Robin's feet, serious as though in anticipation of a sword-touch to the shoulder.

"I'm not a knight," Robin reminded him. "Can't knight *you*, either."

"Hold still," Edwin snapped, and flicked the green light at Robin's scratched leg, where it tickled deliciously.

"That felt nice," Robin said. He sat, heavily and all at once, so that he could beam right into Edwin's face. "Do it again!"

"Dammit, Bel, what did you tip those arrows with?"

"Some mixture or other from Whistlethropp's," said the angel addressed as Bel, who had alighted nearby. "Such a droll picture on the label, you'll laugh when you see it."

Robin laughed obligingly in anticipation.

"Shop-bought," Edwin muttered. "Can't be too strong, at least."

"*I'm* strong," said Robin happily. "Shall I show you?"

He stood and then threw himself forward. Peals of approving laughter greeted his attempt at a handstand, which made up for the fact that he quickly overbalanced and ended up on his back, grinning up at the sky. There were more people around now. More voices. The more the merrier.

Edwin's frown appeared between Robin and the clouds.

"Wasn't that impressive?" Robin tried to poke at Edwin's chin. "Aren't you impressed?"

"Euphoria, but at least you're lucid," said Edwin. "Hm. Sage will take something like that; they used it in field medicine—

hold still." His fingers moved to build up another flick of cupped light, this one blazing yellow. Robin didn't want to hold still. He wanted to race around the house.

Edwin had one bony knee resting hard on Robin's thigh, holding him down with a meagre strength that Robin would have been able to shake off in an instant. But . . . that might have hurt Edwin's feelings. Instead Robin relaxed and chuckled, making little patterns in the gravel with his feet and hands as Edwin muttered to himself.

"Angels," Robin said, thinking about lying in the snow. He craned his neck to see if Bel was within view.

"She's not an angel," said Edwin. "She's my sister, and she should know better than to assume someone who's never played her games is going to know to hold still when she fires a charmed arrow at them."

"It'll wear off soon. All in good fun," said a hearty male voice. "Must be a new record, my dear fellow. Not here ten minutes and you're already turning on the lectures."

Robin lifted a hand to pat at Edwin's apricot hair, and missed.

There was a high-pitched female laugh. "See, Bel's done you a favour. Made you a friend, even if it did take a game of Cupid to get the thing done."

"That's a bit much, Trudie," said a milder voice.

"Will all of you please be *quiet*," said Edwin. His fingertips tucked themselves under Robin's jaw, cool and quick, then pulled away and began a new pattern in the string. Robin was more than happy to watch the dance of Edwin's fingers. The spell was hesitant to start and stayed small when it was done, a tiny red glow like the tip of a cigarette.

"I don't smoke," Robin said. "Used to. Gave it up."

Edwin reached down and opened Robin's mouth with his thumb. Robin felt his eyes go hooded, felt his chest rise with a breath of promise and pleasure.

Edwin shoved the red spark into Robin's mouth, and Robin swallowed mostly on reflex.

Ten minutes later, Robin was seated on his own suitcase in the entrance hall, vacillating evenly between a feeling of angry indignation and the desire to burst out laughing at the absurdity of the whole situation. The anger had so far stifled the laughter, for the simple reason that nobody at Penhallick—with the exception of Edwin—seemed to think that Robin had any *reason* to feel angry.

Robin had been properly introduced to Mrs. Belinda Walcott—née Courcey—and her laconic and elegantly moustachioed husband, Charles, along with a handful of their friends. William—"Call me Billy, everyone does"—Byatt was a densely freckled sandy-haired chap hovering in Charles Walcott's shadow, and the smile he gave seemed amiable enough. Then there was Francis Miggs, a stout fellow with a reddish complexion who looked at Robin with a beady gamester's eye, as if thinking of placing a bet on him. The only other woman was Trudie Davenport, the sharp-featured brunette with a da Vinci nose and an actress's high laugh, who even on ten seconds' acquaintance gave off the air of a marble set loose in a bowl—always trying to return herself to the centre of things.

"I didn't realise Bel was having one of her parties," Edwin said to Robin. "I thought it'd be quieter."

"You should have telegraphed!" Belinda's angelic face was rendered decidedly less so by the jut of her lower lip. "Really, Win, it's *too* thoughtless of you. My numbers were already thrown off because Laura's ill and Walt's up from town with Father, and now you've dragged another fellow up here, too, when you *never* bring guests." She eyed Robin with frank curiosity. "If you'd only let Mother and Father know you were coming, I'd have told Charlie to invite his cousins. Ghastly simpering bores, the pair of them, but at least they'd have balanced the table. And you could have amused them for me, I suppose."

"Myself being equally boring," said Edwin in a colourless tone.

"Precisely!" said Belinda, and bundled the two of them off upstairs to dress for dinner, with a parting shot of: "Not that way, Win—I've put Miggsy in your room; the view's much the best on that side of the house—wasn't expecting you—never mind, you'll do very well in the south corridor. I suppose you'd better take the willow rooms."

Robin was following Edwin up the stairs and so had a perfect view of the way Edwin's knuckles paled in a fist by his side, quickly released.

"Of course" was all Edwin said.

"Win," said Robin, after a moment. His theory held: the knuckles whitened again. "Or not," said Robin easily, "if you don't care for it."

A pause. "No, I don't."

"I'm surprised it's not Eddie."

They'd reached a landing; the footsteps of the servants transporting their bags were already receding down the corridor on the next level. Robin admired an Oriental-style vase in blue-and-white porcelain set atop a wooden display stand. He added, "Charlie, Trudie, Miggsy, and Billy. I'll be lucky to escape the weekend without being Robbied or Bobbyed."

"I did warn you."

So he had. The aggressive informality was odd, like plunging right into a cold pool at the public baths, but Robin much preferred it to the alternative. None of them had shown the least intention of Sir-Roberting him yet.

The willow rooms were a pair of matched bedrooms tucked down the end of a corridor. The furniture was modern and thin-limbed, the walls painted a pale green from waist height down and papered above that in a pattern of willow boughs.

In the room assigned to him, Robin ignored the bustling of the upstairs maid who was clearly doing her best to prepare a room on five minutes' notice, and went to run his hands over the wallpaper.

"This is William Morris."

"Yes, sir," said the maid, somewhat unexpectedly. She was—Robin blinked hard—lighting a fire in the grate, by magic. She cradled like Robin's attacker had: with no string at all. She blew the sparks into shy flames and looked over her shoulder with a smile. "Most of the rooms here are done up with it. Mrs. Courcey wouldn't hear of anything else."

Mrs. Courcey. Robin wondered that Edwin's mother hadn't come out to play hostess herself, but perhaps she was one of those women who took an hour to dress for dinner.

Which was what Robin was meant to be doing, he realised. Country hours and all that.

"Thank you, ah . . ."

"Peggy, sir."

"Peggy. Can you finish this later? I don't want to be late for dinner."

She stood. "D'you want me to fetch one of the footmen, sir? Mr. Courcey's man, Graves, is the only proper valet in the house, but he's—"

"I'll manage," Robin assured her. "Though I will need these trousers mended. I'll leave them on the clothes-stand, shall I?"

The arrow graze on his leg had already stopped bleeding. There was no time to have anything ironed. Most of the creases of Robin's shirt were hidden by the black waistcoat and dinner jacket.

Evening had truly fallen and the corridor was lamp-lit when Robin closed the door behind him, smoothing his hair back with a palmful of pomade.

No. Not lamp-lit. A fist-sized ball of creamy light like one of van Gogh's stars hovered at the level of Robin's eyes, helpfully off to one side so as not to blind him. When Robin stepped forward, it moved forward. When he halted, it halted.

Something larger than laughter and emptier than pain lodged between Robin's ribs, a feeling that was new but felt, in an indefinable way, mundane. Human. He looked again at the ball of light—*magic, magic*—then screwed his eyes shut, leaned his arm against the wall and his head on his arm, and breathed like he was learning how.

"Is it the curse?" Edwin asked, behind him.

Robin flinched; he hadn't heard Edwin's door open or close. But he couldn't dredge up any shame. His dignity had flown out the window somewhere between the attack of pain in the train carriage and rolling around in the dirt under the influence of Belinda's arrow. And none of it was his own fault. He refused to feel bad about it.

He shook his head.

"Or the flu?" There was no clue in Edwin's tone as to whether he'd believed Robin's prevarication about a recent illness.

Robin shoved it all aside and straightened up. A second light had appeared, this one hovering over Edwin's shoulder.

"I'm still not entirely sure I won't trip over my feet, bang my head, and wake up to find it's all been a dream," Robin said. "But I suppose if pain was going to shake me out of it, it'd have done it by now."

An ironic look widened Edwin's eyes. "Endure the dream for a few days. I'll have you back to your life as soon as I can."

Of course he would. Robin was an off note—a book that had been thrown to the ground. Edwin wanted to tidy him back to where he belonged. That had been clear all along.

"This light is spying on me," Robin said.

"It's a guidelight. It's a charm tied to the room, and now to you. It'll light your way if you want to go somewhere after dark."

"Even if it's only to dinner?"

"You might be glad of it on the way back."

"Seems as though it'd make some of the after-dark activities of your typical house party rather more difficult to carry out in stealth, if everyone has one," said Robin before he could seize control of his tongue.

There was a pause. Edwin glanced at his feet, then back up. No smile had appeared, but the irony was dancing in the blue of his eyes now.

"Tell it to stay, and it will stay," he said.

Feeling utterly foolish, Robin turned to his guidelight. "Stay," he ordered, and took an experimental step. The light began to drift back to the position just outside the room's door, where it had been when Robin emerged. "Come to heel?" Robin suggested, to the light's utter disinterest.

"Amusing as this is," said Edwin, "they'll be waiting on us for dinner."

"Tell me the truth," Robin said. "Is my fork going to take it upon itself to deliver my peas to my mouth?"

"Only if Belinda's still feeling playful," said Edwin. He led the way down the corridor, his own guidelight bobbing along with him, before Robin could decide if he was joking.

7

Robin Blyth liked the house. That much was obvious.

And despite his attack of—nerves? misgivings?—upstairs, he was at ease at the dinner table, dropping comments when called for and falling into polite silence whenever the conversation tripped off into areas of interest only to magical society. His only misstep had been at the beginning of the meal, when he asked if they were waiting for Mrs. Courcey to join them. The room had suffered an expanding awkwardness before Edwin's father said, "I'm afraid my wife is indisposed this evening," with a glance at Edwin that said, quite plainly, that Edwin was failing to tidy up his own messes.

Now Edwin drank his soup without tasting it and watched Robin's smile dimming and broadening as the ambience dictated. It was the smile of someone who knew exactly how to handle himself in company, even when the company was strange. Never mind his parents' enemies, and never mind the Home Office—the *Foreign* Office should have snatched up the owner of that devastating smile and cultivated him like a hothouse plant.

For his part, Edwin was considering himself lucky to keep the food down. He always forgot, when he was in town. He always forgot how it felt to step past the Penhallick sign and have his magic shiver in confusion, and for his blood to tug at his veins. Penhallick House had been built on land handed over by the Crown a century ago to someone missing their Cornish roots, and handed over again—name and all—when it was bought by Edwin's parents. Now it was his family's land, young to magic, and every minute he spent here he could feel it trying to *know* him, trying to find power where so little power dwelled. There was an unsettling sense that the grounds themselves would rise up and buck him off like a skittish horse. It always felt identical to the message in his father's eyes: coded on the best days, and blatant on the worst. *I see what you are, and you are not enough.*

"I thought it was that Gatling boy who had the liaison job," said Walt. "Got sick of facing up to his own uselessness, did he?"

It took Edwin a moment to realise that his brother was speaking to him, and another to quell the stupid, juvenile flutter of panicked wariness. He should be past this cowardice. They were grown men. Walter Courcey was their father's trusted lieutenant in business and a member of the Chief Minister's advisory council; he had better things to do with his time now than think up creative new ways to torment his younger brother.

Edwin told himself this, silently and deliberately. It didn't help. It didn't change the fact that, dangerous curse or no, Edwin would have hesitated before coming to Penhallick at all if he'd known Walt would be here too.

"I don't know," Edwin said. "I haven't seen Reggie for weeks."

"A real blow for Sylvester Gatling, that was," said Edwin's father. The table fell quiet, faces turning respectfully. Clifford Courcey was not a large man, but he held himself with the aggressive self-assurance that Walt and Belinda had inherited. His unmagical business associates probably mistook it for the weight of money, but Edwin's father had been born with the power that underlaid his poise. Earning his fortune had only gilded it.

He went on, "His only son too. Terrible thing, to see a branch of English magic dry up like that."

"His daughters might make up for it in time," offered Billy Byatt. "I heard the older one's to be married."

"No guarantee of the bloodline, all things told," said Mr. Courcey darkly.

Heat climbed Edwin's neck. He kept his mouth shut as a new course was laid on the table. Billy met Edwin's eyes and quirked his lips in sympathy. Next to Edwin, he was the least powerful of the magicians in the room, and Edwin couldn't help but read pitying fellow-feeling into the fact that Billy had always been the friendliest to him of Bel and Charlie's set.

"Perhaps you can shed some light on the man's whereabouts, Sir Robin," said Walt. "Is Gatling a friend of yours? Sad to say, some people never quite get the knack of friendship, but *you* don't strike me as that sort."

His small smile invited Robin to play along with the jibe at Edwin's expense. It was familiar enough to be exhausting. More than anything Walt liked to pause and admire the sites of his own previous victories, and by the time Walt left school he'd already torn up two of Edwin's tentative friendships by the roots: one by simply presenting the choice of being tormented alongside Edwin or of escaping it, and the other—subtler—by poisoning them against him with half-truths. He'd left the earth salted in his wake; Edwin learned his lesson, and didn't try to make any more connections that might prove tempting targets. It was fine. He'd always been most comfortable in his own company.

"I'm afraid not," said Robin. Perfectly polite, but no longer warm. "I've never met Reggie Gatling."

"*Blyth*," said Walt, after a pause. "I don't believe I know any Blyths. Is the magic on your mother's side?"

"I, ah," said Robin, and skewered Edwin with a wide-eyed and transparent request for help.

Edwin had been chewing over how much of this to tell. Belinda and Charlie's set were heedless gossips—no worse than the average, but nothing told to them could ever be considered a secret. It would spill through their level of English magical society like tea across a page.

He'd introduced them to Robin as the new liaison and left it there, and Robin's company manners were doing a good job of hiding his ignorance, but there was no hope that they'd get through an entire weekend without revealing its totality and depth. Not with the kind of entertainments that Belinda enjoyed.

"Robin doesn't come from magic at all," said Edwin. Best to have that part out quick and clean. "Someone in the Home Office assigned him to us by mistake. He's only been unbusheled a few days."

Cutlery paused. The quiet of the table thickened.

Walt was looking at Robin carefully. After a moment he smiled, calling up a chill of association that made Edwin want to hide his fingers in his lap. To an unbiased observer it was probably a normal smile, peacock-tinted by Walt's guidelight, which glowed cosily in the glass jar that sat next to his water glass. Tonight the jars in front of each place setting were all from the same set, an abstract mosaic of greens and purples.

Robin's empty jar seemed suddenly like a rather unfortunate metaphor.

"And you brought him here," Walt said.

"As good an introduction as any, if he's to do the job," said Edwin. He forced himself to hold his brother's gaze. Anything to do with the curse could wait until tomorrow, and Walt and their father planned to return to London then anyway.

"I suppose it is rather nice for you, Win, not being the one in the room with the least magic," said Bel.

Trudie turned to Robin with the expectant air of a child whose nose was pressed between the bars of a zoo cage, hoping the elephant was going to do something diverting. "It must be absolutely fresh and strange and wild to you, then."

"The game of Cupid was something of a surprise," said Robin.

Both Trudie and Bel went off into gurgles of laughter.

"No wonder you dodged, you silly thing!" said Bel. "It's a game of nerve. The imbuement on the arrows is for them to seek movement. They won't hit you, if you freeze in time. If you flinch, you're more likely to be scratched, and you take the punishment."

"Like the instincts of hunting dogs," said Robin blandly. "Just scratched?"

"Nobody's died yet," said Francis Miggs, and laughed as though he'd said something amusing. His elbow jogged Edwin's as he reached for the sauceboat, and Edwin avoided his eye. Miggsy was easy to set off, once he'd had a few glasses, and his sense of humour had coarsened but not progressed in spirit since the schoolyard.

"It's best played in couples," said Bel.

"Quite so," said Charlie. "Not the thing to entrust the safety of one's wife to another chap's spell, after all."

"So one partner shoots, and one controls the . . ." Robin made a floating motion with his knife.

"The lady shoots," said Charlie. "Can't expect a female to handle a directed levitation, can you? That takes training. But some of them are a dab hand with a bow." He beamed, wide and complacent, at Bel. She beamed back.

Robin asked a few questions about how the spell worked; Charlie demonstrated, wiping butter from his fingers before beginning the cradles. He explained what he was doing in a condescending tone, getting several of the technical details wrong. The spell worked anyway, sending Bel's chair hovering a good three feet above the table while she clutched her wineglass and sipped theatrically.

"Not at dinner, Charles," said Edwin's father, but he didn't sound displeased.

Charlie and Bel kept Robin involved in lively conversation after that. Charlie always liked people more once he'd explained something badly to them, and Bel just liked things that were Edwin's.

After dinner, Mr. Courcey withdrew to his study and Charlie proposed a game of pool and a bottle of port.

"Not for me," said Edwin. "I'm going to go and see Mother."

"I'll come with you," said Robin. "That is, if you don't mind. I'd hate to go to bed without having paid my respects to the lady of the house."

Edwin couldn't think of a reason, under the eyes of everyone else in the room, to refuse. "All right," he said.

Though once they'd been left alone, Edwin's guidelight having been decanted from its keeper to its place above his shoulder, Edwin didn't bother to hide his annoyance. "What are you doing? I thought you'd appreciate being in company. Go and drink with the others—go and play pool."

"I'd be afraid of being scratched by a cue, without having you there to fix me. How does one play pool at a party like this? On the ceiling?"

"One cheats. Though I doubt Billy or Miggsy can provide much competition to Walt and Charlie, if they're playing under Killworth rules. Ivory's difficult to imbue without a lot of blunt power. They may be playing it straight, tonight. I'm sure you'd be in with a chance."

"You're trying to get rid of me," Robin said, pulling up short. "I was only—I honestly—is she very unwell, then?"

Edwin could have rid himself of Robin in another two sentences by implying that Robin was rudely imposing himself on a private family affair. Which he *was*. But Edwin remembered Robin's rounded shoulders outside their bedrooms and looked at the tension around the man's eyes. Robin was quite capable of being rude to *Edwin*, if nobody else. If he wanted to go with the others, he'd have gone.

"I don't know precisely how she is at the moment," Edwin said, relenting. "But she likes meeting new people. Come on."

Morton the tortoiseshell was standing in the middle of the smaller staircase, staring at a point halfway up the wood panels of the wall, as they walked to Edwin's mother's suite. He let out an interrogative yowl, paused, flicked his ears, then yowled again.

"I think your cat's smelled a mouse," said Robin.

"No, he's only talking to the ghost."

"Ghost?"

When Edwin turned, the expression on Robin's face matched the resignation that had suffused his voice. It was the look of a man so drenched by the rain that he'd tossed his umbrella into the gutter and was opening his collar to the storm.

Edwin steered his thoughts away from the prospect of Robin's bare neck adorned with columns of rainwater. It was—a slip. Understandable. He was tired. He was worried. He hated the countryside and the way both Penhallick and his brother made him feel. Hell, he'd been standing in the damn storm himself since he walked into Reggie's office that Monday morning.

But he was going to cling to his umbrella for all he was worth.

"Ghost," Edwin affirmed. "Don't worry. They're not dangerous."

"Back in town, you said they didn't exist. That they were nonsense."

"*Visible* ghosts are nonsense," Edwin said. "You can't see them. And they can't talk to you unless there's a medium around, and there's maybe three true mediums in the whole of England."

Robin glanced at the wall. "Then how do you know they're there at all?"

"The cats, mostly. There are detection spells you can do, but cats are simpler."

When they were admitted to Mrs. Courcey's rooms, with a smiling admonition from her maid Annie not to keep her awake too long, Edwin's mother was sitting in her chair rather than in bed. That was heartening. Even more so was the pristine curl of her hair, and the gleam of rubies at her ears. With the shawl flung around her shoulders she might have been a matron tired by the exertions of an evening ball instead of someone who'd likely not moved from that chair all day.

Edwin crossed the room to kiss her cheek and smelled the lilies of her scent.

"Hello, darling," she said, returning the kiss warmly. "You should have let us know you were coming."

"I wanted to surprise you."

"And so you have." She peered at Robin, who was hovering just inside the room. Annie had many jobs, and one of them was to funnel the house gossip directly to this room. "Sir Robert Blyth? Welcome to Penhallick."

"Thank you, ma'am," said Robin. "I'm sorry to hear you haven't been well."

Mrs. Courcey indicated the arm of her chair. After a pause, Robin came and perched on it, awkwardly. He made her look even thinner in comparison, even more swallowed by the velvet. He glanced at Edwin, on her other side, and Edwin had the unpleasant feeling of being part of a set of bookends. His reunions with his mother were usually private.

But he hadn't been lying. She did like new people. And she certainly liked Robin's immediate plunge into asking after the willow-bough wallpaper, and the particular inlaid wooden surface of the long dresser in the entrance hall, and the tiles around the basin in his room.

"You have an eye for design, Sir Robert," she said, delighted.

"My parents had an interest in art. I became more interested than I meant to," said Robin. It sounded like a practiced answer. "I haven't ever seen a house so completely dedicated to the new styles. It's extraordinary."

Florence Courcey's eyes were tired but bright. "I tore out its guts, when we first bought the place. Attics to cellars. And then marched in with half the creations of Misters De Morgan and Morris in my pocket."

"Daring," said Robin with a smile.

"You probably know that my husband made his fortune in the American railways. We spent quite a few years over there, when my health allowed that kind of travel."

"I didn't know that," said Robin, with a *go-on* kind of air. "Edwin didn't tell me he'd lived in America."

"It was before I was born," said Edwin.

"It was a wonderful time. We even had the pleasure of be-friending the great Mr. Tiffany," his mother murmured, her gaze going distant. "Even since returning to England for good, we've commissioned a great many works for the house from his studio."

Robin lit up. "I thought so. The little jars at the dinner table?"

"Yes! One of my particular treasures, though of course we could hardly explain what an ornamental guidekeeper is, when we placed the order. I miss the sight of them—oh, I do wish I had the energy to join the family at dinner more often—do feel *keenly* that I should be present—"

"You can't be expected to put up with Bel's set, Mother," said Edwin. "Don't think anything of it. I'll dine with you while I'm here, shall I? We can make a picnic of it."

"No! No, darling, I can't think of imposing such tedium on you."

"And if I said I preferred it?"

Her eyes were Bel's eyes, a paler blue than his own. There was nothing in them but love, and yet Edwin felt like a paper-cut the whisper of her disappointment. "Edwin, darling. You mustn't let them tease you."

"Blyth. Robin," said Edwin. "I'd like a moment alone with my mother."

Robin stood at once. "I'll wait outside," he said. "After all, I left my guidelight outside my room, despite Edwin's warning me not to." He winked at Edwin as he left.

"What a nice young man." Edwin's mother patted the folds of her shawl. "I'm so pleased to see you bringing a friend here, darling."

"He's not a friend." Edwin sat at her feet, as he hadn't done for months. The first touch of her hand on his hair made him want to cry, but instead he took another deep breath of her perfume. "Can I give you a secret, Mother?"

"You know how I love secrets," she murmured.

Edwin looked into the fire and let his mother card her frail and swollen fingers through his hair, and told her the uneasy story of Robin Blyth, baronet and civil servant, new to magic and already marked by it in baffling circumstances. It felt better to have told someone. It felt right, normal, for it to just be the two of them, Edwin and his mother, holding things close against the world.

"Poor boy," she said. "And what a bother for you! You could hardly do otherwise, of course. Best to have this dealt with. I suppose you'll give him lethe-mint, when it's sorted out?"

"Of course," said Edwin.

"It may take more than the mint, if it's been a week. I'm sure you know what's best, my dear. And you can always ask Charles to do the spell itself."

Edwin breathed in. Out. "Of course," he said again.

He would happily have fallen asleep there, but he had a guest. He bid his mother good night and let himself out. Robin was inspecting the coloured panes of the closest window, darkened though it was by night. Edwin would suffer through a conversation about Tiffany glass if necessary.

But then Robin turned and Edwin saw the question hovering on the man's lips.

Edwin said, "It's a form of rheumatism. It gives her pain, and it saps at her strength." Broad; inarguable. That was as much as a stranger needed to know. The fits of melancholy had been mild, by all accounts, before the rheumatism got its claws into her. Now there were weeks when she refused to change from her nightgown, or to have the curtains drawn, or to raise her voice to dictate a letter. Edwin had done the imbuement on her pens himself. They were sensitive to even a whisper.

Edwin wrote to her more often, not less, when the gaps between her letters yawned wide. It never seemed to drag her out of it more quickly. He wrote nonetheless.

They had just turned into the south corridor when Blyth halted and swayed on his feet, eyes wide. He did not clutch at his arm, or curl around it as he had in the train and as Edwin had half feared he would during dinner. Instead he simply stood, slumped against the wall and staring at nothing, the colour gone from his face just as it had done in Hawthorn's house. He was breathing, but shallowly. Edwin felt, for a long few heartbeats of startling terror, entirely useless.

And then it was over, whatever it was. Robin blinked and was behind his own eyes again.

Edwin guided them both down the corridor and into the closest of the willow rooms, which was Robin's. The guidelight still shone motionless outside the door as though set in a bracket.

"All right," said Edwin when the door closed. He was fed up and worried in equal measure. "Tell me what's going on. Should I send for a doctor?"

Robin sat on the edge of the bed. "No. I'm not ill. At least, not in the normal sense."

"Do you have fits?" Edwin demanded, not bothering with delicacy. "Do you hear voices? Whatever it is, I'm hardly about to have you kicked out of my family's house in the middle of the night. Tell me."

Robin's voice shook. "I see things. Not just *see*—I'm plunged into them, I suppose. It feels like being transported somewhere else, in a rather horrid way. It started the night I was attacked."

"What sort of things?" Edwin asked, sharp. He was already trying to cross-reference immersive visions with any kind of curse he'd ever read about, and failing.

"This time it was a hedge maze," said Robin. "Large. Well-trimmed. The kind of thing you can find on the grounds of houses all over the country, I dare say. I saw the maze, and the sky, and—something moving, just on the edge of it all."

"This time. The others were different?"

"Yes. Different each time." Colour washed Robin's cheeks. "All just brief glimpses of places, or people. And no, I don't hear voices. There's never any sound."

"Tell me what you've seen."

Robin's voice gained an edge. "I'll *paint* them for you, if you insist, but perhaps it can wait until tomorrow?"

"You should have told me about this," Edwin snapped. "A curse that makes you have visions—that's a *detail*. That could be *vital*. How am I supposed to learn how to counteract it when you're withholding information?"

Robin glared at him. "No matter how many times we call one another by friendly names, *Edwin*, I don't know you. I didn't know if I could trust you. I still don't."

Edwin stared back. "You . . . came here." Hardly eloquent, but Robin seemed to take his meaning.

"Yes. I am here, aren't I? In a house full of strangers who can do magic, when the last magical strangers I met put *this* on me."

That was a fair point. Edwin was momentarily startled at the fear crowding in Robin's eyes, behind the anger; then he was startled that this was the first time he'd seen it. Stubborn sportsman Robin Blyth. Physical courage he clearly had in handfuls, but this was something else. Edwin swallowed a wash of guilt and climbed to his feet, feeling his own fatigue seep through him as he did so.

"Get some sleep," he said. "I'll start my research in the morning."

Robin nodded, shoulders slumping. He rolled his head on his neck where he sat, eyes falling closed, elbows resting on solid spread thighs. A few strands of hair rebelled against their slick styling and fell over his forehead.

Edwin bit the inside of his own mouth and turned away. He could allow himself these slips as long as they stayed firmly inside his own head. Tomorrow he would do what he always did with problems: he would hurl himself at books and interrogate them until they rendered up the solution. He would work this all out; he would let Robin wake up from this bad dream. And then Edwin's life, too, would settle back to normal.

8

The breakfast room contained the smells of buttered toast and sausages. It also contained Trudie Davenport and Charlie Walcott, Trudie spooning sugar into tea while Charlie talked and stroked his moustache simultaneously. They both looked up when Robin entered.

"*Sir* Robin!" said Charlie heartily. "Slept well, I hope?"

As cold-plunge informality went, Robin reflected, that was a middle ground he could live with.

"Very well," he said. "Good morning, Miss Davenport."

She flicked a look at him that was flirtatious in an impersonal way, a pole thrust out to test the depth of a puddle. "*Trudie*. I insist."

Her teaspoon stirred the cup with a rattling clink, and without any help from her. Belinda's Cupid game had been a spectacular introduction, but not, it seemed, characteristic. Most of the magic here was smaller, more offhand, completely enmeshed in the lives of the people.

And all of it *hidden*. There must be scores, perhaps hundreds, of country houses and townhouses where the magic was like this, kept inside walls or within the bounds of the estate, just another secret moving like a minnow beneath the surface of society and flashing a fin only where necessary. National interest. Briefings to the PM, like the one Robin had done earlier that week, where Asquith—with his long nose and hooded eyes—had looked as though nothing had ever surprised him, nor ever could.

And yet there was a word for magic's revelation to the unenlightened. As though one were Saul on the road to Damascus.

Robin piled up a plate of food from the covered silver dishes at the sideboard. He ate at a faster pace than his digestion usually agreed with, and nodded along as he was informed that Mr. Courcey and Walter had already left in order to catch the first train back to London, and that the other members of the party were yet to show their faces.

"Aside from Win," said Trudie. "The servants were already taking tea into the library when I came downstairs."

"Some people don't feel social at breakfast," said Robin.

"*Some* people were born without a social bone in their body," said Trudie.

It was momentarily difficult for Robin to keep his expression pleasant, hearing this echo of Walter's dig at Edwin the night before. Robin hadn't known quite what to make of Edwin's brother. Everyone else had deferred to him, but it was more than the usual deference to a favoured and charismatic eldest son. There had been a strange, balancing-act tension in the air that casual sibling animosity couldn't explain. It had put Robin's teeth on edge, and it was a relief to know that Walt wouldn't be a regular member of the house party.

"Bel's leaving everyone to their own devices this morning, but she'll insist you both join us for boating on the lake after lunch," Charlie said to Robin.

"I don't know if we'll be—" Robin started, but Charlie said, "Nonsense!" and turned back to his bowl of kedgeree.

Robin swallowed half a cup of tea in two gulps, winced at the spasm of complaint in his throat, and murmured something noncommittal as he escaped the breakfast room.

When he found the library, he stopped a few feet inside the door in order to stare. He'd been in manor-house libraries before. Even Thornley Hill had a modest one, and he'd been envisaging something like that: a room stuffy with dust and gloomy with solid last-century furnishings, shelves packed with matching sets of untouched leather-bound books.

The library at Penhallick House was two storeys high, with a narrow balcony running along the two walls that were lined with bookcases stretching from the floor to the ceiling. Another wall held arch-topped windows, their curtains caught at the waists to allow morning light to spill into the room. A single rug was set well back from the fireplace that dominated the final wall, a mouth of wrought iron surrounded by tiles patterned with white vines on vivid orange. The rest of the floor was an intricate and angular pattern of inlaid wood, blond and amber-brown shades set at angles to one another, crawling in regular lines from one wall to the next.

That was what you saw looking straight ahead. Looking up, all you saw was books. Robin remembered, belatedly, Edwin saying that they had one of the largest private collections in the country.

Hawthorn had called Edwin a librarian and clearly meant it as an insult. But Robin felt like he was viewing a page from a book on exotic creatures, demonstrating how the patterns of their hides allowed them to blend into their surroundings. Edwin stood near the centre of the library floor, shirtsleeves rolled to mid-forearm, one hand turning the page of a thick book splayed open on a table while the other scratched at the back of his neck. Looking at him, Robin realised that before this moment he'd never seen Edwin Courcey look even the slightest bit *comfortable*.

Robin let the heavy door swing noiselessly shut behind him, and cleared his throat. Edwin's head rose.

"There you are," said Edwin, as though Robin were a tardy schoolboy. "When you said *paint*, were you joking around?"

"Good morning to you too," said Robin. "What paint?"

"Last night, you said you could paint your visions."

Robin had been joking, more or less. He was a mediocre artist at best. But he thought about trying to cram *words* around what he'd seen, with Edwin's impatient eyes needling him, and suddenly the alternative didn't seem like such a bad idea.

"I can try drawing one of them," he said. "If you've pencils?"

A nod. "I do. Now, come here and roll up your sleeve."

So it was Edwin who wielded the pencils first, while Robin held out his bared right forearm and Edwin copied down the runes of the curse with painstaking care. Neither of them commented on the fact that it reached fully to Robin's elbow now. Curled up in the corner of Robin's soul, like a summer-basking snake, was the fear that had opened its eyes when Hawthorn first said, *It'll keep getting worse.* Every time the pain claimed him that fear shed its skin and grew larger.

Edwin took the piece of paper with him halfway up the ladder leading to the balcony. He *shouldn't* have blended in, Robin thought, watching him. There was no sense to it. Edwin wore a white shirt and a waistcoat backed in ivory satin, his long legs clad in cloud-grey flannel that looked soft to the touch. He was overdressed for this country party; Charlie had worn a sports jacket at breakfast. Edwin was a slip of a figure, insubstantial and underpigmented against the richness of the shelves and books.

Edwin said, "Hm. Zeta twenty-nine four," and the ladder flew sideways on its runners as though pushed by an enthusiastic hand, carrying Edwin to the corner of the library.

Robin pulled a piece of paper in front of him and began to draw the vision that he remembered most clearly. The glass floor, with its dark geometric lines. The view upwards; the many pairs of feet crossing to and fro.

All right, it wasn't the one he remembered most clearly. But he was hardly going to draw *that* one.

He was absorbed enough in his task that he didn't look up when Edwin dropped a small pile of books onto one end of the table. He *did* look up when Edwin said, sharply, "When were you at the Barrel?"

"Beg pardon?" said Robin.

Edwin slid the paper out from Robin's hands. "That's the view from the ground floor of the Barrel. The building that houses the Magical Assembly," he added, in light of what was probably a blank expression on Robin's face. "We call it the Barrel, because—but you must have been there."

"Me, I'm an accident of paperwork," said Robin. "Remember? I haven't been anywhere except where you've been dragging me. This was in the first lot of my visions."

Edwin frowned down at the paper. He traced one of the dark lines with a finger. "A real place you've never been. That rules out waking dreams. You could be seeing through someone else's eyes, in that moment, but why a curse—"

"That's not it," said Robin. "The first time it was—lots, at once, and all different. And . . ." He swallowed, and told Edwin about the vision he'd had of Lord Hawthorn on the boat, while standing in the doorway of Hawthorn's room.

"Did he look older? Younger?"

"Not visibly."

"Past, present, future," said Edwin. He didn't seem to be talking to Robin anymore. He dug in a pocket of his waistcoat and pulled out his string, looping it rapidly around his hands. "Not the present. Perhaps one of the others."

"That's possible? Seeing the future?"

Edwin's mouth thinned. "No. Yes. Foresight's not even proper *magic*, nobody knows where it comes from, and it's too rare for there to be any hope of studying it properly. Half the confirmed cases in history weren't even in magicians. There's one in India at the moment, and one in Germany, and I haven't the foggiest about any others. People with it get . . . snapped up. They're useful." He shot Robin an uneasy look. His thumbs were moving in a graceful dance. "I've never heard of it being induced. If someone knew *how* to induce it, through a curse or by any other means, they'd make a fortune."

"And wouldn't go around bestowing it willy-nilly on people they're trying to threaten, one assumes," said Robin.

The cradle formed between Edwin's hands wasn't glowing, but the air caught within the string shimmered like the space above a hot pan. "Pi sixty-seven, pi sixty-one, kappa fourteen two, beta zero one seven through nine." Edwin clapped his hands, crushing the string between them, then made a flicking motion.

A sparse rustling sound like the wind in half-naked trees came from the bookshelves, and books shouldered their way out from the shelves like audience members called eagerly onstage to participate in—well, a magic show. They floated over to the table and settled in a row, ready to be opened.

Robin felt like his entire face was a question. It must have been; Edwin looked at him and began at once to answer it.

"When I was twelve I spent an entire summer coming up with my own tables of classification based on subject matter. I've had to expand the system several times since then." He glanced around. "Luckily one can just keep adding more numbers. An alphabetisation charm is—well, more complicated than you'd think, the notation takes up half a page. But it's been designed. It's easy to implement. It's just not sensible for a reference library. Where did you study?"

"Pembroke," said Robin. "Rah, Light Blues."

Edwin nodded. "I presume the Cambridge libraries are arranged much like the Oxford ones. Indexed by shelf position in the stacks?"

"Haven't the foggiest. I'd assume so." As far as Robin was concerned, you requested books and they were fetched for you. He'd spent as little time in the library as possible.

"Not any more sensible, if you want to browse by topic. There's a man in America who's published a similar kind of classification system based on numbers, actually. And I thought I was so ingenious, when I came up with this one on my own." A wisp of bitter self-mockery in his voice.

Robin said, faintly staggered, "You were *twelve*."

"The ladder's imbuement is keyed to the classification system. And I've marked each book so that the indexing spell knows which ones to fetch." He stroked his fingers down the spine of the book in his hand. A briefly glowing $\Pi67$ appeared, and then faded.

"You invented this system? You applied it?" Robin looked around them at the hundreds, *thousands,* of books. "And you carry the whole thing around in your head?"

"I made a catalogue." Edwin indicated a small hand-bound volume he hadn't once touched. "And if you're going to suggest that I was a very dull child, let me assure you that it would by no means be an original insult."

When Robin was twelve, he'd spent his summer trying to invent the game of indoor cricket, much to the distress of several antique urns and at least one window, and leaving beetles in Maud's bed. He had a sudden flash of a pale, bookish boy—the kind that he'd have barely noticed at school, except to wonder why they couldn't be more *fun*—creating tables and patiently inscribing book after book, forcing the sum of his knowledge to fall neatly within the dictates of his mind.

"Remind me not to make an enemy of you, Edwin Courcey," he said, smiling to show he meant no sting. "I think yours is probably the kind of brain that could run a country."

Edwin wasn't smiling, but something about the way he ducked his head suggested that he was pleased, and not sure how to handle being pleased.

"That would involve people, and I'm less good with people. I'll settle for knowing all the things I want to know," Edwin said quietly. "When and how I need to know them."

"Can you fetch me something like that?" Robin asked.

"What?"

Robin cast around for ideas. He just wanted, for no reason he could explain to himself, to see Edwin's fingers create that commanding hot-shimmer again. "Any good stories in this library of yours?"

Edwin looked at him for a few seconds. Robin prepared himself to be told off for wasting research time. Then Edwin rearranged his string, coaxed the shimmer into existence, and said, "Alpha ninety," his blue eyes fixed on Robin with the incurious gaze of a Byzantine saint.

A new pile of books floated over and formed itself in front of Robin. Most of them had battered, much-loved covers, and smears down the edges of the pages. Fairy tales. Books for children. Two of them were thicker; the largest and most imposing was called *Tales of the Isles*.

Edwin sat, abruptly. There was a faint sheen of sweat to his brow.

"Are you all right?" Robin asked.

"I'm fine. Read your stories."

"Is this indexing spell a particularly tough one, then?"

"No." Edwin's voice was thin ice. Robin remembered Belinda's sweet comments at dinner. *The one in the room with the least magic.*

"Does the string—magnify the effect of the spell?" he hazarded. "Is that why you use it?"

Edwin's unfriendly expression sharpened and then, all of a sudden, relented. "No," he said. "But I can see why you'd think so. You can get away with imprecision in your cradles if your power fills the gaps. I can't. And magic is like any other kind of strength. If you use too much of it, you have to wait for it to replenish. So if a dragon crashes through the library window in the next hour, *you'll* have to save us."

"A *dragon*—"

Edwin looked at him. Some of that irony was seeping in through the edges.

Robin grinned. "You sod. You really got my hopes up."

"Dragons live in books," said Edwin, nodding at the one in front of Robin. "I'm going to see if I can find out anything about your curse, and your—foresight."

The index mark, Q90, was also pencilled on a bookplate inside the cover of each book. Robin flicked first through those of them with coloured illustration plates, looking for dragons, but didn't find any. He cracked *Tales of the Isles* instead and became rapidly absorbed in the contents page.

The Tale of the Flute That Fell Down a Well.
The Tale of the Queen's Seven-Year Dance.
The Tale of the Stone That Never Cracked.

He looked up to find that Edwin was no longer seated, but doing idle laps of the library floor, pacing and pausing and sometimes even spinning on the spot, or doing a half step like a dance. All the while holding a book up to his face and occasionally turning a page.

Robin didn't say anything, but his gaze must have been palpable. Edwin paused, book lowering.

He said, defensively, "It helps me think."

"Cheaper than coffee, at any rate," Robin said. He'd meant it as rather a hint—he was starting to feel peckish, and could have done with some biscuits to nibble on—but Edwin just turned around and took himself over to the window seat that filled the central and largest window, where he settled as though in stubborn refute of his own claim.

Edwin probably wouldn't allow him to get crumbs on the precious books, Robin reflected, and turned back to his own reading. He flicked back and forth in the book, dipping into stories, letting the words and ideas wash over him. None of them were very long, which suited Robin. It was like filling a plate with small quantities of food from a buffet table; no flavour lasted long enough for him to be bored of it.

He couldn't have said how much time passed, himself engrossed in stories and Edwin crossing occasionally to the table to fetch more books back to the window seat. The curse grabbed once at Robin's arm, and he counted his breaths and closed his throat on his whimpers until the pain released him; Edwin never looked up. The sounds of footsteps came faintly from elsewhere in the house. Once or twice Robin heard a raised woman's voice that could have been either Belinda or Trudie, or a member of the domestic staff. Mostly, the library had the quiet that managed to fill libraries like a solid presence.

All of a sudden Robin's eye caught on a title buried in the dense list. *The Tale of the Three Families and the Last Contract.*

He turned to the page indicated. That particular tale was much like the others: short and not too fanciful, as though the author were more interested in collecting the facts of the matter than dressing it up to be read aloud for entertainment. It described the last court of fae making the decision to leave the mortal realm and return to their own, and the formal contract made between these fae and the three greatest magical clans of Britain, to preserve some magic for the use of humans.

A small printed illustration was set within the text. The black-and-white lines were an unimpressive depiction of the three items that the story claimed were the physical symbol of the contract—one for each family. A coin, a cup, a knife.

Robin jumped when something moved in the corner of his vision. It was a different cat to the one they'd found in conversation with the ghost on the stairs. This one was white with ginger patches, and it prowled with purpose towards the window seat, which as the sunniest spot in the room seemed likely to be a regular haunt. It paused in feline affront when it found the cushioned seat occupied by Edwin.

In a single decisive motion, the cat leapt up into Edwin's lap and nudged its head demandingly against the book.

A smile stole over Edwin's face, piecemeal. One side of his mouth rose and then the other. It was a very small smile, and looked as though it didn't often venture forth from confinement. Edwin folded the book in one hand. With the other he reached out his slender fingers and rubbed the cat beneath the jaw. At the same moment, the sun must have peeked from beneath a cloud, because the light spilling into the window seat changed.

Robin realised he was staring, but he couldn't stop. Edwin's colourless self had taken up the white-gold of the sunlight and he looked close to ethereal, like a fairy from the book. A witch, with his familiar.

Robin's first impression was still correct. Edwin was not handsome. But from this angle, with that smile like a secret caged in glass, he had . . . something. A delicate, turbulent, Turner-sketch attractiveness that hit Robin like a clean hook to the jaw.

"Edwin," Robin said. It came out thinner than he'd meant. He crossed to the window seat and showed Edwin the story he'd found.

Edwin's brow furrowed as he read. "I remember this," he said. "Every magician in Great Britain is supposed to be descended from one of these fabled Three Families, down one tributary of blood or another. Now, the men who attacked you, you're sure they said that precisely? The *last* contract?"

"I . . . think so."

"It's most likely a coincidence. This is just a story."

"Magic is just a story," said Robin. "If magic exists then surely the fae do. Or did."

"That's not a logical progression," said Edwin, veering into tutor territory again. "We have no more concrete proof of the fae's historical existence than we do of—dragons."

"Except the people looking for this contract *don't* live only in books," said Robin, irritated.

"Which is no guarantee that they're not on a fool's errand—" Edwin visibly relented. "It's true that we do see a similar kind of origin myth arising in other cultures. The idea that magic was never *ours,* that every spell used to be the result of bargains struck between us and a race of magical creatures. The contractual nature of this particular rendition is very . . . English." That small smile again. "It's in Dufay's poem. *We hold the gifts of the dawn, from those now passed and gone.*"

"That's right. You were going to show me the rest of it."

Edwin glanced at the books as if tempted to continue the tutorial. "We have more useful things to be doing. I don't want to find out how much worse that curse of yours is going to get if we can't remove it, and I can't imagine you're keen on it either."

Robin swallowed and his mood soured as another squeeze of fear was wrung from him like lemon juice. Somewhere in the house a clock struck the half hour. "No."

"Curses laid in the air that appear on the skin fall under a certain category of rune-magic," said Edwin. Now it was his turn to show Robin a page of his book, though God only knew what he expected Robin to glean from it. "Though I still can't find a single reference to foresight being induced. I think you should keep your head down about that. It doesn't much matter if we tell the others about the curse, but true foresight is too rare. You'd have half the Magical Assembly on your doorstep as soon as we got back to town if there was a murmur it might be that." A humourless smile. "And I don't think any of Bel's friends know how to *murmur* anything."

Robin thought he was doing very well indeed dealing with a houseful of magicians at leisure. He shuddered at the idea of being dragged off by—*political* ones.

"I can keep my mouth shut," he said.

"Leave this with me," Edwin instructed, hefting the *Tales*.

Robin sighed and abandoned the most interesting book in the place to join a whole pile of very dull-looking ones. For a while longer he wandered both levels of the library and browsed in the unmagical style, pulling things from the shelves and enjoying the incomprehensible novelty of their titles. His stomach was beginning to rumble in real demand for lunch, and the sun through the window was making his legs itch with longing to be properly stretched. At a normal house party he'd have suggested a game of cricket, but perhaps magicians didn't care for anything so mundane. Or perhaps they played with a ball that would dodge the bat and try to slam itself against your pads.

If there was no real sport to be played, then messing around in boats like Charlie had mentioned didn't sound too bad, after a morning spent indoors. Even a bracing lake swim would be something.

His attention elsewhere, Robin fumbled the precarious row of books he'd idly drawn halfway out from the shelf, creating a pointless pattern of indented spines. Several of them fell to the floor and Robin hurried to pick them up.

"Wait, bring them over here," Edwin said. "Did you damage the covers?"

Robin tried for an apologetic grimace as he carried the books to the table. The pages of one looked strangely jagged and uneven, and Robin's stomach lurched in disproportionate panic, but he realised that in fact a much smaller book had been tucked into the large one and was now slipping free.

He pulled it clear. It was a thin bound pamphlet. The cover was purple.

His fingers released it as though burned, and he let it fall to the table. Then he realised that this action was the most revealing thing he could have done.

Robin looked up. Edwin didn't look horrified, or embarrassed, or even faintly curious. Edwin's expression held a wary nothingness. He studied Robin's face and Robin saw the moment when he made a decision based on what he saw there.

He'd wondered if Edwin might try to bluff it out. Instead Edwin said carefully, "I'd forgotten I'd brought any of those here. You'd better hold on to it, in case someone else stumbles across it."

"Yes, I imagine there's practically a queue of people panting to get their hands on . . ." Robin flicked back to the frontispiece of the larger book and read aloud. *"A Treatise on the Major Variants of Temporal Clauses in Thaumokinetics."*

"Indeed. Light reading," said Edwin dryly.

Robin's laughter startled out too quickly for him to snatch it back. That small smile flickered on Edwin's face again. Robin opened the purple book to see its own title, which was set above the smaller-type words BY A ROMAN.

"*Exploits of a Cabin Boy*. I think I remember this one. Heavy on the, ah, whippings."

"I—" said Edwin, and there was a sharp, casual rap from the library's open door.

"Look at you fellows, startling like someone's set off a lightning charm," said Billy Byatt. "Stir yourselves and wash up for lunch: Bel's orders. What's so bally important that you've spent the whole morning cooped up with books, anyhow?"

"Government work," said Edwin. "Research. I'm sure you'd find it dull."

"No doubt," said Billy cheerfully. "Chop-chop!" and was gone again.

Robin slid the Roman tract back into the treatise, and together they returned the mistreated books to the shelf before they left the library. The atmosphere between them had become both lighter and more weighty, somehow. What Hawthorn had implied about Edwin, the purple tract had confirmed. And it would have been far more than that, for Edwin. It would have been tantamount to *realisation*—a first dawning glimpse of the fact that Robin, too, was a man who sought the company of other men, or at least was familiar with one of the more popular writers of homosexual erotica distributed through an otherwise reputable shop on Charing Cross Road.

Robin thought about the string that Edwin used in his spells: how a particular cradle might have five or six or eight lines of the pattern joining one hand to another. Binding them close. Robin and Edwin had already shared a handful of secrets, and now they shared another, and this awareness of their common nature—in a way that had nothing whatsoever to do with magic—hung delicate and unspoken between them as they left the room.

9

The lake was edged with boggy reeds and stretches of coarse sand, with seven small rowboats scattered around its shore like compass points. The day still looked bright and idyllic, but a cool wind had picked up.

Robin had his hands thrust into his pockets as he and Edwin followed the others down the path to the lake. He cast a glance at Edwin and said, as though it had been on his mind, "You really don't like this place. The outdoors bits of it, at least."

"No," said Edwin shortly. He certainly didn't like *boating*, and yet here he was. After what had happened yesterday with the arrow, he didn't trust his sister to safely involve someone unmagical in her games.

"I never know how to feel about Thornley Hill, myself," said Robin. "Haven't been back for years, and we only ever had a few winters there when I was a boy."

"My family's blood-pledge to this land is almost younger than I am. My parents did the dedication ceremony when they bought it, because that's what one does. But power fills the gaps in this as well. And I haven't enough, and the land knows. I didn't know any better until I went away to school and suddenly it was different, suddenly it was . . ." Like he could take a full breath for the first time. Like the incredible loudness of a perpetual noise ceasing. "It's better in the city. More distractions." Edwin closed his mouth. He'd said more, and more easily, than he'd intended.

"Chin up," said Robin, clapping Edwin's shoulder in a rah-the-Blues kind of way. "I suppose we city fellows must grin and bear these things from time to time."

He demonstrated the grin in question, sunny as the sky. Edwin felt a prickle of pleasure at the sight, and hastily quashed it. He wasn't searching for kinship. He wasn't looking to have things in common with Sir Robert Blyth, who was pleasant and hearty and probably born with an oar in one hand and a cricket bat in the other.

But you have a taste in common, a treacherous voice in him murmured. *You know you do.*

Edwin dragged his eyes down to his own feet, cursing his complexion as it heated. He'd honestly forgotten that he'd brought any Roman tracts to Penhallick from the city.

It didn't matter. It didn't *matter,* any more than it mattered that Robin's hair shone like polished wood in the sunlight, or that he'd rolled his sleeves up past his elbows again and Edwin wanted to trace the veins and tendons of those well-cut rower's forearms with his own fingertips, learn their textures, make a small sensory memory for himself to pull out on quiet nights in front of the fire. He'd felt like that a good handful of times at school—at university—and for the most part he'd known to avoid those boys and those men. Even when it was mutual, attraction didn't conjure respect from nowhere. Where contempt existed, attraction could even deepen it.

No, Edwin's body couldn't be trusted to make decisions.

They joined everyone else at the side of the lake. Bel had explained the basics over lunch—or rather, she'd begun to explain and then Charlie had taken over, with a touch to her wrist and one of those benignly bestowed smiles that said he didn't want to tax the little woman's intelligence. Each of them would have their own small boat. Bel and Charlie had drawn up a large map of the lake and divided it into squares, each one representing a section of the water about six feet in each dimension. Many of those squares had been set with charms, either friendly or not-so-friendly—"Nothing irreversible!" tinkled Bel. Some of them held floating lilies that would unfold, at a light tap, to reveal prizes. A few of the lilies would be decoys; there was no way to tell without rowing out to them and trying your luck.

One of the groundskeepers had rowed out and planted the lilies in the lake, held in place with hanging weights. Charlie had cast each trap-charm, folded them small and embedded them into the map, then overlaid a thorough sympathy that flung the spells invisibly out to haunt their positions in the lake like ghosts.

It was a fiddly, pretty piece of magic. All the prettiness of it was probably Bel's. The bulk of the magic, of course, had been Charlie's. The two of them had taken a sip of lethe-mint nicely calculated to cover the time they'd spent preparing the map, so that they could play alongside everyone else. A friend of Edwin's mother had been known to do that in order to attend the same play every night of the week, or read her favourite mystery novel ten times over. It probably did the mind no favours to use it in that cavalier fashion, but nobody writing in English had ever studied these substances with the proper rigour, to Edwin's irritation.

Edwin took the blue boat, next along the lake's circumference from the red one Robin had claimed. He wrangled an oar to shove himself off, immediately won himself a splinter, and winced. By the time he managed to get the boat pointing towards the centre of the lake, Robin was already heading towards the nearest lily with a smoothness that Edwin would never be able to mimic.

Robin hadn't gone far, however, before he jerked and began to laugh. And laugh, and laugh, doubling over in the boat. Laughter was coming from some of the other boats as well, and shouts of advice or mockery. The warmth of Robin's laughter was beginning to take on the helpless edge of hysteria by the time the momentum of his boat drifted him out of the square and he was able to calm down.

"All right?" Edwin called.

"Tip-top!" Robin returned with a hint of wheeze.

"Billy's trying for your lily." Edwin pointed. Robin gave a cheerful curse and began wrangling himself expertly again.

Edwin ran into a blinding illusion and nearly lost one of the oars through the ring-lock by the time he'd fumbled for his string and managed a basic illusion-reversal by touch. His sight flooded back and he grabbed for the oar. Miggsy was close to a lily, cursing and rowing hard against some unseen magical current. Billy had the hiccups. Trudie was complaining loudly about her sleeves; her oars and hands were coated in green slime. Near the shore farthest from Edwin, Bel was laughing, teetering in her boat, but it just sounded like her usual laugh.

Robin was *gone*—no, there he was, emerging from a curtain-spell, right next to one of the lilies. He tapped it with his hand, then reached into the unfurled flower to pull out a fist-sized twist of coloured paper.

This was met with cheers. "Which is it?" called Charlie.

"Caramels," called Robin, rustling the paper open. "I'm almost afraid to try one."

"Oh, the prizes are safe. They're *prizes*. I'll have one even if you won't," said Billy, who had managed to bring his boat almost up against Robin's.

Robin handed over one of his sweets, and dangled the twist of paper in Edwin's direction as Billy took off towards another lily. On his way over to accept one, Edwin acquired a spontaneous and non-illusory fire in the bottom of his boat, which he extinguished with a few handfuls of lake water rather than bothering with his string.

He pulled up alongside Robin's boat and his intended thanks died in his mouth. Robin was staring into space, hands lax on the oars, with the unseeing blankness that meant he was in the grips of the foresight.

"Robin," Edwin said.

Robin blinked, and focused. His face had paled. He met

Edwin's eyes and nodded, then brought up a good attempt at a smile.

"Foul! No conspiring!" bawled Miggsy.

"I'm all right," said Robin to Edwin. "I'll tell you later. Here."

Edwin took a caramel from the proffered parcel. The strain in Robin's face bothered him. Robin had been correct, last night: none of this was Robin's fault, and he deserved distraction if he wanted it. He'd been enjoying himself with the game until that vision, whatever it was.

Robin had barely moved a few firm strokes farther towards the lake's centre when a miniature fountain erupted beneath the red boat, like an account Edwin had read of the great water-spouts of whales. It sent both Robin and caramels tumbling into the water. The cheers and hoots were far louder this time.

Edwin rowed gingerly to what he calculated was the edge of that charm's radius. He reached over and grabbed the edge of Robin's drifting boat; it had landed right side up, at least. Just as Robin swam over and reached for the other side, Edwin gave it a daring yank out of his reach.

"What—" Robin looked drenched and befuddled, his hair darkly otter-slick.

"Rah," Edwin said with precision. "Dark Blues."

Robin's face transformed into a grin and he splashed a handful of water up at Edwin. "So you *do* have a competitive streak," he panted as Edwin steadied the red boat's side so that Robin could struggle back aboard. His shirt clung, transparent, to his chest. "Didn't think I'd have to pack boating flannels," he added, plucking at it. "And I don't think they come in mourning colours. Damn, that wind's got a bite to it, doesn't it?"

"I can warm you up," said Edwin.

Robin stared at him. Edwin felt his face fill with mortified colour.

His voice cracked as he said, "I meant—I can do a drying spell."

"Oh," said Robin, with a hint of crack himself. "Yes! Much obliged. If you would."

Edwin dropped the cradle twice before he managed the spell. It warmed his palms and parched the skin there; he raised his cupped hands to his face, and blew as though to snuff a candle. The spell billowed invisibly out and over Robin, and a half-lidded expression of enjoyment fell onto his face and nearly distracted Edwin into losing his focus.

"There," Edwin said when it was done, trying not to sound too winded. He had the wrung-out feeling that meant he'd drained his power and wouldn't be able to muster the smallest of spells for the rest of the day. Perhaps it had been a waste. But Robin looked delighted, his sunniness restored. And his shirt, Edwin noted with a pang, once again opaque.

Robin ruffled his now-dry hair with one hand and said, "Right-ho—let's try for a second," and sculled himself determinedly off into a new stretch of lake.

Edwin put his abandoned caramel in his mouth and let it soften there, sweet and buttery. The breeze had picked up, but it wasn't unpleasant. Trudie had her hand in an open lily. A small contained rainstorm was soaking Charlie, near the lake's centre; Charlie flung up an umbrella spell, then laughed and let it dissolve, tipping his head back.

This was . . . not terrible. Edwin felt almost fond of Bel and her imagination and her tireless dashing after diversion.

Bel herself pulled her boat up near his, breathing hard. She too had a bedraggled look to her hair, and she waved an oar, sounding gleeful. "I *thought* I'd have laid the Pied Piper on one of them."

Edwin followed her gaze to where Robin was undergoing an ornithological bombardment. Every duck and coot and moorhen on the lake had taken an intimate interest in the red boat, and those that weren't paddling at it as though scenting bread had already begun to flap their way out of the water and into the boat itself. Robin was laughing and trying to shove them back out again, collecting angry quacks and pecks for his troubles.

It wasn't just waterfowl, either. Smaller birds dotted the air, flitting and curling, calling out in every voice from fluting to harsh. They seemed to be trying for a perch on the boat, or on Robin himself.

"I'm going to be Noah's Ark if this keeps up," shouted Robin. "Oh—blast," and ducked as a blackbird swooped right for his face.

The water around the red boat was frothing with the motion of curious fish. Edwin had exactly enough time to wonder uneasily about eels before the inevitable happened: one too many birds, one sudden movement too far on Robin's behalf, and Robin was toppling into the lake. Again.

Belinda shouted with laughter and buried her face in one hand.

"Robin?" Edwin shouted.

"Ah—help?" came from Robin, somewhat muffled.

"Oh, *Lord*," screeched Trudie.

Belinda laughed harder—all the others were laughing, too, and Edwin was trying to suppress his own helpless amusement at the sheer ridiculousness of the spectacle—

And that, of course, was when the swans appeared.

There was a single elegant pair of them, and they'd been crossing the lake at a serene pace, reaching the scene of the hubbub like a couple arriving late at a party to ensure that their entrance was noted.

Robin waved one arm and shouted something that was difficult to make out from within his local storm cloud of beaks and feathers. He was likely flailing for effect, playing up to the crowd. If he really wanted to escape, it would be easy enough for him to dive and swim clear of the charm.

One of the swans spread its considerable wings, hunching up. A hiss came from the snowy throat, loud enough to be audible even above the outraged din of the other birds and the gales of laughter from the boats. The second swan began to follow suit. It was—large. Somehow one didn't think of swans as that large.

Edwin found himself clutching his oar. He'd thought his magic drained to quiescence, but something new was churning within him, a feeling like sandpaper being applied to the underside of his skin.

"Something's wrong," he said.

And in the next terrible moment before the swans charged he saw Robin's face, very clearly, and it was white and stiff with dread.

"Bel!" Edwin yelled. "Something's wrong, will you—Billy, *help* him!" and turned his boat, badly, furious and scared and being scraped raw by the urgent impetus of a magic that he'd never had cause to feel, never had a hope of recognising for what it was, before now.

He kept glancing over his shoulder as he rowed, trying to tell himself that he could still see Robin's head, sinking below the surface and then rising again, and then sinking—

Someone was still laughing. Edwin wanted rope to erupt from his fingers and choke them for it.

Edwin rowed with panic and no grace through a cold-charm and some kind of auditory illusion that he barely had time to notice. By the time he reached the Pied Piper square, Billy was there, floating on the outskirts of the fray and building an illusion that—wouldn't work on animals, the *idiot*.

"You need a negation—no, a reversal," Edwin said. "Second-class, give it a radius of at least ten feet, hurry it up," and took a breath and cursed his life for a nightmare before leaping into the water.

He regretted it immediately. The hiss of the swans was unbearably loud, their wings a blinding maelstrom of violence, the strike of a webbed foot against Edwin's neck almost brutally painful. The water was cold, and unmentionable slimy things writhed against his ankles, and Edwin had no idea how one rescued a heavier and more athletic man from swan-induced drowning, and he'd used up his magic on that bloody drying spell—why hadn't Edwin *thought*, why was he so *useless*? And that horrible urgent scrape of sensation still had him and was driving him on.

Edwin's hand touched a moving limb. He took a handful of fabric and hauled upwards with the strength of desperation. Robin's head broke the surface, spluttering, just as Edwin's forearm cramped.

"*Fucking*—" Robin gasped, and *then* Billy finished the reversal, and every single bird tried to exit their vicinity at once in a whirlwind of flaps.

And then it was, at least, quiet.

Edwin panted with the effort of staying afloat. He felt like he had grown extra limbs solely so that they could ache. His trousers were fighting him. Robin was spitting out water.

It took Charlie and Billy together to haul Robin into Billy's boat, and Edwin swam after them towards the lake's edge, abandoning his own; someone could charm it in later. Robin managed to step ashore on his own legs, but they wobbled and sat him down hard on the sand. Edwin, trailing filthy weeds, went and sat next to him while Charlie helped Bel and Trudie pull up their boats. Edwin's neck throbbed nastily where the swan had kicked it. Robin's bared forearms sported more than a few red grazes.

"Got another of those drying thingums up your sleeve?" said Robin hopefully.

"No," said Edwin, low and short with frustration. "What the devil *happened*? Why didn't you swim clear?" A thought hit him. "It was the curse. Or a vision."

"Neither, this time," said Robin. "I couldn't move my legs. They felt like they'd been turned to lumps of lead."

The spell casually dubbed Dead Man's Legs was a favourite of most boys when they learned it. The idea of it being used on someone trying to stay afloat in water was horrifying.

The others were all on the sand now, murmuring concern. For the most part.

"Well, Sir Robin can't say we're not providing adequate amusements," said Miggsy.

"*Amusements*," Edwin started, hearing it come out halfway to swan-hiss, and then Robin grunted and ducked his head and Billy said, sharp, "What's the matter? Did one of those beastly birds get a good bite in?"

Even by the time the words had left Billy's mouth, nobody could have mistaken Robin's pain for anything but a bone-shaking agony. His lips peeled back from his teeth and his eyes were screwed shut as he clutched his arm close to his body. Edwin put his hand on Robin's sodden, shivering shoulder, and forced it to stay there. He felt flayed by his own helplessness.

It took many endless heartbeats before Robin's eyes opened and the white claw of his hand uncurled. Edwin lifted his own hand free.

"I thought I was getting used to it," Robin gasped. "It appears—the opposite, in fact."

"What on Earth, Bel?" said Trudie. She'd taken a few steps back, as though Robin's suffering might be catching.

"Don't look at me," said Bel. Her pale blue eyes were momentarily as cold as their colour, fear and anger lifting the veil of vivacity. "It's a *game*. We'd never put something truly painful on the map."

"No, just something thoughtless and dangerous," snapped Edwin, climbing to his feet. "Attracting swans, Bel, really? And Dead Man's Legs on top of it?"

Bel glared. "What do you mean, on top?"

"Don't speak to your sister like that, Edwin," said Charlie.

"Sir Robin," said Billy. "What is the matter?"

Robin's eyes, lucid and bright with something that was close to trust, turned to Edwin. Edwin knew how to lie, but he was no good at doing it on short notice.

"Robin's been cursed," he said. "Show them. We might as well see if anyone's got any bright ideas."

There was a murmuring somewhere between scandalised and concerned as Robin extended his arm, baring the rune-curse to the sky. Edwin summoned his wits and gave a deeply edited version of how it had been laid in the first place, eliding most of the details, suggesting it was a case of mistaken identity—and watched, too tired and cold to dredge up much in the way of hope, as the men frowned down at the runes and took it in turn to shrug their ignorance.

"In any case," Robin said, "Edwin's going to find a way to get it off, soon."

A pathetic trickle of pleasure found its way into Edwin's chest at that blithe vote of confidence.

"I did wonder why you'd shut yourselves up in that stuffy library," said Trudie.

"Yes," said Charlie. He set a hand under Robin's arm and helped him up. "Let's get you dried off, old man, and we'll find something to do that doesn't involve swans or books."

Edwin waited until everyone began to move back in the direction of the house, then went and stopped his sister, keeping her in place until the others were out of earshot.

"Bel," he said. "You felt it, didn't you, when Robin went under?"

"Felt what?"

Sandpaper, Edwin wanted to scream. How aren't you *pulped* by it, why aren't you *shaking,* your magic is five times mine and you felt *nothing?*

"A guest of ours almost died on our territory," he said, terse. "You're a Courcey, Bel. Our parents pledged blood to this land. It was telling us, so we could prevent it."

Bel's hair was still a half-tangled mess, and her frightened irritation was already sinking beneath the surface of her usual unconcern. A memory stirred in Edwin of a much smaller

Belinda, glancing with this exact look between Edwin and
Walt, and making the decision to retreat. To ignore. To sing
more loudly to herself, when Walt laughed and Edwin cried;
to leave her younger brother as the sacrificial barrier between
herself and the source of her fear. She sought protection. It was
who she was.

"It was barely a sting," she said now. "Nothing to make a
fuss over. You know I'd never mean a guest harm, Win."

Do I? Edwin bit back. *I don't know that at all.*

Bel headed for the house and Edwin watched her go. He
didn't *want* to believe her capable of it. So: suppose she and
Charlie *hadn't* decided to cast two dangerous spells on one
square of the lake, where any one of the players could have
been the first to trigger them. Perhaps one of the others had
taken the opportunity to scare the non-magician; Edwin
wouldn't put it past any of them, as a prank. But Robin had
been targeted already, in the city, by someone wanting to scare
him into cooperation. How many frights made a pattern? How
many coincidences made a plot?

Edwin rubbed his aching neck, then knelt and tangled his
fingers through a tuft of grass. He closed his eyes and concentrated, straining, trying for the first time in his life to call out to
his mother's blood, his father's blood, spilled in this dirt before
Edwin was alive. With the abrasive surge of guest-in-danger
gone, all he could feel was the same old itch of disappointment.
Not Courcey enough. Not anything enough.

He looked down. The edge of a grass blade had sliced the
pad of his forefinger open, forming a red line thin as thread.

"All right," Edwin said, soft. "All right. I'm keeping him
safe. I'm trying."

10

Robin dreamed of the swans.

He spent the afternoon after the boating game playing pool and talking sports with Belinda and Charlie and their friends. He drank a few more gin cocktails than was his custom. He almost managed to pretend that he was in his club, or at a party with his own friends, except for the occasional jolt when someone used magic. Even Belinda and Trudie could light a cigarette from their fingers, though their cradles were looser and less complex than any of the men's.

Belinda's set of magicians had the uninhibited manners of the freshly moneyed, and treated Robin's title as though it were an amusing hat he'd donned for the occasion. Robin might have found them refreshing if he wasn't fighting a headache and a tendency for his swan-pummelled ribs to catch at his lungs halfway through a breath. And if it wasn't for the undercurrent of casual, unthinking malice to the conversation whenever it turned to other people: gossip with a sort of aniseed edge to it.

Other people included Edwin, who made himself scarce until dinner. Through the games of pool Robin kept turning his head whenever someone entered the room, not bothering to examine the niggle of hope that was quashed when the newcomer turned out to be one of the footmen bringing more drinks. Edwin had seemed frantic when Robin was in danger, angry that it had happened, and fascinated as ever by the curse and the visions. But he'd not sought out Robin's company. Whether he

was in the library or with his mother or elsewhere, he wanted
to be there on his own.

Robin took his headache to bed early. The next morning he
woke shaking, with his legs gone to wax and lake water in his
mouth and his arms sore from where he'd tried to defend himself against the crushing blows of the swan's wings, and his
ears full of that terrible hiss and someone shouting and laughter carrying across the water—

No. It was a dream. Not even a vision: a bog-standard nightmare. Robin's legs were tangled in the bedclothes. He was dry
and breathing and alive and . . . as safe as he could be, in a
house full of careless magicians, with a curse that was getting
stronger and more painful.

Robin politely turned down the invitation at breakfast to
join the others on a morning walk and picnic. He lingered
alone, dissecting a kidney omelette with his cutlery and drinking excellent coffee, until Edwin appeared.

Edwin was wearing a waistcoat in a dull shade of grey, and
did not look as though he'd slept well. Unfortunately, it suited
him. Robin was already restless; now his thumbs ached to be
pressed to the circles beneath Edwin's eyes, or run across the
sharp cheekbones. He wanted to catalogue the changing agricultural shades in Edwin's hair, to see what kinds of light
would bring up the colours that lay between bright wheat and
murky barley.

It was incredible what difference it had made, that moment of
unspoken connection over the Roman tract. It shouldn't have.
Even aside from the mysterious tangle of curse and contract
that hung urgently over them, Robin was hardly going to make
any kind of overture without encouragement. And Edwin was
still himself: cool, prickly, resentful of Robin's presence in his
life, thin and quiet and studious and carrying around an air
of being invisibly shuttered. And quite clearly more intelligent
than the rest of the house's inhabitants put together, with bony,

agile fingers that Robin could close his eyes and see hooking magic out of string.

"I want this curse off," Robin said, too distracted by trying to banish the image to manage a more normal kind of *good morning*. "I want you to try. Today."

A frown. "I haven't done enough—"

"Keep at it. I'll help. I'll do whatever you say. I'd rather you attempt it and fail than twiddle our thumbs another week while it gets worse and worse. I dare say if it were left up to you, you'd *never* feel you've done enough research to even give it a try."

Edwin's blue, bruised gaze had nothing readable in it.

Robin said, with difficulty, "I'm—afraid of the pain. Is all."

Edwin said, "I'd like some breakfast."

He brushed very close to Robin on his way to the sideboard, close enough for Robin to smell his hair. It took Edwin until he'd swallowed his first mouthful of bacon and another of marmalade-laden toast, washed down with tea, to say, "You're right."

"Hm?" Robin was onto a fourth cup of coffee and wondering, as his pulse hammered gaily away beneath the skin of his neck, if that had been a wise decision.

"Perhaps I could read every book in the library and never stumble across the exact form of runes. It's your arm. It's your pain. I'm willing to give it a try, this afternoon." Edwin inspected the crust of his toast. "By which I mean, I'll ask Charlie to do it."

"I'd rather it was you."

The sheer surprise in Edwin's lifted gaze was like a needle to the heart. "No, you wouldn't," he said, but mildly. "You want the person in the house with the most magic to do the actual spell. I'll put it together for him. I'll write it down; I'll make sure he does it exactly."

That launched a discussion—a miniature lecture, rather, but

Robin didn't mind—about the difference between runes and cradling notation, which took them through breakfast and into the library again, where Edwin slid behind the table with a near-audible sigh of relief. Robin sat down also, pulling a book towards himself at random to show willing.

Edwin said, "I meant to ask how you are. Any damage from—what happened yesterday?"

There were bruises blossoming beneath the scrapes on Robin's arms. His head still ached. He still felt on edge, though that might have been the coffee.

Instead of any of that he found himself saying, "I've not often been the butt of the joke before."

Edwin said, with an odd lightness that didn't sting as much as it could have, "More used to being the bully than the bullied?"

"Well, I wasn't one to step in and stop that sort of thing, when I saw it happening at school." Robin shrugged. "I'm not proud of it. Tried to do better, when I—when I woke up to the fact that it wasn't really funny, I suppose." When he began to understand that what he was seeing at home, when his parents gathered well-dressed people into sparkling rooms and made pretty speeches about charity, was the adult version of the same game, only half of which was played to the victim's face. The other half was the whispers; the casual venom. The two-facedness. The brutal construction of one's reputation on the shreds of those you flattered with one hand and tore down with the other.

"Dead Man's Legs is a good spell for bullies," Edwin said. "Walt was very fond of it for a while, if I ever looked too keen to dodge out of whatever light humiliation he'd planned for that day."

Robin tried to find a good response to that. Edwin had spoken matter-of-factly, but his shoulders had lifted: he was offering Robin a sliver of vulnerability. And after seeing the way

Edwin was treated by everyone in his family but his mother, Robin couldn't pretend to be surprised.

"Did you and your brother overlap at school, then?"

"For two years," said Edwin. "And no amount of scolding about using magic when away from home ever stopped Walt. Most of his crowd were magicians, too, and he was good at finding corners."

Robin remembered how that went. Every school had those corners, conveniently out of sight, and out of hearing range of the masters' offices.

To steer them elsewhere, Robin asked more about learning magic. A great many questions had been building up in the aftermath of his initial shocks. Edwin's shoulders relaxed as he explained the ways in which boy magicians learned cradling and its notations.

"There's a curriculum, of sorts. But everything past the basics depends on one's tutors. And how ruthless one's parents are about lessons during holidays, if they send you to a normal school as well."

"Your mother doesn't strike me as ruthless," said Robin, smiling.

A shadow crossed Edwin's face. "She's the reason I was *allowed* to spend my summers under tutorship. Father didn't consider me worth the expense. I was never going to amount to much."

Robin glanced around them, at this edifice to knowledge. "What about university?"

"There's no university of English magic," said Edwin. "You can study apprentice-style from other scholars, if you wish. But I enjoyed Oxford. For its own sake. And there's been nobody doing really original magical work in this country since the turn of the century. Nobody making *advances*. Nobody who could have taught me more than I found out for myself." He stirred the pages of a book with his fingers. A bitter smile touched his mouth. "I never had enough power that I had to be taught to control it."

Control was a word that hung on Edwin like a half-fitted suit. In some places it clung to him; in others it gaped, in a way that made Robin want to hook his fingers into the loose seams and tug. He didn't want Edwin to stop talking.

"There must be scholars in other countries?" he ventured.

"Yes, but it's the same as any area of study. Often there's no common language. I've enough French to struggle through a few arguments with members of their Académie, but that's all. And correspondence is slow."

Robin had a brief vision of wax-sealed letters floating across the ocean like so many gulls. He supposed that rainstorms could be a problem.

"What about your pen?" he asked. "Couldn't someone in France do a spell so that it wrote down—whatever they wanted you to know? Or could you have a set of them, one each, where one of them copies what the other is writing?"

Edwin stared at him. Then rubbed a hand over his face. Robin expected one of those university-tutor sighs; it took him a moment to realise that Edwin was *laughing*, in a small silent way.

"Of course," said Edwin. "Trust you, Sir Robin Blyth, to accidentally stumble onto one of the central problems of magical progress. No, I'm not joking. It was a good idea. Here. The problem is *distance*." He set his hands on the table, shoulder-width apart. "How much do you know about natural sciences?"

"Er," said Robin.

"Gravity? Sir Isaac Newton?"

"The apple chap?"

Edwin visibly shredded his planned explanation into shorter words. "Forces act strongly if two things are close together. Much less so if they're far apart. And magic is the same. You can imbue an object and let it be—there are plenty of magical objects—but you can't change its properties, or directly control it. You need to be close, for that. Not even Charlie could have cast that sympathy with the map from anywhere but right next to the lake." He picked up a piece of scrap paper and tore it into the rough shape of a person, then cradled up a spell that he smeared over the paper figure. "Touch it."

Robin touched the paper, gingerly, and felt something like a snap of static. The paper figure sprang upright on the table. Robin snatched his hand back. The paper man's arm gave a flap in imitation.

"Sympathy," said Edwin. "See?"

Robin, mostly to prove he'd understood the thing about distance, stood and walked steadily backwards across the floor. The figure jerkily copied his movements for the first two steps, then faltered, then rippled and fell to the table, lifeless. Robin waved from a distance and nothing happened.

"That's rather weird," Robin said. He couldn't help thinking unsettlingly of the man with the fog mask and the glowing string, and the way Robin's body had felt, entirely unresponsive to the demands of his mind.

"Hm," said Edwin, looking at the limp paper figure.

"Hm?"

Edwin cradled up the indexing spell and summoned books from two different corners of the library. He directed Robin to look through some ghastly tome called *A Comprehensive Survey of European Runic Evolution* for any symbols that looked anything like the ones on his arm.

"I thought you'd been through this one already," said Robin.

"William Morris," said Edwin, distractedly, flicking through one of his new acquisitions.

"Pardon?"

"You've an eye for pattern." Edwin paused, but didn't look up. "You might catch something I missed."

Robin sighed, found the sketch Edwin had made of the curse the previous day, and prepared himself to stare at inked symbols until his head ached. Meanwhile Edwin summoned one of the maids into the room and spent some time getting her to demonstrate what seemed to be a spell for removing stains from rugs, while he stared at her fingers and copied their motions.

Perhaps the strongest magician was the best choice, but Robin trusted the instinct that had led him to prefer Edwin when it came to his own safety. There was a deliberation to the way Edwin worked, an insistence on perfect angles, that reminded Robin of Penhallick House's wallpapers: overcomplex from a distance, but rewarding closer inspection.

Once the maid was dismissed, Edwin went away to the window seat with another book and his imbued pen, which hovered and took notes as Edwin murmured snatches of incomprehensible words to it. The day was grey and dull, with a sodden heaviness to the clouds and the occasional distant rumble of a storm rolling around the vicinity. The light falling onto Edwin was not the golden Turner light that had first grabbed Robin's attention.

It didn't seem to matter. Robin still wanted to stare at him, framed as he was by the wood, one leg thrust out across the wide cushion of the seat, head bent over the open book.

This was becoming ridiculous.

Several chapters' worth of meaningless symbols later, Robin found himself half wishing that the foresight would strike; it would at least provide an alternative to the endless movement of his eyes between page and sketch, with frequent detours to land on Edwin, who had once again taken to doing thoughtful laps of the library floor.

Robin's vision on the lake the previous day had been an unsettling one: a stretch of flat, muddy land under an equally muddy dusk. Winter trees, motionless. Flashes of light and plumes of smoke in the distance. As with the other visions, there'd been no sound, but something about the scene had given Robin the sense that there would be little to hear. The landscape had felt eerily uninhabited, as though someone had tried to paint the Temptation in the Wilderness and forgotten to add the figure of Christ.

Ever since the first evening, the visions had come one at a time. That was something.

"Anything?" Edwin paused by the table.

Robin flicked back to where he'd used a paper scrap to mark a figure of runes that had some of the same curlicue flourishes joining one symbol to the next, though none of the individual runes looked even slightly like those on Robin's arm. Robin had tried to read the dense text accompanying the figure. He'd given that up after the first paragraph, which held a grisly description of exactly how the depicted curse had been thought to boil a man's blood within his veins.

"Possibly," said Edwin, in an obvious effort at politeness.

"I'll keep at it," said Robin.

By the time one of the downstairs maids knocked to ask if they'd prefer to have sandwiches brought in, it was drizzling. Their lunch—in the dining hall, at the insistence of Robin, who was feeling restless again—was interrupted by Belinda's cheerful and lightly rained-upon group, who descended on the piles of sandwiches and cold cuts without bothering to change out of their damp clothes. Trudie began an embellished, tinkling version of how she'd slipped on pebbles and *nearly* fell halfway down a hill.

"Plans for the afternoon, chaps?" asked Billy, beneath this recital. "And *don't* say the library."

Edwin said, loud enough to be heard by the whole table, "We were hoping to take the curse off Robin, actually."

Trudie's voice faltered as eyes swung their way. Billy's eyebrows shot high. "Cracked it, have you?"

"I've an idea worth trying." Edwin cleared his throat. "Charlie, we'd be glad if you did the honours."

Charlie drew himself up like a pigeon chest-puffing out of a puddle. "Of course," he said, through a mouthful of ham and cress. "Now, if you ask me, the best thing for a general reversal—" And he rambled on from there, insisted on seeing Robin's arm again, and called upon Belinda to remember a time when he'd removed a dancing imbuement that someone's drunken uncle had laid on the cutlery at their wedding dinner.

Edwin sat quiet in his seat dabbing crusts through a smear of yellow pickle until the appearance of warm treacle tart and clotted cream distracted Charlie into a sticky silence.

"Something like that" was all Edwin said then.

"Well!" Trudie clapped her hands to summon the room's attention. "It's not a game of charades, but it's not something you see every day, is it?"

So they all ended up in the library after all. Robin's lunch sat uneasily in his stomach. He *did* want the thing off, he *did* want Edwin to try now.

"One of these days a brainy type like Win here is going to work out how to let one magician draw on another's power," said Billy. His affable, freckled face smiled up at Robin from where he was sitting backwards on a chair. "And then our Charlie won't be so much in demand."

Charlie snorted. "You mean I'd merely be in demand as some sort of—cart horse, or motor-engine. Someone else holding the reins? Rather *not*. You have the power you have, and that's an end to it."

"Is this another of those central problems?" Robin asked Edwin, who nodded.

"Theoretically, it should be possible," Edwin said. "But it's never worked in practice. Not in the entire history of magic."

Robin struggled to recall the explanation Edwin had given that very first day in the Whitehall office. At least he had the excuse of lifelong ignorance. "It isn't just a matter of contracts?"

"Should be, shouldn't it?" said Billy. He gave Robin an appraising look, as though he'd unexpectedly done a trick. "You're settling into this like a natural, Sir Robin. Honestly, a commendable lack of gibbering."

"Win's probably been lecturing the poor boy for days," said Belinda. "Some of it's bound to have sunk in."

Edwin looked steadily at Robin. "Yes. Contracts. But how do you define a person, with the precision needed? How do you define their magic? Either it would be so complex it would take ten magicians a year to build the spell, or it's something so simple we'll never think of it. It's impossible. We work around it." He tapped his fingers on the table and glanced at Charlie. "We make do."

"We rely on the brainy types," said Miggsy. He said it much less pleasantly than Billy had. "Are you sure this is going to work? There are plenty of curses that last until death, you know."

Robin's throat tightened. Edwin's glance to him was shuttered, as Edwin's company-glances were, but Robin could have sworn that what the shutters had closed on was guilt. So Edwin was withholding some information.

"I'm not a child," said Robin. "You don't have to protect me."

Instead of answering, Edwin frowned at Miggsy and said, "And there are plenty of curses that do not, and each of *those* had a first time when someone cracked their removal. Should we give up without even trying?"

Miggsy raised his hands in mocking surrender. Trudie gave a stifled giggle. The eager attention of their eyes reminded Robin of laughter on the lake, and suddenly he felt more exposed, more vulnerable, and more angry. He wasn't anyone's to put on display. Not anymore.

"I'd prefer it if it was just Edwin and Charlie," he said. "If you fellows wouldn't mind?"

Trudie had the nerve to pout. None of them argued, though Belinda lingered near the door as though she were thinking of doing so.

"Go on, darling," said Charlie. "A man doesn't care for a

female to see him in pain, does he? You wouldn't sit around gawping at him having his tooth pulled."

"Thank you," said Edwin dryly as his sister left the library. He handed Charlie a piece of paper half-covered with the symbols of cradling notation. "Shall we get on? It's built on a reversal framework, but you won't be applying it to the curse itself. I've defined the three stages. The first is an exact copy, ink onto paper—you shouldn't have any trouble with that. Then a deep sympathy, like the one you used on the map of the lake. I've had to guess at the defining terms for the curse, but it should hold. And then this one, with the reversal folded into it."

Charlie skimmed his eyes down the paper. "I've not seen that one before. That clause—is it dissolution?"

"It's a domestic spell." The corner of Edwin's mouth curled: a small piece of pride. "Your maids likely use it to lift stains from your tablecloths. You lift the ink away, once the sympathy's applied, and we hope to blazes the curse comes away with it. You see?"

"I say, that's rather neat," said Charlie. "So it starts . . . ?"

"Don't just *waft* your finger like that. Here."

It took another ten minutes while Edwin frowned and adjusted Charlie's fingers in the same way that Scholz adjusted a man's stance in the boxing ring. Charlie, in the absence of his wife and friends, took the corrections more amiably than Robin had expected.

Robin, hating the constant winding of his nerves with the delay and not at all keen on the image of tooth-pulling that Charlie had dropped into his head, sketched the eerie landscape of his last vision on the back of some more of Edwin's notes.

Finally Edwin pronounced himself satisfied. Robin rolled up his sleeve for what he hoped was going to be the last time.

"I really can't promise—" Edwin said.

"I know," said Robin. "Is there anything I need to"—he waggled the fingers of his free hand awkwardly—"do?"

"We could find you a belt to bite down on," said Charlie.

"*Charlie,*" said Edwin.

"A joke! A joke, old man."

Robin tried to sit on his free hand in a way that was surreptitious, then gave it up as a bad job and simply squeezed it between his thighs.

"Right-o," he said. "Give it a try."

It was almost fun, to begin with. Edwin spilled a small pool of ink onto some paper as Charlie cradled the first stage of the spell. Robin felt a queer ticklish sensation as though the runes were being traced by a wet feather, and he watched with interest as the large blot of ink split and rearranged itself into a perfect copy of the curse, including all the new curls and densities that had developed overnight. The second stage, the sympathy, called up no sensation at all. Edwin's eyes were slits of concentration, watching Charlie's hands as though he could see the phantom string that he himself would have used.

"Stains from tablecloths," murmured Charlie, winking at Robin. "Shall we?"

He splayed his hands flat above the ink-copy, then tugged suddenly upwards as though yanking a net of fish clear from water.

Robin heard a scream like metal under strain.

It was him.

It felt as though the symbols were *alive,* all teeth and heat, burrowing their way through Robin's flesh. The hand that had been between Robin's thighs gave a pang, and Robin realised he'd jerked it so hard it had struck the edge of the table.

"*Robin,*" Edwin was saying.

The pain ran out of fuel in Robin's forearm and headed north. Robin had the sudden conviction that if it reached his chest, his heart would stop. A wash of fear weakened him entirely. He gave another scream, this one coming out muffled through his teeth, and then the pain took gleeful hold of his muscles and he spasmed all the way out of his chair.

He didn't remember hitting the floor, but he must have. When he opened his eyes the left side of his head was pounding as someone rolled him onto his back. His left wrist throbbed in tandem with it. His entire right arm felt like water at a low simmer.

"I'm fine," he said weakly. "I can sit." The arm behind him was Charlie's, helping him upright. Edwin, on his knees on the rug, looked a curdled mixture of fear and relief. One of his hands was gripping Robin's ankle.

"Is it—?" said Robin.

"No," said Edwin. "I'm sorry."

Robin made his eyes focus. The runes of the curse had spread, rapid and angry as ants in a poked anthill. They wrapped around both sides of his arm, now, and reached half-way up the span between elbow and armpit. The snake of his fear swelled and writhed.

"Rotten shame," said Charlie with genuine sympathy. "Chair or feet? Or stay where you are?"

"Chair," Robin decided, and winced his way into it with Charlie's help. "Thanks for trying, Charlie. You should proba-bly let the others know I'm still alive and whole; I'm fairly sure I was yelling my head off, there."

Charlie waved a *don't-mention-it* kind of hand and left, looking transparently glad for the excuse. Robin exhaled. It felt like the first time he'd remembered to do so since regaining consciousness.

"I made it worse," said Edwin, flat.

"It was getting worse anyway."

This did not appear to help matters. Edwin's pale face was pulled tight with unhappiness. "Perhaps I should take you to the Assembly after all."

Robin remembered what Edwin had said about the Magical Assembly and the rarity of foresight. "I'd rather you had an-other go at it," he admitted. Edwin looked taken aback; Robin shrugged. "Why not?"

"Why *not*?"

"I'm the one who insisted you try today. And I'm sure you're on the right path. You've been nothing but . . . precise." That was it, the word that fit Edwin better than *controlled*. He was thoughtful, and dedicated, and precise, and Robin found it unspeakably comforting. His usual love of spontaneity was taking a serious battering, here and now, when it was his own well-being at stake. He managed a smile. "Who else am I going to entrust my good bowling arm to?"

"You don't have to be so—" said Edwin, and stopped.

"Stubborn? Lost cause, I'm afraid."

"That's. Not what I meant."

"Oh?"

Muscles worked under the skin of Edwin's slender neck. "You say you don't want to be protected. All right. I say you don't have to be careful of my feelings."

Robin bit back the words *Someone should be,* because he could tell they were going to come out the wrong way. "My head's hurting like the dickens," he said, standing. "I'm going up to bed. See if a rest does it any good. Tell the others I'm still not feeling quite the thing, will you?"

He tucked himself beneath sheets that smelled of lavender and smoke. Sleep stayed out of reach; Robin managed to dip his aching head beneath the surface of a doze, thoughts unspooling like a dropped roll of thread. Like glowing string.

The pain came again, an hour before the bell rang for dinner. While it lasted, it wiped everything else away.

11

Edwin's mother declared herself well enough to join the general dinner table that night. It was a rare enough occurrence that the room felt respectful and festive; even Trudie and Miggsy managed to keep the scrape and hoot of their voices to reasonable levels. Which only went to show that the rest of the time they *could* have—Edwin considered, chasing peas around his plate with his fork—but were choosing not to out of sheer delight in their own loudness.

Florence Courcey sat with Edwin at one elbow and Bel at the other, and Robin sat across from her. The fact that Edwin had failed so completely to remove the curse was the main topic of conversation.

"What did I say?" Miggsy said. "Some curses can't be snuffed until the bearer has been, you know. Just getting the chap's hopes up, pretending otherwise. Not meaning any offence," he added, to Robin. "But I'm one for facing up to facts. Always have been."

Edwin saw, and couldn't have explained how he saw, a remark that was going to be both straightforward and unpleasant rise to the edge of Robin's lips, hover there, and then evaporate in the sheer warmth of Robin's company manner.

"Perhaps you're right," Robin said. "Me, I'm one for clinging on to hope, I suppose."

Edwin's mother turned to him. "I'm sure you'll come up with something, darling," she said, low. "You're so clever. My clever boy."

Edwin smiled at her, not trusting himself to speak. Sometimes he had the horrid, disloyal thought that she'd have preferred him dull-minded and casually powerful, if only to provide Walt with less of a target. Like Bel, their mother had perfected avoidance for self-preservation. Every time she sat at table with both her sons, Edwin saw stamped on her face how much she hated her inability to step between them, but it was useless to expect her to change. The shape of the Courcey family had been ironed in place years ago, and trying to rearrange it now would do nothing but leave dangerous holes in the fabric.

His mother raised her voice again. "You mustn't think very highly of us magicians as a species, Sir Robert, given your experience of us thus far."

There was a snort from Trudie's direction, which buried itself, thanks to an elbow emerging from Bel's beaded confection of a dinner gown, in a fit of coughing.

"Not at all, Mrs. Courcey," said Robin. "I'm sure I'm not the first fellow to take a beating on another's behalf because he's thought to know more than he does. Nothing magical about that."

"Well, you've gone practically native," she said. "I see you've decided to bring your guidelight along tonight."

"I'm accustomed to the thing now. It *is* very handy." Robin conveyed a heroic portion of lamb to his mouth and managed to smile with his eyes as he chewed, gazing down at his guidelight. The table was set with the Tiffany guidekeepers again.

"I always forget how lovely this room looks when it's full of people. Full of light."

"It does look lovely tonight," Robin agreed. "As do you." He sounded neither flirtatious nor flattering. Entirely sincere.

Edwin watched the smile tremble across his mother's face, then firm out into the strong and luminous expression he always tried to remember her as wearing. In that moment he would have carved a curse onto his own arm as a favour for

Robin, who had made his mother smile. At the same time he felt an ugly backwash of jealousy in his stomach; he couldn't remember the last time she'd smiled like that for *him*.

She did look well, carefully dressed in a pale-green gown with layers of ruffles that disguised the thinness of her arms, with her favourite set of pearls glowing around her neck. She was also playing an even more genteel game of croquet with her peas than Edwin was. Edwin told one of the footmen to ask the kitchen for another round of buttered French rolls, as she'd at least eaten all of her bread.

For some reason Billy and Charlie were batting around the thought experiment of power transference again.

"But surely," Billy was saying, "you can't deny that it would be useful, to be able to pool the power of many and place it at the command of one. Spells that require difficult coordination in a group could be done much more simply by an individual."

"Not necessarily," said Edwin. "Each of us grows up accustomed to controlling our own amount of power, and no more. If I suddenly had all of Charlie's magic . . . perhaps it'd be easier for me, but perhaps I'd try something as simple as making a light, and end up burning the skin off my face."

"Convenient, isn't it?" Miggsy said. "That kind of sour-grapes attitude about it, for someone like *you*."

Edwin sensed the tiny wince that went through his mother. Every surface inside his mouth went bitter.

"As I said," pronounced Charlie. "You have the power you have. Dangerous to mess with that."

"I *do* agree, Charlie," said Trudie, eyes luminescent with hope that she'd be able to drag the conversation on to something more interesting to her. "And we all know what happens when too much power goes bad. Think of what happened with the Alston twins."

"Alston?" said Robin. "Lord Hawthorn?"

"You've had the pleasure?" Trudie tinkled a laugh. "I suppose he's more likely to be in your circles than ours. Won't have a *thing* to do with magical society since he got back from the war. You'll have to tell us what he's like these days, Sir Robin. The worst kind of dissolute, I hear."

"I've spoken to the man for less than ten minutes altogether," said Robin. "I certainly didn't know he had a twin."

"Lady Elsie." Bel shook her head. "*Such* a tragedy, what happened to that poor girl." Everything about her begged to be asked the next question. Trudie's brown eyes glittered in anticipation of chewing over someone else's misfortune.

For the first time, Robin looked something less than perfectly at ease. Edwin wondered if the man was going to flatly refuse the hook, but he said, "Oh?"

"Perhaps it was always going to end badly," said Bel. "Lord Hawthorn was strong, but Lady Elsie was *enormously* powerful—more magic than had been seen in hundreds of years, they said."

"A shame," said Charlie. "Females simply can't be trained to that extent. Of course it unbalanced her."

"She burned all the power out of her own brother," said Bel, "when they were trying some kind of twisted experiment. Hawthorn wasn't well enough to leave the house for months afterwards, and as for Lady Elsie . . ." Belinda lowered her voice. "Nobody ever saw her in company again. Poor thing, she only lasted another year. Leapt from the roof of their manor house. It was *awful*."

Edwin had a memory, sudden and wild as a summer rainstorm, of Elsie Alston, with her tangle of brown hair and her infectious laugh. A laugh that she and her brother would bounce between them like an amplification clause built into a cradling. Edwin had been a small child when the Alstons were the darlings of English magical society, and only thirteen when Elsie died. He remembered chasing the twins across the Cheetham fields, unable to keep up. He remembered the tall, magnificent young woman who'd been a fixture in their lives one day—not seeming unbalanced in the slightest—and vanished into sickness and seclusion and scandal the next.

Edwin's mother, who still exchanged letters with the Countess Cheetham, said nothing. A fresh bread roll sat entirely untouched on her plate.

"It does sound like a tragic business," said Robin. He fixed Edwin with a look that said, clear as glass, *Help me change the damn subject.* "Edwin told me that you're born with magic or without it. What happens to the people born with great big buckets of power who never get trained? Surely it must pop up from time to time among families where there are no other magicians?"

Miggsy groaned. "*Must* we have all the great debates over dinner?"

"Sir Robin's allowed to be curious," said Charlie.

"I've tripped over another of those central questions," said Robin, quirking a smile at Edwin. "Haven't I?"

Edwin said, "You're more or less right. We have to assume that a small number of natural magicians are born outside of registered families, but are never trained, and so never know."

"Think of someone born with a great musical gift and never put in front of a piano," said Charlie. "But one can hardly go around testing the general population just in case you unearth the occasional natural case of magic, can one? There'd be no way to keep ourselves hush-hush."

"Very occasionally there's an accident that's probably some child's magic going wrong," said Billy. "And then the Assembly has to send people around to fix it up and smooth things over. It's one of the things that your office is supposed to pick up on."

Over the course of several seconds, Robin transparently remembered the existence of his civil service position. Edwin resisted the urge to laugh.

It was true, though: hush-hush was the rule of it. There were hundreds of years of near-disasters to prove that. Edwin had read reports from the liaison office's records, including one of a mass unbusheling in Manchester in the 1850s that had nearly started an urban war and had resulted in two cotton mills and a meeting hall burning down, an extremely difficult cover-up, and a good third of the city's magicians packing up and leaving.

"Tell me if this is a silly question," said Robin, "but I hadn't even thought—I mean, Edwin's told me about your Assembly, but—is there magical *work*, officially? Positions of employment?"

Charlie plucked that question up and settled into his favoured role of explainer. Edwin was conscious that he had told Robin exactly no more than the fact of the Assembly's existence and that they wouldn't have much in the way of scruples if a smiling example of foresight on well-developed legs presented himself in front of them, full of ignorance, ready to be exploited. He kept forgetting how *much* there was, if one hadn't grown up with it.

"I'd have thought there'd be potential for industry," Robin was saying, in the first gap that Charlie had managed to leave so far.

"Steam and gas still do more work, more consistently, than a magician can. And these electrical gadgets do even more," Charlie said. "And transmuting a thing to another thing's a tedious job. Far too much bother per penny."

"Energy per mass," clarified Edwin.

"You could spend your life changing dirt to gold, but it's a lot less exhausting all round to go out and—"

"Invest in railroads," finished Bel smoothly. She gestured around the room with her knife, illustrating the fruits of their parents' endeavours.

"That girl of yours works at the Barrel, isn't that right, Billy?" said Trudie.

"Not my girl any longer," said Billy to his water glass.

"Oh, that's right. I'd forgotten."

Bollocks you had, thought Edwin, watching Trudie's sharp smile.

"I'm sorry to hear that, William," said Edwin's mother.

"Power's the thing, isn't it?" Billy shrugged. With his shoulders curled in he looked smaller than usual. "My family's not got the pedigree that hers does, apparently. Her grandfather's got his heart set on some toff from the colonies for her. Made her break off the engagement. Not much a chap can do but bow out gracefully, is there?"

"Rotten luck," said Robin sincerely. "We should take your mind off it. Tell me more about what Edwin and I have been missing, toiling away in the library. Is there much to see around these parts? Any hills with a view worth the climb?"

"We went up Parson's Mount today—that's not bad," said Bel. "I suppose there's a handful of ruins around, if you like boring old stones."

"It's not the best time of year for it, but there are some estates with famously good gardens, if you go further afield," said Florence Courcey. "Audley End, and that abbey with the walled garden—oh, and Sutton Cottage. The grounds there are really sublime, they say, though I've not seen them myself."

"The Sutton hedge maze is supposed to be a grand puzzle," said Bel. "Not as large as Hampton Court, but not far off it. We should make a day trip of it, Trudie, don't you think? Perhaps in the spring."

"Sutton Cottage," said Robin. "Mrs. Flora Sutton? Edwin, wasn't she the one writing to Gatling? I could have sworn that was the address."

It took Edwin a few moments to remember the rose-scented letter in Reggie's pile of correspondence. "I can't recall."

"Well, that's only natural," said Edwin's mother. "Flora Sutton? Yes, she was a Gatling, before she married. She'd be Reginald's great-aunt. The Suttons have no children of their own, I believe, so—" She gave a couple of dry coughs. Some of her faint, sparkling energy seemed to leave her with them.

"Mother, are you sure you're feeling well?" asked Edwin. "Do you want to retire?"

"Nonsense, darling. I'm sure I can remain upright at least until the end of dinner." She turned, chin high, and struck up a bright conversation with Trudie about hats.

Robin caught Edwin with a touch on the shoulder as the dining room was emptying. "Sutton Cottage is worth a visit, don't you think?" said Robin. "It's not as though the bushes are crawling with possible leads, when it comes to Gatling's vanishing act. And—hedge maze," he added, nonsensically. "It doesn't seem like something we should ignore."

"Hedge—*oh*." One of Robin's visions. Edwin said slowly, "You'll be expected at the office tomorrow. And back home, I'd imagine."

"I'll send a telegram home. And one to Miss Morrissey—I say, we should ask her to post that letter from Reggie's aunt here too. I wish I'd opened the thing now."

Edwin tried to shake off the warmth summoned by that *we*. "You want to stay on? It's not going to get any quieter, I'm afraid." For all Robin's talk of Saturday-to-Mondays and magical jobs, Bel's set were not overly burdened with employment. Edwin had no idea when they planned to quit Penhallick. Possibly when they got bored.

Belatedly Edwin remembered that *quiet* was not an advantage, to someone like Robin. But Robin just grinned at him and said, "Then we'll go day-tripping, and avoid the fuss," as though the prospect of chasing down Reggie Gatling's dubious relatives with Edwin was honestly appealing.

Like Robin with the pain from the curse, Edwin had hoped he was becoming immune to that grin, when in fact the opposite was true. A hot, greedy pulse of want tried to make itself known in Edwin's intractable body.

No. Edwin pushed it down and focused instead on the guilt that had sprung up when Reggie's name was first mentioned. Reggie, who was still missing; Miss Morrissey would have sent a message to tell them if he'd resurfaced. Edwin had been distracted by the more immediate danger of Robin's worsening curse. But it was all part of the same damned mess, wasn't it? The thought cooled the breath in Edwin's lungs to a thickening mist of real fear about Reggie's fate.

Not least because Robin's attackers might very well intend Robin to share it.

Robin dashed off a message for Maud immediately after dinner, and left it folded on the dresser in his room. He and Edwin could call at the telegraph office in the nearest town before they set off for Sutton Cottage the next morning.

Mrs. Courcey had confided to him over the dessert course that she hoped they could have a telephone installed within the next few years. Robin imagined such a thing could make a world of difference to a housebound invalid. He thought about the way Edwin looked at her, as though storing up grain for winter. Edwin saying, *It's better in the city*. Robin was only now realising how much Edwin must dislike everything else about being at Penhallick, for it to trump even his beloved mother's presence.

Guidelight bobbing above his shoulder, Robin followed a footman's directions to a large parlour, where the others were gathered for drinks and cigarettes and, from what Belinda had been saying at dinner, some new sort of game. Robin's afternoon doze had left his mind grumblingly awake. He didn't fancy groaning his way through another bout of the curse's punishment in company, but even less did he fancy retiring early to the willow-bough room and staring at its ceiling. He liked being with other people. Too much time alone and he felt his colour leaking out.

All right, he was coming around to the strong opinion that he didn't *like* this crowd overmuch, but they were better than nothing. And even though he was smartly wary of Belinda Walcott's games, he thought his chances of being shot at or drowned or swan-mauled were fairly low, indoors.

The parlour was a striking room even by the standards of Penhallick House. The Morris paper on the walls held a dense pattern of leaves and clusters of flowers in red and blue and yellow, woven through with thorny tendrils studded with ti-nier flowers in startling white. It filled the walls in wide panels between dark, carved wood that stretched from the floor and formed arching ribs where it met the ceiling. There were shelves cunningly set into the wall to show off books or glasswork or panels of mosaic. Plants grew from enormous brass pots; rugs formed a rough chessboard over the floor. The furniture was slender and upholstered in cloth embroidered to within an inch of its life, and most of the chairs had fabric flung over them to create yet more contrasts of pattern.

There were almost no paintings. Robin felt a brief, unex-pected pang of longing for his own family's house in London, but banished it. This room didn't need paintings. It would have smothered them. It was almost too much even on its own—almost, but not quite. Robin had no doubt that you could scrape twenty people off the street and most of them would proclaim this entire endeavour to be in ludicrously bad taste, but he adored it. It was jubilant and restorative. It was impossible to feel colourless, surrounded by so much colour.

Robin turned away from inspecting the nearest shelf to acknowledge Billy's greeting, and stopped.

There was a motorcar parked in the middle of the room. It had not been there when he entered; Robin was reasonably certain that even he would have noticed a car before the wall-paper. But there it was, gleaming innocently from tyres to top, as though a country house's parlour were a normal showroom.

Trudie smirked and walked *through* the car, towards him. Watching the dark-green bulk of metal swallow her to the collarbones made Robin's stomach squirm, but she emerged unscathed as though from mist. "We're playing at illusions," she said, waving a glass of sherry. "Charlie's got *such* a knack for them. Doesn't it just look as though it's about to speed into the fireplace?" Her dark gaze was full of an expectant amusement that seemed to say she was waiting for Robin to entertain her—or rather, for something entertaining to happen *to* him.

Robin nodded his admiration of Charlie's work, but didn't move to join the group. Instead he wandered over to where Edwin was seated in a kind of nook formed by sofas. Edwin had removed his necktie and his dinner jacket. Robin knew enough now to guess that the small green jars dotting the room's low tables contained the group's decanted guidelights, but Edwin's was loose, hovering above his shoulder. The reason was obvious: Edwin had a book in his lap. He was also taking notes, the unmagical way. Robin failed to dredge up the tiniest scrap of surprise.

The cigarette in Edwin's other hand was another story. Robin enjoyed the drooping angle of it, the casual pinch of Edwin's fingers.

"You smoke?" was Robin's greeting.

"Only in company," said Edwin. He correctly read Robin's surprise and went on, almost amused. "Yes. Indeed. Not often."

"Give us one, then," said Robin, settling himself on the nearest ottoman.

Edwin blinked and held out a carton. Robin pulled his gold lighter from his pocket and lit up. It had been long enough that the first taste of smoke made him cough.

"I thought you said you'd given it up," said Edwin.

"I did. I don't smoke." Robin smiled at him. "Apart from sometimes. In company."

Edwin's eyes strayed back to the lighter, which Robin tossed in his hand. "It was a gift from Maud, when I sat my second Tripos. For luck."

Edwin's tiny smile flickered at the side of his mouth. He

took a drag from his cigarette as though to banish it, and looked back at his book.

Robin opened his mouth to suggest that Edwin could give himself a night off research, but closed it again, silenced by the twin realisations that Edwin still felt guilty about his failure to lift the curse today, and that Edwin wanted the excuse not to join in the parlour games.

Edwin said, without looking up, "Actually, this one's a history of the magical families of Cambridgeshire. It's recent and atrociously pompous and full of spiteful digs at the author's distant cousins. But it's the only thing in the library that might tell us something about the Suttons."

Robin felt a warmth that had nothing to do with the fire, which was crackling away within a deep tiled recess. Edwin's wry, professorial humour was something that Robin didn't think many people were allowed to see.

It was Miggsy's turn in the illusion game when Robin next looked up. He extended a hand to help Belinda out of the chair where she sat, and cradled a spell. The chair filled at once with a gauzy version of Belinda herself, leaning sideways to laugh at something.

"I say, that's neat."

Edwin followed his gaze. "That's an echo, not a constructed illusion. It's a fiendishly fiddly spell, but if you cast it over a chair and define the time as five minutes ago, it'll show you who was sitting there."

Robin's mind filled instantly with penny dreadfuls and police stories. "You could catch a few criminals that way, wouldn't you think?"

"I suppose so. You'd have to be precise about the parameters, or else stand there doing it over and over to find the right time. And it takes an immense amount of power to see further back than a day or so." He glanced at Robin. "It's like the law of distance, only more so. Time and magic interact . . . oddly. We don't understand it well."

Belinda showily pretended to kiss her past self farewell as the image faded. Miggsy began another spell at once, in the clear hope of holding her attention, but Belinda had already flitted off in response to Charlie's wave.

"I think Miggsy's sweet on Belinda," said Robin.

"Oh, yes," said Edwin. "He's been in love with her for years."

At times like this Robin could feel the pull of gossip, the heady temptation of it. It would be so easy to glide from statement of fact to judgement, sly and sweet on the tongue. He did *know* the appeal. He'd just seen it used as a weapon too many times to have any appetite for it.

Charlie hovered over his wife's shoulder as she built her own illusion, keeping up a stream of talk and sometimes adjusting her hands. Robin would have been tempted to drive his elbow into the man's face, but Belinda seemed to brighten under his attention. The butterfly illusion she created was pretty enough, but its movements were wrong. It rose from her cupped hands like a sack being hauled up on a rope.

The butterfly had hardly shaken itself into nothing when Charlie declared it his turn again, and cradled for almost half a minute before a steam-powered carousel sprang up, to general laughs and more clapping. The carousel was miniaturised, man-height yet still filling half the room, an intricate and eerily silent whirl. Belinda stood trailing her fingers at its margins, a fresh cigarette in her other hand. Trudie grasped Charlie's elbow and gushed her admiration.

"And Trudie, with Charlie?" Robin ventured.

"Bel and Charlie surround themselves with people who are in love with them," said Edwin. It didn't sound like malice. It sounded like tired statement of fact. "They can't stand not to be loved."

And then there was Billy, whose perpetual smile was more interesting given that he was apparently nursing a broken heart and a broken engagement. To be found inadequate by the beloved's family was a familiar story in any society, whether the deficit was breeding or wealth or—in Billy's case—magic. Perhaps his cheerfulness was armour. You wouldn't walk around with open wounds in this crowd any more than you would in one of those South American rivers full of fish that would nibble your bones bare.

Robin felt an uneasy wash of familiarity. He'd had that thought, about the blood-sensing fish, before. All these casual currents of game-playing were a smaller version of the social world that his parents had built around themselves—their own carousel, full of sparkle and mirrors and meanness, all too ready to collapse in the end.

He settled himself on the arm of one sofa and watched Charlie's illusion for a while longer. Light glinted off the curling golden poles above and below the plaster horses in a way that would have had one of Robin's art-masters shouting about amateur awareness of light sources: it was a definite sunlight glint, here in this gas-lit and fire-lit—and guide-lit—room. One of the perils of working entirely from memory, Robin supposed. What did it feel like, to work on a creation like this, to paint it in one's mind and call it into being? And then see it blink into nothing? And then raise your hands and do it again, entirely anew?

"You know," said Edwin quietly, "that's the first time you've looked envious. Even a little."

Robin looked down at him. Edwin's finger kept place in the book as he lifted the last inch of his cigarette to his lips, and an unabashed flare of heat settled into Robin at the sight of it.

"Envious?"

"Of magic. Of magicians." Edwin's mouth quirked. He stubbed his cigarette out on a green glass saucer. "I think it's why the others are taken with you. You're playing it rather cool. Being pleasant and sociable and unimpressed is not the usual response to an unbusheling."

"I wasn't unimpressed," said Robin.

The quirk deepened. Edwin looked away, a sudden twitch of his head, then back down at his book.

It was true. Robin hadn't thought that he might be acting in any way out of the ordinary. But he supposed that in a society where more power was transparently desirable, Robin's attitude might seem like that of a bootblack standing among the silks and perfumes of Court, sipping Champagne and cheerfully declaring how content he was with the freezing attic room he shared with five brothers.

Magic, Robin reflected, was different things to different people. For Mr. Courcey it had fitted exactly into that comparison: something like money or political power. The more the better. For the people in this room, though, Robin had the sense it was closer to the way that most people he'd met thought about religion: a social glue, a bedrock. And for Edwin it was clearly both science and art. An academic passion.

Bits and pieces of the dinner conversation tumbled through Robin's mind and he wondered how Lord Hawthorn thought of magic these days. Lord Hawthorn who had said he'd *never liked* Edwin's family. At the time it had sounded like another insult; now it seemed evidence of good judgement. The way these people had gossiped about Hawthorn's sister was enough to make Robin's teeth ache.

No, that wasn't an ache. It was hot tension—it was tingling pepper on his tongue—it was the sensory weirdness that preceded the visions, light dancing at the corners of his eyes. He was noticing it earlier. He had time to anticipate.

"Edwin," Robin said weakly, and leaned forward on his elbows, head drooping, just as the foresight took him. He managed to think, with a throb of irritation: *Why can't this be* useful—

A narrow street, a line of shop fronts in the glumness of fog. City lights glowing like the eyes of beasts. Grubby signs and brass trim, and a window full of clocks, almost dreamlike through the murky air. Clocks spinning and ticking and pendulum-swaying. A slim male figure wrapped in coat and hat pushing open the door in order to enter the shop; a bell at the door's top set into feverish tinkling motion.

Change. An elderly woman in a strangely small and windowless room, dressed in impeccable black silk, backed up against the wooden panels of the wall. Fear in her face, and then an angry smile emerging from the wrinkles that carved lines away from her thin lips. She flung out a hand and something flashed—a spell, a thrown knife? The next moment there was an answering flash, a glow of pink light around her neck, and the woman crumpled and fell.

Robin gasped back into himself. He felt Edwin's hand first, the painful grip on his arm. Then he noticed the quiet that had fallen in the room.

"Still among the living," said Robin, raising his head. He couldn't suppress a wince.

"Still feeling the effects of Win's experiments?" asked Belinda.

"Or was it that curse again?" put in Billy.

"To be frank, I've not been feeling the thing since taking that dunking yesterday." Robin put a hand to his own head. "Perhaps I'm coming down with a cold."

"Come on," said Edwin quickly. "I'm sure we've a remedy or two in the kitchen."

Nobody asked them to stay. Billy and Trudie were already trading amiable barbs about each other's illusions as they left. So much for Belinda's friends being *taken with him*. Robin was a little sad to quit the glorious parlour before he'd had a chance to poke his nose into all its corners, but he wasn't sad to be alone with Edwin again.

Ten minutes later they were upstairs, in yet another parlour that Robin hadn't entered before, cosily arranged near the fireplace. A servant had been dispatched to the kitchen with specific instructions as to which herbal tea Mr. Edwin wanted, and that it was *not* to be added to the water, but served alongside.

A tea trolley was wheeled in before long. Alongside the tea set and the pot of water were a plate of iced gingerbread and a small decanter of brandy.

Edwin upended the bag of leaves onto a spare tray, and spread the green-grey mass of them to form a thin layer. Robin, nibbling gingerbread, watched with interest as Edwin pulled out his cradling string and built a spell that created a syrupy rainbow shimmer between his hands, like petroleum on puddles. Once it vanished into the leaves, Edwin dumped the lot into the teapot and stirred vigorously before replacing the lid.

"This is an imbuement," said Edwin. "It has to be on the leaves, you see. Any kind of potion with magical properties has the magic applied to the plant ingredients first. Magic tends to adhere to life, or at least a place where life was. It can't do much to clean water, and even less to an alcohol base. Infusion's easier all round."

"Magic and life," said Robin. "I suppose it makes sense."

"I've just got hold of a book by a last-century Japanese research magician, who wrote a lot on that subject," said Edwin. "They're doing so much more in other countries, they have *academies* . . . anyway, Kinoshita's work was on the specific properties of living things and where they interact with magic. Of course, a lot of their plants are different, but—" He cut himself off with a jerk of his chin like a bottle twisting off the flow of wine. "Sorry," he muttered. "I can—talk."

"Don't be," said Robin. "Shall I be mother, then?" He poured the tea, careful with the strainer as it caught the sodden leaves. The imbued tea was a deep yellow. It had an odd background note that was almost buttery, and a sharp aftertaste that shot up to Robin's nose like ginger. He wouldn't call it delicious, but it wasn't unpleasant. Halfway down the cup he became aware of warmth spilling down the muscles of his neck and shoulders, like sinking into a hot bath. He'd been wondering when to point out that he didn't in fact need a cold remedy, but this was delightful nonetheless.

Edwin drank steadily. He looked about as tired as Robin felt; perhaps *he* was the one who needed the soothing effects of the potion, and had seized the excuse. Robin didn't want to chew over the failed attempt at lifting the curse, so he struck out in the direction of another topic.

"Sounds like a rotten thing, what happened to Lord Hawthorn and his sister."

Edwin made a noise of agreement.

"Is that why he's—how he is?"

"No, he was like that before. But there was no cruelty to it. He wanted you to push back. He never truly wanted to hurt."

"Were you close to his sister, at all?"

"Not close. But friendly. And Charlie was talking utter *rot,* at dinner, saying her magic sent her mad. I don't know what happened to her, but it wasn't that. She was born for that power. Both of them were. And Elsie had all of Jack's energy, twice his charm. It was very easy to like her."

Edwin's low, fierce voice cracked on the word *easy.* Robin reached out and touched Edwin's forearm, purely on instinct. He froze the next second, ready to draw away—ready for Edwin to draw away—but instead there was a small loosening of Edwin's fingers, and an even smaller nod of his head: acknowledging comfort, giving permission. He even gave Robin a look that was, while a little surprised, almost friendly.

Robin smiled at him and took his hand away before he could trample on the moment. He wanted to memorise the details of the friendliness. A crinkle at the side of Edwin's eyes. A softening around the mouth.

This was so deeply awkward. Usually one simply *knew,* when acquaintanceship was turning to friendship. It wasn't the kind of thing men discussed at length. Robin had no idea whether Edwin would characterise them as friends; quite possibly not. But all of Robin's muddled feelings, which had been set on a giant fairground swing during the past two days, now churned and bubbled in his chest and finally announced that they were going to be vocalised, and Robin had a few more seconds to decide exactly how.

"Thank you," Robin blurted, which seemed safe.

"It's barely anything," said Edwin. "Even for someone like me. These leaves will take—"

"Not for the tea. For everything. I know it's a beastly bother for you, coming here, and it's even more beastly the way these people treat you." It felt a relief, to say it aloud. "And I dare say most magical chaps would have simply—tipped me into the midden, as Miss Morrissey would say, or at least tipped me into the hands of that Assembly of yours, instead of spending so much time and effort trying to help me."

Edwin's lips were parted in what looked like astonishment.

Robin felt foolish enough that he contemplated upsetting the teapot as a diversion.

"Robin," said Edwin finally. "I dragged you out to the countryside. Where you have been shot, magically drugged, set upon by wildlife, half-drowned, endured an escalating amount of pain from a curse that I can't remove, and managed to smile through a number of activities with my sister and her ghastly friends. I'm thankful you haven't hit me across the face and stormed back to London."

Robin managed to hold his tongue on something truly un-wise like *You look like a Turner painting and I want to learn your textures with my fingertips. You are the most fascinating thing in this beautiful house. I'd like to introduce my fists to whoever taught you to stop talking about the things that in-terest you.* Those were not things one blurted out to a friend. They were their own cradles of magic, an expression of the desire to transform one thing into another. And what if the magic went awry?

Robin took a long sip of tea, instead, and smiled at Edwin through the steam. "I'm not going anywhere," he said.

12

They took the motorcar to Sutton Cottage the next day. Neither Walt nor Bel were keen drivers; Edwin was sure their father had only bought the thing and learned the basics of its workings in order to be able to discuss it knowledgeably with his business associates. The Daimler gathered expensive dust in the converted carriage-house, and the chauffeur had given notice out of sheer boredom after a handful of months.

A chauffeur was not needed. Robin referred vaguely to friends of his who owned motorcars and had taught him the knack of it in Hyde Park—"Though the speed limit's only ten miles to the hour, in the Park. And it's twice that in the country! This should be a lark."

Edwin, who wished Robin had betrayed this boyish and limb-threatening enthusiasm *before* they'd pulled out onto the road proper, pulled his hat more firmly down onto his head and fiddled with his cradling string, trying to remember if he'd ever read anything about how to unbreak a broken skull.

They stopped in town and sent their telegrams. Once back on the main roads they passed a few carts without mishap, and even another motorcar full of men around university age, who applied themselves to the horn and waved their hats until Robin waved back at them. Robin seemed to have a sense of what he was doing, and no desire to go at reckless speeds. Edwin managed to relax enough to direct their progress from the map.

"I hope this does get us closer to Gatling," Robin said

abruptly, into what had been a pleasant silence. "I know you must be worried about him."

"Yes," said Edwin.

A pause. Robin's hands shifted on the wheel of the car. "Are you and he ... ?"

Edwin morbidly considered flinging himself from the vehicle, but settled his nerves with the force of habit and will. So Robin wanted to talk about it after all. He shouldn't have been surprised. And it wasn't an unreasonable assumption for Robin to make. "No," he said. And heard himself add, "Reggie doesn't care for other men—that way."

"You can't always tell."

"Sometimes you can tell," Edwin said. "One way or another."

"Can't argue with that." After another pause, more tentatively: "And Lord Hawthorn?"

Edwin closed his eyes. Oh, what did it matter? Hawthorn himself had gleefully freed this cat from its bag and given it a kick to speed it on its way. "Hawthorn is a thing unto himself. And—yes. For a little while. It would have been three—no, four years ago."

Edwin had been fresh out of Oxford, Hawthorn two years out from the military service that had been his first attempt at violently ignoring the magical world. Edwin had thought that he wanted the old version of Jack Alston, thought that version was still there, and kept digging for him beneath the mockery; thought he could risk opening himself in turn. He'd been wrong. And who knew what Hawthorn himself wanted. It hadn't been Edwin, that was certain.

Robin said, "It's never been someone in particular, for me. I mean to say—at university, there were a few fellows. But all my encounters were, ah. Well. It was understood that there were limits."

"Furtive and athletic." Edwin opened his eyes and watched the fence poles and trees gliding past. "I can imagine."

He could, unfortunately. Robin in a soaked rowing vest, shorts pulled to his ankles, leaning against a shed by the river. Handsome face twisted in pleasure, one large hand on the head of the fellow rower who knelt at his feet, working at Robin's cock with hand and mouth—

Edwin clenched his jaw and forced himself not to move. Not to cross his legs. Not to draw any attention at all.

"I'm wondering if I should be offended, but that does rather cover it," said Robin, ruefully. "And the same since, I suppose. Bathhouses and the like. One has to be careful, but one makes do."

Yes: one had to be careful. It was over a decade since Wilde's trial, but one still had to face the possibility of being pulled up before a jury, and considering oneself lucky if the charge was merely *gross indecency* and not *buggery.*

If one weren't someone like the Baron Hawthorn, with enough money and clout to make such problems go away, anyhow.

"You've never wanted a future with someone?" Edwin asked.

"I've never been a future sort of person."

Edwin stared at him. He was wondering if he'd actually have to point out the irony; then Robin's mouth convulsed helplessly, and then they were both laughing. Edwin leaned back in the seat, feeling the car's motor thudding gently into his body in counterpoint with the laughter that shook his rib cage, and wondered at it. He hadn't thought he'd missed this, out of all the things he missed in his weaker moments of remembering those months with Jack, but he had. It was refreshing to be able to *talk* about these things, in fellowship.

Edwin supposed his inclinations were an open secret among their level of magical society—he'd heard Miggsy say once that at least it wasn't as though Edwin was ruining any girl's hope of marrying into strong blood. But even if sometimes Edwin felt his skin seethe with a loud, desert-hot hunger, he knew himself. He knew his weaknesses, how easily he could let his walls down when offered something that he craved.

And oh, how firmly he was having to patrol those boundary walls these days. He could feel them blurring. Every time he was surprised by how easy it was to be softer and more open in Robin Blyth's presence, his wariness flew up in equal measure, as though on the other end of a lever. *Stop here,* it shouted. *No more. Be safe.*

And it was. It was ten times safer, a hundred times simpler, to assume that Robin's warmth was fellowship and nothing else.

They drove. The wind tossed leaves in handfuls, and the colours of autumn were muted under the grey sky. It wasn't precisely quiet, what with the noise of the car, but something in Edwin that had loosened itself with the laughter remained loose.

"Shouldn't be more than a few minutes away now," Robin said. They turned onto what, according to Edwin's map, was the lane leading directly to the Sutton Cottage grounds.

Edwin shifted in his seat. He was restless in the way he was when he'd missed something, when he'd skipped some essential step in constructing a spell, and his mind was trying to bring the fact to his attention.

"Perhaps this wasn't a good idea," he said.

"Why do you say that?"

"Why would some elderly relation have any idea what Reggie's been up to?" A sluggish unease was alive in Edwin's stomach now. "This is a waste of time. I could have skimmed through five more books. Turn the car, we'll be back early enough not to have wasted the day."

"I'm not turning the car." Robin frowned. "We should find out what she knows. It's not as though any of your books are going to say This Way to Reggie Gatling. At least Mrs. Sutton wrote to—"

"We have to *stop*," Edwin said, close to panic. A rough line of elms was approaching and beyond it Edwin could see the crisp, rich green of well-tended hedges. "We shouldn't be here."

The car slowed as some of Edwin's alarm finally conveyed itself to Robin. Edwin felt ill. "We shouldn't have come. We have to turn around." How could he make Robin understand? "There's nothing here—"

The car inched past the tree line.

Edwin sagged back into his seat, his breath catching on a gasp. He felt like someone had thrown cold water over his brain.

"Robin," he said. "That was a warding. Stop the car. We'll keep going, but—I need you to stop."

Robin stopped the car without another murmur. "What's going on? A what?"

"A warding, and a strong one. Someone doesn't want visitors." Edwin climbed out of the car. "You didn't feel it?"

Engine having puttered to a stop, Robin climbed out after him. "I heard you rabbiting on like you were trying to change your own mind. I didn't *feel* anything."

Edwin was already cradling a basic detection spell, but although he could feel a vague tug of his hands towards the tree line, it wasn't likely to provide more information than that. He reached up to touch the yellow-splotched dangling leaves of the closest tree, and let the spell collapse, then tucked his string away. He was more interested in what would happen if he stepped back through the line.

"Come here," he said. "Take my hand."

Robin took Edwin's outstretched hand in his own. Edwin ignored the flood of physical awareness that tried to clamour in his bones, the way his whole body wanted to turn towards Robin's.

"If I try to pull away, don't let me. If I start to run . . ."

"Wrestle you to the ground?" Robin suggested pleasantly. His thumb moved over Edwin's. Edwin looked away.

"Yes. I'm presuming you included rugby in the list of sports

you spent your time excelling at while your family was paying
for the improvement of your mind."

"Message received," said Robin, amused. "Get on with it."

Edwin stepped between two of the elms.

The feeling of violent wrongness flooded back at once. He
knew he was in the wrong place. He should be anywhere but
here.

Edwin held tight to Robin's hand and managed to propel
himself back onto the other side of the warding with a wrench
of stumbling effort. He dropped Robin's hand and turned to
touch the trees again. *"Fascinating."*

"I'm sure."

"You don't understand. That kind of ward has to be constantly re-laid, and the amount of power it would take to maintain it along the entire boundary of a property—or perhaps it's
just this particular row of trees—"

"Edwin," said Robin. "I utterly refuse to spend the rest of
the daylight helping you hop back and forth between trees just
because you want to test a theory. Entertaining as it would be
when you inevitably got stuck halfway over a fence."

Edwin sighed and returned to the car. "It'd be simpler to ask
Mrs. Sutton how it's done," he allowed.

"Ah," murmured Robin. He followed Edwin and applied
himself to starting the engine. "But where would be the intellectual challenge in *that*?"

To his surprise, Edwin found himself flushing at the tease
without feeling like he wanted to make himself small, or meet
the barb with coldness, or seek out a quiet space where he'd be
unbothered by anyone's company but his own.

"No need to be like that simply because you wouldn't recognise an intellectual challenge if you tripped over it in the
street," he said, trying to mirror Robin's tone, and Robin
laughed as he climbed back behind the wheel.

They drove the rest of the way without incident. Sutton Cottage itself was one of those coyly named places; it was nearly as large as Penhallick House. And the grounds were as impressive as advertised, a grand sprawl in the best English tradition. They drove past a rose garden where a pair of gardeners were at work removing spent blooms, tidying and trimming in readiness for winter. The famed hedge maze could be seen briefly, before the drive curved around and the maze was hidden by a gentle hill dotted with trees. And there was the fountain, set in the centre of a scrupulously neat parterre that dominated the area in front of the house.

Two elderly couples were being helped into a carriage as Robin and Edwin pulled up in the motorcar. The women's old-fashioned bonnets were tied firmly onto their heads and one was clutching a guidebook.

"Looks to be a popular place," said Robin. "*They* certainly weren't persuaded to turn around before they'd even arrived."

"No," said Edwin. A different kind of unease had taken over now. He suspected he knew why the other visitors had been unaffected, and it brought up a whole host of new questions.

The carriage pulled out. A man in servant's livery approached the car. "Here to see the gardens, sirs?"

"Yes. No." Edwin craned his neck up at the house. The grey stone of the frontage crawled attractively with ivy. "We need to speak to Mrs. Sutton."

A genteel cough. "My apologies, sir, Mrs. Sutton does not generally see visitors. She is not interested in selling the estate. If you are members of the Horticultural Enthusiasts Association, she does appreciate receiving letters—"

"I quite understand." One of Robin's most comfortable, sunny smiles accompanied the calling card he handed over to the footman. There was a pause where the man visibly digested the words *Sir* and *Baronet*. "We're here on family business, about Mrs. Sutton's great-nephew. Reginald Gatling. We'd consider it a great favour if she'd see us."

Edwin barely remembered that he owned calling cards even when he was in London. "Edwin Courcey," he said, in response to the footman's inquiringly open palm.

They stood under the high, glowering clouds until the footman reappeared and ushered them into Sutton Cottage itself. Flora Sutton received them in a large parlour crammed with vases full of fresh flowers. She was older than Edwin had expected: a small white-haired woman with a bluish translucent look to her wrinkled skin. Her hands trembled. She looked like a piece of crumpled tissue paper, right up until her cloudy, rheumy eyes fixed themselves on Edwin and he had the unnerving sense he'd been instantly understood and classified.

"Thank you for seeing us, Mrs. Sutton," said Robin.

"Are you the Courcey?" she demanded.

"Yes," said Edwin. Her eyes hadn't shifted from him, even when Robin spoke. "We're here about Reggie."

"Mm. So Franklin said." Now the piercing gaze travelled between the two of them. "Reggie did say there would be others, soon enough. You may dig up every square inch of the grounds, gentlemen." Her chin lifted. "You are too late. It is safe now, far away from here."

"What is?" asked Edwin.

Robin was quicker. "The last contract," he said. "Whatever the blazes it really is, Gatling had it from *you*?"

Mrs. Sutton pressed her lips together and bowed her head. The shake of her hands worsened for a few moments. When she looked up, half of the vivacity had left her face. "I think you boys should leave," she said, suddenly querulous. "I cannot help you."

"You don't know what we want help with," said Edwin, feeling wrung by guilt, but irritable nonetheless.

A sigh like rustling leaves. "Please—"

"I was raised by liars, Mrs. Sutton. I'm afraid you'll have to do better than that."

Edwin looked at Robin, startled. Mrs. Sutton was doing the same. Robin looked apologetic and charming and yet, somehow, like a rock planted amongst crashing waves. He was already shrugging off his jacket, unfastening his shirt cuff.

Robin went on, "We don't mean you any harm, you have my word. There are people after this contract, and they think I know where it is. And they're not too concerned with the niceties of how they go about getting their information."

Mrs. Sutton gathered her spectacles onto her nose and gazed at the bared curse. She was controlling her face now, but she still looked shaken.

"You wrote to Reggie, didn't you?" Edwin said. "At the London office. I'm the Assembly liaison," he added, into her hesitation. "I work with Reggie. He's been missing for the past three weeks." Hastily, he explained the circumstances—who Robin was, and how he'd become involved. How the contract was mentioned for the first time when Robin was cursed, and how they'd found her letter, rose-scented, in Reggie's mail.

"Yes, I wrote to him. I wanted to—check in," said Flora Sutton. The spectacles dropped again. Now she sat like a fairy queen in a bower, keen as fresh-cut grass. "He didn't send me a single word after he left with it in his pocket. And I'd kept it safe so long, I felt anxious over it."

Myriad questions hung thick in Edwin's mind, and he was dizzy with urgency at the promise of finally having them answered. He snatched at the first that came to hand. "How did Reggie know you had it in the first place? All of this, the threats, the curse—it must be because the contract can't be found with any kind of spell." He thought of the tantrum of spilled paper and overturned furniture in the office.

Mrs. Sutton hesitated a moment more. Edwin struggled to trap the rest of his questions behind his teeth, his breath held, waiting.

Then a spark entered the old woman's eyes, and she seemed to come to a decision. "That rather depends on the spell. You. Courcey." She nodded to Edwin. "Go to that cabinet and fetch me the stone in the uppermost drawer."

Edwin did as directed. The room was lined with book-shelves. One didn't notice them at first beyond the sheer, col-ourful, nose-itching extravagance of the flowers. The standing shelves alternated with panels of dark-stained wood carved in a pattern of ivy.

The stone in question, nestled in a velvet-lined drawer in a pretty wooden cabinet, was a flat and sharp-edged chunk of grey rock. Etched into its surface, most visible when angled into the light, was a branching fern.

"A fossil," said Robin. He quirked a smile at Edwin's sur-prise. "My parents liked the occasional antiquity along with their art. I think we've a nice stone seashell or three in one of the parlours."

"This plant is long gone, but you can tell where it lay," said Mrs. Sutton. Her manner was quicker now, more eager, as though she'd given in to an impulse to indulge herself by ex-plaining a theory to a willing audience. "An object of power has a weight to it, and will warp the normal lines and channels of magic around itself. *That's* what you look for, if you know how. Even if the thing's removed, if it's been there long enough"—a nod to the fossil in Edwin's hand—"the shape of it remains."

"Like one of those echo illusion spells?" said Robin. "An imprint of the past, turned into something you can see?"

That got him a sharp look from Flora Sutton. "This is how we found the contract in the first place. And the imprint is stronger if the object rests in a place of power. Like Sutton." She glanced around the room, pride heavy in her gaze. "Two channels of magic cross one another here."

"Channels of magic." Edwin's mind was spinning. He needed two hours and a notebook to make sense of all of this. He needed to fling himself onto the rug at this strange old woman's feet and refuse to budge until he'd absorbed every-thing she had to teach. "You're talking about ley lines. That's— nobody bothers with ley lines anymore. That sort of magic hasn't worked for generations."

"Certainly it doesn't work, when you men try to wrench it into your neat little boxes and cradles." Flora Sutton sniffed. "Sutton's power makes it a perfect place to enchant as a hiding place, but also makes a—heavier footprint. Easier to locate, once one knows the trick. It was always a risk." She sighed. "Reggie said that the people he was working with hadn't quite got the knack of it, but they were starting to triangulate the pieces. And Reggie saw their maps and figured it out, because he knew I lived here. And so he came." She spread her hands. "To warn me."

"And you gave him the contract to take away with him," said Robin. "Left with it in his pocket, you said."

"He took the danger away with him too," said Edwin. "That was noble."

"Was it?" said Robin. He was watching Mrs. Sutton, as he had when he'd accused her of being a liar. "I have to assume there's some reason everyone's after this thing, and prepared to do violence for it. And you've told us a great deal for someone with little reason to trust us, but you haven't told us why the contract's so important."

He was right.

The wrinkle-lined mouth tightened. "Ignorance of its purpose is the only reason to trust you at all. Safekeeping works until the moment it doesn't, Sir Robert. Reggie told me he didn't like the people he was working with; he'd stopped trusting their intentions, but he couldn't stop them from coming here eventually. The best he could do was to stay a step ahead. We agreed he would move it to a new place, where it hadn't rested so long, and so make it more difficult for them to find. And I refused to let him tell me where that would be."

"Well, if it helps at all," said Robin dryly, "you and your great-nephew have certainly made these people very angry. So he must have hidden it well."

"Of course. He swore on his name that he'd do his best to keep it safe from them, and he put blood into the swearing.

Besides," said Mrs. Sutton, "I'd be a sorry excuse for a magician if I didn't trust my own secret-bind."

Edwin blanched. He'd only seen a secret-bind laid once, on an unmagical woman who'd seen some things her lover wasn't supposed to let her see, and who'd been past the temporal window when lethe-mint would have been effective. It had been a sloppy job; Edwin and Reggie had been involved in the debacle for all of two days before it got kicked up the chain of command to someone else in the Assembly, but the image of the woman stood out painfully in Edwin's mind. The tears ravaging her face, and the way she tried to clutch at her own swollen tongue where the brand of the bind sank further every time she tried to explain what had happened.

"A bind, so he wouldn't talk," said Edwin. The mist of his fear thickened abruptly to a sickening, mind-numbing fog. "And now nobody's seen him for weeks. He might be in hiding, yes, but how do you know he hasn't been *killed*?"

Guilt illuminated Mrs. Sutton's face like lightning: no tears filled her eyes, but remorse twisted her lips. Edwin couldn't muster much sympathy for her. You didn't lay a bind on someone unless you thought they might be either tempted or coerced into giving up the information.

Sure enough, the next thing Mrs. Sutton said was: "I did suspect people would start to die."

Robin flinched. He rubbed his forearm convulsively, then clenched his fists by his sides. "*Why?* What is this contract? Does it have anything to do with that fairy story? What does it *do*?"

Mrs. Sutton's hands made bony landscapes of tension as she gripped the arms of the chair. Ludicrously, she and Robin looked like two people on the verge of battle. Part of Edwin wanted to slip away and hide.

"On its own, one part of it does nothing. Even if the wrong sort of people do get their hands on it, my piece alone is hardly going to do them much good. But if they came close to finding me, they could find the others." She inspected the middle distance, face drawn. If *she* was seeing a vision of the future, it was nothing good.

Robin ground out, "Will you just *tell* us what—"

"No," said Flora Sutton, a whip of finality. She lifted a hand when Robin began to protest again. "The contract should have stayed lost; failing that, it should have stayed secret. It could be used in ways that would harm every living magician in Great Britain—could cause *unspeakable* damage, and the very *idea*—" She looked grey. "It's despicable. We didn't *know*, when we discovered it. And as soon as we realised what it could mean, we stopped. No. I won't help another soul another step towards it, and that includes you two gentlemen. No matter how sympathetic you claim to be. It will be safer for everyone that you not get involved."

"I *am* involved," snapped Robin. "These people, whoever they are, believe that I can find this contract. There's every chance they'll come after me again for it."

"I am sorry for that, Sir Robert," said Mrs. Sutton. She did sound sorry. She also sounded like someone who had no intention of letting Robin spill any secrets if and when this happened.

Robin started forward; Edwin put a hand on his arm to stop him.

"All right," Edwin said. "We won't press. Mrs. Sutton doesn't know where Reggie is either; that's what we came here to find out."

"No, we—"

Edwin squeezed hard and Robin subsided. "Will you tell me about the warding on this estate?" Edwin asked.

Her thin silver eyebrows shot up. "I beg your pardon?"

"You must have been trained. Not many women in this country could do a secret-bind. Did your husband teach you?" The book he'd read the previous night had told him a little about the Sutton family. Five generations of them in this cottage;

the late Gerald Sutton had been powerful and well regarded, and sat on the Magical Assembly for a term or two. The book had contained nothing at all about Flora Gatling, who'd become Flora Sutton when she married him.

"He taught me as much as he could." Her face showed the first signs of softening. "Everything else, I taught myself."

"The estate warding," said Edwin, lowering himself onto an ottoman. "How did you do that? It only works on magicians, I assume?"

"Yes." Up went the eyebrows again. "I rather thought you'd have unravelled it, to get through it in the first place. You didn't?" Her eyes went distant for the space of a heartbeat, then regained their sharpness. "Hm. You didn't. However did you get past it, then?"

"Thank goodness for motorcars," said Robin.

"No, thank goodness for *you*," said Edwin.

"Ah," said Mrs. Sutton. "Yes. The more magic you have, the stronger the push." Her glance was a question—Robin answered it with "Not a drop."

"And I've only a few drops," said Edwin. "Perhaps a teaspoon." It didn't hurt as much as he expected. He wondered what would have happened if he had as much magic as he'd always wanted. For all he knew he might have grabbed the wheel from Robin and crashed them into a ditch.

Mrs. Sutton summoned a second pair of spectacles from a table across the room. The magic was fast and neat and casual; moreover, she did it with *one hand*, and with a gesture that Edwin had never seen in his life. He burned to ask her to repeat it, but she was already donning the glasses, which somehow had the effect of doubling her gaze's intensity.

She reached out an imperious hand. Edwin thought stupidly about calling cards. Then he shifted closer and laid his hand in hers. His arm thrummed with tension, ready to draw back.

"Oh," she said, after what seemed like an age. A small smile broke her face for the first time. "You've an affinity like mine,

Mr. Courcey. I expect you've a thumb green enough to raise oaks."

"I—wouldn't say that, no," said Edwin.

Now her hands, paper-dry and cool, landed on Edwin's cheeks. He forced himself to sit still. Up close, he could see the cloudiness of her eyes in detail, the yellow tinge of the whites.

"There are more kinds of power than the men of this country have bothered to know," she said kindly. Her hands dropped. Edwin's breath gusted out. "You asked about the warding around the estate? I grew it with the trees themselves. I had to help their growth along as a secondary factor, of course, but I made the contract with the first seedlings and it held when I took cuttings. In combination with this being Sutton land, it was enough."

Half of that made no sense at all, drawing on impossible and irrational assumptions, but the other half was pinging off bits and pieces from Edwin's own reading, including Kinoshita.

"Wait, wait," he said, fumbling after the mental shape of it. "You imbued the living plants? And you've never had to re-do it? How is that possible?"

"I believe I just told you," she said, schoolmarmish. "Start when life starts. Beginnings and endings are powerful. Liminal states. You can create profound change if you slip in through the gaps."

"Spin it from twigs," Robin said, suddenly. "Like the saying? Like an orchard?"

It shocked a laugh from Mrs. Sutton, just as sudden. "I suppose I did. And the maze as well, and there's far more than warding in *that*. I wouldn't want to be the magician who set foot in there. The visitors love it, of course. Someone wrote a lovely article about my gardens for *Country Life* magazine last year."

"All that to keep magic-users off your estate," said Edwin. He thought about the kinds of people who tucked themselves away from other magicians. He knew why Hawthorn did it—or, at least, he knew as much as anyone, and more than most. You did it because magic had hurt you, or someone of yours, beyond the bounds of what you could bear to be reminded of.

Or because you were keeping a danger at bay.

"All that to keep my part of the contract away from dangerous hands," said Mrs. Sutton. "The maze is where I kept it."

"How mythological of you," said Robin. "Building a labyrinth to keep something enclosed."

A tissue-crumple of dimples. "I rather thought so."

Robin gave Edwin a look that might have been a question. Edwin had no answers for him, but a moment later he rather wished he'd said something anyway.

"I'm having visions," Robin told Mrs. Sutton. "I think I might have had one of your maze."

"Visions? Come here, boy. What manner of visions?"

"Foresight," said Edwin. "Or at least it would seem so." He didn't trust this woman, but it was Robin's curse, Robin's business, and Edwin could hardly blame him for grabbing at the slimmest chance of help now that Edwin had failed to provide any. So Edwin explained that part of the story, including what Hawthorn had said and what little he'd managed to work out from his own research. He let Robin describe the visions—and the pain, which made Mrs. Sutton wince. *Good*, Edwin thought, fierce.

Robin weathered the direct stare through the second pair of glasses, first at his face and then at the bared curse.

"Hmm," was Mrs. Sutton's verdict, a full minute later. "You boys will take tea with me in an hour. Go for a walk—go and see the grounds, while you're here. I will need to read a few things."

Edwin cast a longing glance at the bookshelves and nearly asked to stay in the room and help. But he did want to inspect the maze, to see if he could glean anything more about this idea of twinning spells to plants as they grew.

"Mr. Courcey," said Mrs. Sutton when they were almost out of the room. Edwin turned. She was sitting very straight, very proud. For an agonising moment she reminded Edwin of his own mother. "I'll be interested to hear what you think of my plants. And don't go *into* the maze, for heaven's sake. I won't have anyone else's death on my conscience today."

Edwin wondered if this was a joke. It didn't appear so.

The grounds were even more obnoxiously lovely than they'd seemed from the car. Robin and Edwin didn't encounter anyone else as they made their way towards the hedge maze in what must have looked like a comfortable, leisurely stroll. It didn't feel comfortable. There was too much that could have been said; Edwin had no idea where to begin, and when he didn't know what to say, he said nothing. Cowardly, he was hoping that Robin would take the plunge.

Robin had slung his linen jacket over one shoulder. He seemed very interested in the rose garden and the pretty wilderness that followed it, dotted with autumn colour and early berries and even some flower beds in bloom.

"What do you think?" Robin said eventually, nodding around them.

Edwin's voice came out thistle-spiked. "I think if *my* name were Flora, I'd have avoided anything this obvious."

Robin stopped. He was a few steps ahead, beneath a trellis archway of greenery. "This has rather shaken you up, hasn't it?"

"Oh, don't," snapped Edwin, throat scratched with guilt. "Don't go being *nice,* how can you constantly *be* like this, when it's your arm and your visions and someone else's bloody mess—and I made it *worse*—and Reggie might be *dead,* and here we are dancing like sodding debutantes around the fact that you might be next, and who knows what—"

"Edwin. Shut up," Robin suggested.

Edwin did, gratefully. He snagged two fingers through a gap in the trellis, sagging the weight of his arm there, trying to formulate an apology. Robin put his hand between Edwin's shoulder blades, patted twice, then let it stay.

"I hope that wasn't you trying to be comforting," Robin said after a moment. "Because you're dashed miserable at it, if so."

Edwin made a small, pained noise that was trying to be a laugh, and let himself lean back into Robin's palm. As a rule, he did not enjoy physical contact. It usually seemed an intrusion, or mistimed, or compounding whatever distress or insult or small condescension the touch had been meant to mitigate. He was still full of an off-balance ambivalence, a tingling awareness of Flora Sutton's fingers on his cheeks.

It seemed completely bizarre that Robin could reach out and touch Edwin like this, a casual hand on his back, and it could be perfect. Just as the touch on his arm last night, over tea, had also been perfect. Exactly what he needed in that moment and had been unaware of needing.

Edwin pressed his lips together and made a memory of it: a small thing to store and bring out later, when Robin was safely back out of his life. Then he moved away.

"Come on," he said. "I do want to look at this maze."

Not that he could make more than a stab at knowing anything about the plants themselves—yew? was that what one made mazes from?—but he halted near the maze entrance and didn't mind the immediate wrench of wrongness in his stomach. It was something to be *studied*, and that meant he could endure it.

"It doesn't look easy to cheat," Robin said admiringly. The maze was, indeed, dense and leafy and half as high again as either of them. Robin trailed his fingers along the outer hedge. "It looks square, from here—how far back do you think it goes? I'm going to try and walk around."

His footsteps crunched away as Edwin cradled the same detection charm he'd used at the estate boundary, and crouched down. Given what Mrs. Sutton had said, he assumed he'd have a stronger sense of the spell the closer he was to the roots, though this kind of charm couldn't hold a candle to a nice thorough spell notation.

Again he felt a warming tug of his hands. He hooked one portion of the string with an index finger and changed the angle, concentrating hard on the idea of visibility. His magic moved sluggishly, then more smoothly. If he knelt right down and peered underneath the lowest portion of the hedge, like someone seeking a dropped coin beneath a low sofa, he could see a faint pink pattern cobwebbing the trunk of the plant.

The gravel crunched again with footsteps and a shadow fell over Edwin's hands. He shook the spell clear and began to straighten up.

"Honestly, all this has done is given me twenty more questions for the lady her—"

The blow came like a pendulum, sideways and fast. It knocked Edwin down when he was halfway to standing. He managed to catch himself on his hands, but struck the side of his forehead unpleasantly hard on the ground.

His head spun. His heart was thundering. His cheek was pressed into the gravel; there was dirt on his lip. He was staring at a pair of black shoes, well polished, soiled with dirt. For a long moment the surprise of the attack alone froze Edwin to the spot, lying sprawled on his stomach over his awkwardly bent arms, and then pain blossomed simultaneously in his scratched palms and the side of his head.

He heard, dimly, a shout of alarm that might have been his name. It was enough for him to force himself to move, first pushing himself to his knees and then all the way to his feet.

Edwin's attacker was a tall man who looked to have been dipped in shadow: all black, from shoes to gloves. Above the shadow was the fog. Robin hadn't managed to convey the sheer *oddness* of the fog mask, the way it made one's eyes ache with the effort to focus on something that couldn't be seen.

The man's attention was no longer on Edwin. He had set one foot inside the entrance to the maze, and was now struggling to free it. One of the plants had sent out a thick thorny tendril, which was wrapped around his ankle and climbing.

"Hey there! Edwin!" came another shout from Robin. "What's going on?"

The fog mask turned in Robin's direction, then back to Edwin.

Edwin had no idea what to do. Hit the man? He'd never thrown a punch. Try to help the maze and hold him in place? His hands were shaking and scraped and he felt as though he'd cracked like an egg, when he hit the ground, letting all of his energy spill out.

Robin was running towards them now, closing the distance fast. The man in black made the decision for all of them. In a single violent movement he wrenched his foot free of the grasping plant, stumbled forward, and grabbed hold of Edwin's clothes. Before Edwin could do anything more than freeze in further alarm, the man yanked Edwin sideways and hurled him through the wide entrance and into the maze itself.

Edwin stumbled, tripped, and once again sprawled on the ground. His breath coughed out of him. This was *ridiculous*. This sort of thing was not supposed to happen.

Robin skidded to a halt in the maze entrance, gaze swinging between Edwin himself and where Edwin's attacker was clearly escaping the scene. Something was wrong with Edwin's sense of scale, because the hedge seemed to be growing, the entrance shrinking. No: it *was* shrinking. The hedge was bulging, expanding like boiling milk into the gap.

"Follow him!" Edwin wheezed. "Don't you want—" *to find out what's happening, to shake some information out of him—* but it turned into a coughing fit, which ended unpleasantly in retching. The warding-wrongness was still grumbling away in his gut.

Then something like rough wire wrapped itself around his right wrist, and pulled.

Edwin heard himself grunt as his arm straightened at an uncomfortable angle, and he tried to tense his arm and pull back. He couldn't gather the nerve to look at it. He kept looking at Robin instead, hoping to glare the man into sense. The rising drawbridge of the hedge's defences was still in motion, the gap ever narrowing, but no tendrils touched Robin.

It had the inevitability of watching a tall object begin to topple. Robin hovered, a look of naked indecision and concern on his face that all at once firmed into determination.

"*Don't*," Edwin said, or tried to say. It came out as another cough.

The hedge was almost closed off now. If Edwin had two free hands, or any presence of mind, or more than a few bare fucking teaspoons' worth of magic, he'd have thrust something, *anything*, through the gap. Something to throw Robin backwards for long enough to keep him where he still had a chance of being safe and useful.

But because Edwin was who he was, and because Robin Blyth was who *he* was, that didn't happen.

Robin leapt forward, landing at Edwin's side, and wrenched his arm clear of the hedge just as it writhed itself into a green wall with no gap in it at all. No way out.

13

Robin, breathing hard, knelt by Edwin's side. "Are you—"

"You *complete and utter idiot*," said Edwin.

Edwin looked a fright: scratched and covered in dirt, and struggling to kneel. Robin's stomach had lurched horribly when the man in the fog mask had flung Edwin through the maze entrance. There had been something so awfully *relaxed* about the motion, as though he was used to moving inconvenient people, and be damned to the damage he might cause along the way.

But Edwin was alive enough to be spitting prickly insults, and to be fighting back against the equally prickly tendril of hedge that was now looped twice around his wrist. Robin grasped it a few inches from the first loop and tried to snap it, but it had the stubbornness of young things, and simply bent and wriggled. Robin would have swapped half his meagre inheritance in that moment for a good sharp penknife. He gave up on wrestling and simply used his teeth: unpleasant, but effective.

When he finally bit through the green twig, the plant punished him with a recoil that split the soft inside of his upper lip. At least the coils around Edwin's arm were loose and dead now, easily shaken off.

Robin helped Edwin to his feet. He wasn't expecting effusive thanks, but he'd have appreciated something more than a snappish, "You should have followed him!"

"A magician?" Robin snapped back. "What makes you think I'd have any more luck than you, against him?"

"Then you should have gone and told Mrs. Sutton. She'd have been able to get me out."

"And I'm sure you'd have been *fine* in the meantime!" Robin punctuated this by swatting hard at another tendril that was making a play for Edwin's collar. The tendril dodged with the patient, sluggish non-fear of summer midges, and crowded immediately back again.

Edwin dodged as well, a few seconds too late. He looked ashy, the bones of his face chiselled. Most of Robin's annoyance evaporated.

"Edwin, you look ill."

"It's the secondary warding, I think," said Edwin. "I felt it even at the entrance. No magicians in the maze. She did tell us."

"You hardly threw yourself in here on *purpose.*"

Edwin managed to summon one of his superior-knowledge looks. "Imbuement isn't sentience, I told you that the first—oh, blast this plant!" He stomped hurriedly on a few more tendrils, which were making a play for his ankles.

"We could try yelling," Robin offered. "There's gardeners around. *Hoy! Help! Mayday!*" He had to pause to gulp in air and energy, and to get himself in front of the next incursion of the hedge on Edwin's space. It didn't shy away this time. With a scratch of gravel beneath his shoes, Edwin jogged further into the maze; there was only one direction available to them, at this point.

"Maybe Mrs. Sutton will sense it anyway," Edwin said. "You're not a magician. The maze has no reason to hurt you. And if you're in serious danger, it might come up against her family's blood-pledge with the land." He met Robin's eyes, skittish, then glanced away. "I felt it, at Penhallick. When you were in the lake. And I've barely anything to feel *with.*"

"Doesn't mean she'll do anything about it," said Robin. His

instincts, when it came to Flora Sutton, were all confused. He knew her as a liar. He'd felt the edges of her ruthlessness, at odds with her faded appearance. But ruthlessness in service to a truth, to a *cause,* was not necessarily the same as cruelty.

There was a rustle from the direction they'd come. Robin turned back to look at where the entrance had been, and realised with an unsettling lurch that the maze seemed to stretch a lot farther than the few yards they'd moved from where the entrance had boiled closed. The path curved away and around, far enough that it was draped in shadow.

A cold wave of familiarity washed Robin's bones. This was the vision he'd had. This sky, this maze.

And *this* particular sense of something moving, just out of the corner of his eye, with an awful, unseen, predatory intent that took hold of every hair in the nape of Robin's neck and flicked it upright.

"I think we should—" said Edwin, strained, just as Robin said, "*Um,*" and they moved, scurrying backwards, to the end of their current green corridor and round the sharp bend of the corner. It helped a little to be out of that particular sight line. Not a lot. Robin's neck continued to prickle.

"Can you do anything? Blast a hole?" he asked Edwin. "At least we know we're only a single hedge's thickness away from the outside, at this point."

"I can . . ." Edwin's dubious expression grew a tinge of horror as he patted his pocket. "I—I had it in my hands," he said. "When he knocked me down the first time."

"Do you need the string?" Robin demanded. "I know it helps. Do you *need* it?"

"I haven't—" Edwin started, white-faced, then made a choking sound as dust flew up in fountains around him. This time the plants erupted from the ground itself: the same thorny vine-like growths, like grasping fingers seeking the light. In the time it took Robin to register the sight of them, they were already up to Edwin's waist.

Robin lunged between the nearest two and grabbed Edwin's arm, gripped tight, and ran.

When the maze's paths branched off he chose the one that looked least forbidding, or at least the one where he could see the most ground ahead. Only once did they find themselves faced with a blunt dead end, and by that time Edwin had found his reflexes. He pulled them up sharp, yanked at Robin's sleeve, and got them moving back the other way.

They raced around three more corners. Now the maze looked closer to normal. The space between the hedges was a normal distance. Robin's instincts were still muttering that they were being chased, but at least it was a mutter rather than a shout.

Edwin was out of breath. Robin didn't realise he was eyeing the man incredulously until Edwin shot him a poisonous, defensive look in return.

"We can't all be athletes. And—the bloody warding." Edwin dragged a tired hand across his forehead. He still looked faintly bilious, and now a sheen of sweat had been added to the picture.

"The warding on the estate stopped working on you as soon as we crossed the tree line. Why is this one still at it?"

"At a guess, it's an emanation, not a boundary. From the centre, I think." The centre, where they were heading.

Where we're being driven, a corner of Robin's mind provided.

"I suppose in the absence of other options, I can empty my guts onto one of the bloody plants." Edwin turned a look of sickly hatred onto the greenery.

"Holly," said Robin, realising.

"What?"

"It's not yew anymore. It's holly."

"Superb," said Edwin, dry. "Now if—"

"Watch out!" Robin lunged, but Edwin still cried out in pain and alarm as the wall of dark, waxy leaves bulged, bubbled out like hot porridge—and *burst,* with a flurry of edges and thorns. Edwin had flung his arms up to protect himself; when Robin groped through the dust and splinters in the air and managed to grip one of them, he could feel the ragged edges of shredded cotton, and prayed that the flesh beneath had weathered it better.

"Edwin?"

"Still among the living." The words were rough with pain. "Run."

And they did. The bulges of holly were forming on either side, catching Robin in the range of the splintery explosions as often as they caught Edwin. Robin risked a look over his shoulder only once, saw hints of movement among the gathering shadows, and gave that up as a terrifying mistake. The corridors were shorter, the corners tighter. They must have been nearing the centre.

"Another dead end," panted Edwin. "Turn around."

Robin turned. His breath rasped hot in his throat. The constant stop-and-start of it all, not to mention the fact that his body was tensed against damage, was draining his strength as no rugby match or regatta ever had.

He turned again. And again, circling on the spot, until he was facing the same way he'd started. There was no path anymore. Just the holly hedge, rising up on all four sides. "Well, running's stopped working," he said. "Time for magic."

"I can't—"

"You have to do *something,* because my best left hook isn't going to do much against a sodding *bush.* What would you do? If you had your string?"

"Fire," said Edwin promptly.

"Fire—God, I'm a congenital *idiot.*" Robin dug in his pocket and pulled out his lighter. "Can you do anything with this?"

At least Edwin no longer looked on the verge of tears or a shaking fit. He'd solidified, somehow. Robin remembered Lord Hawthorn's words: *Courcey here just loves a good puz-*

zle. Edwin jerked himself away from a fresh grasping branch, which left deep pink scratches across the side of his neck, and gazed with narrowed eyes at the holly. "I don't think it will be enough," he said reluctantly. "Even if I managed a magnification, it takes a hell of a lot of power—a lot of heat—to get green wood going."

"What if it was drier?"

"Drier?"

Robin gestured impatiently and kicked another tendril away from Edwin's ankle. "After I fell in the lake, you—"

"*Oh.*" Edwin looked down at his hands. "Yes. All right. Stand close behind me."

So Robin did, one hand holding his lighter at the ready. All around them the hedge crept inwards and upwards, tiny rustling sounds layering themselves into something almost animalistic. A growl of thorns. Edwin was shaking.

"You can do this," Robin said. "I know you can."

"You don't know anything," Edwin whispered, but it sounded like *thank you.*

He lifted his hands haltingly, palms together, then drew them apart. He cradled slowly, freezing whenever Robin moved; Robin managed to get his own trousers partially shredded, diverting the holly that was trying to wrap itself around Edwin's legs, swallowing down the urge to scream at Edwin to work *faster.* Another minute and there'd be no space left for them to be standing in at all. But Edwin kept going, and soon there was a soft yellow glow between his palms.

"It's working!" said Robin.

"It's worked," said Edwin.

He raised his glowing hands to his mouth, took a breath, and blew.

The drying spell that had swept over Robin in the boat had been a warm, pleasant breeze. This was obviously something more. The plant reared backwards at an angle. The hot wind gusting from Edwin's lips swept, and swept, and kept sweeping—and the dark green turned the middling brown of dry, dead things in a patch a yard wide.

Edwin dropped his hands. His next inhalation was like the breath taken to save oneself from drowning.

Robin flicked at his lighter the four times it took to produce a flame. He held it up in mute invitation. Edwin dragged the flame in front of him by grabbing at Robin's wrist. The holly shivered and growled around them. Just as slowly, though much less hesitantly, Edwin cradled a second spell.

"Magnification," Edwin murmured. "Like the snowflake."

"Very good, don't care," said Robin. Edwin could explain the damn spell clause by clause *later,* when they were *out.*

"Hold it steady," said Edwin. "This might hurt a bit—sorry."

It did hurt. A bit. Robin's standards for pain had changed somewhat over the past few days. The flame balanced on the lighter grew and grew, and Robin's forehead broke out into first sweat and then the unpleasant sear of standing too close to naked fire.

Robin held on until Edwin gasped, *"Throw it."*

The dry yard of hedge went up with a sound like sucking air and breaking rocks.

Robin jammed his handkerchief over his nose and mouth and tried to peer through the shimmer and smoke. On either side of the dried patch the still-green holly had drawn back, as though from someone coughing on the Underground, and there were two thin gaps.

"There!" He was prepared to do more grabbing and pulling, but Edwin didn't hesitate. One after another they leapt and scrambled around the side of the burning holly. The heat of the flames was uncomfortable, the smoke a dirty sting in Robin's eyes, but he moved fast and was through, stumbling into an open space, before he knew whether he'd been burned.

They were in a wide square of gravel, surrounded by hedge on every side. Dead centre stood a marble statue of a woman:

neoclassical, taller than life, the falls of stone fabric looking almost soft, her hands held close to her body and cupped together. Between those hands was a dark hole, as though one could reach into her body. A space for secrets kept safe.

Edwin was coughing. Now, with effortful breaths, he managed to stop.

"Out of the frying pan . . ." He gestured.

Robin's objection that they had, if anything, gotten out of the *fire*, died on his tongue. The square of gravel was shrinking. The dry holly was already burning itself into glowing twigs and embers, but it was still too high and dense to shove through. And the gaps were gone. All of the non-charred holly was squeezing in: warily, gradually, as if they'd put it on its guard.

They'd reached the centre and now there was nowhere to go.

"I'll try a ward." Edwin screwed his eyes shut and worked painstakingly through the spell. He winced and started over twice, and held the final position for a long, long few seconds, during which Robin tried to convince himself that he could see coloured light, or anything at all, sparking into being in the cradle. But he couldn't.

Edwin's exhalation was one of defeat. "No, that's it. The drying spell took most of my magic. Anything large enough to be useful now is going to take more than I have left." He shook his hands out as though loosening the string that wasn't there. "Any other bright ideas, Sir Robin?"

Perhaps he was going for sarcasm. It sounded like a plea.

"Get behind me" was the sum total of the ideas Robin had left. "It's after you, not me."

"It's going to go *through* you," said Edwin. "And—it doesn't have to. You could simply get out of its way."

Robin glared his utter contempt for this idea. "I thought you said it wouldn't want to put a guest in serious danger? How about you tell it not to hurt me, and *then* get behind me."

Edwin's voice was nearly shrill. "This isn't *my* land!"

"We don't need all of it to be yours!" said Robin, teetering on the edge of hysteria. "These few square yards would do
nicely!"

Edwin opened his mouth, no doubt to spill out a lecture as
to why Robin was making an ignorant suggestion that was in
no way going to save them from imminent, creeping horror.
Instead he made a short, breathless, seasick sound.

"Oh, and why not," he said.

With his dirtied clothes torn and hair swept everywhere,
Edwin looked positively wild. He kicked at the gravel until
he hit finer dirt and then knelt down to touch the bared patch.

Robin realised that he was pressing himself back against
the statue. The air above the scorched holly had begun to look
thick, somehow, and the air around them was very cold, as
though something made of ice was breathing damply. Robin's
skin crawled and his neck muscles locked up with a dreadful,
instinctive refusal to turn his head to either side, for fear of
what he might see.

"Not to rush you . . ."

"Blood, need blood," muttered Edwin, a man actively bleeding in at least three separate places.

"Try your right cheek—yes, *there.*"

Edwin swiped at his cheek and shoved his hand down into the
dirt, braced on hands and knees. "The words," he said blankly.

"*Edwin.*"

"I've never done this before!" Edwin snarled.

"You've read it." Robin tried to shove his surety out through
his voice. "You've read everything. You *know* this."

"I—yes. Yes." A breath, a pause, almost impossibly long,
scraping like a bow against Robin's screaming nerves. Then
Edwin spoke in a tumbling rush. "I, Edwin John Courcey,
claim the witnessed inheritance of the magicians of Britain,
and I make blood-pledge for myself and my heirs with"—
another incredulous, bitten-back sound—"as much of this land
as will have me, even if it's only these few fucking square yards.

Mine to tend and mine to mend, and mine the—the pull and the natural right." He turned his head to look at Robin. He looked ghostly, ghastly. "This man is a guest. He has no magic. He means you no harm."

Everything was getting darker, as though storm clouds were mustering. There was a yawning chill like the drawing-back of waves preparing to crash against rocks. The only sound was the crack-click rustle of the holly, shoving past the charred corpse of its brethren, crowding them in.

Fighting the drag of his terror, Robin shoved off the statue and grimly prepared to put himself between Edwin and the worst of it.

Edwin bowed his head over his hand. He said, in a voice that had nothing left in it but desperation, *"Please."*

The world shook like a tapped glass of water, and then—

Went still.

Robin had squeezed his eyes shut, braced. He cracked them open. The grey, bright daylight was back. The holly hedge had retreated on all sides by a few feet. A snatch of birdsong in the middle distance came like a shock, obscenely normal.

Edwin stood. He looked like a wrung rag, and swayed on his feet. Something was strange about his eyes, about the colour of his face, but Robin couldn't have said what. He reached out one hand, absent, as though to keep his balance.

The hedge curled gently away from Edwin's fingers. Robin's skin shivered with an indefinable change in the pressure of the air. The sense of something impossibly large, inhaling. Robin didn't want to run from it, this time. He didn't know what he wanted.

"Let's get out," Edwin rasped. "Please."

Robin didn't know if Edwin was talking to him or to the maze, but he stepped in and let Edwin grab at his arm for support. Edwin's hand was a filthy mix of dust and blood.

Just as the maze had been guiding them to the centre, now it seemed equally willing to aid their exit. The plants leaned away rather than leaning in, benignly opening up the path. The terror had washed out like the tide. Robin kept both of them moving until they were stepping back out into the open garden, the gravel louder under their feet, the sudden expanse of middle horizon a palpable relief.

Edwin disentangled himself and walked stiffly to the nearest patch of lawn, which was dotted with oak trees. Robin followed and chose one to lean against. He hurt in too many places to count.

"Well," Robin said presently. "That could have gone . . . worse?"

Edwin turned his scratched, incredulous face on Robin, and there was a moment where Robin didn't know which way the moment would tip; whether Edwin was going to be angry at him all over again, for rushing foolishly in, in the first place.

"I can't believe we were almost killed by a hedge," Edwin said, halfway between plaintive and outraged.

Robin cackled with laughter that seemed to grab bodily hold of him. He let the tree take most of his weight. "I just"—he managed—"thought of the phrase *hedge witch*." It was like when he'd been struck by Bel's arrow: the fuzzy, happy sense of floating.

The happiness redoubled when Edwin began to laugh too. Surely it was the first time, Robin thought. The first time he'd seen Edwin laugh properly. But no, that wasn't right; they'd laughed in the motorcar on the way here, barely an hour ago. A hundred years ago. Now Edwin leaned his hands on his knees and laughed like a brook, looking alight and alive and wonderful in the sunshine.

"Are you *sure* you don't want to go back to London?" said Edwin, wheezing mildly.

"I'm collecting near-death experiences, me," said Robin. "Though I am giving serious thought to that suggestion about hitting you in the face."

"Oh, no." Edwin straightened. His tone was dry. Gingerly

he wiped a hand over his scratched face. "And ruin these good looks?"

A moment of hilarious silence, and both of them collapsed into laughter again. This time Edwin almost stumbled, and steadied himself again on Robin's arm. His grip lingered, stayed.

Distance, Robin thought giddily. *Falling apples. The effect of proximity on natural forces.*

It seemed natural, after all, for Robin to pat Edwin comfortingly on the back, and then to let his hand slide down to the man's waist and rest there. They were alive. They were laughing. The enormity of Robin's fear was leaching out through his feet and into the soil, leaving him feeling invincible. Edwin's body was warm and he swayed forward willingly, his chest coming to rest against Robin's. His eyes were bright as cobalt.

It was like tumblers falling into place in a lock. The invincible feeling surged, sharpened, and became a *want* so large it pushed at the boundaries of Robin's skin.

Edwin had gone still. Tense. Unmoving: neither forward nor backward, even as the familiar wariness swam over his features.

Robin still had one arm around Edwin's waist. He lifted the other and traced the fine line of Edwin's cheekbone with his thumb, as he'd wanted to do for—oh, hours, days. A hundred years. It came away with a few flecks of blood, and Edwin's lips parted in something that was an exquisite cousin to pain; Edwin's thin chest filled, and his chin lifted by a bare fraction of an inch, calling attention to the line of his throat.

It was almost like foresight. A vision, elbowing aside all of Robin's other thoughts, that reached only a few moments into the future. He would keep hold of Edwin's face and pull it forward, he would let the heat of Edwin's body between his legs sear itself into memory, and he would set his lips to that neck, that mouth—

A woman's scream sliced the air, from the direction of the house.

14

The same footman who'd greeted them in the driveway came hurrying up as they approached the house. He had the harried look of a man who intended to hustle the visitors back into their car with a thousand apologies. He stopped dead at the sight of them, however, and Edwin suspected it was only years of training that kept his jaw from dropping outright.

"We heard a scream," said Edwin. "What's happened?"

"I . . ." The footman's gaze swung pendulum-like between them. If Edwin looked half as bloody and bedraggled as Robin did, they might as well have been actors who'd wandered off the stage of *Titus Andronicus*.

"We were attacked," Robin said. "And not just by the maze. There was—a man, in a"—he waved a hand near his face and Edwin supplied—"illusion mask."

The footman, visibly deciding to escalate this above his own station, burst out—"Mrs. Sutton, she's—there's been—you'd better come with me, sirs."

Edwin's head swam as they followed him into the house. Not the least of it was the way his body was clamouring to relive the moment when he'd realised exactly how close they were standing and exactly what Robin's hot, intent gaze heralded. Part of him wanted to ignore the rest of this wretched situation, implausible and dangerous and bewildering as it no doubt was, and snatch hold of Robin's shirt and try again.

Now, now. Can't let standards slip just because of a little near-death experience, Edwin thought, and had to bury a burst of strangled inappropriate laughter in a cough.

It died in his throat as they entered Mrs. Sutton's parlour. The room seemed busy with people, though there were only four of them. A girl in a maid's uniform was sobbing; the sound grated on Edwin's nerves. He heard a sharp inhalation from Robin, who'd preceded him into the room, and then an older woman moved aside, turning at the sound of their entry, and Edwin saw what had caused it.

Flora Sutton sat in the chair where they'd left her. She seemed to have shrunk; the velvet was vast, cradling her. Her eyes were open and as unmoving as every other part of her body. There was no blood, no marks. A violent stillness rang in Edwin's mind.

The smile on her dead face had an edge that Edwin would almost call triumphant.

"What on Earth" came from the older woman in a sharp tone. Housekeeper, by her dress and her dignity. "Franklin, get these . . ."

She, too, trailed off as her gaze travelled over Edwin and Robin.

"They're visiting on family business, Mrs. Greengage," said the footman. "The mistress"—no more than a soft break in the words—"met with them." He introduced Edwin and Robin, note-perfect on Robin's title, habit managing to overcome whatever shock he was feeling.

"Courcey," said the other man in the room, whom Edwin had already mentally labelled as *butler.* The name was question and relief all at once. Edwin supposed it would have been the outside of enough, for this household to have to deal with un-magical garden enthusiasts in the immediate aftermath of . . . whatever this was.

"Yes. Mrs. Sutton was looking into something for us." Edwin gestured to the new pile of books on the table at the corpse's right hand. A small vase with a sprig of red leaves had been pushed aside to make room for them. "We went to look at the maze while we waited. We were going to have tea."

"Our maze doesn't care for magicians," said Mrs. Greengage. Her arm was around the sobbing maid, but she frowned at Edwin. "How'd she not warn you of that, Mr. Courcey?"

"Has—look here, has someone sent for a doctor?" Robin demanded. "The police?"

The fact was hauled once more into Edwin's consciousness: this wasn't Robin's world. He didn't know how it worked.

"No police," Edwin said, trying to promise explanation at a later time with his frown.

"We've telephoned for Dr. Hayman, but he was out on a call. Left a message with his wife," said the housekeeper. Edwin nodded. Not his mother's favoured doctor, but Hayman had provided the occasional second opinion on her rheumatism. There weren't many unbusheled doctors in any given county; they tended to be busy.

Edwin's eyes drew back to the pale and smiling face of Flora Sutton. Time was not exactly of the essence. She was dead, and nothing was going to make her less so.

"I knew" came from the maid, who'd managed to stop sobbing. "I *knew*. I was polishing in the hall and it went *quiet-like*, all of a sudden." A wet hiccup. "It was the clocks. All of them."

"The clocks stopped," said Edwin.

It was something he'd read about, but never thought he'd see. Generations of magicians in a house saturated it, made the blood-pledge sink into more than the soil. The clocks of Sutton Cottage were attuned to their mistress. She stopped; they stopped. Edwin managed to bite his tongue against asking the girl if she'd noticed the mirrors misting over as well.

The maid nodded. "I came running, fast as I could. And I—found her—" Dissolving into tears again, she buried her face in her apron.

Robin stepped forward, tentative, moving closer to Mrs.

Sutton's chair. The sudden loss of his body heat brought Edwin tumbling back into his own body, aware of his senses. Everything *hurt*.

"Sir Robert, you mentioned a man?" said Franklin.

"Someone shoved Edwin into the maze," Robin said. "Someone who has—attacked me, before. Or is associated with those who did. I don't know where he went. He ran. He might have . . ." Robin trailed off. Nobody contradicted or corroborated him. When the fog-faced man had come here to confront Mrs. Sutton, while they were in the maze, he'd clearly evaded the staff on both entrance and exit.

The silence in the room might as well have been a shout: *Did you bring this down upon us?*

Did they? Had they?

I did suspect people would start to die.

No blood, no marks. But dead blue eyes open and fixed on something, or someone. A woman who would let her great-nephew die to keep the secret of the last contract, and who'd probably have let Robin do the same without more than gentle regret. Edwin didn't think for a moment that Flora Sutton's death was due to natural causes. And she'd been expecting it, he realised with a start, unable to look away from that smile. Ever since Reggie visited and took the contract—*part* of the contract—away with him.

Reggie hadn't taken the danger with him at all. Or if he had, Robin and Edwin had brought it right back.

All that keen-eyed intellectual passion, all her knowledge of old and natural magics, snuffed in an instant. Angry sorrow welled in Edwin. What a damned *waste*.

"We shall have to wait and see what Dr. Hayman says," said the butler. "In the meantime, if you gentlemen—"

"There's something in her hand," said Robin. He knelt on the rug. His hand hovered above her clenched one, then touched the wax-white skin with a gentleness that made tears seize abrupt and unexpected in the back of Edwin's nose. "May I . . . ?"

Nobody said anything. Edwin moved closer; something was, indeed, peeking from the side of her clenched fingers. Robin turned the dead woman's hand over and prised the fingers open, one by one. Then he snatched back his fingers as if they'd been burned, and shook them hastily.

Mrs. Sutton had died with a handful of silver. It was a necklace, the chain of it all looped and held secure beneath the pendant, which was a circular shape about the size of a half crown, with neat folds and blackened patterning.

"A rose," Robin said.

"Ah, yes. It's—an heirloom," said Mrs. Greengage. Too loudly, and too quickly. She swept forward and bent to take the pendant. She, too, snatched back her fingers with a startled noise as soon as they came into contact with it.

Edwin lifted his hands to try another detection charm, in case that would provide any clues. There was no telling what kind of imbuement Mrs. Sutton might have laid on an object she was clutching at the time of her death. Then he remembered that he'd lost his cradling string, and that even if he managed to do without it in situations that *weren't* driven by fear of death, he'd used up his magic. It would be hours yet before he could manage another spell.

Well, touching the rose didn't seem to have caused *harm*. Just discomfort. And to magician and non-magician alike. Curious. Edwin considered asking them what they'd felt, but didn't want his own observations tainted by what they said. They could compare notes afterwards.

Taking a deep breath, Edwin reached out.

"Edwin—" Robin started.

Edwin's fingers made contact. His arm was tensed, ready to draw back, but . . . nothing happened.

No, that wasn't right. Something was happening. The silver rose was warming beneath Edwin's touch, and not just warming, but *vibrating*. A soft, subtle hum like the fall of horses' hooves far down a road. He lifted the pendant clear and closed his fingers on it, letting the chain dangle, the hot buzz shivering right down to the bones of his hand. The sensation became jerky, as though it were trying to push itself in a particular direction.

"What's it doing?" asked Robin.

Edwin snuck a look at Mrs. Greengage, whose expression had solidified into something between hostile and hopeful. She didn't look like a likely source of information.

"I'm not sure," Edwin said. "It feels like—there's a hiding game, like this. It's an easy charm. Hot and cold. Hotter is closer." It didn't explain why the charm hadn't wanted anyone else to pick the pendant up, but Edwin wasn't going to put it past a single item on this entire damned estate to be capricious at best, given its mistress.

He moved around the room with arm outstretched, letting the rose heat and cool and buzz more and less demandingly in his grasp. Soon enough it was obvious where it wanted to lead him: a tall mirror hung on one of the ivy-carved wood panels of the wall, large enough to show Edwin himself from hair to boots. He was mussed and scratched all over, unkempt as a boy come from climbing trees. The mirror's frame was made of the same silver, and with the same design of roses, impeccably polished. There was no obvious place to put the pendant, no convenient empty space in the pattern where it could be nestled.

Edwin thought first of the stopped clocks. There was no mist on this mirror, at least. Then he thought of the illusion mirror that led to the back of Len Geiger's shop, and reached out the hand containing the rose to touch the glass surface. His cheeks glowed with warmth like sunburn as his fingers brushed it, and for a moment there was something odd, something different, about his reflection.

Even as he tried to focus on it, the glass dissolved into nothing and left an empty space. A frame that could be stepped through. There was a much smaller room beyond, barely four paces to each dimension, with a small desk and a squat bookshelf.

Behind Edwin, it sounded as though all the domestic staff inhaled at once. He ignored them, because he could just see a name on one of the spines—was that *Howson*? A high step brought him into the room, where he skirted round the desk and crouched by the bookshelf. The lowest shelf was all notebooks bound in black leather with gold embossed dates—records, diaries?—but the top two were books, and *what* books. Treatises that Edwin had only ever heard of, names he'd never thought to see attached to printed works at all. A copy of the same Kinoshita he'd been so thrilled to pick up from Geiger's; that gave him a stab of irrational annoyance.

"Mr. Courcey?" came from the room behind him.

With a sigh, Edwin stood again, climbed back out of the frame, and blinked. Every single person in the parlour was staring at him. Robin had taken a seat, legs sprawled tiredly. The maid had her hand to her mouth.

It dawned belatedly on Edwin that he'd just spent a good few minutes poring over a dead woman's book collection while her corpse cooled and the question of her death still hung in the room like poisonous vapours.

"Er," said Edwin. "Was it . . . common knowledge that this room was here?"

"Yes, sir," said the butler, rather stiff.

"Ah. Good. I want to buy those books," Edwin blurted. Then winced, mostly because Robin was wincing. Being a normal polite person was proving even more difficult than usual, buffeted as he was by the shocks of the day's events and the tentacles of sheer intellectual greed that were telling him to snatch up Flora Sutton's private library and never let it go. "Not that I'm saying—I don't mean *today*—of course, it'll be a question for whomever inherits the place."

A choked giggle came from the maid. The butler and housekeeper exchanged a look that contained encyclopaedias and also, somehow, an argument. Edwin didn't know who won it, but it was the butler who took a fraction of a step forward and coughed. He was a tall man with greying fair hair receding back from a high forehead.

"I'm afraid I'm not as familiar with the connections between the families of the area as I should be, sir," he said in a tone that implied the opposite. "Did you say you were here to see Mrs. Sutton on family business? Are you a relation of the Suttons?"

"No, not at all," said Edwin. "I know her—knew her"— God, the amount of past tense in this entire situation was horrifying—"great-nephew. Reginald Gatling."

Another information-dense look was exchanged.

"The Rose Study," said the butler, with impeccably enunciated capitals, "is one of those parts of the house which respond only to the owners and their heirs. So you see the purpose of my question. Sir."

"What are you implying?" said Robin, sharply.

Edwin shook his head. Much as he would have simultaneously loved and hated to believe his father was not his father— and there had been times in his childhood when the sheer prospect of being only *half*-related to Walt by birth would have made him forgive his mother any amount of straying from the marriage bed—there was too much resemblance to hope for that.

"I'm not—" he said, then stopped. A different sort of impossibility bubbled up and presented itself to the part of his mind that was always looking to make sense of the senseless.

Surely not. *Surely.*

"What is it?" asked Robin.

Edwin looked from one of the servants to the other. It took all the courage he had never possessed to say the next words. "I made blood-pledge. With the ground beneath the hedge maze, to stop it from attacking us." He swallowed hard. "I thought it would just be the maze, I thought—honestly, I didn't *think* it would work at *all*."

"Begging your pardon, sir, but you should touch the mirror again," said the maid.

"*Mina*," said Mrs. Greengage, sharp.

Edwin turned and did so, with the hand not holding the pendant. The illusion of glass was back in place. It wavered, as if unsure what Edwin wanted, then held. Edwin's face heated again and this time he saw on his reflection what he'd barely glimpsed last time: the flush of blood in his cheeks, over which the white marks of two hands stood out like tracks in snow.

One hand on each cheek, exactly where she'd laid them. *An affinity*, she'd said.

Edwin spun and stared at the corpse of Flora Sutton. Slowly, he felt the marks fade.

"I . . . don't understand," said Robin.

"Neither do I," said Edwin. Thin hysteria was frothing in the back of his mouth. He managed to choke it back with a laugh. "It should have refused me. If it'd had any sense . . ."

Sense. As if an estate were a rational being, which would make conscious decisions or be argued with. As far as Sutton Cottage was concerned, Edwin had planted his blood in the soil and wildly sworn himself to as much of the land as would have him, on an estate far more magical than he himself had ever been, in the moment when its mistress had just died without heirs and in the hour after she'd laid her hands on his cheeks. The maze hadn't settled because it was trying to protect Robin; Robin had never been its target in the first place. It had settled because it was refusing to harm *Edwin*.

From somewhere in the house came a dull knock, followed by the sound of a bell. "That'll be the doctor," said the butler, and vanished from the parlour.

"*Edwin*," said Robin. He had that storm-soaked look on his face again, the one that meant he was coming to the end of his store of credulity for one day. "Tell me what's going on."

"Oh, nothing of consequence," said Edwin. "I've merely inherited one of the oldest magical estates in Cambridgeshire."

15

By the time the doctor left it was close to dinnertime, and the prospect of driving all the way back to Penhallick in the dark was something neither Robin nor Edwin felt up to facing. The household offered to make up rooms for them to sleep in.

"It might be easiest," Robin said. "It'd be a game to explain why we look like we've been dragged behind horses through a briar-patch, if we went to an inn somewhere closer."

"You could show them your calling card," said Edwin, but it came out of the shallows of his mind, murmured and barely meant. By now he was a bundle of pains, of bodily exhaustion and leftover nausea, of feeling simultaneously emptied of magic and as though a magic not his own was pressing around him, eager and impatient, demanding recognition. It was nothing he'd ever felt before and he would have preferred to escape it. To step back across that line of trees and be normal once more. He felt irrationally as though if he slept at Sutton Cottage he'd wake up woven into the wallpaper.

But Robin looked just as tired as Edwin felt. And a core of Edwin managing to make itself heard beneath the fear was saying that Edwin had entered into contract, no matter how impulsively, and abandoning the land before the sun had set on that contract would be . . . rude? Impolitic?

Unhallowed. The word swam up and laid itself like an oil-sheen over the waves of Edwin's exhaustion.

"Mr. Courcey?" Mrs. Greengage was holding herself straight, not providing much clue as to whether she would prefer to welcome the estate's unexpected new owner or kick him out on his ear.

Edwin nodded. "We'll stay. Thank you."

"And we apologise for the bother of it, on top of all the shocks you've had today," said Robin, in tones far warmer than Edwin had managed. "Do let us know if there's somewhere we'll be out of your way."

They were tidied out of the way into a small sitting room, cold from having its curtains drawn, presumably to prevent the fading of several tapestries and large watercolours that Robin inspected immediately.

Edwin sat on a sofa and let his head rest in his hands. *Robin* should have been the one to have an estate crash into his grasp. He needed money; Edwin didn't. He knew how to be nice to people, to make them feel appreciated. Edwin was lucky to remember to nod at acquaintances in the street.

Dinner was quiet, the meal obviously prepared in a heroic effort to cater to young male palates from a kitchen stocked mostly by the tastes of an old woman. Afterwards, they were shown up to rooms that had the musty and faintly surprised air of places where the dustcovers had only just been whisked off the furniture.

Edwin poured water from ewer to basin and splashed some onto his face, pushed back his hair, and stared blankly at the thin face in the dresser's mirror, scored with red marks. The darker red of the jacquard silk dressing gown did his pallor no favours at all. His clothes had been taken away to be cleaned and mended; they'd not changed for dinner, having nothing suitable to change into. The gown still smelled faintly of mothballs. In its pocket Edwin had stowed a new loop of string, which he'd begged from the housekeeper. He dipped his fingertips in and touched it for comfort.

The guidelight had split into two when Edwin first entered the bedroom. Half had remained in the bracket in the hall, but the rest had followed him inside and found its place in an old-fashioned guidekeeper, a cylinder of amber glass with a bronze handle so that one could move it around the room by hand. The light was strong enough that there was barely a need to do so. When Edwin's hand came near the keeper, the light flickered and brightened further, and a warm sensation spread up Edwin's arm. It was a cousin to the sandpaper rasp that had heralded Robin's danger in the lake, and also to the everyday itch of existing on Penhallick lands. At the same time it was nothing like either of them. It felt, too much, like *power*.

When he turned his gaze from the mirror to the windows, the curtain-ties unhooked themselves and the curtains gave a twitch towards their centre as if to ask: *This? Is this what you want?*

Edwin closed his eyes. If he told himself that the coaxing glow of magic was no more than something to be studied, he might be able to keep the enormity of the situation at bay. He knew a little about how estates could be, if they'd been inhabited for generations by an unbroken line of magicians. Stopped clocks were only the least of it. When he'd visited Cheetham Hall as a child, Jack and Elsie had competed in the ballroom to see who could flatter the floorboards into tilting beneath the other's foot. Elsie would win far more often than not, and Jack would lie back on the floor and shout with begrudging laughter, curling his fingers wickedly until the rug twitched from beneath Edwin's spectator feet and sent him sprawling as well. Jack Alston, a dark, wild boy with all the power of his inheritance at his command, and a family who loved him without question.

Edwin had learned to want him, then, and also to fold his resentment in that want like a glass shard in layers of tissue.

A knock came on the door, followed by Robin's voice pitched low. "Edwin?"

"Come in."

Robin's hair was wet through, his own scrapes standing out stark on his freshly washed face, within which the hazel of his eyes shone like the surface of a lake. The dressing gown that had been found for him was dark green, quilted fabric tied with a black cord. He'd pushed up one sleeve, baring the curse to the air. He was rubbing over it with one thumb, hard enough to crease the skin.

Edwin nodded at it. "Is it . . . ?"

"Just once, a few minutes ago," said Robin. "I'm counting my stars that it didn't go off when we were in the maze. So it really could have been worse."

He'd said that when they first emerged. Just before—before.

"Yes," Edwin said softly. "It could have been."

"So are you glad I plunged in after you now?"

It was an impossible question, coming at the end of an impossible day, and Edwin's emotions crowded him like birds trapped in a cage, beating and beating against his usual inability to express them. Strangest of all was the fact that for once he didn't feel afraid. Perhaps his fear, like his magic, had a finite volume, and he'd drained it all in the maze. They'd both almost died. And even if they'd been half the world away, with no blood-pledge to hold Edwin responsible for keeping Robin alive, he'd still find the idea of Robin coming to further harm—unacceptable.

"No, I'm not glad," he snapped, a wild and unstoppable lie. "I *knew* you would be nothing but trouble."

Robin was smiling, because Robin didn't know what was good for him. That was how he ended up like this, with the scratches on his face and his hands, and—and Edwin couldn't stop himself from reaching out and tracing the worst of the scabbed red lines, half-flattered and half-guilty and all-over angry with the world for putting him here, now, richer than he'd been at the start of the day by one of the oldest magical properties in England and by *this*, Robin Blyth lifting his palms willingly to Edwin's inspection, displaying the evidence that they'd both bled out of desperation today. Edwin was so angry it filled his skull like hot water. He couldn't breathe past it.

"Edwin," Robin said hoarsely, and Edwin pressed blindly forward and kissed him.

It was a bad angle. It was a bad kiss. Edwin hadn't kissed anyone in years and it was like a language long unspoken in his mouth, coming out with the wrong cadences and with the grammar all askew. Robin's lips were soft beneath his. Edwin let himself stay for a quick count of two, which was as long as it took for horrified self-preservation to overcome the impulse that had shoved him forward.

He pulled away. He tried to. He'd barely created a distance between them when Robin closed it again, fast enough that Edwin couldn't focus on his face; couldn't classify the expression there. Robin's arms were tight around his back, wrapping him up, solid and inescapable. Once again it was exactly what Edwin needed. His body melted into it, need rising up through him like vines. And then Robin's mouth was on his again, and all of a sudden the grammar of the thing fell into place.

Somehow Edwin's back was against the wall, and they were still kissing. Robin was pressed in close enough that Edwin could feel Robin hardening against his hip. One of Robin's hands brushed up into his hair, the other arm still snug in the small of Edwin's back. Edwin realised he had no sodding clue what his own hands were doing—ah, there they were, holding on to Robin's broad shoulders for dear life.

Robin sucked on Edwin's lower lip and then drew away, pulling a sound from Edwin's mouth along with it. Edwin froze, but Robin just made a kind of low growl and ducked his head. He mouthed at Edwin's jaw, the side of his neck, heat and tongue and suction. Edwin's cock hardened and he felt, rather than heard, the exhalation that was almost a sob of pleasure by the time it escaped his mouth.

Edwin moved his hands to Robin's chest, and pushed. Gently, but firmly. Robin pulled back, and finally Edwin was able to look him in the face. Robin's lips were wet and the lakes of his eyes gone dark, and he was staring at Edwin as though Edwin were an undiscovered wonder.

A thrill completely unlike magic chased from one end of Edwin's spine to the other. He could feel that neediness threatening to overwhelm him. He wanted to collapse into it, to tilt back his head, to throw his body into feeling something that wasn't pain or fatigue or tension. Pulling himself together in the face of that want was like dragging a weight uphill.

Edwin swallowed and put his hands at the sash that held Robin's gown shut. "Can I—?"

"Yes," Robin blurted. "God, *yes.*" He was still wearing drawers, beneath the gown, but nothing else. He leaned in and kept snatching kisses, hungry and disjointed, but stopped with a low moan when Edwin's fingers closed around his cock.

It had been a long time since Edwin had done this for someone else. He experimented, gentle strokes alternating with firmer tugs, watching the way Robin's throat moved as he swallowed, listening to the soft curses that emerged from his lips. Robin put a hand on the wall by Edwin's shoulder and rested his weight there, giving Edwin just enough space to work his hand in between their bodies.

Edwin's breath shuddered in his chest with the intoxicating smell of Robin's skin. His eyes caught on small details: the evening shadow of Robin's jaw. The trim at the collar of the gown, now gaping to reveal Robin's chest. The action of his own hand now moving steadily back and forth along the thick shape of Robin's cock, which was just beginning to leak at the tip.

Robin bent his head, looking down as well, and they bumped foreheads. Edwin hastily loosened his grip. "Sorry, is it—"

"Yes! Fuck, it's—I—I want to see, is that all right?" Robin licked his lips and flicked his gaze down, then up again. "I like your hands. I like watching them."

The easy vulnerability of the admission startled Edwin. But of course Robin was brave in this, as he was brave in everything else. Of course he'd throw himself that open without a second thought. If someone tried to mock him for what he wanted he'd probably just *laugh*.

The startlement was followed by a shy, deep flutter of pleasure. Edwin found himself smiling.

"Is that so," he said. He still had his fingers crooked around Robin's cock. It seemed like it would have been rude to release it, at this point.

Robin nodded, his eyes darkening further. "If you had any idea how distracting it is, when you do things with that string . . ."

Edwin kissed him, once and hard, trying to think. He knew how to think. He did. There had to be *some* blood spare in his body to power the cells of his brain, even if most of it was thickening his own cock and dancing in his limbs.

"Here," he said. "I've an idea. Come and sit on the edge of the bed."

Walking with an unsteadiness that widened Edwin's smile, Robin did so. He wriggled out of the drawers entirely and hesitated over the robe before keeping it on. There was an almost luxurious indecency to the sight of him as he sat down, the front of him bare and exposed but framed by the green fabric. His legs were strong, a shade paler than his arms. There was a raised scar on one knee.

Edwin climbed onto the bed and knelt behind Robin. A schoolboy memory took brief hold of him as he settled, his bent knees snug against Robin's hips, his chin on Robin's shoulder. The first time he'd ever taken someone else in hand had ended like this, and begun the way he supposed these things always began. You leaned over and replaced another boy's hand with your own, and no words were uttered about any of it. Probably Robin—*furtive and athletic*—had never known anything except this sort of exchange.

That thought was enough for Edwin to let himself linger, to get comfortable. Enough for him to rest his hand on Robin's bare knee, ignoring the breath of complaint as Robin let his thighs splay wider, and to brush his nose back and forth beneath Robin's ear. He felt calmer now. More in control. He trailed his fingers up Robin's thigh to where the skin was sensitive, close to the groin; a muscle jumped beneath his touch, and Robin's next exhale was shaky.

"Please," Robin said when Edwin paused again. He was staring down at Edwin's hand.

Edwin hid a smile in the crook of Robin's neck, and settled properly into the business of giving Robin pleasure.

It . . . didn't look *bad,* Edwin had to admit. There was absolutely nothing special about his hands, but he could happily watch *this*—the slide of skin beneath his fingers as they moved on the flushed length, spreading the wetness that now leaked steadily from the tip—for hours. He tightened his grip, increased his pace. Robin rumbled encouragingly, his shoulders settling more heavily back against Edwin's front. Robin's own hands gripped his legs hard enough to dent the skin.

The sight of that, of Robin's tense restraint because he wanted Edwin to do this, was *letting* Edwin do this, was somehow even more arousing. Edwin bit his lip. He felt hot all over, immersed in the tingling satisfaction of being the one to set the pace, allowing himself free rein to drink in the angles of Robin he could see. Edwin's own cock was straining against his own drawers now, his hips trembling with the desire to push forward and rub against Robin's arse.

He felt Robin's body stiffen, and tightened his grip even more; he was rewarded with the soft choking sound that Robin made, and then the pulse of Robin's cock, messy white fluid spilling between his fingers and onto the gown, the sheets, Robin's body.

Robin turned his head; it took Edwin a moment to realise that he was being kissed, and to tilt his own head to allow it. Robin's hand came up and buried in Edwin's hair and the kiss was looser, deeper, than the previous one had been. Robin shrugged off his gown and let it fall to the floor, then turned bodily on the bed, a little awkward, never surrendering Edwin's mouth for very long. He knelt up and pulled Edwin in against him and Edwin shuddered and bit down on Robin's lip when his cock made contact with Robin's flat stomach. He took handfuls of Robin's shoulder blades. He wanted to burrow beneath Robin's skin and never come out.

Edwin knew his weaknesses as old friends, and here was the bare bones of them: he'd never been any good at keeping himself contained, in bed. He'd years of practice holding himself back behind shields raised against insult or injury, but *desire* was another matter. His body betrayed him when it wanted something, and now it wanted everything. It wanted Robin Blyth's hands—not to look at, no, but to respond to.

He leaned back, using his body weight to drag them both down until his head hit the lower edge of the pillow. It was just enough impact to remind him that someone had struck that head, earlier today, and the throb of renewed pain made him wince.

"Are you—"

"Yes, fine," Edwin said, impatient, and wrapped himself around Robin like ropes.

Robin's mouth descended to his again, one of Robin's hands sliding beneath Edwin's neck. Robin's body was weighing him down, pressing him into the bed. The thick silk of the gown felt like water on Edwin's skin. Something in the room was making a sound almost too high to hear, a singing vibration, and if it was Edwin himself then he was going to expire of embarrassment, but he had a terrible feeling it was—strings, silver, mirrors, something both tangible and external. Something in Edwin's new house, baffled by the soar of Edwin's blood and trying to find a way to match it.

"You're far too dressed for this," Robin said after a particularly savage stint of kissing.

"You cannot imagine how little I care."

Laughter, and Robin rolled off him and leaned his head

against Edwin's shoulder. But he was also at work opening Edwin's gown, clumsy in a way that had to be deliberate, so many sparks and shivers did it call up when Robin's knuckles rubbed against his hardening length. Edwin sat up enough to wriggle free of the gown and kick it to the floor, then lay back again.

"How—how do you like it?" Robin asked. It was nearly a rasp. He was intent and shadowed with a smile still tugging at his mouth, almost unbearably handsome. He shoved the last fold of Edwin's drawers out of the way, skin met skin, and they both inhaled as though in a race for the oxygen between them.

Edwin froze, his instinctual wariness momentarily winning the struggle it had been waging against the tidal force of his need. He could feel it, that dangerous temptation to open himself fully to sensation. He could barely think. He forced himself to think.

He'd let Robin come waltzing effortlessly across his boundaries, just as Sutton had. And like Sutton, Edwin could muster secondary wardings. He could fall back to other defences. If they both wanted this then surely, *surely* Edwin could have it without giving away too much of himself—but only if he was careful. If he kept himself in control, he could still scrape together a few ways to keep himself safe.

"Edwin?" Robin said, faltering.

"Fast," Edwin said, breathless. He pushed up into Robin's hand, making it a demand. "Fast and hard."

"Oh, hell," Robin whispered.

Robin took direction like the athlete that he was. Fast and hard was how he gave it, the small calluses of his fingers almost unbearably good against Edwin's cock, his thumb circling the head and his pace ruthless. Edwin could do nothing but clutch at him, his nails dragging up Robin's spine, and let the sensation thicken and simmer up through his body in waves until he was panting, gasping, frantic for it to be over and wanting it to stretch out forever.

Edwin opened his mouth against Robin's bare shoulder as

he came, turning a cry into a bite. He squeezed his eyes shut and even then felt something like the flash of a camera, white light painting itself onto the inner surface of his eyelids, before everything went dark.

When he surfaced from the trembling decrescendo of his pleasure, the room seemed smaller. Cosier. The flicker of the guidelight created shadows in every corner and, incidentally, allowed Edwin to see the red, saliva-wet mark left by his teeth on Robin's shoulder. As though what Robin was in desperate need of was *more wounds.*

Edwin realised he was touching the mark, and snatched his finger back. "I'm—so sorry. Ah. Heat of the moment."

Robin tried to curl his own shoulder forward to look at it. "That's a first," he said, buoyantly cheerful. "I've not had anyone do that to me since Maud was going through her savage phase, age approximately five."

Edwin collapsed and buried his head in the pillow. "I'm *sorry.*"

A hand ruffled his hair, and he nearly swatted Robin for the sheer indignity of it, but he owed Robin whatever Robin thought was fair, for—for *biting* him. Dear God.

"You can tell me if this is against some kind of magician etiquette," said Robin, "but what happened with the light?"

Edwin turned his head. "The light?"

"When you, er." Robin made an unfortunate gesture. "The guidelight went very bright, and then went out like a candle. And then recovered itself. Does that happen every time?"

Edwin bit his tongue against admitting that he hadn't noticed, or rather, that he'd thought he'd imagined it. That it was some new effect on his nerves of having been brought to a more satisfying and overwhelming completion than he'd experienced in years. He had enough energy to glare at the guidelight, but not nearly enough to launch into an explanation of his vast and ludicrous ignorance on the usual sequelae when one was having fantastic sex in a magical estate that one was wearing

like an ill-fitting new suit. One thread of his mind managed
to wonder if Sutton Cottage had ever done that for Flora and
Gerald Sutton, before abandoning that line of thought in a recoil of horror.

"Not in my experience."

"Ah," said Robin. His cheerfulness had taken on a smug
edge. Edwin's first and uncharitable instinct was to shove back
against it, to deflate it, somehow.

He rolled onto his back, the air of the room abruptly cool
on the damp patches of his inner thighs. The glow of desire
was ebbing and on its shoreline he felt uncertain, anxious; he'd
forgotten what you did, in the aftermath, with someone that
you liked. And who seemed, strange as the concept was, to like
you in return.

Robin was grinning. Edwin tried to meet it with a smile of
his own, and didn't manage to look away from Robin's mouth,
and the thought struck him like the fall of an icicle into a snowbank: *Lethe-mint. You're helping him get free of the magical
world, and then you're going to help him forget it. Don't get
entangled. Pull the threads clear.*

A louder and more selfish thought clamoured: *If he's going
to forget anyway, that makes it even safer, doesn't it?*

It only occurred to Robin to think about his vision after the
fact. At no point in the proceedings had he gathered enough
concentration to plan more than the next glorious moment, let
alone to try and match what they were doing to the vision of
Edwin he'd had on that very first night, in his sitting room in
London.

At the time he'd thought it ludicrous. Unthinkable, that the
prickly porcelain figure of Edwin could be unwrapped and en-
ticed into this kind of exchange. Even that very morning, if
pressed, Robin might have said Edwin was likely to be cool in

bed: welcoming enough, but passive, with his responses kept tightly under a lid. Robin had had partners like that before. The men who were struggling with themselves about their preferences, or even those who seemed to think it would be somehow uncouth, *not the done thing,* to show simple pleasure.

Cool fish that he was, Edwin had run scorching hot, and Robin was going to be bringing himself off for weeks at the memory of Edwin's fierce concentration, his hand firm on Robin's cock. The sound Edwin had made into Robin's shoulder at the moment of climax, like his soul was being ripped from him.

The heat of his abandon was cooling now. Edwin rolled off his side of the bed and walked to the washstand in the corner. He kept his back to Robin, and something about the hunch of his shoulders hinted at embarrassment. Perhaps even regret.

"Edwin?"

"What?" Edwin asked, a little stiff. At least he turned.

"I'm wondering what sort of blind idiot I was, not to find you attractive when we first met," said Robin.

Colour touched Edwin's cheeks. The smile that tugged at his mouth was the same one he'd worn when Robin had admitted to being fascinated with his hands: faintly incredulous, but mostly pleased. It wasn't an expression of regret. It did make Robin want to drag him back to the bed, pin him down, and murmur praise into his skin until it inked itself there like the opposite of a curse.

"Ah," said Edwin. "Whereas I am neither blind nor an idiot."

It took Robin a second to recognise how neatly Edwin had bounced the compliment back at him. He grinned, shoulders relaxing as the tension between them mellowed.

Robin took his own turn at the basin, shivering as the water slid over his skin. Edwin found a pile of blankets in the large chest at the foot of the bed, then crouched by the fire. His hands looked hesitant, forming the cradles without string, but it seemed he'd barely begun the spell when the fire gave a small leap in the grate and began to burn more fiercely. He added a couple of logs and brushed his hands off as he stood.

"I've been thinking," Edwin said.

"How very out of character."

Another tugging smile. "Someone knew we were here. They knew how to find us; or you, rather. I'm not under any illusions that I was meant to escape that maze intact, and they may not have been counting on your attempt at heroics. They wanted you alone."

Both of them slid under the blankets, sitting up, the spare ones wrapped around their shoulders. This was Edwin's room, but he didn't suggest by so much as a sidelong glance that Robin should leave. Robin hadn't shared covers since boyhood, excluding a few nights when Maud had been particularly in need of whispered nonsense to distract her from where she was chafing against their parents' plans for her future.

Robin had known Edwin a week, even if it felt longer. It was an odd, off-balance kind of domesticity to be discussing the events of the day in bed.

The events of the day, which had involved death and neardeath. Nothing about this *wasn't* odd.

"Or they wanted us distracted, so they could go and demand information about the contract from Mrs. Sutton, now we'd led them to her," Robin said. "In which case they succeeded."

"Either way, they found us. You."

Edwin's raised eyebrows finally dragged Robin to the logical conclusion. "Everyone at dinner last night heard us plan to come here."

"Yes."

"That doesn't make sense. If one of Belinda's guests wanted to get me alone, they've had ample opportunity."

"And if they wanted to hurt you," said Edwin bleakly, "they could have cast the Pied Piper and Dead Man's Legs on the same square of the lake."

Robin blanched at the coolness with which Edwin seemed to accept that his sister and brother-in-law might be involved in this malicious plot. And yet—*Charlie tried to remove the curse,* Robin's brain whispered, with equal coolness. *And what happened then?*

"The problem is," Edwin went on, "the man who attacked us today managed to get past the estate warding."

Robin felt stupid. It had been a long day, and he was sore. But Edwin's had been just as long and *he* was much less physically fit; he'd sustained the same amount of damage, and here he was with his brain racing capably around like a cat after mice.

"I—didn't think of that," Robin said. "You think he wasn't a magician?"

"It's possible to cast an illusion mask on someone else, I suppose. I didn't think of *that*. I assumed . . ." Edwin frowned, tilting his head back to rest against the wall. The lines scored across his throat by the thorned vines were disconcerting. He could have been a decapitated saint in a devotional, the carmine line of the wound painted in to hint at the manner of martyrdom. "I wondered if the curse could have a tracking clause," he finished.

Robin looked at his arm. By now the runes had begun to creep up his shoulder. He had nearly a full sleeve's worth of intricate black pattern.

"That might overcome a warding," said Edwin, having switched easily into lecturing mode despite sitting with blankets pooled in his lap. "It's a matter of one sort of spell having priority over another."

"If they cast a spell to follow me, they could follow it even if the boundary spell was telling them not to?"

Edwin nodded.

"Then they didn't need advance notice of where we were going," said Robin, with relief. While he might not *trust* any of the members of Belinda's party, he didn't want to believe any of them capable of murder.

It did leave them without any more clues as to who was responsible, though. What clues had been in this house had died with Flora Sutton.

Robin thought suddenly of the vision he'd had of an old woman—a *different* old woman—black-clad and bright-eyed, being attacked in a small space. Something about the defiant edge to her smile had been the same as Mrs. Sutton's.

"About Mrs. Sutton," he said, tentative. "Did you have the feeling she didn't give up whatever that chap wanted from her?"

"Yes," said Edwin. "Or else she gave the answer he *didn't* want, and then took herself out of the picture."

That was a kind of courage that Robin wouldn't have ascribed to many people. Certainly not to himself. When he'd punched the men in illusion masks, that first evening in the London streets, he'd been more surprised and affronted than anything else. Now, after six days of pain and confusion, he wondered if he'd still do the same thing. And if that wasn't exactly what the curse's pain and visions had been intended to inflict.

As much as Robin had wanted to shake the secrets out of Flora Sutton's skirts—to know why he'd been cursed, and what Reggie Gatling might have died for—he'd seen the fear on her face, when she talked about the contract and what it could lead to.

Was leading to.

"I'll have to go through her books," said Edwin, brightening marginally. "I wonder if Sutton Cottage would let me take a few of them home." He glanced around the room as if expecting a response to his musing.

It seemed completely mad, that Edwin had acquired an estate on the basis of some blood and one woman's hands, but there it was. Magical inheritance law, it appeared, was two parts sympathy and one part paperwork. The housekeeper had unlocked a desk drawer in a dusty study, before dinner, and there it had been: Edwin's full name, in stark copperplate, on an official will. That sort of charm was possible because Edwin was a registered magician, Edwin had explained. Though there'd been an edge of uncertainty to it, as though they'd strayed into areas for which even Edwin's life of reading had not fully prepared him. Perhaps it was something to do with Sutton Cottage itself, like the way the guidelight had flared up when Edwin climaxed.

Thinking about that, Robin wanted to put his lips to Edwin's again. But he was entirely at sea in the etiquette. What came after sex and before sleep? What fell into the bounds of acceptable behaviour?

"No visions today?" Edwin asked.

"Not yet," said Robin. Thank goodness one hadn't decided to strike mid-coitus. "I'm getting more of a warning, when they come. I'd have time to"—he waved a weak hand—"sit down. As it were."

"What kind of warning?"

"Sparkling lights at the corners of everything. Like when you take a tumble to the mat and stand up too fast." Robin licked his lips. "And a taste like pepper. And usually some kind of smell, but that one varies. And—it's hard to breathe. Pressured. Not quite like being winded, but close."

"Could you bring one on, do you think? Purposefully?"

"Why?"

"You saw the maze," Edwin said. "It was important. You could see something else."

Robin didn't relish the idea, but that was inarguable. He settled further down in the bed and closed his eyes. "Where do I start?"

"With what usually starts it," said Edwin. His voice had the usual confidence of knowledge, but hushed. The sound of it was a comforting thrill, like rough flannel dragged over Robin's skin.

Robin rubbed his tongue against the roof of his mouth, striking up a heat that he could pretend was the hot taste that heralded the foresight. He screwed his eyes tight shut until the light prickled. He inhaled, deep—no scent but the dusty lavender of sheets long kept in a linen chest, and the murkier one of bodies and their closeness—and held it.

Held it. Held it. Eyes tight.

He willed his mind to plunge into a vision, but couldn't focus on anything past the sensation of his lungs pressing against his ribs, straining, the stubborn burn of them followed all at once by a flood of panic—any moment his mouth and nose would fill with water, he wouldn't be able to breathe even if he tried—

He gasped his eyes open and flailed in his haste to sit up and lean forward. Edwin's hand touched his shoulder. Robin was expecting an eager query about whether it had worked, but Edwin just rubbed small circles with the heel of his hand.

"No good," said Robin when he had his breath. "Sorry. Felt too much like the bloody swan-pond, even trying."

Edwin lifted his hand away. He looked very tired, and as though he was having trouble deciding on what he wanted to say. What came out, carefully arranged as a dinner service, was: "I wish I could make this better."

"You're trying," said Robin.

The thin lips thinned further. "Failing."

Robin thought for no real reason of Maud, who'd throw herself into every new endeavour and passion as though it were the first. He swallowed a terrible surge of guilt. He was supposed to be there for her, supposed to be sorting out their family's future, and where was he? Tucked away in a manor house in Cambridgeshire, drinking up Edwin Courcey with his eyes and pretending that his own problems were the only ones in the world.

"Trying's what counts," he said.

Edwin yawned. The room was warming, since he'd stirred up the fire; that must have been the reason he let the blanket slip down from his shoulders. Robin let himself drink his fill.

Edwin's skin was smooth and pale, the wings of his collarbone making Robin's mouth water. He thought about that particular vision again: Edwin, nude and writhing, on his back against sheets. *These* sheets? How was he supposed to tell? Sheets were sheets.

"What? What's that look for?" Edwin's limbs were curling up, self-conscious and self-protective. Robin was far too distracted to say anything but:

"I was thinking I'd quite like to suck your prick."

Edwin's breath caught. His bent knee softened, as Robin stroked a hand up Edwin's leg. Robin was already reaching for him, already moving down in the bed to find a good position, when Edwin's hand landed on his wrist. Edwin had a look on his face that Robin couldn't read at all.

"I—thank you, but I would rather you didn't," said Edwin.

Robin stared at him.

Edwin licked his lips and went on, hastily, "That said, I'd like to. For you."

"You shouldn't feel obliged—"

"I don't." A trace of a smile now. "I'm not lying to you, Robin. I would very much like to do that."

Robin had never in his life come across any fellow who had an objection to having his prick sucked, and felt a moment of indignant wounded pride; he'd seldom made that offer before. But he was hardly going to push any kind of activity on someone unwilling, and Edwin was eyeing Robin's cock—it throbbed in anticipation—with the sort of intensity he'd previously applied only to books, so what was Robin going to do, refuse him?

"Well," he said, helpless. "Thank you awfully, I suppose?"

"Always so polite," said Edwin. He leaned down and kissed Robin, a single sharp meeting of mouths.

If asked, Robin wouldn't have thought that *precision* was the quality he'd have most desired in a bed partner who was about to apply his mouth to Robin's cock. But then, he'd never have conjured up the way Edwin held Robin down with a palm splayed low on his stomach, and worked with calm, thorough care from the root to the tip, laying open-mouthed kisses and gliding his tongue against the sensitive skin as though shaping words in a new language. As though painting runes into it. Even the air of the room seemed like a caress, now, as though Edwin's new house was bending itself to Edwin's will and creating for Robin a room the exact blood-warm temperature of his body.

Edwin kept a hand on Robin's slick length, paused between mind-sparkling little sucks of the head, and rolled his own blond head on his neck as if ironing out a knot in the muscle. The action was a casual, fussy one. Robin had seen Edwin do it twenty times when they were in the library as he closed one book and reached for another. Robin laughed silently, his stomach vibrating beneath Edwin's hand, and Edwin shot a glance up at him, instantly wary. Robin licked his dry lips and tried to stare his gratitude out through eyes that felt gritty with pleasure.

"That feels incredible. Honestly." Robin slid his fingers into Edwin's hair. "Do you mind . . . ?"

Edwin didn't push into Robin's hand, nor did he pull away. He *thought* about it. There was no reason for that to be arousing, but it was. And when Edwin said, "Not at all," with a whisper of hoarseness to his voice, Robin groaned and let his hand tighten, tugging Edwin back down onto him, and stopped thinking entirely.

16

Robin fell asleep almost at once after returning to his own room, and woke on the verge of sunrise as the curse took him in its awful grip. He struggled back to himself from a crimson haze in which chopping the damn limb *off* was beginning to sound like a legitimate solution.

There was no getting back to sleep after that. He dragged a chair over to the window, which looked out onto a surprisingly lovely sunrise in watercolour shades of pink and yellow that stretched across the gardens. Rose-fingered dawn. Robin might have been a mediocre scholar, but some things stuck.

The butler delivered Robin's clothes. His shoes had been polished. Trousers, shirt, and waistcoat had been washed and brushed into respectability. The tears in the clothing had even been mended with stitches so tiny and neat it was tempting to call them magical. Robin ran his thumb over the lines of repair as he dressed. He made a note to ask Edwin more about domestic magic—a note that disappeared promptly from his mind when he entered the breakfast room and his nose, scenting kippers and curry, informed his grumbling stomach that he was *famished*.

After breakfast Edwin spent some time shut up with the butler and housekeeper, presumably sorting out further business related to the legalities of inheriting an estate via blood, soil, and silver pendants. Robin, extraneous once more, went for a walk in those parts of the garden that did not contain mazes. He struck up a conversation with one of the under-gardeners, of which he learned there were *four,* and that the number of visitors happy to pay for a tour of the house or grounds was enough to make this position much sought-after among the gardeners and groundskeepers of the county.

Edwin had not inherited a magical mystery so much as, it seemed, a legitimately lucrative tourist attraction.

By the time they set off for Penhallick, Edwin had filled the boot of the Daimler with a double armful of books from the hidden study behind Flora Sutton's mirror. He was quiet during the drive: not quite skittish but preoccupied, and speaking only to give direction from the map unfolded across his knees.

Robin didn't want to press against what seemed a deliberate drawing-back. Should he assume that Edwin would say something, if he wished the topic to be broached at all, or was Edwin waiting for him? Should Robin simply ask if what had happened between them could happen again, or if it could even be the start of . . . what? Robin's mind was trying to fit itself around an unfamiliar shape, an implausible future as fragile as Edwin's snowflake. All he knew was that he didn't *want* to let this slide beneath the surface of their tentative friendship as though it had never happened.

No game of Cupid awaited them at this arrival to the Courcey manor house. It was raining desultorily, soft patters of it against the roof of the car. Edwin stirred from where he'd been gazing out the window, sometimes idly cradling his fingers and dropping them before any spell could be fully formed, and sat up.

"Five pounds says they didn't even notice we were gone," he said.

"Why not make it ten? Now you're a man of means and all."

"Don't remind me." Edwin paused. "As a matter of fact, I'd prefer it if you . . . kept quiet on that score. At least for the moment. I don't know how my family's going to take it, and I want to tell my mother first."

Edwin went inside while Robin stowed the car in the converted stable and remembered just in time that there was nobody to look after it. He found a rag and gave it a quick wipe-down before heading into the house itself. He intended to go straight to the willow rooms and change clothes—perhaps even find Edwin in the middle of doing the same, and find some tactful way to gauge the man's interest in a revival of the previous night's activities—but Edwin himself, still in yesterday's clothes, met him a few steps inside the front door.

Edwin's eyes were wide and his shoulders were held brittle and stiff. "There's been a complication," he said.

"What kind of—" Robin began, and then heard a burst of familiar laughter coming from inside the parlour, and knew exactly what kind.

Most of the Walcott party was arranged on various pieces of furniture. Every one of them was wearing a different expression; every one of them turned to look as Robin entered the room, Edwin on his heels.

"Sir Robin!" said Belinda, looking effervescent and modern in a pink walking suit. Her expression was one of delight with an edge to it. "Look who's turned up and agreed to come boating with us this afternoon."

Robin turned his attention to the girl next to Belinda. Her attire was much more sombre: the dark grey of mourning wear. She rose to her feet when she saw him.

Robin said, "Maud?"

She was already halfway across the room, face pinching into a frown, and she snatched up one of Robin's hands in hers so that she could press it. Robin let her hold tight enough to steady the fine tremor of her fingers that meant there were too many unfamiliar eyes upon her. She could turn her laugh on like an electric light, but she couldn't quash this. Robin wanted simultaneously to embrace her and to shake her, but she'd have appreciated neither.

"Robin!" said his sister, aghast. "Darling, whatever happened to your face?"

"I had a disagreement with a hedge," said Robin. "More to the point, Maudie, what are you doing here?"

"I'm here for the shooting season. What do you think, Robin? I'm here for you."

"How—what—how did you even know where I *was*?"

"Your typist told me," she said promptly, releasing his hand. "Miss Morrissey. I liked her."

Robin opened his mouth with a storm's worth of further one-syllable questions building inside it.

Maud went on hastily: "I went to the Home Office. And I asked, and asked, and asked, and eventually someone managed to track down your new office for me."

"*Maud—*"

"I didn't lie," she said. "Although . . . I may have let some very nice men make a *teensy* few incorrect assumptions about the nature of the home emergency that led me to be trying urgently to find you."

Robin's head was threatening to throb. "Home emergency?"

Maud cast her green eyes down, then peeped them up at him. She looked altogether forlorn. Robin could only imagine half of the civil service turning gruffly avuncular in the face of this look, and the other half tripping over their tongues to make themselves agreeable to the owner of those eyes.

"I broke Mother's favourite vase," she said meekly.

Robin stared at her, anger and disbelief bubbling up through him, but somehow by the time it hit his throat it was laughter. He exhaled a long chuckle, helpless, and Maud's eyes creased with relief.

"Did you honestly?"

She nodded.

"The—" He gestured a bulbous shape.

"The hideous one she inherited from Great-Aunt Agatha," Maud confirmed.

"Don't tell me you walked all the way here from the station," cut in Edwin.

"No! Win, it's the most amazing joke!" said Belinda. "The dear thing arrived at the station with a packed bag and simply asked around the shopkeepers until she found someone who would bring her here in a pony-trap."

"Asked and asked and asked," muttered Robin. One of Maud's dimples peeked out unrepentantly. "If you're not here to tell me about the untimely death of Great-Aunt Agatha's vase, then why did you need to come on such an adventure?" he asked, though it was a weak question. With Maud, the adventure itself was the point.

"You think I don't know when you're hiding?" Maud demanded. "I *told* you I wanted to go to university, Gunning's been calling every day to press you for decisions on the estate, and you make weak noises for two days and then run off to the country on some excuse about work? And it's ever so dull, at home, without you—and with Mother and Father gone."

Her eyes were almost artfully wide and pleading. Robin dearly wished that the mere prospect of believing him to be a member of the secret service would be enough to dissuade his younger sister from rushing headlong into the unknown. He also didn't believe for a minute that she'd run here only to seek comfort, though it clearly held water as an excuse with the others, who'd see only an impulsive young girl in mourning clothes. *Dull* was a very carefully chosen truth.

"And now," Maud went on, voice rising, "I find out you've been keeping some kind of *magic* from me?"

"Ah," said Robin, who had been trying and miserably failing to come up with a way to ask whether the household had been playing at normal since Maud's invasion. That ship had clearly sailed in their absence. Maud looked far more excited than scared, at least.

Behind his shoulder, Edwin gave a pained sigh. "After all that grief about unbusheling," he said grimly. "I am going to murder Adelaide Morrissey."

Robin, who rather thought he recognised a punishment for tipping-in-the-midden when he saw one, said nothing.

"Why don't you sit down, old chap?" said Charlie, catching Robin's eye. "We were going to have some tea and sandwiches, take the edge off before lunch."

They sat. A trolley full of food was brought into the parlour, and Billy demonstrated an illusion-spell for Maud. Her fingers were still, in the easiness of being one person's focus; and a handsome young man's, at that. She was full of questions, which Billy tried to answer and Charlie ended up answering instead. She rolled her eyes at learning that women were in general not expected to practice magic seriously, and it was only recently that some female magicians had begun to insist on studying it to the same extent as the males. Charlie's tone indicated that such females were being humoured, but nobody expected much of them.

"Of course," Maud said, with a pointed look at Robin.

"Here, Maud, you must try this lemonade," said Belinda, reaching for a metal jug with a stylised etch of flowers. "It's a specialty of Cook's. The secret is the mint from our own gardens."

Maud took the proffered cup with a smile, but didn't have a chance to voice her thanks. She made a noise of stifled surprise when Edwin stepped in and took the cup from her hand, setting it back on the tray.

"It's a prank," he said.

"Come off it, Edwin, don't be sentimental," said Charlie.

"They serve it unsweetened, Miss Blyth, just to watch you spit it out." Edwin stared hard at his sister. Belinda stared back at him, and then her face melted into a *got-me* kind of smile.

"A bit of fun," she said.

"Quite," said Edwin. "Now, if you'll excuse us, Robin and I were stranded at Sutton Cottage last night without a change of clothes, and we're in desperate need of fresh shirts. And I'm

sure he and his sister would appreciate some time alone, so that
he can . . . explain things. *Gently.*"

Somewhat to Robin's surprise, Maud didn't argue with this.
She cast a longing look at the sandwiches, but allowed Robin's
hand at her elbow, steering her out of the room. They'd almost crossed the threshold, Edwin once again close at Robin's
shoulder, when Belinda spoke behind them. She didn't raise
her voice. Robin wasn't even sure he was meant to hear it.

"It's kinder than the alternative, Win," she said. "You know
it is."

"Did you bring luggage, Miss Blyth?" said Edwin, ignoring
his own sister.

"Yes," said Maud. "The housekeeper took me up to a room
with birds and strawberries on the walls."

"Come with us, for now." Edwin led them up the main stairs
to the corridor containing the willow rooms. Robin pulled to
a halt before any doors could be opened. Maud had dug her
fingers into his arm.

She said, "You've been very rude and not properly introduced
me, Robin, but I'm assuming this is Mr. Edwin Courcey?"

Frankly, it was a miracle anything about the preceding half
hour had shown any resemblance to the normal proceedings of
polite society. Robin managed, "Um. Yes, that's right."

"Good." Maud dug into a deep pocket of her skirt and
pulled out a folded letter, which she handed to Edwin. "Miss
Morrissey said it was for the both of you, but she wrote Mr.
Courcey's name on it, so I suppose he gets first look."

Edwin broke the seal and unfolded the note. Some of the
colour left his face as he read. He raised his eyes to Robin,
and Robin again, *again,* wanted to touch him; wished to offer comfort, wished they'd had more than a night, wished he
could bring his mind to focus on what was clearly a potentially
serious matter while his body murmured memories of the taste
of Edwin's skin.

"State secrets?" Maud asked, not budging an inch.

"No, Maudie. But secrets related to my job. I need to talk to Mr. Courcey. I'll tell you the parts of it you can know, I promise."

She made a small face, but stepped into the willow room when Robin opened the door, and didn't protest when he closed it. He was almost certain she wasn't going to press her ear to the door—they trusted each other more than that—but he let Edwin beckon him a little farther down the corridor anyway.

"Looks like she'd have swallowed it if you said state secrets," said Edwin.

"I don't lie to the people I care about," said Robin. "What is it?"

"Reggie's dead." Edwin's hand tightened on the letter. The paper made a small, dry sound. "They found his body two days ago."

It wasn't a surprise, after everything. Robin said "I'm sorry" anyway. Edwin didn't meet his eyes, but gave him the letter. Robin read quickly. "Handed over to the Coopers? What does that mean?"

"Investigative branch of the Assembly," said Edwin. "Perhaps the rest of the bloody Gatlings did decide to take his disappearance seriously. The Coopers will make sure the usual police don't push too far, and they'll pick up the case themselves, if there's something to pick up."

Edwin didn't sound encouraged by this, nor did he suggest they could return to London and shove this entire mess into the hands of these magical police, who were surely far more qualified. Of course. Robin was still having visions, and Edwin was trying to keep him out of their sight for as long as possible.

Honestly, Robin gave it another two days before he found himself demanding that they take the risk if there was the slightest chance these Coopers could get the curse off him. But he trusted Edwin's judgement.

The rest of Miss Morrissey's note was a dry assurance that if they were making headway then they might as well stay out of London, as there was no pressing need for Robin's presence. The PM had left for Cardiff and wouldn't be back within the week, so wouldn't be needing his usual briefing.

A few more days in the library, with an extra set of books this time. It might make the difference to Edwin's attempts. Though now Robin had his sister to worry about on top of everything else.

"Edwin," he said. "What did Belinda mean, kinder than the alternative?"

Edwin's face set into the coolness that meant he was trying not to react, or was worried about someone else's reaction.

Robin said, "Don't lie to me. Please."

"Lethe-mint." Edwin swallowed. "That's what would have been in the lemonade. It's what Charlie and Bel drank after they set the traps in the lake, so that they could play the game. So that they wouldn't remember where any of it was."

"And giving it to Maud was another of their games."

A long pause. "Not really," said Edwin. "It's what ends up being used, most often, after an accidental unbusheling. There's a time limit on lethe-mint's use. After a while, the only option is casting a spell directly on the mind, and those can be—difficult. Or else letting the person keep the memory but binding their tongue to protect it. Lethe-mint *is* the kindest option."

Robin was surprised at how personal his anger felt, how close to betrayal. He'd tear apart anyone who harmed his sister, of course he would, but the fact that it was *Edwin* defending Belinda's actions . . . that hurt. For the past week it had been the two of them against the world. And now it was clearly Edwin's world against Robin's.

"So they were going to just—take her memory of all this? Let her think, what, she'd been *drugged*?"

"Tell her she'd been offered Champagne and drank too much of it," said Edwin.

"And you'd be perfectly fine with that?"

"I *stopped* them," Edwin snapped. "As you'll recall."

Robin forced himself to breathe. Some of the steam left his head. He rubbed at his face. "Yes." He managed an ungracious "Thank you."

"Talk to your sister," said Edwin. "I'll talk to mine."

Robin had no idea, even when he opened the door to the sight of Maud sitting in the room's single upholstered chair, how he was going to *start* said talk.

Then he tasted pepper, and realised the decision had been made for him in a spectacularly inconvenient fashion.

"Oh, blast," he said weakly. He managed to stagger in the direction of the bed and—possibly—even sit down on its edge, although the vision swooped in and claimed him before he could register the sensation of sitting.

The young woman was tall, with blond hair tucked up in a fashionable nest of a hairstyle, and she wore a dark skirt with a high-collared white shirtwaist peeping from beneath a dark-red riding jacket. She held her skirts in one hand and slowly climbed a few stairs to a landing, her gloved hand trailing against the wooden panels of the wall.

She turned on the spot. She began to cradle a spell, laughing and directing a warm flash of smile at someone. Green light glowed at her fingertips with equal warmth, and then she spoke.

It was as though she summoned the pain with her silent voice. It seemed to come up from the depths, rising and rising until the vision wavered and plunged into blackness, Robin no longer a set of disembodied eyes but instead disembodied agony, perhaps a pair of lungs—perhaps a distant throat, choking. Mostly, the pain. The hot wires sinking through him again and again, slicing his flesh into burned shreds.

It ended.

Slowly, the rest of Robin's body faded into awareness. He was panting. He opened his eyes. He was lying on the bed, on his side, his sister's hand tight on his shoulder and her terrified face close to his.

"I'm all right, Maudie," he said at once. He winced at the scratch in his voice. "It's passed now."

"*What's* passed?"

Robin sat up, slow. His arms shook.

"Robin," Maud said, looking scared and small and *his,* on his side; they were always on the same side. Robin couldn't deny her anything, he'd never been able to, and he knew what she was going to say and what his answer would be. "Robin, please tell me what's going on."

17

If he'd known any of this would happen, Edwin thought, he would have turned and walked right out of the Office of Special Domestic Affairs and Complaints as soon as he saw someone that wasn't Reggie sitting behind the desk. He could have saved himself a lot of bother.

He certainly wouldn't be standing here having an honest-to-goodness argument with his sister and her husband. They were both giving him a surprised look, as though at a pigeon that had suddenly begun a tap-dancing routine in the middle of Trafalgar Square. Edwin finally managed to get them to agree that they wouldn't do anything to Maud, *anything*, while Robin was here, and that Robin needed to stay until they'd sorted out the curse.

Edwin swore full personal responsibility for the Blyths and their memories. Bel had never much cared for responsibility; she all but dusted off her hands, and resurrected her smile.

"I know you don't spend much time with the family, Win," she said in parting. "I suppose it's easier for you, all things considered, to live like one of *them*"—she waved her hand—"but do remember, won't you, that you're one of us?"

"Yes, Bel," said Edwin.

He wanted to shout that she knew nothing about his life, nothing about what he found easy and what was difficult. But Charlie was frowning and nodding behind her shoulder, and Edwin was not, in the end, at all brave. It wouldn't have mattered even if he had yelled. Bel and Charlie had always had that perfect immunity, like a waterproofing charm cast at birth. Criticism slid off.

It was only when they wandered away, arm in arm, that Edwin realised they hadn't asked him *why* he and Robin ended up staying the extra night at Sutton Cottage. Why Edwin's face and arms now itched with shallow scabs.

Edwin had never really convinced himself that Charlie and Bel could be involved in this entire business of murder and contracts and curses and secrets. Now he rather thought it was impossible. If they knew what had happened, surely they'd at least bother with the pretence that they didn't.

They didn't know. And it simply didn't occur to them to care.

Even so: Edwin wasn't about to drop his guard entirely at Penhallick. Miggsy had more than enough nastiness running through him to be dangerous, Billy seemed easily led by stronger personalities, and Edwin didn't think he'd ever seen a *true* emotion of Trudie Davenport's. She performed as she breathed. She could be hiding almost anything.

He went to his mother's rooms next, but her maid Annie told him she'd just fallen asleep and that she'd barely caught a wink the previous night. Edwin promised to return later, and let his feet take him to the library. He recognised that he was hiding. The last few days had represented the most time he'd spent constantly in the company of another person in years. Robin was surprisingly easy to be around, but even so, part of Edwin felt like the Gatlings' oak-heart clock: run-down, out of power. Needing refreshment to be any good at all.

And this, the large lavish space with its silence and the soaring shelves of books—each one bearing his own hand's symbols, his own catalogue painstakingly charmed into them—was the refreshment he needed. The usual itchy Penhallick sensation had been both stronger and less uncomfortable since he returned, like how he imagined it felt to don a pair of reading glasses and see words come into focus when one had been straining after them. He didn't know what he'd expected. For Penhallick to be *jealous,* somehow? For it to have disavowed his blood? No—plenty of families had multiple properties.

He'd have to research it. Thoroughly. After all of this was over, of course.

One of the servants had delivered the pile of Flora Sutton's books to the library. Edwin had taken her three most recent volumes of journals, and a handful of those books that seemed most likely to refer to rune-curses, foresight, or the technicalities of magic as contract law. So far he'd had no luck at all concentrating on the curse; now at least they had a clue to the larger picture.

Edwin fetched *Tales of the Isles* and opened it to "The Tale of the Three Families and the Last Contract," locating the illustration. Three objects. Physical symbols of the contract between the magical families and the fae. Coin and cup and knife.

My part of it alone is hardly going to do them much good, Flora Sutton had said. Was that it? Three pieces, and all of them needed?

Which part had she hidden in the maze's heart, then let Reggie carry away with him, to be hidden in turn?

Even if they learned that, it still wouldn't tell them what the pieces were needed *for.* The terrible purpose that Mrs. Sutton was convinced the contract could be turned to, which would hurt every magician in Great Britain.

Edwin opened one journal, then closed it again. If the dead woman had been telling the truth about the scale of this, then surely it was too big for him. He was one barely powered magician with nothing but a tendency to let books replace people in his life. He didn't know how to own an estate, or to unravel deadly mysteries, or to hold responsibility for the minds and well-being of perfectly nice unmagical people within his hands.

He scrubbed at his eyes. He touched one of the scratches on his hand.

He had to try anyway. If Edwin *had* turned and walked away from Robin on that first Monday, Reggie would still be dead, and Edwin wouldn't have even the smallest scrap of a notion why. Robin would still be cursed.

And Edwin wouldn't have spent a week being mocked and half-killed and overwhelmed and—looked at like a miracle, and kissed like an explosion.

Edwin dragged himself back to his purpose. He used the index-spell to summon Perhew's *Contractual Structures in the Common Magicks*, stacked it atop one of the Sutton books, and took them both over to the window seat. Fat raindrops chased and swallowed one another down the leaded panes. Edwin removed his shoes and rubbed his feet on the embroidered cushioned seat, letting himself be distracted by colour: the dark navy of his socks against the red and amber-yellow and brighter blue that formed the pattern of stitching on the cushion. He wondered what it was that Robin saw, looking at things like that.

Edwin bit at the soft flesh of his inner cheek and opened the first book on his lap.

"Don't be foolish," he said quietly.

Penhallick House, around him, said nothing at all in return.

Any amount of time could have passed by the time a loud throat-clearing hauled his attention up from the well of words.

"How did I know you'd be here?" said Robin. He read the book's title and made a face. "Rather you than me."

"It's not as dry as all that," said Edwin. "Though for the first time I wish I'd read Law at Oxford. I was a Natural Sciences man."

"*And* spent every spare moment teaching yourself to create new spells, I expect," said Robin, sliding into the other corner of the window seat, close to Edwin's tucked-up feet. "I'm no longer surprised you creak like a rusty gate when trying to make friends." His smile was warm and conciliatory. It made up for the tease of the words themselves; Edwin wasn't sure if it made up for the startling sense of being rendered as transparent as the window behind him.

"Is that what we are?" Edwin moved his toes, edging up against Robin's leg. It felt daring.

Robin's smile widened. "Belinda and Trudie are taking Maud on a tour of the house. You'd tell me, if there was a chance of my sister being turned into a pincushion or a Tiffany lamp."

"They'll behave," said Edwin. "I made Bel promise."

"I should probably apologise to her," said Robin. "I didn't intend to have my family invade your property."

"Bel's probably delighted. She wanted a balanced table." Edwin managed to swallow the acerbic edge to his own tone before he said, "I see the urge to just rush in headlong runs in the Blyth family."

"Maud's been after me to let her go to Newnham College, and she thinks I'm shirking the answer." He rubbed at his hairline, mussing some brown strands. "She's right."

A large part of Edwin wanted to pull the conversation back to practicalities and research, but this felt like one of those discomforts that had to be pushed through in the name of discovery, like the hundreds of times he'd made his own hand spasm painfully while he was working on nerve-spells. *Friends,* Robin had said. Friends were allowed to discuss things that were important.

"I know what it's like to want that terribly," he offered.

"You were probably born with a book in each hand," said Robin. "I never thought of her as that sort."

"Maybe she deserves a chance to try."

Robin's hand had moved and was resting over Edwin's ankle. His thumb made two thoughtful circles over the bone there, barely felt through the wool of Edwin's sock. Edwin's foot tingled as though waking from sleep. Robin exhaled through his nose and said, "Our parents would never have let her."

"You don't talk about your parents much."

"I am—trying very hard not to speak ill of the dead."

"Sod that," said Edwin, clear and low. It startled a laugh from Robin. "You told Mrs. Sutton you were raised by liars."

Another few slow circles of Robin's thumb. A shadow flickered in his expression. Edwin wondered, from nowhere, what it would look like if Robin's heart was breaking. It was a terrible thought to have. He had it anyway.

"I made a pact with Maud," said Robin after a few heartbeats. "She knocked on my bedroom door one night, after one of Father and Mother's charity dinners. She'd been lying awake for hours. She asked me if I thought our parents really cared for her. *They were so nice to Mrs. Calthorpe tonight, but I heard them talk about her when the Duncans were here last week, saying such awful things. Do you think they talk about me, when I'm not there?*" Robin pressed his mouth tight. "I promised her, that night, and she promised me. We made a pact to always say what we meant. Never to lie."

Edwin tried to imagine never lying to his siblings. Never being lied to. The image shivered and collapsed.

"You're right. I should give Maud a chance, if we can afford it," said Robin. "I want her to have what she wants out of life."

"Because you couldn't?" It seemed the obvious question.

"I don't mind—no honestly," with half a smile. "What else was I going to do? I've no great gifts. I wasn't clearly destined for anything in particular."

"Then why the civil service?" Edwin asked. "If it wasn't about the wage, to begin with. Why did your parents want that for you?"

"It was the service half that mattered. I doubt they cared a penny about what kind of government work I actually *did,* so long as they could talk about me as something else they'd donated to the British Empire out of the goodness of their hearts. I thought about the military, but I'd have had to move away from Maudie."

And he wanted to be there for her. To protect her. It was excruciatingly congruent with everything that Edwin knew of Robin's character.

Edwin's leg cramped and he stretched it out, farther into Robin's half of the window seat. Robin's hand settled at once on Edwin's calf, adjusting absently so that Edwin's ankle lay across his thighs. There was nothing suggestive about the posture, but Edwin's heart still thumped. He looked at Robin's fingers, sinking into the memory of the previous evening's events for a quick, hot moment, like a metal tea infuser held briefly in a pot of water.

He said, not letting himself overthink it, "You turned out very decent, considering how they probably treated you."

"They *didn't*," said Robin. "Nothing like the way your father spoke about you the first night here. They were cruel to other people, but . . . I honestly think they saw us, me and Maud, as something like that man you cut out of paper. An extension of them." He spoke as though piecing the thought together for the first time. "Things to be moved around in whatever way would make them appear in the best light. We had to be real to one another, because I don't think we were real to them."

Edwin touched the back of Robin's other hand with his fingertips. He felt painfully awkward. He'd never had the knack of knowing how, why, when to extend this kind of touch. But Robin, of course, made it easy: he turned his hand up and clasped Edwin's in his own, squeezing it.

"That sounds awful."

"It wasn't . . ." Robin's grip tightened past pain. Relaxed. His next laugh was off-balance. "All right. Yes. It was bloody awful. And I always thought one day I'd turn around and tell them what I thought of them, and now—now I can add on top of it the fact that they didn't even *try* to plan for our futures; they let the estate be mismanaged in whatever way would let them spend more on their parties and paintings, and give the biggest and most obvious donations to the charity of the moment. And now—we're here. Nobody's going to give Maudie a *scholarship* to Cambridge, and I'm not nearly smart enough to turn things around in a hurry, but nobody else is going to do it, and I'm so . . ."

It wasn't a broken heart. It was more like broken glass: a bottle, smashed, letting everything flow out from where it had been long corked and fermenting. Robin was gazing far past Edwin, into the future.

"Scared," said Edwin.

So there it was. He'd found the thing that scared Robin Blyth.

"Yes," said Robin.

Lunch was served not long after, and by the time the last course had been removed the rain was heavier than ever. Bel sighed and abandoned the idea of boating, then allowed Charlie to talk her and Trudie into a walk around the grounds, so long as he promised not to let a *drop* through the umbrella-spell.

Edwin, fortified by roast beef and syllabub, took Maud Blyth to meet his mother. She managed a cheerful greeting and smiled with honest delight when Maud, who one-on-one had Robin's knack for society manners—*paper men*, Edwin thought, and it soured the moment—complimented her hairstyle and the lace at her collar.

"Annie's gifts are wasted out here in the country," Florence Courcey said, splitting her approving look between Maud and the maid. Annie sat tucked in the corner cleaning spots from ribbons and sashes. She blotted them with a rag dipped in a bottle, then cast a simple version of the dissolution spell that Edwin had thought might work on the curse. "She should be attached to someone who's going out visiting every day, where her handiwork can be seen and admired."

His mother was sitting stiffly, not moving with ease. She was exerting herself on his behalf, spending energy she didn't have, like a gambler refusing to rise from the table. Edwin caught

Robin's eye, and Robin made polite noises about letting Edwin and his mother exchange news in private, and took Maud out of the room.

Annie brought over a tonic as soon as the Blyths had left. Edwin's mother closed her eyes and let discomfort make a mess of her features while Annie adjusted her cushions.

"I'm sorry, Edwin, darling," she said. "I did think I might be more myself, after a good sleep."

"Don't be silly," said Edwin. "I'm tiring you, I won't stay long. But I have another secret for you." He drew up a chair to sit on, trying to work out the easiest shape of the story. "This one's awfully large."

"That's all for now, Annie." His mother dismissed the maid with a nod. Her eyes were already brighter, though it was a brittle brightness: another coin laid down that she'd have to account for later. Her anxious look scanned his face. Edwin kept forgetting the scratches there, except when they itched. "What is it, darling? Is this about—did I hear you had an argument with a hedge?" Of course that had already whispered its way back to her, through Annie's army of gossips.

"You know we went to Sutton Cottage," said Edwin, and let the story pour out from there. He underplayed the danger they'd been in, not wanting to worry her, making the hedge maze and its antipathy for magicians seem more like one of Bel's pranks. It probably made it sound pathetic, that he'd gone as far as trying to make blood-pledge with someone else's property in order to escape, but that couldn't be helped.

"Sutton Cottage," his mother breathed. "I knew it was old, but . . . Nobody I know has been there, not since Gerald Sutton passed away."

"No, it's warded," said Edwin, and wondered for the first time if that was entirely due to Flora Sutton's desire to guard her piece of the contract, or if she'd had other reasons to want her fellow magicians to leave her in peace. It wasn't as though Edwin couldn't see the appeal. He'd worn string-scrapes on his fingers as a child, and tired his eyes with reading, trying to find a ward that could be set on his own bedroom door and keep certain parts of the world at bay.

The world, meaning Walt.

"You really think it's that powerful, darling?"

"Yes." Edwin caught the yawn from his mother, and the aches of the previous day's exertions settled back into his shoulders. "It's nothing like Penhallick, Mother. It felt like if I stood there long enough, it would pull parts of me into the soil like roots." He hadn't meant to let that out, but the uneasy whimsy slid off his mother's attention. "And I'm wrong for it. I think Mrs. Sutton grew half those gardens from magic, and God knows I haven't enough to maintain them, or to have the slightest clue how she did it in the first place. It's just going to be something else for me to disappoint. And after all that, I *still* haven't managed to do anything about the curse on Robin."

"I'm sure you will," she said. "And I'm sorry about the Gatling boy. Sounds like such a nasty business, darling. Once you've sorted out Sir Robert's problem, I hope you can keep yourself well clear of it."

Edwin wanted to agree with her. He thought about Flora Sutton's blue needling stare, and her hands branding his cheeks with her expectations. He thought about the sheer affronted anger that had sprung to life in his belly when he was shoved into the hedge maze. It was, he realised with a start, still there: an ember smouldering away beneath the ash of fear and futility.

He stood and kissed his mother's cheek, and went to hide in the library again until dinnertime. Robin didn't seek him out, this time. Edwin told himself he was glad.

He dressed slowly for dinner, listening for the sounds of Robin getting ready in the room across the hall. He couldn't hear any: the doors were good wood. The walls were reasonably thick.

He was listening so hard that the knock on his door seemed abnormally loud.

"Cuff links," said Robin when the door was opened. He was juggling them in one hand. "Do you mind?"

It was a transparent excuse. Edwin managed not to smile as he let Robin in, and managed not to smile as he fastened the cuff links for Robin, and managed not to smile as Robin sat on the edge of Edwin's bed and looked in every corner for inspiration before finding, somewhere in the wainscoting, the idea of inquiring if Mrs. Courcey's health had taken a turn for the better.

"Perhaps. She has ups and downs."

"My mother would have loved a painful illness," Robin said, bitter. "She could have raised hundreds of pounds in her own name, and had someone wheel her around the hospital wing with her name on it while she looked brave and interesting. God. That probably sounds—sorry."

Edwin looked at Robin's head, now buried in his hands. It had been, yet again, a long tense day, and they still had the evening to get through. He went over and touched the nape of Robin's neck, two fingers tucked beneath the rise of the starched collar. Robin went still at the contact. Edwin moved his fingers, a light brushing back and forth, somewhere between comfort and invitation and apology.

And admission, even in his own head: *I am nothing like you, and yet I feel more myself with you.*

The word inked by a certain hand on Edwin's heart was *affinity*. It was almost enough to make him bolt from the room.

But Robin's skin was warm and Robin was looking up at him, now, with eyes like unshielded flame. Robin took hold of Edwin's forearm, a thumbprint at the wrist, moving it until he could press an open-mouthed kiss to the dip of Edwin's palm.

Edwin pulled his hand free. Robin let him.

There was a silence crowded with the sound of Edwin's pulse, and the tightening of all his nerves, and the throb of blood in his cock.

"Come down here?" Robin said, a bit rough. "I want to kiss you."

"It's not long until dinner." Edwin gestured to his clothes, though a small howling part of him despised the rest for a spoilsport and a coward. His knees were weak. He wanted to climb astride Robin's lap and rip Robin's buttons open and kiss him until both of their mouths were far too wrecked and obscene to be seen in public.

Robin stood and took Edwin's face in his hands, raising his eyebrows. "My deepest apologies. If I promise not to crease so much as an inch of sir's clothing, does sir think I might possibly—"

"Oh, stop being an ass," said Edwin, feeling his lips twitch.

The kiss was careful enough to be a tease in itself. Like all of Robin's teases, it made warmth spill down through Edwin. Edwin let himself feel the heat, let himself lean in only a very little. He could remain in control of this much.

Robin held Edwin in the cradle of his fingers like a spell that would snap into nothing unless handled with care. Edwin heard the first breath of sound, a musical whine, try to escape with his own breath. He made the mistake of trying to crush it by letting the kiss get looser, more urgent, closer to the roar of desire that he was refusing to give in to in any other way.

Robin muttered a curse against Edwin's lips and released him. Edwin stared at him, rendered mute by hunger. If he turned to the mirror he was almost certain he'd see Robin's handprints there, white as Flora Sutton's had been, marking him.

"Later tonight," Robin said, a low promise. "Now, as you said, dinner."

18

Maud's assigned bedroom in Penhallick House really was covered in strawberries. The wallpaper was a Morris design that Robin had once seen on a cushion, all greens and blues and curious birds, with eye-catching blobs of red. The four-poster bed and dresser were made of glowing walnut. Maud looked oddly at home there, taking pins from her hair and dropping them one by one into a jar with tinkling sounds like the overture of rain.

Robin, remembering that the strangeness of magic had given him whiplash long after he'd thought himself accustomed to it, lingered in the room.

"Are you sure you're all right, Maudie?" he asked when she raised her eyebrows in clear invitation for him to leave her alone.

"You're waiting for me to declare that I'm dying to be a magician," she said. "You needn't worry. Mrs. Walcott—Belinda—explained the lay of the land. And I don't need magic. University, remember?"

"I'm taking you back to London," Robin said. "As soon as . . ." He raised his cursed arm. Maud's eyes softened.

"I'm sorry I barged up here," she said. An unusual offering.

"I'm sorry it looked like—I'm sorry I *was* running away."

Robin felt more lighthearted than he had in a while, as he left Maud's room with his own guidelight bobbing above his shoulder. The things were convenient, you had to admit. Anticipation tingled within him. He undressed down to socks and shirt and trousers in the fire-warmed willow room, then knocked at Edwin's door.

A longish pause met him before Edwin said, "Yes?"

Edwin looked over his shoulder when Robin entered. He was seated on the edge of the bed; his shirt was all the way off, and Robin had a good view of his pale back and the nearly elegant thinness of his arms. His face was a curtain rapidly drawing over an expression of wan misery, and it furrowed into apology at whatever he saw in Robin's. He stood.

"What is it?" Robin asked.

He watched Edwin's mouth try to form the word *nothing*, and fail. "I think it just hit me all at once," Edwin said. "That I'm never going to see him again. Reggie."

"You really . . ." Robin tried to adjust course, tried to remember the conversation about Gatling they'd had in the car. "Had feelings for him?"

A neutral twitch of Edwin's head.

"Wanted him?"

Edwin swallowed. "He was . . . safe."

When Robin had first been coming to terms with who he was and who he wanted, there'd been an older boy at school he'd thought of like that. A glorious, impossible, untouchable fantasy. And when Robin thought about something more than physical release, someone to *be* with—

But he'd never in his life let it get past the thought. For men like them, only the impossible was absolutely safe.

"I understand how that goes," Robin said.

"Yes," said Edwin. He was holding his own elbows. The look on his face struck Robin like the withdrawal of a knife so sharp that the entry had gone unnoticed. "I believe you actually do."

"I'm sorry," Robin said, feeling a heel. "I'll go."

"Don't," Edwin said quickly.

"I don't want to intrude."

"You're not. You can't. It's extremely irritating." Edwin stepped close, very close indeed.

"What's irritating?"

Edwin said, "Every time you touch me it's exactly what I want."

Robin's heart pounded as the anticipation took hold of him again, redoubled and delighted. He laid his thumb in the hollow of Edwin's throat, beneath the scratched lines, his fingers light at the side of Edwin's neck. Edwin closed his eyes and tipped back his chin. Robin could feel the movement of Edwin's breath, the almost-shudder of his body.

"Really?"

"Yes. Exactly." Edwin sounded cross. Robin pulled him in gently, leaned in himself. He watched the line of Edwin's mouth, then brushed over it with his own lips, wanting to savour the moment when Edwin's tension melted into eagerness. He slid his other hand around Edwin's back, greedy for the expanse of bare skin. Edwin had his hands between them, unbuttoning Robin's shirt, the softness of his mouth surrendering fraction by fraction by fraction.

As ever, there was no warning before the pain started.

"Bloody *fucking* hell," Robin managed just before agony closed his throat on speech. He jerked himself away. He saw Edwin's face, kiss-smudged mouth and naked surprise, and then crumpled to the floor as his vision greyed out and the curse took over.

What scared him the most was that when he opened his eyes again, he had no idea how long it had been. He'd actually blacked out this time. And how long since the last attack, which had overlapped with the foresight? Hours only.

"*Robin.*" Edwin was crouched by his side, paused halfway through a cradle.

"Ow." Robin squeezed his eyes against tears, satisfied himself they weren't about to spill down, and pushed himself to sit upright against the side of the bed.

Edwin lowered the string. His face was white and taut. "It's lasting longer," he said. "Isn't it? I thought you might not come back from it this time."

Robin swallowed half of his own fear in the need to reduce Edwin's. He could at least do something for Edwin's obvious anger at his own futility.

"Do you have anything cool?" he asked, nodding at his arm. "It's—still feeling hot." Another new, alarming sign. For the first time it felt as though the cage of glowing wires had burned so hot and so long that it needed time to return to normal.

Edwin nodded and created the opening loops of a spell. He cradled a swirl of subtle mist and smeared it over Robin's arm. It was like the relief of turning one's pillow over on a hot night.

"Thank you."

"I hate this," Edwin said. "I hate that this is what magic is to you. What it's done to you." He was winding his string in absent, fretful motions around one thumb; he sounded irritable, almost wistful. "It's not supposed to be bad. It really is— something marvellous."

The mist was gone, but the cool swirl of it was still sinking into Robin's arm. He could have tried to tell Edwin how lovely *that* spell had been, how soothing, but instead he reached out and took one of Edwin's hands, gentling his thumb over the back of it as he drew it towards his mouth. Edwin didn't resist; his breath caught, distinct in the silence, and it was enough to bring Robin's arousal sweeping back over the horizon from where the pain had banished it. He found a holly-scratch over one of Edwin's knuckles and traced it with his lips, then his tongue.

Edwin took his hand back. His eyes were hot, the furrow of his brow more thoughtful than fearful. He darted a look down Robin's body and up again.

"I have an idea," he said. "Will you trust me?"

"Of course," said Robin.

"It'll be easier if you take your clothes off."

Robin could no more have resisted that suggestion than if he'd been magically compelled. He took his clothes off and lay down, and Edwin sat on the edge of the bed beside him.

"This is experimental. I've only ever done it on myself," Edwin said, and Robin could hear him talking himself out of it, so he grabbed Edwin and pulled him down for another kiss to distract him.

It worked rather too well. Robin emerged gasping, nearly having lost his own concentration to Edwin's skin sliding hotly against his, the taste of Edwin's tongue, the way Edwin panted when Robin tightened his grip in the silky-fine fairness of Edwin's hair.

"Whatever it is, I want you to do it." He smiled and nipped at Edwin's lower lip with his teeth. "I'll try anything once."

"How completely unsurprising," Edwin murmured. "No, you need to understand this before you agree to it."

"All right," Robin said, flopping back defeated into the pillow. "Tell me."

Edwin explained that his spell had been built to target the ends of nerves, and the signal of it would travel down those nerves just as normal sensation would. Except . . . magic. It all sounded like a lot of unnecessary bother to Robin, given Edwin could just have *touched* him and probably had the same effect, but Edwin looked animated and interested and like he'd forgotten about Robin's stupid bloody curse, so Robin was happy to go along with it.

"Do you consent?" Edwin finished formally.

Magic was contract. Robin thought about the difference between Edwin's impeccable care and the way Belinda had laughed when the Cupid arrow turned Robin giddy. He thought about Edwin spitting his full name into the earth along with his blood.

"I, Robert Harold Blyth, consent to you using your completely experimental but—knowing you—completely safe and well-researched spell. Will that do?"

"Thank you," said Edwin. He was already cradling a glow of pale blue light. It matched his eyes, Robin thought ridiculously, and then Edwin touched one glowing finger to Robin's wrist and he wasn't thinking of anything at all. A sensation that was something like the snap that followed rubbing your feet on carpet, and something like the perfect fire of swallowing good brandy, was moving all the way up his arm and through his shoulder and—"*Fuck*," Robin gasped—burrowing itself to a triumphant end exactly between his shoulder blades, where it faded.

Edwin looked anxious. "Was that—"

"*Do it again.*"

This time Edwin touched one of Robin's toes, and the sensation slid all the way up Robin's leg—he hissed as it seemed to pass within a few inches of his cock—and into his lower back. It glowed there longer, this time.

They both grew bolder after that. Robin sucked two of Edwin's glowing fingers into his mouth, then gasped hard around them and forgot not to bite, because he could feel the sparks burying themselves somewhere in the nape of his neck.

"Sorry!" he said, once Edwin had snatched his hand away.

"No damage done," said Edwin. He sounded rather hoarse.

Another handful of light. Edwin shifted back down the bed and reached between Robin's legs, and Robin cried out as Edwin cupped his balls with agonising gentleness. The path of the blue-light sensation was short but very, very targeted.

"You said you—did this to *yourself*?" Robin panted. He could see it: Edwin's hands shaking on the strings, Edwin's long legs splayed open, feet slipping on the sheets. "What, with a Roman tract propped open on the bed in front of you?"

"Actually . . . yes, once," Edwin said. "I believe it was the story about the plucky young reporter who was caught spying, tied to the evil lord's bed, and tortured with the fascinating collection of glass phalluses."

Robin's lip flashed with pain as he bit down on it. He knew

that story; it hadn't exactly been torture, by the end. He couldn't help imagining how much better, or worse, this would have been if Edwin had tied him up first.

"Keep going," he said.

Edwin did. The blue light carved lines of ticklish pleasure that softened and burned from every point on Robin's body, always heading inwards, each one a breath of air on the fire of need building inside him. Sometimes Edwin paused and used the cooling spell again. Sometimes he followed it with a similar spell of soft heat, calling up contrasts that made Robin groan and want to roll away and roll towards them, both at once.

Always Edwin returned to the blue light, letting Robin feel the full length of each nerve as distinctly as if he were drawing them there with ink. As though Edwin were mapmaking and using Robin's flesh to do it. The spells he cradled were always small, controlled; Edwin seemed determined to eke out as much effect as possible from his modest supply of power.

Robin drank up the motions of Edwin's fingers and the intent delight on Edwin's face, until it reached a point where even that was too much effort and Robin could only lie there, hot and wrecked, taking fast gulps of breath, incandescently aware of every mapped inch of his body. This had already gone on twice as long as any sexual encounter with another human being in Robin's life. His cock was hard, and fluid beaded at its tip. If he took himself in hand it would be over in three good strokes.

He didn't.

"I wonder," Edwin murmured.

"Yes," Robin agreed instantly. "What? Yes."

Edwin left the bed, but he was only going over to the dresser, and he returned with a small bottle of hair oil. Robin's heart kicked hard in delight. Edwin was still wearing his trousers, though Robin could see where he was straining against the front of them. Now he stripped with efficient movements, and when he was naked he laid his string hesitantly to one side with the clothes.

"Legs apart?" he suggested.

Robin planted his feet on the bed, thighs in a V, and told himself sternly to hold still and not embarrass himself. Whatever this was, it was going to be *amazing*.

Edwin knelt between Robin's legs, coated his hands with the oil, and began, with care, to build the spell without string. It took him a few tries, and when he succeeded the blue light was fainter than it had been before. It looked on the verge of blowing itself out.

In the moment before it did, Edwin pressed his middle finger deep into Robin in one quick slide.

Robin actually *shouted,* hands slamming down against the bed. His hips bucked up as he came in hot spurts all over himself.

Edwin held him through it with his other hand on Robin's mess of a stomach. His finger was still spreading oil, gently stretching Robin open, as he pulled it out. He looked somewhere between startled and gratified.

"You have—the best ideas," said Robin.

"Well, that's it," Edwin said, and sounded rueful about it. He was wiping both hands on another fold of sheet. "That's my magic done. I won't be able to manage any more tonight."

Robin flapped a forgiving hand and lay there, trembling. His nerves had caught the trick of it and kept sending faint echoes of the sensation through him, chasing from skin to spine and sometimes back again. His cock didn't seem to have realised that the show was over; it was at half-mast and throbbing needily.

"Robin. If you had any idea how you look," Edwin said, low.

"Like a railway accident?" Robin said. "That's how I feel. But good. A *good* railway accident."

Edwin laughed. He was lying on his side next to Robin; his own cock was hard between his legs, but he seemed content to ignore it. Robin felt gloriously selfish, impossibly lazy. It was long past Edwin's turn. That was only fair.

"Give me half a minute," Robin said. "I could—or," struck by inspiration, "*you* could." He rolled onto his stomach to make his meaning clear.

Edwin looked surprised. Robin remembered Edwin declining to be sucked, but no refusal was forthcoming here; Edwin's lips parted and his cock jerked. Robin eyed the length of it in new assessment. Yes. Yes, Edwin *could*.

"Are you sure?"

"I've done it before," Robin assured him. "I enjoy it." Not every man did, Robin knew. But Robin hadn't encountered many things he didn't like. He gathered enough strength to push himself into a better position, elbows and knees, in invitation. His cock was definitely stiffening again, heavy between his legs. If this was an aftereffect of the spell, Edwin didn't need to invent library catalogues or discover how to make snowflakes, or inherit a grand estate. He could make a fortune off this alone.

Robin tried to arrange all of that into helpful words, but it came out as a caught-back whimper when Edwin moved to kneel behind him, Edwin's hands clutching at his hips.

Edwin paused. And kept on pausing.

"What are you waiting for?"

When it came, Edwin's voice was a rasping whisper, prompting. "I, Robert Harold Blyth . . ."

"Oh, you utter bastard. Yes. I, Robert Harold Blyth, fourth baronet of Thornley Hill, if that helps, consent to . . . *ah*." Another small jolt of leftover pleasure shook him. Edwin's fingers were digging in hard.

"Yes?"

"Anything," Robin gasped, "fuck, *anything*, Edwin, please."

"You shouldn't." Edwin sounded wrecked. "I could take so many things from you, with a contract like that."

"I really fucking wish you *would*," said Robin. He could feel the prickle of sweat at the back of his neck, and Edwin's cock nudging up against him. He was going to go mad with wanting.

His breath left him in a groan as Edwin pushed into him, the stretch barely painful at all. The long rub of Edwin's cock was like the satisfaction of scratching an itch that had been plaguing one for hours. The heels of Edwin's hands felt nearly as good, in their firm, clumsy slide up either side of Robin's spine so that he could clutch at the muscles of Robin's shoulders.

"Oh," Edwin breathed, a broken sound. His breath was hot at the side of Robin's neck, the weight of his body resting on Robin's. He straightened, but the grip of his hands tightened. The change of angle made Robin's elbows shake as Edwin's cock pressed against something inside him. Edwin made another noise; Robin stared blankly at his own splayed hands and tried not to die.

Edwin went on, "You feel—I have to—" And then he did, fucking into Robin in long erratic strokes, pulling Robin back to meet him, burying himself fully each time. It was less than half a minute before he froze, gave one more urgent shove, then held himself still as he gasped out his release. The sounds were almost as good as the spell, burrowing straight to Robin's blood from his ears, until Robin felt he would explode.

He opened his mouth to beg, but Edwin was there already. One of his hands fumbled down and closed around Robin's cock; Robin heard himself make a sound like *gnh,* and followed him over the edge. He was dimly aware of himself clenching around the length of Edwin still buried inside him, and even more dimly aware of Edwin's ragged breath.

Edwin pulled himself clear and sat up, still catching his breath. Robin thought seriously about moving, and decided instead to collapse his cheek into the pillow and his body fully onto the bed. There was a large wet spot beneath him. Robin tried to care and failed.

"Bloody hell," said Robin. "*You've* certainly done that before."

Edwin went a darker shade of pink. "A few times. Not with—not recently. And I haven't ever used that kind of magic on someone else."

Perversity made Robin say the name that Edwin hadn't. "Not even Hawthorn?"

"No, he didn't want me to do magic around him. He liked that I didn't."

Robin felt warm all over at the idea that Edwin had done this with nobody else; only with him. His whole body was still coming down from the effects of it, his heart going rapidly, still trying to live out the last of the dance. "Could you slow my pulse with a spell like that?" he asked, curious and flush with daring. "My breath?"

Edwin blinked. Robin rolled onto his back, took Edwin's hand, and guided the fingers—tacky with Robin's own release, which had quite the opposite effect on the heart rate in question—to press beneath Robin's jaw, where his blood was pounding away close to the surface.

"Oh," Edwin said.

They'd begun this with Robin's fingers at Edwin's throat. Now here they were caught in the mirror of that, Edwin not pressing hard but not being careful either, Edwin's eyes sharp in his flushed face and blue enough to drown in—Robin's breath caught without any effort expended, magical or otherwise, from either of them.

Edwin pulled away. "I have done that on myself as well. To—calm myself down." In far less pleasurable contexts, Robin assumed. "But I'd be risking your life if it went wrong."

"As opposed to risking your own."

Edwin said, dry, "I rather think we've had this argument twice this week already."

"Yes—you say I shouldn't risk it, I say I'm going to anyway. I told you. I'll try anything you have up your sleeve, if it feels half as good as that blue thing does." Robin spread his arms wide and Edwin's eyes caught on his chest, then on the black marks of the curse, and then Edwin looked away. Into the silence leaked the small sounds of night outside the window. Faint footsteps above them could have been maids in attic rooms preparing for their own rest.

"You should be found in your own bed tomorrow morning, I think," said Edwin.

Robin sighed and began the mildly sticky process of wiping off, gathering and re-donning his clothes. He spared a thought, bitter in a way that he thought he'd grown immune to since his schoolboy days, for all those couples who would never have to think twice about spending the night together after an evening of pleasure. As house parties and their winked-at transgressions went, it wasn't as though Robin and Edwin were breaking any vows of marriage. Nobody was being betrayed.

But the facts of existence for men of their inclination were a sore old enough to have turned to callus. Robin threw Edwin a final smile, and let himself across the corridor. No point in dwelling.

It wasn't until he was lying in his own bed, beneath the identical wallpaper, that he wondered if Edwin had simply wanted him out of the room. Edwin Courcey seemed to grow *more* layers as Robin unpeeled them; Robin didn't know what to do with Edwin's swings between cool reserve and that naked, affection-starved need. The way he reacted when Robin touched him. The quiet, desperate sounds he'd made as he fucked into Robin, as though he would never be sated.

Robin shifted in the bed, enjoying the ache of awareness in his backside as he enjoyed the ache of his shoulders after a long session in the boxing ring. *He* felt sated, certainly. Aglow with it, wanting to linger in the memory like a warm bath. He was still tired and scared and cursed, still caught up in a plot that refused to reveal itself fully, but part of him was insisting that he felt happier than he had in years.

You really must have been in desperate need of a good fuck, he told himself, feeling his mouth curve. The words landed in his mind like bad notes on a piano. Apparently Robin recognised lies even when he was telling them to himself.

Because it wasn't the physical act alone. It was the way he felt watching Edwin read; it was the feeling he had every time his eyes sought Edwin in a room and landed on any angle of the man's face, any movement of those delicate fingers: *There you are. I've been waiting for you.*

Only the impossible was safe. This was merely implausible, and that made it dangerous. But Robin could die tomorrow, or next week; the curse could writhe up his neck and burn his mind out with pain, or someone with fog for a face could take his arm on a busy street and decide to finish the job. He felt greedy for more nights like this, as many of them as he could cram into his existence.

And unlike shadowy attackers and mysterious tattooed runes, the way he felt about Edwin was a danger Robin was able to do something *about*. He could already feel the jubilant, contrary, Blythian urge rising within him: to rush headlong, as Edwin put it. To grin right into danger's face and see what would happen next.

One of the downstairs maids was making up the fire and opening the curtains in the library when Robin entered it the next morning. It was early enough that the morning light was dim and watery, the house's corridors cold and filled with deep grey shadows. Robin had been awake for at least an hour, unable to convince his body not to lie in tense anticipation of the curse striking again, and the thought had tumbled heedless and whole into his mind: this *wasn't* a danger he had no choice but to mope around and brace against. He was going to be more than a curse-marked deadweight that Edwin was dragging around the country. He was going to *punch back*.

Flames began to lick in the fireplace. Robin cleared his throat and the maid straightened at once from the grate, her hand disappearing into a pocket of her apron as she did so. Robin wondered if he'd find string in there, if he told her to turn it out; he wondered if there were punishments meted out by the housekeeper for needing string to manage domestic spells, if the scorn for such a crutch stretched across class boundaries in the magical world. There was so much he didn't know.

"Sir." She bobbed a curtsey. "Can I help you, sir? Anything you need?"

"No," said Robin.

Perhaps she was too well trained to look surprised, now she was over her initial startlement. Perhaps the downstairs staff of Penhallick House merely assumed that Mr. Edwin's strange unmagical friend from London was just as prone to haunting the library at odd hours. Either way, the maid nodded, cast a critical eye over the room as though marking dust to be attended to later, and slipped out of the double doors, leaving Robin alone.

The slim catalogue was where Edwin had left it on one of the tables. A section of it was, thankfully, alphabetical. Robin flicked to the F section. *Foresight: Π61.*

No neat indexing charm for Robin, but Edwin had a tendency to leave his books lying around if he thought he might want to refer back to them, and there was a clear edict against the servants clearing them away. It took no more than ten minutes of digging through the active piles and checking the marks on the bookplates for Robin to find a couple of candidates, and he settled down grimly to do what he should have been doing all along: working out how to get *himself* out of the mess, instead of letting Edwin do the work for him while he took the opportunity to escape his responsibilities in the city.

Edwin had all the experience, all the intelligence, all the knowledge of magic. But Robin had one thing that Edwin lacked: the very dubious gift that magic had bestowed on him in the first place.

Robin could see the future.

Edwin had asked, *Could you bring one on, do you think?* and he wouldn't have asked idly. He didn't do anything idly.

Edwin had left scraps of paper as bookmarks. One marked a mention of those people in the history of English magic known to have possessed true foresight. Another noted that it was thought to be present in the magical population all over the world, and most of the reports of deliberate wielding came from the greater Asian continent, with one or two possibly originating in South America.

The book prefaced these reports, in a stuffy tone that Robin's Cambridge-educated mind had no trouble translating into the wheezing voice of a Pembroke don, as unreliable, and no such possibility had yet been conclusively proved by civilised minds.

Perhaps Edwin had a point about the complacency of English magic. For the first time in his life Robin wished heartily for the existence of thorough research.

It was thought—the book grudgingly went on, once it considered the reader duly caveat-ed—that some possessors of foresight were able to wield it at will, and nudge it to focus on a particular person or subject or event. However, this caused the foresight to become less of a window onto the certain future, and more about *possibility*.

At this point the text devolved into words of a length and pompous complexity that made Robin's mind try to shy away and think about cricket, an automatic reflex left over from university. He managed to digest the sentence: *Reports exist of consciously directed foresight becoming temporally unmoored.*

Whatever that meant. Robin thought of the painted boats afloat on the lake. He flicked through the rest of the books, but none were any more forthcoming on the subject of foresight's deliberate use.

It was lighter in the room by now, though still well before the usual breakfast hour. Robin settled himself in the window seat, feeling oddly intimate as he did it, remembering the feel of Edwin's ankle beneath his hand and the trickle of raindrops on the window. The morning chill was trying to creep in through the glass and the heat of the fire had barely spread. Robin rubbed his hands together and tucked up his knees.

Edwin had suggested that he start where the visions always start. Robin didn't fancy holding his breath again, but he could concentrate on the palette of sensations that came before. The taste. The heat. The prickle of light.

Robin had never tried to deliberately clear his mind. He had the absurd image of taking a broom to waves on a seashore, trying to sweep the water back out across the stones. Might as well stand there like Canute and order it.

No. Concentrate.

The future. What kind of future was left to them? *Either this curse comes off me or it doesn't,* Robin thought. *There are people after this contract. Edwin's involved now, and they know it.*

What is going to happen?

He breathed in. Breathed out. Let his thoughts break like waves.

When the taste of pepper came, it was fainter than usual. The vision was so indistinct that Robin thought at first he was seeing another foggy day, but it wasn't that. The lines of the library could still be glimpsed as if through a heavily grimed window. Trying to focus on the foreground, the vision itself, struck a match of pain behind Robin's eyes. He gritted his teeth and pushed harder.

What is going to happen?

Moving shapes. A silvery blur dotted with flashes of maddening colour that never cohered—a stupid, useless pointillist picture of a vision—was that a tree? a chair? Pepper burned on Robin's tongue and his skull throbbed with effort. *I'm going to make this work, dammit, dammit*—

A room. It should have been awash with flowers, and wasn't. The parlour at Sutton Cottage. Edwin was stepping through the frame of the mirror leading into the hidden study. The glass had liquefied to allow him through, but like a rippling pond it still reflected things in a distorted fashion. There was at least one person, perhaps another, in the room. Edwin's hand was tight on the frame; he began to glance over his shoulder, speaking—

A very young man with a head of dark curls and a poor-fitting suit, shoulders hunched as he stood in the eaves of a closed street door and scribbled fast in the kind of notebook you saw emerging from the pockets of journalists. He leaned frequently around the frame of his shelter, as if expecting someone, or afraid of being caught—

Priscilla, Lady Blyth: youthful and alive, dimples cradling her loveliest smile as she accepted the fur placed on her shoulders by her husband. Pearl buttons on her long gloves. The way that smile slipped into annoyance as she glanced upwards through the banisters to where her oldest child was crouched, watching, aching—

An explosion that sent smoke and mud in a growling cloud against the sky, a field crawling with uniformed soldiers—

Edwin lying sprawled and lifelessly white on a gravel path between perfectly manicured lawns, a group of men in evening wear straightening up from inspecting his body and looking, in eerie unison, down the path to see—

Spring sunlight sparkling like diamonds on the Cam, the view from Arthur Manning's second-year room where it overlooked a green-cosy bend like Millais's *Ophelia*, the prow of a punt just floating into view—

A blond woman with hectic colour in her cheeks and the side of her hand in her mouth, ecstasy soaking her expression, the other hand caught in the elaborate skirts of an evening dress—

Robin was losing his grip. The part of him that was still *him*, that was a mind dimly aware of its existence beyond the images playing themselves out, had just enough sense left to worry. The visions had gone on too long. They were becoming, if anything, more immersive. And moving faster and faster, like the flickering spin of a zoetrope. Blurring together. Dizzying.

The last image that appeared for long enough that Robin had a chance of paying it proper attention was, again, Edwin. His hands were brimming and burning with a light so bright it looked as though it could set fire to a forest. Edwin raised those hands, drawing them back as if for a blow. The look on his face was utterly unfamiliar, a snarl nearly animal in its ferocity.

And then—

And then—

19

Edwin didn't have a habit of remembering his dreams. The rare exceptions were the bad ones: hiding uselessly in a version of school gone darker and less familiar, crouching with knees drawn up, hearing Walter's voice drawing near. Sometimes those dreams began as more mundane things in which Edwin was sitting university examinations, but they always managed to end in the same place.

This particular morning he woke with scraps of dream disappearing like sun-touched mist, and he could feel enough of their fading edges to suspect that the dream had been a good one. More than good. Pleasurable. Or perhaps, given the previous night's events, it was only memory. Either way, Edwin closed his eyes and savoured it: warm desire like melted honey, and the phantom ache of someone else's body pressed to his.

Last night had not gone as Edwin had expected. He was grateful that Robin had been so easygoing, so happy to let things play out as Edwin steered them. He'd made no attempts to push at Edwin's boundaries or his stated desires.

Edwin brought his own hand up to his throat and let his fingers rest there. It was early; he wasn't quite awake yet; he was safely alone. He could let himself wonder if he'd *wanted* to be pushed, and what he would have done if Robin had pressed the full force of his so-caring, so-trustworthy self up against the walls that Edwin had been frantically erecting even as the seas of lust tried to erode their bases.

Here, now, Edwin could examine what lay on the inside of

those walls. There were so many things he wanted. Sometimes his whole body was a drawn-back bow of wanting. But telling Robin even a single naked truth—*Every time you touch me it's exactly what I want*—had been terrifying enough without Edwin making himself prove it.

And it hadn't mattered. It had been satisfying, bordering on glorious, giving Robin that taste of a spell that Edwin had created. Edwin wasn't going to be able to look at Robin's shoulders again without remembering the view of them from behind. The firm muscle bunching. Robin begging. The tightness of him as Edwin pressed in.

That was a sense-memory to keep under glass, the prize of Edwin's collection.

There was a knock on the door. Edwin's mouth curved into the start of a smile.

"Are you awake? Mr. Edwin?" It wasn't Robin's voice. The girl knocked again, louder, which stirred Edwin's curiosity. The staff had instructions not to disturb the household at this hour.

"Yes." He threw on a dressing gown and slippers, and opened the door. One of the maids stood there, hands clutched taut in front of her, looking even less comfortable than Edwin felt.

"Mr. Walcott says you'd better come down to the library at once, sir. It's Sir Robert."

"What? What about him?"

The girl swallowed. "I don't know. I think—he's gone all funny, sir."

"Funny?" Fear harshened Edwin's tones. He regretted it when she flinched. "No. All right. Thank you. I'll be right there."

He fetched and pocketed his cradling string, then jogged down the main staircase and towards the library. The wide doors were closed, and a rustle of voices came from behind them.

The tableau that encountered him when he pushed open one door—a small group of people, including two servants, clustered around a single figure—made Edwin's knees weaken and panic cram itself into his throat. He steadied himself on the door handle. He couldn't be sure where he was, which house on whose blood-sworn land, whose body he was looking at.

This is my fault, he thought, quite distinct.

"Win!" said Charlie, straightening up. He, too, was gown-clad. Bel was properly dressed, but her hair tumbled unbound down her back. Edwin experienced an unbalancing moment of being glad to see his sister and brother-in-law; more to the point, to see *only* them. Small mercies. He wouldn't have been able to cope with Miggsy or Trudie at that moment.

Charlie went on, "Don't suppose you can shed any light on this, old man? He's taken rather ill, I'd say. Is it that curse?"

Ill wasn't dead. *All funny* wasn't dead either, if Edwin had been thinking. If he'd been *able* to think past the sheer wrench of terror. He hurried forward. Robin was slumped in the window seat, looking at first glance as though he'd lost himself daydreaming, his half-lidded gaze focused somewhere beyond the glass. His face and shirtfront were wet, beads of water clinging to the brown hair that hung over Robin's forehead—sweat?—and the only movement was the rapid rise and fall of his chest.

"He won't wake to prodding," said Charlie. "Or slapping, come to that."

"Or water dashed in his face," said Bel. "I thought of sending to the kitchen for one of Mother's reviving inhalations, but I don't know what would be best."

"Perhaps rosemary done over with—" Charlie started.

Edwin said, "How long has he been like this?"

"We don't know," said Bel.

"He's been in here at least an hour, Mr. Edwin," said the housekeeper. "Mary said he came in when she was lighting the fire."

"Is it the curse?" repeated Charlie. It was rare enough that Charlie asked Edwin's opinion on anything, let alone seemed genuinely keen to hear the answer, that Edwin took a moment to enjoy it. And then felt terrible for enjoying it.

"Yes. It's the curse."

He was, in a way, lying.

Last night, when Robin had collapsed in the curse's grip, he hadn't looked like this. He'd blacked out entirely; he'd been curled around the arm with the curse markings, even in his unconsciousness. This blank, perplexed expression, this half-waking unresponsiveness . . . Edwin had seen this on Robin before. He'd also stolen a glimpse at the books splayed open on the table.

This was foresight. Some horrid, stretched-out form of it. And it had Robin trapped as surely as they'd been in the maze.

At least an hour, Edwin thought, numb.

He said, "Has anyone told his sister? No—don't," as the housekeeper turned towards the maid. "Let her sleep. Thank you. That's all."

He didn't watch as the servants left the room. He sat in the window seat, near Robin's tucked-up bent knee, and tried to think. Someone getting lost in foresight was as far outside of Edwin's experience as the runes on Robin's arm. All he had to work with was the curse's presence. The curse had brought the visions. Banishing the one should banish the other.

This felt like an examination dream. Solve the problem. Time ticking away. And as in dreams, thinking was like pushing through a crowded street against the flow of people, and meanwhile Robin was stuck halfway between sleeping and waking.

Liminal states.

It took Edwin a few moments to remember where he'd heard those words spoken, and to call up the rest of what Mrs. Sutton had said. *Beginnings and endings are powerful. You can create profound change if you slip in through the gaps.*

Edwin's thoughts were working again. He had the grinding, half-painful half-wonderful sense that meant facts and precedents and logic were slowly finding one another in his mind, sliding into place, presenting a solution. Things said, over the past few days, unnoticed. Unconnected; now connecting. He was afraid to breathe in case he disturbed it.

"I have an idea." He watched Robin's unmoving face, the new dullness of those hazel eyes that had laughed at him; *you have the best ideas.* "I'm going to try again to lift the curse. Charlie, can you remember the spell I showed you last time?"

Charlie shifted, but the disapproving expression on his face wilted at Edwin's glare. He nodded.

"Show me."

"Win," snapped Bel. "There's no need to be rude."

Charlie glanced at Robin, and demonstrated, with no magic behind the cradles. It was close; and Charlie was, after all, a profoundly powerful magician. If it was the right spell, if Edwin could create the right conditions, it would work. Edwin himself could control his power minutely, could lean into the reassuring tension of his cradling string, but he knew—he had it etched into his bones, from years and years of bitter experience—that control could only take you so far if the power behind it was missing. And Edwin would have to do the most dangerous part of this himself, with his own hands. No room for error or mistrust.

He had that wrenching sense of displacement again. He was on the wrong land. He was—

No. No. He was a Courcey of Penhallick; he was, as Bel insisted, *one of them.* And he had *something*, he'd felt Robin's danger abrade his skin where Bel had felt barely a sting, and—

Another piece slid inexorably home in a mind still attuned to pattern. Was *that* it? Not a lack of connection, but *more* of one, the land pushing and pushing and Edwin, for years, closing himself off from it in shame?

An affinity. From a woman whose land had spun itself orchards from twigs and charms from saplings.

It had to mean something. He was going to make it mean something.

"Don't touch him yet," he said, whip-sharp, and dashed out of the library. He didn't need to go far. The nearest exit was the front doors themselves. Edwin ran out into the rain, flinching at the first gust of drops dashed against him by the wind, and dropped to kneel on the gravel of the driveway. His slippers were already crusted with dampness and dirt.

Blood. He needed blood. The echo was so absurd that he nearly laughed. He lifted a hand to his cheek, which was wet with entirely the wrong substance.

Edwin pulled his string from the pocket of the rapidly soaking dressing gown, and cradled a very small sharpness. He drew it across the back of his hand—one more scratch to join the rest—and scooped up the tiny welling of blood with one finger while scrabbling in the gravel, creating a small crater to the dirt beneath.

"I, Edwin John Courcey, belong to the line of Florence and Clifford Courcey, who made pledge with you years ago. I know you're still new to magic. I know I should have—tried harder, and sooner. I'm sorry. But a guest of this estate is in danger, and if there's anything in my blood that you recognise, then help me. Help me now."

Did he feel anything? Any crackle of agreement in the blood-dotted finger? He couldn't tell. Perhaps; perhaps he imagined it. He'd have to try anyway.

He dripped tensely back to the library to find that Maud Blyth had woken up after all, and come in search of her brother. And found him.

"You have to *help* him," Maud was demanding of Charlie. She had one of her hands on Robin's shoulder. She was shrill and pale and really quite absurdly young, and Robin loved her more than anything else in the world, so Edwin managed to swallow a series of impolite words and said, "We're going to try."

Maud pressed her lips together, but she didn't ask *how,* for which Edwin was grateful. He was aware of how horrific it might sound if he tried to explain.

Edwin had to rip Robin's sleeve open to the shoulder in order to bare the entire curse. Despite his churning worry, his cheeks burned. It felt obvious that he'd already touched this arm, this skin, this man.

They quickly completed the first part of the spell, the ink-copy and the sympathy, and Edwin had Charlie build the dissolution spell and hold it at the ready so that they could move as fast as possible. Speed was going to be everything here.

Miggsy had been absolutely correct. Some curses would only die when the sufferer did.

Liminal states. Working in the gaps. Birth was a beginning; this was the ending.

Could you slow my pulse, with a spell like that?

Perhaps Penhallick didn't think Robin was in danger yet, but Edwin was about to change its mind.

"Bel," he said. "Fair warning. If I do this right, it might be uncomfortable for you." And for their mother. He hated the thought, but shoved it aside. He'd find a way to explain it to her, to apologise—later. If it worked.

He seated himself again with his legs in contact with Robin's, looped the string around his hands, and looked at his fingers. They didn't shake at all. He took a deep breath and began.

When he'd done this to himself, it had felt like tiny invisible threads reaching out from his fingertips, hooking into the muscle of the heart, shivering with each beat. Allowing Edwin to gently, so gently, push his magic down the threads and persuade the muscle to take a longer interval between twitches. He'd read all he could find on the physiology of the heart.

Some of it had been beyond him—he was no physician—but he'd read anyway, until he had a mental picture to work with.

Now Edwin let the light of the spell build and slink down those threads like dew down spider silk. It was strange not to have the thump of movement in his own chest, to know that the twitch he felt was the beat of Robin's heart, steady and fast, held in Edwin's hands.

Beat. Beat.

Edwin kept his eyes on Robin's face and concentrated harder than he ever had in his life. Nudging. Slowly. Slowly.

Beat. And pause.

Beat. And—now longer—pause.

Robin's eyes had fallen closed. His colour had changed; he looked ashy.

Beat.

Bel made a low, surprised noise and hugged herself, arms around her stomach as though having cramps. Edwin wanted to scratch his skin off; it had hit suddenly, urgently. He gritted his teeth and ignored it and felt the invisible threads twitch, sluggish, slower and ever slower, until Robin's heart gave one last pound and then—nothing.

Nothing.

"Charlie," Edwin said. "*Now.*"

Charlie laid his spell-glowing hands over the ink-copy and lifted.

Edwin had been braced for Robin to scream again, but instead Robin's body gave a silent jerky shudder that was even worse. There was a sobbing cry from Maud. Edwin didn't look at her. He looked at Robin's arm, where the black runes were—Edwin nearly sobbed himself, in sheer relief—fainter, and fainter again, washing away like chalk marks in rain.

Edwin forced himself to wait until there was no sign at all of the curse left. Then he took hold of the invisible threads and tugged.

He lived an entire lifetime in the gap between his signal—go, twitch, *live*—and the response. But respond it did.

After three full, normal beats, Robin shuddered again, and thrashed his way through an inhale like a man pulled from drowning. Maud made another sound. Robin's eyes opened.

"Hold still, Robin, *please*," Edwin heard himself babbling. He satisfied himself that Robin's heart was once again beating on its own, withdrew the threads of the spell, and let his hands fall into his lap. He felt as though he'd run up and down three flights of stairs. His thumbs were tingling; he'd held the necessary loop so tightly that he'd cut off the circulation.

Which was nothing at all compared to what he'd done to Robin.

Robin was coughing, looking around. "Did I—" he started, voice dry as leaves, and was cut off as Maud flung herself into his arms. Robin hugged her and Edwin swallowed a harsh, useless jolt of jealousy. Robin looked over her shoulder at Edwin, then Charlie, then Bel. Then Edwin again. "What happened?"

"Second time's the charm, it turns out." Charlie sounded as ebullient as ever. "Quite literally in this case."

The moment of realisation was another jerk. Robin withdrew his right arm in its ruined sleeve from where it was wrapped around Maud, and stared at it for a long time. The smile that broke onto his face was a painting of relief and joy.

"You tried again? And it worked?"

"Mr. Courcey did something to you to make it work," said Maud, unexpectedly. Edwin hadn't had any idea she'd followed the proceedings. He and Charlie hadn't exactly been explaining the steps. "It was frightening. You looked positively ghoulish. But," she went on, hesitant, "I suppose for you lot it was quite an everyday thing?"

Bel laughed. "Oh, by all means. We lift curses every second day."

Robin rubbed at his arm. It was a motion that by now

seemed part of the fabric of him. He said to Edwin, quietly, "How did you manage it?"

Charlie and Bel were still there. Maud was there. Edwin considered lying; and, as usual with Robin's gaze on him, was unable to do it.

"I killed you," he said. "Briefly."

"You did *what*?" said Maud.

Edwin said, "Slowed your heart," and held Robin's gaze until he saw the realisation there. "And then sped it up again, obviously. The curse thought you were dead. That was enough."

Robin squeezed Maud's hand. "Well, I'm not. I am ravenous, though. Go and finish dressing, Maudie, and I'll see you at breakfast."

"You're sure you're all right?"

"I've a devil of a headache," said Robin. "Otherwise, yes. I'm fine. I'm better than I've been all week."

Maud left. Now that the show was over, Bel and Charlie followed suit, though Bel shot curious glances over her shoulder at Edwin. She was looking at him with more interest than she had in years. It was discomfiting.

The library doors closed. Edwin and Robin sat in the window seat, not quite touching. Edwin had no idea what to say. He wanted to sit there for another week, staring at Robin safe and unmarked and free.

"You *killed* me?" said Robin finally.

"I—yes. I know. Oh, God. I'm going to have to write a paper about it. A *book*." Edwin could feel a hysterical, triumphant laugh trying to emerge. "I didn't know if it would work at all. But I couldn't think of anything else. You wouldn't wake up." He took a sobering breath. "You were just staring into nothing, Robin. And . . . it *was* the foresight, not the pain?"

A guilty expression washed Robin's face. He nodded.

Edwin tilted his head to the books on the table. "What were you trying to do?"

"Force it," Robin said. "Make it show me something useful, something that would give us more information about the last contract. Or the curse. Anything."

Edwin stared at him, aghast. "You ended up *comatose*."

"We weren't exactly swimming in leads. I wanted to try something more than leafing through books."

"That doesn't mean the answer was for you to go throwing your mind into a kind of magic you don't know anything about, without anyone's guidance. You might have—if—are you *completely stupid*?"

He bit his tongue, but it was out there now. Robin settled farther back. From a distance this arrangement, the two of them, probably looked cosy. There'd be no indication of the sudden drop in temperature.

"I know I'm not clever," Robin said. "But no, I'm not stupid."

Edwin's traitorous tongue was now a lump in his mouth, frozen in fear that he'd make things worse. He wanted Robin's smile to come back. He wanted to reach out in conciliation and touch. He wanted to be touched. It was unbearable.

Robin's eyebrows arched; there was just enough humour there that Edwin knew he was luckier than he deserved. "This is when you say, *I'm sorry, Robin*."

Edwin's intense contrariness suddenly wanted him to do nothing of the sort. He made himself say, "I *am* sorry."

Robin pushed himself to his feet. "And then I say, thank you, Edwin. Thank you for being brilliant and—saving my life, I expect." He leaned down slowly enough that Edwin could have evaded the kiss, if he'd wanted.

He didn't. Robin's lips were dry, peeling a little. It was quick and soft, no more than a gesture.

"Edwin," Robin said, husky. That voice was a whole conversation being cracked open like the top of an egg. It promised all sorts of things that Edwin wasn't equipped to hear. He had the ludicrous urge to ask Robin to write them down; to bind them up and give them to him on paper.

Edwin slid out from the seat and went over to the table, where he began to close the books that Robin had left open. "You're welcome," he said lightly. "Now, I need to get dressed for breakfast. And you should change your shirt. Belinda threw water on that one, and that's *before* I had to ruin the sleeve."

There was a pause that might have been Robin noticing the dampness for the first time.

"Good idea. I really am starving," Robin said, and there was a different promise in those words, full of heat and light. Edwin didn't allow himself to look up to meet it.

"Mm," he said, to the familiar leather covers of the books. He tidied a small stack of them. Edge to edge. "So am I."

There had been two separate instances in childhood when Robin had broken one of his arms. He only dimly remembered the pain of having the bones set and the limb wrapped in linen strips, soaked in plaster that hardened to a cast. What he remembered with startling clarity was the moment when the shudder of the surgeon's plaster-saw finally cracked the cast in half, and his arm emerged from it, limp and pale as that of a girl who'd spent her life under parasols.

The curse was gone. The knowledge felt like having a bone new-knitted beneath white flesh. Robin found himself still rubbing at the shirtsleeve with his thumb, wondering. He didn't care that a headache had buried itself behind both his eyes since he was wrenched awake in the library. For the moment, he didn't care that the Last Contract was still out there, and people would still kill for it. *No more pain.* No more fear that the next attack would be the last. A weight that had been dragging at him was gone. He wanted to shout and laugh and scull from Putney to Mortlake and back again.

Edwin caught up with him just outside the breakfast room. He was shut away inside his clothes, hair smoothed

back, looking far more composed and far less touchable than
he'd been in the library. Always, with Edwin, this drawing-
back. He drew close and lowered his voice. "I didn't ask—*can*
you remember any of what you saw? It went on a long time."

"It was all rather scrambled, after the beginning," Robin
said. "I'll jot down what I can after breakfast."

Once again Robin's curse and its dramatic removal were the
talk of the table. Charlie was explaining the ink-spell to Trudie
and Billy, while Miggsy made an elaborate show of floating the
coffeepot down the table to serve Belinda a fresh cup. Maud sat
apart, not talking to any of the magicians, pulling grapes from
a cluster and eating them one by one. She shot Robin a smile,
though, when he sat opposite her, and she eyed his overfull
plate with approval. Robin's hunger was no joke; he'd taken
huge servings of everything hot, and liked his chances of going
back for seconds. Maud poured him tea as he took the first
forkful of devilled kidneys, followed by another of bacon and
fried potatoes, heavily dusted with salt and pepper. He took
two more mouthfuls, barely bothering to chew, and regretted
it when the middle of his chest complained about the amount
he'd gulped down all at once.

Robin coughed and set down his cutlery. He was reaching for his tea when the smell hit: a wrong note in the morass
of savoury odours that filled the room. This was like petrol
fumes. Like damp stones.

No. It couldn't be what he thought. The food was well sea-
soned, and he'd eaten it too fast. He was seeing—light glittering off the silverware and the window, that was all.

It was done. It was *off*. It was—

An Indian woman, neatly dressed in shirtwaist and skirt
with a blue tie at her neck, seated behind a desk in an office. She
was arranging a pile of paper and speaking to someone, while
the typewriter on her desk flung its keys up and down without
a finger applied to it. She looked up and her face broke into
a smile. When she stopped speaking, the typewriter paused

too. Her face had the faintest echo of familiarity, as though she were a sketch copied many times over from a well-known original. She began to stand up.

"—bin? *Robin?*" It was Maud, voice high with panic.

The breakfast room swam back into focus. Everyone was staring at him.

"Yes. Sorry." Robin's heart was surging into a race. His gaze found Edwin, whose hand was tight around a forgotten muffin, horrified. Edwin had seen this happen far too many times to mistake it.

"*No,*" Edwin said, as though he could erase the last minute through sheer force of words.

Robin scrambled at his sleeve, yanking it up, not caring when he caught his cuff in the butter dish. The skin was still bare of marks. The curse hadn't managed to come crawling back. "How is that possible?" he demanded of Edwin. "The foresight and the curse, they're connected, you said—"

"*Foresight?*" said Belinda, and the word was echoed off-kilter by at least two others on the table. Every pair of eyes was already on Robin, but he felt the keenness of them redouble.

"I didn't say," Edwin said, very thin. "I hypothesised."

"*Mercy,*" said Trudie. "Just think, a foreseer, at one of our house parties!"

"No wonder you've been keeping him all to yourself, Win." Charlie sounded bluff, but there was an annoyed edge to it.

Edwin's face closed off entirely. He was still looking only at Robin. "It seemed logical that the foresight was part of the curse. I suppose it is possible that a latent gift was merely . . . uncovered . . . by your first contact with magic. Unpleasant though it was."

"Unbusheled," Robin said dumbly.

"That's *not* what—" Edwin snapped. "I—there's no precedent, I didn't know—"

"But you did know he had it," trilled Belinda. She waved her fork at her brother. "You've always been like this, you know.

Can't bear to share anything interesting. It's one of your least attractive qualities. Remember that time Mother found the hoard of stones in your bedroom after we'd been to the seaside? And that time you threw yourself on the floor and wailed because Father wouldn't let you keep that watch you'd put in your pocket when Grandpapa died? He was six," she told the table at large. "Thought he was going to *study* it."

Edwin was more porcelain than ever. Robin had the warring desires to defend him and for Edwin to have the guts to defend *himself*, for once.

"Makes sense," said Miggsy. "Been wondering why you decided this one was worth leaving with his memories after all. But if it's for *study*."

"Shut up," said Edwin. His lips were white.

"*Win*," said Belinda.

Robin had picked up his knife again. It took real effort to unclench his fingers and set it back down on the table. It was a surprise, and yet not a surprise. It wasn't just Maud who'd been intended for the lethe-mint. Everyone in this room, everyone in this house, down—he was quite sure—to Edwin's frail and charming mother, had assumed that as soon as Edwin took the curse off Robin, he'd be subjected to exactly the same thing.

"It's a game, you see," said Trudie. "One of us invites someone unmagical and we show them a good time. Show them everything they're missing, in their own world. And then at the end of it we give them lemonade and send them home. Let them think they've overindulged. It's less fun if the unbusheling's happened before they arrive, but . . ." She gave an elegant shrug, but her eyes were as they'd always been: pinned to Robin, cool and expectant. Trudie had been robbed of her fun, Robin realised, by Robin's own phlegmatic acceptance of magic and Maud's rescue from the mint. She was going to watch them react if she had to wield the prod herself, and revealing the game was now the easiest way to do it.

"Lemonade." Maud's voice was quiet and tight. It was how

she'd talked in company when their parents were alive, and it sent another skewer of anger through Robin's heart. "Oh. I see."

"I thought you protected guests," Robin found himself saying. "Blood-pledge, and all that. Doesn't seem to sit right with the idea of bringing people onto your precious land and then toying with them."

"There's no *harm* done," said Charlie, looking baffled. "They enjoy it."

"You're the first time Edwin's brought anyone," said Miggsy. He wasn't baffled. He had the air of someone who knew exactly how unpleasant this was turning, and was relishing it. "He'd not shown much interest in the game before. We were starting to hope the stick up his arse was unbending."

"All right," said Belinda. "There's no need to be vulgar."

"I didn't bring him for that," said Edwin. He didn't look up. "I told you. We needed the library. We needed to get the curse off."

"Yes, obviously." Billy hadn't spoken until now; he'd looked honestly stunned, when the word *foresight* had first been uttered. "But you were hardly going to send him home remembering the whole debacle afterwards, Edwin, surely."

Robin looked at Edwin. Edwin was looking at his plate, where the ruined muffin sat. The moment stretched.

Robin realised two things in close succession. The first was that Billy was correct: that Edwin had boarded that train in London, had invited Robin onto his family's land, with the full intention of wiping his mind clean of it later.

The second was that Robin had been starting to grow a modest garden of hope, in the last two days. Had been starting to cling to a vision that had nothing to do with foresight: that perhaps he could do what he'd never done before, and try to fit someone into his life. He knew some men of their sort did it, but he had never fathomed the appeal. And now he'd been prepared to try. He'd been looking *forward* to trying.

Edwin had been looking forward to . . . what? Taking his pleasure from Robin and then letting him forget it all?

Robin tried to settle his breath. All he could smell was meat and mushrooms and bloody pepper. He'd had enough.

"Maud. Fetch your things and meet me at the front of the house. We're leaving if I have to carry our bags to the station myself."

"You told me you'd take responsibility for these two, Edwin," said Belinda accusingly.

Of course. Of course he had.

"Don't *touch* her," Robin hissed. "I swear to God, I will throttle the first person to cast a single fucking spell on my sister."

The gasp of offended shock from Trudie was a fraction too showy to be real. Robin was sick to his stomach of this place, this beautiful house full of beautiful artworks and false, selfish people.

"I suppose consent's only needed between magicians," he said, direct to Edwin.

Edwin flung his head up. Robin waited for the objection, but it was only in Edwin's eyes, frozen and furious and desperate. Robin felt his anger tipping him towards saying something too personal for this table. There were some things, some hurts, that were still nobody else's business.

"Maud," Robin said.

Maud stood. "Yes. Yes, I'll get my things."

Robin threw his napkin onto his plate, where it began to soak up sauce from the kidneys, a thin, dark blooming.

Then he turned and left the room.

20

Edwin intended to go after Robin, he truly did. He was at the foot of the main staircase when his feet lost their nerve and delivered him to the library instead. Two days ago, cradling an inferno in bleeding hands without his string, he'd thought he might have a scrap of courage to him after all. He'd clearly been wrong. He was much better suited to hiding.

When Robin came in, dressed for travel and carrying his bags as though he refused to trust anything of his to even the servants of Edwin's family, Edwin was curled up in one of the armchairs trying to persuade himself he wasn't shaking. He looked up when Robin entered, and scrambled out of the chair. No matter what this was, fight or forgiveness or farewell, he wanted to be standing for it.

Edwin saw Robin want to give him distance. Then he saw the moment when Robin firmed his jaw and overcame it, and pushed his way into Edwin's space. It was so clearly an attack that Edwin didn't feel ashamed of stepping back.

"You were going to do that to me?" Robin demanded without preamble. "Make me forget?"

Not forgiveness, then.

"No," said Edwin. "I mean—I was, originally, yes. But I changed my mind."

"When? No. I don't want to know that." Robin took a breath. "You said lethe-mint had a time limit on how far back it would erase. What is it?"

Questions, Edwin could handle. Facts. "In its strongest

potency it can only cover ... perhaps a fortnight. It's imprecise, at that strength. There are other factors—"

"It's been nine days."

"Yes," Edwin snapped. "Yes, I still could, is that what you're angling for? I'm *not going to*."

When had he changed his mind? He couldn't point his finger at a single moment. He'd only known that he *had* changed it when the curse came off; when he had to face the size of his own relief. If the second lifting hadn't worked, if he'd killed Robin instead, a part of Edwin would have died, too, and Edwin had no idea what to do with that knowledge. It fell nowhere in the indexed catalogue of his experience.

"I'm not even going to begin with Belinda and the others and their bloody *game,* but I really thought you were different. How could you even consider it in the first place?"

Edwin said, deliberately, "How was your house party, Robin? Did you have a good time? Meet anyone new? In this charade I will be playing the role of your beloved younger sister, by the way. Are you going to lie to me?" He saw that hit home, and pressed his advantage. "There aren't many of us, Robin. We keep our secrets when we have to. It's how we stay safe, keep our world separate from—"

"From my world," said Robin. "I was a paperwork error, and then I wouldn't stay in my box. But no matter. I'm a *fascinating* freak, at least there's that."

"Do you want me to say I don't find you interesting?" Edwin threw back. "I'd be lying. That you're still having visions—of course it's interesting, I won't *apologise* for it."

Robin gave a short laugh. "I don't care. I think *you're* fascinating, I have since the snowflake." Somehow it sounded like an insult. "What I care about is that you brought me here with the intention of discarding me later. Like I was a stone in your shoe, to be removed with all haste. And then I turned out to be a rare kind of stone, worth studying further, worth keeping where you could see it and—stroke it from time to time. Consider its *uses*."

The comment about stone-collecting was salt on the cut of childhood that Bel had reopened with her mockery at breakfast, and Edwin realised—finally, too late—the particular cut of Robin's that had been exposed in turn. It was, after all, how the Blyths had seen their firstborn son. A collection of pieces to be used.

"It's not," Edwin said, thin with desperation. "I don't—Robin, that's not—the foresight isn't all it is. I promise."

"Really? You don't even want me to try and use it without your supervision, and you certainly can't be there every time it happens. I suppose I should stop trying to seize control over my own *mind*, and just let it keep interrupting me at any moment. Just write everything down and send the notes to your precious Assembly? Even if they're about things like—" Robin waved a hand between them, colour in his cheeks.

A chill went through Edwin. "You—you saw that? When? Before we—" The chill doubled. "Is that *why* you . . ." He couldn't finish the sentence.

"No!" said Robin. "Do you think I would just—accept something like that? Go blindly along?"

"Don't you?" Edwin heard himself say. "Go along with things?"

"I certainly went along with it when you kissed me. Another use I could be to you—fucking Gatling's replacement because you couldn't have him."

Some of the blood left Edwin's face; he felt it go, like the stroke of cold hands down his cheeks. "*What.*"

Robin's face was already changing. He rubbed at it with both hands, and when they dropped he looked rueful. "I—no, that wasn't at all fair. I'm sorry. I didn't mean that. It's just . . ." He sighed. "I should go. It'll be for the best. I'm taking Maud, and we'll go."

"Take the motorcar," Edwin said. "Leave it at the station. We'll send someone for it. Or not."

"I'm not going to tell your secrets to anyone, you know," Robin said. "And Maudie won't either, not if I ask her to promise me. I'll put in for a transfer out of the office, like I originally planned to. Whoever's after the contract should have realised by now that I haven't any idea what Gatling did with it. I'll vanish back into my old life and actually look after my family, instead of running away."

"I don't know if you'll be able to vanish that easily," Edwin said. "As far as we can tell, you're still a foreseer. And now the cat's out of the bag in that regard."

He tried to imagine what it would have been like if they had taken Robin's memory, and Robin had kept on having the visions anyway. He'd have thought he was going mad.

"Still a fascinating object," Robin said, resigned.

"I'm saying my world might find you again, regardless."

"Then I'll deal with it."

Edwin wanted to snap at him, to demand that Robin accept his help, that Robin—*go along with it*. Come and be studied. Come and be stroked. Edwin set his jaw and managed to erect his usual coldness. "You're right. It is for the best."

Robin reached out a hand to Edwin's arm, but Edwin was raw with the effort of holding himself calm. He didn't think, he just flinched away.

"*Don't.* Don't touch me. Please."

There was a long, long pause. All the tension that had begun to ebb came rushing back again, as though the room were a cradler's string in hands suddenly yanked apart. A lump of misery bobbed into Edwin's throat.

"Exactly what you want," Robin said, as though solving a riddle. "But not what you *want* to want?"

It was just true enough that Edwin didn't know how to explain the ways in which it was false. Robin looked . . . sad. Not even angry. Edwin wanted to build a spell that would dissolve everything, take it down to atoms and essential forces, so he wouldn't have to look at that expression anymore.

Robin asked, "Do you even like me at all?"

"Y—yes. *Yes.*"

He almost didn't get it out past the sudden echo of memory. He and Hawthorn had bickered, but they'd had very few real fights. Edwin wanted any conflict to end as soon as possible; Jack seemed to want to live in a house built of low-grade needling and casual mockery. They *had* fought at the end, short and sharp like a fist to the ribs. It had nothing to do with wanting to stay. They both knew how unsuited they were, beyond the fact that Edwin had little enough power that Jack could pretend to have escaped the magical world entirely, and Jack was trustworthy in his own abrasive way, and sometimes would look at Edwin almost as though he were handsome, and sometimes would insult Edwin's siblings with breathtaking, gleeful carelessness.

Even so, pulling apart had been like extricating one's clothes from a blackberry bush. Edwin had been off-balance with hurt. He'd said those words, or some very like them. *Do you even like me at all?*

Jack had laughed that cruel laugh of his. *If I ever did, I can't remember why.* And he'd said other things too. He had a devastating eye for weakness, Jack Alston did, and during their ill-advised months together Edwin had come undone under his capable hands and shown him nearly everything there was to see.

Robin was nothing like that. Robin was kind and Robin loved fiercely, but Robin, too, had already seen too much of Edwin. Edwin *couldn't* rip off the last layer. That was all there was left of him. There'd be nothing left but blood.

He said, again, "Yes." It was the very least he owed to Robin, and all he could afford to give.

Robin gave a shaky laugh. "Well, you've an odd way of showing it. Do you have any idea how ghastly I felt, sitting there at the breakfast table with you making me feel like—like a study specimen? Like all these books, I suppose." He gave a twitch of his hand. "A way for you to compensate."

Edwin couldn't call that a lie; couldn't even call it unfair. It wasn't.

"And do you know the worst of it?" Robin went on, inexorable. "I almost want you too much to care. I told myself I wouldn't be anyone else's to be used, and yet here I am, hovering at your side like some damn—" He broke off, staring right at Edwin as though trying to translate the runes of Edwin's face into plain English.

"Robin," said Edwin.

Robin said, very quiet, "Tell me to stay, stay for *you*, and I will."

Edwin wanted to say it, wanted it more than anything, but for the fact that Robin would so clearly have despised the both of them for it in the end. How could a future be built on that? What was Edwin going to do—bind Robin's hands with a Goblin's Bridle? Even with or without all the magic in the world, you couldn't charm a person to stay. Not for long. Not truly. Not and keep yourself safe.

And there was nothing at all safe about Robin. Edwin wanted to take his clothes off and beg to be touched, and held, and whispered to. He might as well have handed Robin a knife and tilted back his throat.

That would be no sort of future at all: Robin always doubting, and Edwin always afraid. Their bodies could fit against one another like lock into key, they could throw themselves daily into impossible pleasure, and still it would be a house with foundations of mist.

So Edwin, again, said nothing.

"Right," said Robin, "that's what I thought," and picked up his bags and left.

21

Len Geiger had already asked twice if there was anything he could help Edwin find, which was a new record. Asking once was generally a polite hint that he was hoping to close the bookshop and get home to his family. Asking twice, when it was barely past noon, might have meant that he was afraid for Edwin's health or sanity.

There was nothing wrong with Edwin's health. The scratches were healing, and he'd dropped by Whistlethropp's shop that morning and picked up a lotion to hasten the process. Similarly, his mind was working as well as it ever had. And that was that. Body and mind: perfectly hale. There was nothing else about him, no other component to feel bruised beyond easy repair, and so rationality dictated that he could not feel that way.

Edwin sighed and closed the book he'd been leafing through without seeing the words. He added it to the pile he'd been amassing: everything he could find that referred to casting spells on living plants, a few entirely unmagical titles on horticulture—the part of Geiger's shop not located behind the mirror made up the bulk of the man's sales, after all—and a few others that had shown up in the bibliography of the Kinoshita translation. It made quite a pile. Edwin arranged for them to be sent to Sutton Cottage; part of him itched to begin reading immediately, but he'd already sent a message promising to return to Sutton the following week and sit down properly with the senior house staff and groundskeepers. It looked as though he was going to be spending a lot more time in the country.

It was Thursday. Edwin had returned to London the previous day, leaving shortly after Robin and Maud. There'd
seemed no reason to stay. Being alone with Bel's friends had
been abruptly as unbearable as it usually was; there was nobody to insulate him from them at the dining table, and nobody to come and find him, to coax conversation and smiles
from him, if he decided to spend all his time in the library.

It didn't take long to become so accustomed to something
that you could describe the exact shape of its absence.

From the bookshop, Edwin walked to Whitehall with his
attention on the small sensations of the city, which he'd missed.
The presence of real noise, human and mechanical. The constant movement. Glass and metal and stone, and splashes of
nature kept within gardens and parks, and the turning colours
of the trees in their framing rows. The air had the thick clam-
miness that signalled fog would climb the streets from the river
that night.

The external typist's room in the Office of Special Domestic
Affairs and Complaints was empty. A rustling noise punctuated by singing, in no language Edwin knew, came from behind the door standing narrowly ajar.

The singing halted and Miss Morrissey looked up as Edwin pushed the door open. She nearly stood, too, but rose only
a few inches before recognising her visitor and sinking back
down.

"Mr. Courcey." She'd drawn a second chair around to the
business side of Robin's desk, nudging the larger one off-
centre. The piles of papers looked rather more organised than
previously. She had a pen in her hand.

"Good—afternoon, Miss Morrissey."

"Sir Robert isn't here."

"I know."

Only when he said it did he realise he'd been hoping otherwise. He'd followed his usual routine, telling himself he *was*
still the Assembly liaison, after all. He'd ducked into the Barrel

that morning to pick up the thin sheaf of notes that had been accumulating in his personal pigeonhole. And here he was, doing his job, draping himself in the normality of it like a cloak and hiding his irrational hope beneath.

Miss Morrissey pulled out a drawer and retrieved yet another piece of paper, which she pushed towards him. Edwin took the seat opposite, where he'd sat not even two weeks previous, when he'd been full of irritation at Reggie's replacement. It felt as though every cell in his body had replaced itself over that span of days, silent and individually unnoticed, forming something the exact shape as the old Edwin that nonetheless resonated at a different frequency.

The piece of paper was Robin's letter of resignation. It was brief, polite, and uninformative. *Regret to inform. Unsuited to the requirements of the position. Cognisant of the honour of being appointed in the first place.*

Cognisant? Edwin mouthed, halfway to forming some kind of tease about Robin of all people using a word like that, but he had nobody to speak it to.

Robin had addressed the letter to the office itself because, Edwin assumed, he didn't want it landing in front of the Healsmith fellow who'd shoved him mistakenly into the post in the first place.

"He attached a note explaining that you'd removed the curse, and asking me to make sure the right person saw the letter," said Miss Morrissey.

A stilted pause. Edwin looked up.

She added, "You knew he was going to resign?" It was a question like those asked by tutors who knew they'd found the holes in your argument and were advancing with fingers ready to be shoved through the fabric of it.

"Yes," Edwin said. The pain of that final parting in the library landed on the impossible bruise of him, and he endured it.

"Hm. At least he remembered that I exist. I wasn't sure if I'd get a letter at all, or merely another new face in the office one morning. Or you, coming in to tell me not to react if I ever encountered him on the street."

There were a host of new probing questions buried in that. Edwin ignored them and pointed an accusing finger.

"You sent his *sister* to my *family*," he said.

The corner of Miss Morrissey's mouth rose. "I was tempted to tag along myself, simply to watch the theatre of it, but someone had to stay here and get the actual work done. The letters do pile up, even the crackpot ones. And you owe me *your* report, Mr. Courcey. One can't be a liaison all on one's own."

Edwin looked back at Robin's letter. The significance of its presence struck him. "You haven't lodged this with Secretary Lorne."

"The Secretary is still on leave."

Another pause. This one was punctuated by the rapid, nervy tap of Miss Morrissey's silver ring against the inlaid leather of the desk.

"I owe *you* my report? I suppose we're calling that the chair of plausible deniability," said Edwin, nodding at the empty chair next to hers.

Miss Morrissey's cheeks darkened a slight amount. "Do you think Prime Minister Asquith will notice I'm not an Oxford-educated baronet, if I wander in next Wednesday and give him the briefing?"

"Cambridge," said Edwin. "I've no idea, I've not met the man."

"Perhaps I can pretend I'm Sir Robert under a spell," said Miss Morrissey. "It's not as though he'd be able to prove otherwise. And I can *do* this job, Mr. Courcey. I can do it very well."

"I've no doubt," said Edwin, and he hadn't. She'd been doing it for months. He dug in his leather document bag and pulled out the pile of notes from the Barrel. "Here. Collate away. And show me what you have."

Miss Morrissey smiled and handed him a few handwritten sheets, neatly arranged under headings. Edwin settled in and read about the usual cluster of novelties, hysterias, and possible brewing troubles. The office combed the newspapers but also had sources in a handful of newsrooms and tabloids, and there was no report that the excitable daughter of a baronet had approached anyone to try and sell the story of her brief sojourn in a manor house full of magicians. Not that Edwin had expected it. If Robin said Maud was to be trusted, then Edwin would trust her.

Miss Morrissey waved her pen in front of Edwin's eyes. He'd been sitting sideways in the chair, staring at one of the filing cabinets, thinking.

"Hmm?"

"So are you going to tell me what it was all about?" she asked. "The curse? The men who attacked Sir Robert?"

Edwin turned the word *trust* in his mind a few times more. Half of him wanted to keep everything contained and secret, but he'd developed an unfamiliar liking for having an ally. He'd spent his lifetime feeling worthless around other magicians, and yet unable to separate himself from magic in the way that Hawthorn had. It had left him walking a sort of ditch between road and field, brushing each side of the world, quite desperately alone, waiting for a better future while taking no steps to find one. He'd thought he was content with it.

He wondered for the first time what Adelaide Morrissey felt, the nature of the ditch that she walked in, having grown up surrounded by magic and passed her awakening-age without manifesting even the smallest drop of it. In Reggie this lack had manifested as a buoyant, curious hunger. In this woman— well, Edwin had no idea.

He touched the pocket where his string lay. *Take a risk. Just try.*

"Fetch us a pot of tea," he suggested. "It's a long story."

Even without the parts that Edwin kept to himself, tucked away in his palm like the tingling press of lips, it took them the entire pot and a plate of currant-studded biscuits to get through it. Miss Morrissey's eyes widened and widened. She was restless by the end, taking her final biscuit on a wander about the room, holding it crumb-dropping between her teeth as she poked through the bookshelves. Edwin thought it was an aimless expression of anxiety until he finished—with a much-edited version of Robin and Maud's exit, lingering on the positive fact of the curse's absence—and Miss Morrissey immediately said, "These people came *here*. They searched the office."

Edwin wrenched his mind back around. "The day after they laid the curse on Robin? Yes."

"For one reason or another, they think Reggie hid the contract—part of the contract—here. It's why they thought Sir Robert would be able to find it."

Edwin nodded and stood as well. The puzzle had its claws in him again, and it wasn't just curiosity that made him want to keep picking at this despite the risks. The ember of his anger had never been extinguished. Walking *towards* danger was wildly unlike him, but perhaps he could pretend that Robin had passed on some of his courage like a talisman.

"Cup, knife, and coin," Edwin said. "If we're to believe the old story, which frankly I'm not sure we should. The hiding place in the statue was small. You couldn't keep anything there larger than a fist."

Miss Morrissey paused opening a box of newspapers. "Would it be dangerous to touch? Whatever it is?"

"Perhaps to non-magicians? No, Reggie carried it away with him. Let's assume not." A thought. "Could he have been carrying it with him? When he was—when he died?"

She blanched and twisted her ring, uncomfortable. "I don't know. You could ask the Coopers."

"No, that doesn't work either. If the people looking for the contract killed him for being secret-bound, they'd surely have searched him afterwards." Edwin shuddered, reminded of the casual force with which the fog-masked man had shoved him into the maze. He thought, uneasily, of Robin, who was just as vulnerable to magic as he'd ever been.

For lack of anything else to do, they took the office apart. Again.

They turned up no knives whatsoever, though did unearth a dusty penny coin tucked between wainscoting and floorboards. Miss Morrissey balanced it dubiously on her palm before handing it to Edwin, who slipped it into the pocket of his waistcoat just in case. He remembered Mrs. Sutton saying, *He left with it in his pocket.*

"It's *very* well disguised, if that's it," said Miss Morrissey.

There were also plenty of cups, though they were porcelain and painted with primroses, and Miss Morrissey swore all five of them had been untidily stacked in the cupboard from the day she started work there two years ago. Edwin inspected them anyway, then handed them back and watched her re-stack them. The bright silver ring on her index finger was not quite regular, he noticed when she took the last cup from him. There was a triangular notch in it, deep and neat enough to be due to design rather than misadventure.

Edwin had seen that ring before.

He picked up her hand to look at it and only realised the rudeness of this when she sucked in her breath. He dropped it at once.

"My apologies," he said. "That ring of yours. Where is it from?"

"My ring?" She tugged it off. "It's not a token from a sweetheart, or anything like that. It was a birthday gift last month, from"—her hand fumbled, holding it out—"Reggie. Only a few weeks late, but you know how he was with remembering dates. Half the time it was a miracle that he had the briefing ready on Wednesdays." A tremble of excitement entered her voice as Edwin took the ring from her. "Do you think it's important? It's not—any of those three things."

Reggie *was* bad with dates, and with keeping time in general.

And just like that Edwin, rubbing with his finger at the ring's notch, remembered where he'd seen its twin. Hanging on the inner wall of the Gatlings' oak-heart clock, which had started going wrong a month ago, as if the oak-heart was running low.

Or if something had disrupted the delicate balance of its magical mechanism.

Edwin's pulse knocked at the groove of his throat. Cup, coin, knife—that was just a story for children, after all, and this was a coincidence too strong to ignore. Reggie Gatling, who had stumbled upon a secret that people would kill for, and who had been one step ahead of those people right up until the moment he wasn't, had passed on two silver rings. One of them hidden away in his family's house; the other hidden in plain sight, right here at the office, exactly where the contract's seekers expected to find it.

Not much could pass a secret-bind. A jumbled clue to location might have been all an interrogator could wrangle before—well. Before. Edwin's skin crawled and he set the ring on the desk, then proceeded to cast every detection-spell that he could think of before his magic whimpered down to the dregs. Nothing. Magically, the ring seemed inert.

An object of power has a weight to it. Edwin thought of Mrs. Sutton's fern-fossil and wanted to growl in frustration at his own ignorance. All he wanted was to know things, when and how he needed to know them. Right now he was failing at that.

Nonetheless, he explained his suspicions to Miss Morrissey, who looked on the verge of donning her hat and coat to come charging the Gatlings' fortress with him. Edwin only managed to persuade her to stay by convincing her that he'd be much better trying to retrieve the second ring by stealth, given he had the excuse of having handled the clock before. Besides, Reginald Gatling's well-spoken Indian typist from the Home Office would be a memorable visitor. Edwin was already in this up to his neck. Nobody had thought Miss Morrissey worth investigating yet; there was no need to drag her into the spotlight now.

Miss Morrissey glared her disdain for Edwin's attempts to shield her from danger, but he repeated the words *curse* and *murder* until she agreed to let him go alone, albeit making him swear up and down that as soon as he had the second ring in hand he'd come back to the office and show her.

It was midafternoon by then, the shadows long and the world clammier than ever. Edwin burrowed into his muffler as he stood on the Gatlings' doorstep. He asked if Miss Anne was at home and was given a disapproving "The family is in *mourning, sir.*"

Edwin hadn't even thought of that. If he knew Anne and Dora Gatling at all, they'd be chafing under the restrictions. The traditions around mourning dress and behaviour had been easing off, in Edwin's lifetime, but there were still plenty of people who would whisper if the family of a recently deceased man continued to pay morning calls in bright colours. Plenty of people who would have been aghast to hear that Maud Blyth had taken herself off to a house party wearing her crepe, too, even if they knew about the Blyth children and their need to kick back against their parents' obsession with reputation.

"Of course," Edwin said. "Would you let Miss Anne know that Mr. Edwin Courcey is here to offer his condolences?" How on Earth *had* he managed to exist without calling cards before now?

By not bothering to have any social acquaintances, he reminded himself.

The butler carried the message and Edwin stood in the entrance hall wondering if any of the clocks in this house—oakhearted or otherwise—had stopped at the moment of Reggie's death. He suspected not; this was a modern townhouse, lacking in history, and Reggie had met his end elsewhere. Or so one assumed.

"I'm sorry for your loss," he said when he sat down with Anne Gatling.

Anne nodded. She looked tired and stiff. She looked like a doll enchanted to do those exact things in response to those exact words: to sit, to nod, to say thank you.

"Have you heard anything about the circumstances surrounding his death?"

Anne looked at her hands. Edwin wished for half of Robin's compassion and ease. Surely he could have made that sound less intrusive.

"Pulled out of the river," she said. "The Coopers visited with Mama again yesterday, but all they know is that it was probably magic that killed him."

"I'm sorry," said Edwin again.

She gave herself a small shake. "Dashed inconvenient; we've had to put the wedding back, of course. Saul's been a brick. Such a help to Mama."

"I meant to ask about Saul and that clock of yours. Did he get it working again?"

"The—oh, yes, he did," said Anne. "He followed the instructions that you left, to pour magic into the mechanism, and for a few days it worked as well as it ever did." She made a small face. "And then it went odd again. Saul said it couldn't have been the power, in that case."

Edwin folded his fingers under themselves as they tried to twitch. He was so close. He didn't know whether the second ring was draining the clock's heart, somehow, or simply throwing it all out of balance, but with any luck he'd be able to study it and find out.

"Is it wrapped in blankets in the linen cupboard, then?"

"No, we sent it to the thaumhorologist. We won't see it for weeks, and it'll cost a pretty penny, but it's the last step before Dora loses patience and guts it to use as a jewellery-box."

Edwin thought quickly. "I've had another thought about what could be wrong," he said, which was absolutely true. "I'd be happy to try and fix it. If not, of course I'd leave it in the specialist's hands."

Anne shrugged. "If you like."

"Do you have a receipt of exchange from the shop . . . ?"

The receipt, when found, was folded around a flat piece of white stone that was charmed to have the same function as the token one received when handing over one's hat and umbrella at a theatre cloakroom. At least the receipt was normal ink on paper, printed with the shop's address and with the Gatlings' name filled in beneath. Edwin slipped it into his pocket.

The thaumhorologist's shop was near Southwark Cathedral. Tense as Edwin was with the nearness of discovery, he didn't fancy making his way that far east only to find the place closed, as it likely would be. He made his way to his own hotel instead, and spent an uneasy night drifting in and out of sleep, restless and aching and thinking about Robin.

Robin, who deserved to *know*, if Edwin found part of the Last Contract. It was Robin's mystery too.

No—Edwin was making excuses. Robin didn't want anything else to do with Edwin and Edwin's world, and he couldn't be blamed for that.

The next morning heralded a grey drip of a day, with a faint fog curling through Mayfair. It was even denser and colder in the streets winding south from London Bridge, and Edwin plunged his hands deep into his coat pockets as much for the warmth as to touch the ring there, turn it with his fingertips.

His destination was easy to spot, even in the narrow street with the fog pierced dully by the illumination of streetlights not yet stifled. The window of the shop was busy with clocks, and Edwin could hear an off-kilter ticking like the mutter of a thousand insects, even before he pushed open the front door and the sound was swallowed by the tinkling of the entrance bell.

The woman behind the counter was peering down into the bowels of a pocket watch spread out on black velvet. She removed her magnifying eyepiece and set her work aside as Edwin shook off his outer layers.

"How can I help you, sir?"

Edwin brandished receipt and stone, and the woman took both. Somewhat awkwardly given that he was asking to take back some of the shop's custom, he explained that he wasn't there to pick up a finished order, but rather to retrieve something he'd offered to fix himself.

"Are you a thaumhorologist?" the woman asked with a hint of sourness.

"Are you?" Her fingers had been steady on the cogs, but the name printed on the receipt had been Joseph Carroll.

"I'm Hettie Carroll. My father's teaching me the trade. Hold tight, I'll fetch it. We're backlogged by a few weeks, he won't have touched it yet. Standing clock, you said?"

He nodded. "Making odd noises at odd times."

Miss Carroll gave him a knowing look, and took the stone with her up a winding metal staircase in the corner, leaving Edwin standing in the small shop full of . . . things making odd noises at odd times. She returned with the clock wrapped in a fold of cloth and placed it on the counter. Her eyebrows raised when Edwin uncovered the clock immediately and removed the back panel as he'd done at the Gatlings' house. Miss Carroll cradled a small light charm, illuminating the contents of the clock for both of them to see better.

It was there. Hanging on the inner wall of the clock, along with the other seemingly random objects. Edwin removed the oak-heart from its bracket first, so that he had better access. The piece of wood was perfectly round and uncannily smooth and showed a desire to roll right off the counter, so he put it in his pocket for safekeeping. Then, with infinite care, he lifted the silver ring from its small hook. He pulled the first ring from his pocket and laid them both side by side on the runner of cloth that covered the counter. Identical. Silver rings— slim, flat things, both with that triangular notch. They looked modern and plain and uninteresting, and not in the least like objects of power that deserved to be hidden from murderers at the centre of a labyrinth.

A tinkle of bells behind him signalled another customer entering the shop. Edwin didn't look around until there was the sensation of someone standing at his elbow.

"Yes, sir?" said Miss Carroll.

Edwin glanced up, then straightened entirely when he recognised the man next to him, who was smiling with affability and the same faint surprise that Edwin was feeling himself.

"Hullo, Byatt," Edwin said. The informality of first names belonged to Penhallick alone.

Billy kept smiling his easy smile. "Hullo, Courcey. Excuse me a moment, won't you?"

And it didn't take more than a moment. He reached out and lifted Edwin's arm by the sleeve, slipped something over his hand, and pulled it tight.

Every part of Edwin's body except his eyes stopped listening to the commands of his nerves. He looked down at his own hand, motionless on the polished shop counter, and the glow of the bridle where it sat snug against his cuff. He felt as though he'd been plunged into a body of water, chilled and nearly dizzy with the suddenness of his fright. He really hadn't given Robin's courage enough credit; this was far more terrifying than Flora Sutton's hedge maze, because at least then he'd been able to move. Fight back.

The smile on Billy Byatt's face had turned faintly apologetic when Edwin looked back up at him.

"I *told* them you'd do all the work for us, if we gave you your head," he said. "You bookish types never do give up on a good puzzle, do you?"

22

"Your head's elsewhere today, old chap," said Fenchurch, lowering his gloves.

He was right. Only half of it was the fact that Robin had been dreading, all through their bout, the pepper-taste and odd smells that would herald the foresight; he'd already tapped out after some dancing lights that were, in the end, only the normal response to having someone else's padded fist land firmly on the side of one's head.

The other half of Robin's distraction was everything he was refusing to let himself think about, starting with the way his skin prickled when he walked the streets alone and ending with the memory of Edwin biting down on his shoulder.

"It is," Robin apologised. "I've a meeting to engage a new steward in an hour, and I'm readying myself to have coals heaped on my head."

Fenchurch landed a commiserating blow on Robin's upper arm. "Will we see you at the club for dinner? Bromley's an inch away from announcing his engagement to the ravishing Miss Gerwich, and we've promised to take him carousing."

Robin laughed. "You'll have to carouse without me, I'm afraid. Family dinner."

"Next you'll be telling us you met someone at whatever shooting party or what-have-you swallowed you up last week."

Robin didn't manage to stop himself from blushing, but did manage to cover it with a lascivious enough wink that Fenchurch would take it in jest. He sponged off and changed and reflected grimly that meeting with Milton, the old—and hopefully new—steward of the Blyth country estate of Thornley Hill, was at least going to be more pleasant than meeting with Lord Healsmith and grovelling for a new position. Robin hadn't gathered the nerve to contact Healsmith yet. Perhaps the man would decide that the Blyths' son had been humiliated enough. If not, God only knew what else he'd have up his sleeve now that Robin had turned down the most obscure-sounding assistant position in the Home Office. Dust-paper man, perhaps.

Robin met with Milton in his study at home. The man was middle-aged and gravel-voiced and all shades of brown and green, like a tree uneasily transplanted into the city. The late Sir Robert had dismissed Milton in favour of a steward less prone to shouting about agricultural mismanagement and the poor conditions of the tenants—a steward who would cheerfully squeeze every last pennyworth of profit from the lands and send it on to the coffers of London's philanthropic darlings, where it would be spent on parties and dazzle and whatever noble cause would allow the Blyths to convert it to the currency they truly cared for. Praise.

Robin had, in turn, let this man know that his services were no longer required, and contacted Milton in order to do his first stint of grovelling. Thankfully not much was needed. It took ten minutes of suspicious squinting for Milton to decide that the new Sir Robert was cut from different cloth than the old one, and a further five minutes for him to clearly decide that while Robin was an idiot on matters of estate management, he was at least a benign one, and willing to be led by experts.

"Can we turn it around?" Robin asked, once Milton had shuffled through the records and accounts.

Yes, was the short answer. The long answer was that Robin could have a very slow turnaround of the estate's income-generating potential, or he could take out another loan in order to throw some money at the problem, and thereby have a faster and riskier one. A slow musing on the mathematical pros and cons of these options got a headache going like bells in Robin's temples, and all the fidgety energy he'd managed to expend in the boxing ring began to gather again.

When Milton left, Robin rang for a pot of tea—he needed something to revive him before lunch—then collapsed in his armchair and felt sorry for himself. He wished Edwin were here. He wished Edwin would rap his knuckles on the door and not wait to be asked inside, but lean against the desk and sort out all of Robin's problems in his cool, exact, intelligent voice.

No. That was one of the things he Wasn't Thinking About. Robin was arranging his future like a man sorting out three generations' worth of junk from an attic; he didn't need to clear a space within it for someone who was willing to lie to him and use him. Someone who, even after all the two of them had been through, couldn't dredge up the courage to admit that they might be allowed to matter to each other, and to show it.

Tell me to stay.

Robin had never said anything like that to a man. And Edwin had said *nothing* in return. All the warmth of him that Robin now knew existed had stayed buried beneath the ice, as though Robin weren't worth cracking for.

Robin exhaled in a sigh and gazed at the framed sketch on the study wall: sweeping black ink on paper, Thornley Hill seen from a nearby peak, done as a gift to the Blyths from one of the artists caught gratefully in their coattails as they ascended the charity scene.

The foresight, for once, might have been waiting in the wings for a convenient time. Robin closed his eyes as the awareness settled in, and was practically comfortable when it hit.

Outdoors. A day with the soft brightness of real heat, the sky baked a dark blue, and a picnic rug laid out in front of a rose garden. Books splashed across the rug as though a stack of them had been kicked over. Edwin and a young blond woman were balancing one of the books across both of their knees as they sat companionably close and cross-legged. For a long time there was nothing more exciting than the fingers of the breeze in the ends of their hair, and the occasional turn of a page. The woman was following the text with her finger, frowning, when Edwin leaned back on his hands and craned up to exchange words with—Lord Hawthorn, the sun finding pieces of ruddy colour in his dark hair, brandishing an apple in his hand. He took a bite from it and kept talking down at Edwin with his mouth half-full, then glanced up—Edwin did as well—as though listening to a comment by someone unseen.

Movement at the sides of the vision. Robin remembered what he'd almost managed once before, and strained to swing the frame of the vision. More movement—birds cutting across the sky—and Robin saw the outlines of two more figures for only an instant, like a photograph poorly taken, before the vision collapsed.

He'd held it for longer than usual. It had felt like the difference between the season's first morning on the river and the morning before race week: an expansion of the lungs, a feeling of sturdiness to the arms, the result of hard training.

Robin opened his eyes to the curl of steam rising from a golden arc of pouring tea. Maud, perched on the ottoman and busy with the tea tray, mixed in Robin's sugar and milk and handed him the cup.

"Ellen said you were asleep when she came in with the tray," said Maud. "Were you asleep?"

"No," said Robin.

She clasped her hands together on her knees. Excitement and worry were warring for control of her expression. "What did you see?"

Robin told her; there seemed no reason not to. "That blond woman," he added. "I've seen her a few times now."

Maud smiled. "Is she pretty?"

"She is," said Robin. He reached out and poked Maud's

sudden dimple with one finger. "Don't you get any ideas. She may not have anything to do with me. I'm seeing the futures of people I've been—spending time with. That's probably how it works. Give it another month and I'm sure I'll start seeing you tossing your cap on the lawns of Newnham."

Maud's dimple danced, but to Robin's surprise this wasn't enough to divert her down the lane of planning her academic career. "Are you really planning to give it all up, Robin? Pretend it didn't happen? It's *magic*."

Lord Hawthorn sidled into Robin's mind. Not the relaxed, unreal version of him from the vision, but the version that Robin had met: even more full of sharp edges than Edwin, renouncing with drawling cruelty the world he'd been born into and which had taken both his sister and his own magic from him. *I'm done with all of that.*

"Ask me again next week," Robin said. "Maudie, how would you feel if we moved into a smaller house?"

Maud adjusted the angle of her teacup handle. "And sold this place?"

Robin nodded.

"It's been in the family a long time," she said, but didn't sound disapproving.

"It's old," Robin agreed. "Which means it's going to need more repairs, and tradesmen are going to charge more to do them. And it's far too large. We've got more servants than we need, keeping up rooms we're never going to use."

"Oh, goodness." Maud, the sole mistress of the house, sat up straighter. "I'm going to have to dismiss people, aren't I? I hate the idea. Most of them have been with us for years."

"It can't be helped. We're not rich enough to be universally adored," Robin said. "We *can't* be philanthropists to that extent."

"No, I know," said Maud. "I'd far rather be known as the most selfish girl in London than have society start expecting us to behave like *them*."

Robin beckoned her closer and dropped a kiss in her hair, grateful for how quickly she'd come on board. "You're not that selfish, Maudie."

"I could break another vase in the new place, to christen it. Like Champagne."

"That's for ships."

Maud giggled and retrieved her tea, and the conversation moved on to where in London they should start the hunt for a smaller house.

After lunch Maud left for a nebulous social event with her friend Lizzie Sinclair. The chaperonage of Lizzie's thoroughly bluestockinged mother meant that the event was likely to be a suffragette meeting or something of that nature, but Robin knew that any expression of concern on his behalf would only push Maud to further heights. Instead of coming home talking excitedly about the rights of women and workers, she'd end up chaining herself to something.

Robin had another meeting. This one was with Martin Gunning; the man of business looked unflatteringly surprised that Robin had sought him out, instead of once again postponing. *Hiding.* Robin made himself pay attention to the numbers, floated the house-selling idea and was rewarded with a slow nod from Gunning, and emerged from the meeting feeling flattened. His head was aching again. Probably there was an imbued tea that would be able to fix that.

A smile dragged at the corners of Robin's mouth as he remembered Edwin sipping tea and expressing his surprise that Robin hadn't hit him across the face and stormed back to London. Always, with Edwin, that surprise. The wariness. The vivid expectation of abandonment; the bone-deep resignation to the fact that he would lose the things he wanted, or else never deserved them in the first place.

"Oh, bloody sodding hell," Robin muttered, and went to find his coat.

Maud was right. He didn't *want* to give it all up. He wanted to be fascinated. Perhaps he and Edwin Courcey could never be anything more than uneasy curios to each other, but Edwin was still the member of the magical world that Robin trusted the most, and in the space of two weeks Robin had tumbled into something that he wasn't prepared to give up without a fight. And he was good at fighting.

He'd drag an apology out of Edwin and then . . . then he'd insist that they start over. Try again. No more lies.

He glanced at his watch. Four o'clock. If he hurried, he'd be able to make it to the Home Office; Miss Morrissey was his only lead. She knew everything. He'd have laid down a month's income that she knew Edwin's address. Robin informed a footman that he was going out, donned coat and gloves, adjusted the angle of his hat like a medieval knight perfecting the tilt of his visor before a chivalric quest, and walked out the front door.

Adelaide Morrissey was down on the street, gathering her skirts to climb the steps of the townhouse.

They stared at each other for a few stultifying seconds, during which Miss Morrissey collected a faint spray of gutter-water from a passing carriage and two double-glances at the colour of her skin. Then Robin managed to say, "Er, won't you . . . come in?"

The third of Robin's Friday meetings was, at least, far from boring. Miss Morrissey strode her way into the house, brandished Robin's resignation letter in his face right there in the entrance hall, and emitted a worried-sounding spiel about the fact that Edwin had taken her ring and gone off to find out if it was actually part of the Last Contract by looking for *another* ring, and he'd promised to come back and tell her as soon as he discovered anything and now it was a full day later—

"And I've been glued to the desk all day in case he turned up, but it's not as if anything more important could be keeping him, and I'm—" She took a deep breath, and her mouth crinkled with concern. "He wouldn't let me go with him because it was too dangerous, as if *he* knew the first thing about dealing with danger, and I don't know where the Gatlings live—*I've* never met them—and now I'm worried he's going to end up dead and dragged from the river, just like Reggie." She said something else, a fluid muttering in a foreign language that had the clear intonation of being unladylike.

Fear soaked Robin like rain. A vision struggled up from the cracks of memory, one of those from the brief lucid period when he'd tried to direct the foresight: Edwin, lying pale and lifeless on the ground, surrounded by people—

No. *No.*

"How can we find him?"

"I was hoping you might have an idea about that," she said. "That's why I've come here. You're the one who's spent all that time with him, and to be frank, there's nothing like a man with a title to open doors when you're—" Miss Morrissey paused. She raised a hand to her mouth and tapped a finger there, a calculating motion. Her gloves were a startling shade of red.

"What?" Robin burst out.

"I'm not supposed to know this. We'd be breaking a few rules."

"Good," said Robin at once. "I mean, I don't care."

She nodded. "We need to go to the Barrel."

"Sir Robert?" said his housekeeper, Mrs. Hathaway, from the top of the stairs. "If you—ah. Beg pardon, sir." She folded her hands in front of her apron and descended like a queen, gaze locked onto Robin in a way that meant she'd already seen Miss Morrissey and was pointedly containing herself. "I'd heard you were going out. Will you be dining at home?"

"We were just leaving," said Robin, conveniently still clad in outdoors gear. "As for dinner, ah . . ."

"I shall *personally* ensure that Sir Robert sends word," said Miss Morrissey, "if he is delayed a minute later than planned."

Her posh voice had somehow acquired a heavy gilt frame of further poshness. Mrs. Hathaway's eyes widened. Robin didn't trust himself to do more than nod. Then they were out the door and on the street.

"Sherborne Girls," Miss Morrissey said after a moment. "If you were about to ask me where I learned to do that."

Robin laughed, and a fraction of his tension eased with it. "By the time that's made its way through the downstairs dining room, they'll be saying I've taken up with the granddaughter of a maharajah."

"What makes you think you haven't?"

Humour quivered in the corner of her mouth, but Robin had a hard-earned sense for jokes that weren't really jokes at all. "Honestly?"

The quiver expanded. "Not quite. He was—there's no word for it in English, but my grandfather was a senior in the magical community in the Punjab before he came to England, and his sister *did* marry a prince. Mama used to tell us she'd come down in the world, marrying a mere colonel."

The morning's fog had grudgingly lifted, but the gloom of it hung in the darkening air. Miss Morrissey told him about her parents as they walked: her grandfather had lugged his family to England for what was meant to be a brief visit, due to the conditions of a will being contested. By the time the legal dispute over the property in question had dragged on for years, the man had become a sort of diplomatic liaison to the British Magical Assembly, and his daughter had met and married Colonel Clive Morrissey in a whirl of minor scandal. The Morrisseys had never been truly rich, or truly accepted in fashionable circles; they had their own circle of magician-peers, like the Courceys did, and moved quietly within that. Both of the daughters of the family had gained a taste for independence at school and had gone straight into civil service.

"It was that or marry at once," said Miss Morrissey, "and both of us wanted to take a breath before we embarked on that. I'm glad," she added. "Reggie's—Reggie was a lot of fun to work with, even if he was prone to haring off around the country on no notice."

"Were you close, the two of you?"

The rhythm of Miss Morrissey's steps faltered. Her profile was burnished in the light of the streetlamps. "As close as any friend," she said. "We worked together for two years. We both knew what it was like to grow up with magic and not have any ourselves."

"I'm sorry," Robin said, honestly. "For your loss."

Her mouth spasmed. Robin wished for the first time that he could have met his predecessor, to work out for himself if this irresponsible man had in any way deserved the subdued longing of two clever people. Perhaps he'd had a smile like a sunrise.

"Thank you," she said. "I'll be quite all right if I can land a kick on one of the bastards who did it."

Robin had a swell of fellow-feeling. "We haven't had much luck at unearthing them. We don't know how many men—er, or women—are involved."

"They're men."

"Why do you say that?"

"Because if even a single woman was involved, they wouldn't have decided that a man who'd been working there *one day* was a more likely source of information than a woman who'd been there for *years*."

It was a good point. Miss Morrissey looked almost offended that *she* hadn't been accosted and cursed.

It took them nearly an hour to reach the Barrel, a tall brick building just north of Smithfield that didn't look like much from the outside. Robin had probably walked past it before and never spared it a second glance. He didn't *want* to spare it a third. When he tried, he felt on the edge of some nasty, queasy vertigo. Best to keep walking, his feet seemed to say.

"Oh! I forgot about the warding," said Miss Morrissey. "Give me your arm."

With one red glove tight at the crook of Robin's elbow, she walked the both of them up the steps. The queasy feeling got stronger and stronger, and Robin thought fuzzily that when they did locate Edwin he was going to congratulate him for managing to keep his wits even *slightly* about him in the Sutton maze, if it had felt anything like this.

The doors were high and heavy, studded with brass. Miss Morrissey pushed one door open and pulled Robin with her across the threshold, grey flagstone giving way to pale marble beneath their feet, and Robin felt normal at once.

Miss Morrissey pulled a shilling from her purse and showed it to him. "Pass token. Charmed to negate the warding; it's not a strong one, just enough to avert curiosity for anyone without magic, which can be a bother for the in-betweeners like us. I'm sure Kitty can get you one of your own, if you—Sir Robert?"

At least twenty feet above Robin's head was a jagged pattern of black lead between thick panes of clear glass, crisscrossed busily by feet. It was the view he'd sketched for Edwin in the library, after seeing it in a vision. The floor where he stood had the dull polish bestowed by years and years of shoes. There were no stairs, no corridors winding away. The marble swept from wall to wall like a field of wheat, and standing within it at random intervals and angles like a parliament of scarecrows were . . . doors. Just doors, of dark wood with bronze knobs, within their frames. From time to time a door would open and one or more people would emerge from it. Sometimes they would cradle a spell before opening a different door, which they would step through into nothing that Robin could see. Attendants liveried in muted dark blue stood around the walls and sometimes stepped in to converse with the people.

Robin found his palms pressed hard to the sides of his legs. Even after everything he'd already been through, the strangeness was tangible. It was like seeing a dog whistle blown: no sound, even as one's eyes told the ears they should be hearing

something. Here Robin's eyes were seeing and his skin was aching, trying to sense something he was born without the ability
to sense. There was just a hint of it, humming and warm, the
bright opposite of the terror he'd felt in the hedge maze.

It felt like standing in the sculpture hall of the British Mu-
seum with the weight of history rising up and pressing in on
all sides, almost brutal in its beauty. The world was larger than
he'd thought.

Miss Morrissey led him a few steps to the side, where a
bench sat snug against the wall, and deposited him onto it. She
sat beside him and began to unbutton her coat in the warmth
of the building's interior.

"I think," said Robin carefully, "that I'm revisiting the
meaning of *unbusheling*."

"The Barrel's office doors are some of the most magical items
in the world. Oak, you know. It can hold a lot of power. We
live in modern times, and in a city as close-packed as London,
magic's often more bother than it's worth. It takes so much of
it to do anything really huge. But sometimes we put the effort
in. Sink the power in slowly. Imbue every inch." She shrugged
her coat off and folded it on her knees. Her voice was soft.
"Everyone deserves somewhere where they can be reminded
of their potential."

We, she'd said, not *they*. Robin tried to put together a question about her heritage, about knowing magic this closely and
having none of it to call her own, but knew he'd only fumble
it. And they were here for a reason. He removed his own coat
and hat.

"How do we find Edwin?"

"We ask my sister," said Miss Morrissey. "Follow me." She
marched them up to a door, seemingly at random, and signalled
to an attendant. "*Good* evening," she said primly, the gilt back
on her voice. "Fourth-floor main entry, please. Sir Robert and
I have an appointment. I'm afraid we were delayed."

Titles and doors, indeed. The man hastened to cradle up a

silver glow, which he smeared across the door, leaving a glowing rune in its wake, and opened it onto an unremarkable hallway. Robin followed Miss Morrissey through.

It was just after five o'clock; they were weaving against the traffic in the building, which was full of people chatting and fastening coats and donning hats. Miss Morrissey led him to an office where two men stood back with a tilt of hat-brims to let them enter, then left via the same door, leaving them with the sound of a woman speaking and the louder sound of a typewriter's keys.

"Wotcher, Kitty," said Miss Morrissey.

The sole remaining occupant of the office glanced up, and Robin's heart jolted. That woman, with her white shirtwaist and blue tie. This room. And this typewriter, paused now, which had clearly been imbued in a similar way to Edwin's note-taking pen. It was the third time Robin had found his own experience lining up with one of his visions; the others had been the maze, and the view up through the Barrel, only minutes ago. Tension locked his shoulders. He *had* seen something relevant. He *had* managed to steer it.

"Hullo, Addy."

"Kitty, this is the new Home Office liaison," said Miss Morrissey, continuing to blithely ignore the existence of Robin's resignation letter. "Sir Robert Blyth."

"Pleased to meet you, Miss—"

"Mrs.," she said swiftly, and yes, there was a ring on her hand. "Kaur. How d'you do." Mrs. Kitty Kaur had an arrangement of lovely features beneath the same coiled nest of black hair. She, if Robin remembered correctly, was the one who'd inherited all the magic that Adelaide Morrissey lacked.

"Kitty," said Miss Morrissey. "Edwin Courcey's gone missing, and we think he could be in danger."

"You know I don't work for the Coopers anymore. Don't you?"

"But you still have access to the lockroom. Don't you?"

A pause. Robin had had enough silent conversations with his own sister to realise when one was happening in front of him. He'd expected a lot more in the way of arguments and persuasion, and was prepared to embarrass himself in any number of ways if it would help, but the sisters Morrissey had a searching shorthand of glances that bypassed all of it.

"Addy," said Mrs. Kaur. "I'll still have to log it, and account for it later."

"Blame me," said Robin at once.

One thick black eyebrow arched.

Miss Morrissey leaned forward and smiled at her sister. "Would you say Sir Robert is a *threatening figure*?"

"Er," said Mrs. Kaur. It was the most diplomatic single syllable Robin had ever heard.

"Are you *afraid for your maidenly virtue*?"

"I'm married, Addy," said Kitty Kaur dryly. "I have none." She eyed Robin. "He does seem the kind of well-built, pugnacious fellow who would follow through on a threat of bodily harm."

"I beg your pardon," Robin began to protest, and then the penny dropped. "Oh. Would it help if I raised my voice?"

"Yes, that would do nicely. Sir Robert strong-armed my sister into bringing him here to seek my help, and threatened us with harm unless I abused my access to the lockroom in order to locate Mr. Courcey. Overcome by concern for his friend, of course, but still. Most brutish behaviour."

"And we are but feeble women," said Miss Morrissey. "Woe."

"Your sister is a magician," Robin said, pointing out what seemed the largest hole in this story.

"*Woe*," said Mrs. Kaur firmly, and Robin recalled what Miss Morrissey had said about the assumptions made by men.

Two more oak doors took them to their destination. The second one required a complicated cradle, which Mrs. Kaur fumbled the first time and then made a face as she began it over again—"The identification clause is a fiddle, and the secrecy one even more so," she apologised, and then: "*Hah,*" with satisfaction as the rune flared into being.

Robin's first thought was that Edwin had probably appreciated the lockroom, if he'd ever been there. It resembled nothing so much as the stacks of a library: a windowless room that had the feeling of being well below ground level, illuminated by pale orange ceiling lights that could have been either electric or magical. Rows of wooden shelves and drawers stretched away from the entrance. There was a peculiar, cathedral-like, anticipatory silence to the air.

"What is this place?" Robin asked.

"This is the Lockroom," said Mrs. Kaur, and now Robin heard the way she said it. Title, not descriptor. "Every registered magician in Britain is represented in this room."

A leather-bound ledger the size of a decent card table lay open on a bench, with words arranged in columns. A pen lifted itself from its stand as soon as Mrs. Kaur stepped close to the book. She raised her hands and moved them through the motions of a new spell, then paused with fingers held at angles.

"Catherine Amrit Kaur," she said, and the pen entered it in one column, then hopped to hover over another. "His full name, if you know it," she murmured.

"I don't," said Miss Morrissey.

"I do," said Robin. For the rest of his life he would be able to recall the exact sight of Edwin kneeling, desperate and pale among closing holly, and hear the sound of Edwin's voice. "Edwin John Courcey."

Mrs. Kaur touched her index finger to thumb, creating a circle, and her hands glowed red for less than a second. There was a faint grinding sound from the bowels of the stacks. A new light sprang up in the distance, like a red ribbon unfurling to the ceiling, tethered at a particular point.

"Stay here, Sir Robert," said Mrs. Kaur. She stepped across what Robin now realised was a threshold, a change from one pattern of wood on the floor to another.

Before long the tap of her footsteps brought her back with a small box in her hands, which was labelled with Edwin's name. Inside was something small and pale, nestled on a velvet interior. Robin reached out to touch it, then snatched his hand back, belatedly trying to teach himself some caution when it came to new magical things.

"It's all right. It's only hair," said Miss Morrissey.

"The *Lock Room*," said Robin. "Locks of hair." He swallowed and looked out at the depths of the stacks. "Every magician in Britain?"

"It's a ceremony, when a child first shows signs of magic," said Miss Morrissey. "A lock is cut. It used to be that your family would keep it safe, but now it's kept here. Centrally. We know every member of our community."

"Could someone do harm, using this?" Robin touched the lock of hair gently. It was like white silk, much whiter than Edwin's hair was now.

"Nothing direct," said Mrs. Kaur. "The hair's dead. It's no use as an active conduit. You can use it to trace because of . . . its memory, I suppose. The Assembly wouldn't keep a potential weapon against its own people like that. But it means we can find and protect our own, when there are no other options." A pointed look.

Robin was full of questions. How did this fit into Edwin's rules about physical distance and the laws governing magic? What happened to the hair when someone died? Were there magicians who refused the ceremony, refused to have their children registered in such a way? What if a magician didn't *want* to be found? The whole concept was more than a little creepy, but he didn't want to be rude, and besides—he was, in this moment, very grateful indeed that the Lockroom existed.

Mrs. Kaur was already building another spell, standing in front of a dingy map of the British Isles that was pinned above the table holding the ledger. When she turned and flung her hands apart, she conjured a much larger version of the map into being; it hung in the air then drifted to overlay itself on the blank wooden panels of the wall behind them. There was some unevenness where the map dipped over the contours of the door and its frame. But it was the Isles, detailed and glowing and sprawled wide.

A phantom cradle lingered in Mrs. Kaur's hands, visible only when tilted at certain angles, catching up both the orange of the lights above and the blue of the map-spell. The dark creases of her palms ran beneath it at different angles again. At her direction, Robin gingerly placed the lock of Edwin's hair into the cradle's centre; he could feel nothing there, but the lock sat and stayed as though caught in a web. Immediately the map pulsed brighter and more purple, changing, rewriting itself on the wall to show a small section of city. Robin stepped close to read the neat text of street names.

"Still in London," he said, excited. "St. James's, Jermyn Street. That's the Cavendish Hotel, I've been there before."

"Mr. Courcey rents rooms there," said Miss Morrissey. "I didn't think he'd—but I'm *sure* he would have come back to talk to me."

"Something might have happened. He—he could be hurt." Robin touched the map, fingertips meeting only wood, and felt his chest tighten subtly. It wasn't the inexorable slide of sensation that it had been before now. It felt like a nudging at his mind, like one of those optical illusions. You could choose to see the duck; you could choose to let your eyes absorb the lines a different way, and see a rabbit. It felt, for the first time, as though Robin had *control*.

He leaned his weight against the wall, closed his eyes, and let it come.

A room, cosy-looking and with books spilling over half its surfaces. A small table laid for tea, with a single cup in a saucer, set out in front of the armchair in which Edwin was sleeping. He looked exhausted and peaceful and entirely normal but for the glowing string around one wrist, the free end of which trailed down to the floor.

Billy Byatt came into view. He sat on the arm of the chair, looking down at Edwin with something too mild to be concern. He took hold of Edwin's shoulder and shook him; Edwin's eyes stayed closed, his head lolling into a lower angle. Billy sat back with a satisfied nod. He reached for the teacup and tilted it to look inside—

Robin wrenched his hands away and came back to himself with enough force that he nearly overbalanced. The map was fading, leaving only a faint trace that wavered when Robin blinked.

"He's not all right," Robin said. He was so angry he had to force the words out. The casual shake. The glowing string. "They've put one of those horrid bridle things on his hand. We're going there. Now."

He turned to see two identical pairs of raised eyebrows. Mrs. Kaur's expression had a layer of shock that her sister's was missing.

"I thought you said you weren't a magician," she said. "What *was* that?"

"Foresight," said Miss Morrissey. "I'll explain on the way, Kitty."

"Billy," Robin blurted, "he's with *Billy*. Billy Byatt."

"Billy Byatt," echoed Mrs. Kaur sharply.

"You know him?" asked Robin.

Her mouth made a strange shape. She exchanged a glance with her sister and said, "I very nearly married him."

23

Edwin didn't use the rose-hip tea from Whistlethropp's often. He kept it in the cupboard of his pantry for those nights when he'd worn his own magic down to the last specks and didn't have the energy to cast a simple charm for sleep, but knew his mind would otherwise keep turning the latest idea over and over instead of letting him rest.

Billy laid his own spell on the tea as well, to enhance it, and heated water in Edwin's hob-kettle instead of removing the bridle and letting Edwin ring down to order some. Edwin watched the tea steep, sitting quiet in his own chair, unable to move except as Billy wanted him to move.

"I am sorry about this," Billy said, pushing the full cup towards him. "But I need to run an errand before we have a proper chat. And you always look as if you could use a nap, you know, Win."

Edwin drank, the half-sweet half-tart liquid spilling across his mouth just the wrong side of too hot. He doubted Billy had done that on purpose. There was something anxious and absent about Billy's smile even then, as though they were merely two young men of passing acquaintance and one was about to ask the other to let him crib off his notes for the Greek exam.

The dispassionate, observing part of Edwin was still trying to cling to that, in order to shout down the part of him that was hopelessly angry and deathly afraid, as the tea leaded his eyelids and he fell asleep.

He woke to evening shadows in the room—he'd lost most

of the day—and the smell of melted butter. Billy was sprawled on the rug making toast at Edwin's fireplace. The scene was cosy. Edwin felt well rested and blurred for the few seconds it took him to ground himself in what had happened, and then his muscles tensed and his pulse flew into his throat, probably undoing all the good that the drugged sleep had done.

"Ah, there we are," said Billy when he noticed Edwin's open eyes.

Then, to Edwin's surprise, he removed the Goblin's Bridle. Edwin didn't even think of hitting him until he'd already moved out of reach; Billy saw the twitch of Edwin's hand and said, reproving, "Settle down, Win."

"It's *Edwin*." He was past accepting a name he hated from someone who wished him ill. "How many of the others knew?"

"The others? Bel and Charlie and all of them? Oh come now, I'm not a fool," Billy added as Edwin began to fumble in his pockets, where he encountered a handkerchief and some lint and the round, smooth ball of the oak-heart where he'd stashed it, but no string at all. Billy dangled the rough brown string from his fingers, then returned it to his own pocket. He settled himself on the low table, nudging the teapot aside. "You *are* a clever one, even if you've not much magic to put behind it."

"How many of them," said Edwin doggedly. So: in Billy's eyes he wasn't a threat. He could behave like not-a-threat. But he wanted *information*.

"I'm the only one of that party who knows about the Last Contract," Billy said, audibly capitalising the words.

Edwin's hands formed fists on the arms of the chair, then relaxed. "What have you done with the rings?"

"They're long gone from here, if that's what you mean. Delivered to a colleague, for safekeeping. No use trying to rush me and search my pockets." He appeared to notice the toast in his hand for the first time and demolished the dripping triangle in a few bites. Edwin's stomach rumbled at the sight. "Clever idea it was, splitting the coin into those rings," Billy went on, through the last of his mouthful. "Don't suppose *you've* managed to work out whether it was the splitting that kept the things unable to be detected by spells seeking magical objects? Or if they're naturally muffled? No?" He shrugged.

Edwin sank further into the chair, mind racing. There had been a coin; there may well yet be a cup and a knife, unless those two had been altered—split—in some way as well. If Billy and his allies, whomever they were, didn't know if the rings being magically inert was an inherent property . . . was that enough to suggest that they didn't have the other two parts? If they couldn't compare?

Too many hints. Not enough clear facts.

"What do these things *do*?" Edwin allowed himself to sound as bewildered as he was. "Why all the fuss? All I've managed to glean is that you need all of them together, and that they"—he corrected himself, careful—"that Reggie's great-aunt seemed to think they were dangerous."

Billy's eyebrows climbed. He wiped a smear of butter from his lip. "I thought you'd worked out *that* much. All our talk at dinner about not being able to draw on another person's power—that's what it does. The contract in its full form. Don't you see?" He leaned forward, eager. "One doesn't need to define the individual if the contract includes all of us."

All of us. *Every living magician in Great Britain.* Flora Sutton's words were the final piece; Edwin's mind shook itself like a tablecloth and laid the solution out, flat and clear and horrifying. If every British magician truly was descended from the Three Families, then it defined them all on the bloodline level; even more horribly, it negated the need to rely on an individual's consent, if you constructed the spell properly. A contract *was* consent, even if it was given on your behalf by your ancestors. Edwin's parents had made pledge with Penhallick, and all three of their children had become part of that pledge without spilling a single drop of their own blood.

The Last Contract defined the terms for an exchange of

power from one being to another, defined its participants, and formalised their consent. Theoretically, if used as a component in a spell meticulously constructed, it could draw every last drop of power from every magician thus defined. And place it at a single person's command.

"But you couldn't wield that much," Edwin said. "Nobody could."

"We can't know the limits until it's tried," said Billy. "Some of the people I'm working with have been trying to crack the secret of power transfer for *decades,* and the contract is the answer. It's what we've always needed, Wi—Edwin. It's an equaliser. If magic can be shared, then even half-pint magicians like you can do the great spells of power."

"Or someone like you," said Edwin as several more pieces fell near-audibly into place, "who didn't have quite enough magic for his sweetheart's family."

Billy flushed. "It's a worthy goal. Try and tell me otherwise."

"You're recruiting me," Edwin realised. "That's why I'm here. That's why . . ." He waved his freed wrist, indicating both Billy's gesture of half-hearted trust and the sheer fact that he'd been put to sleep and contained in his own rooms instead of taken somewhere else and . . . killed. Or wiped clean.

"You've been useful. I *told* them you would be. You're sharp, you're single-minded—it took Gatling weeks to get half as far as you did, and it was mostly luck that his own aunt was involved."

"How did Reggie get mixed up in this in the first place?" If this was truly a recruitment attempt, then Edwin was seizing the chance to go fishing for answers. "I knew he was hiding something, ever since—that trip he took to Yorkshire. That had something to do with the contract? Not ghosts at all?"

"Oh, the bloody ghosts." Billy chuckled. "That's why he went there in the first place. Stuck his nose into every corner *and* was loud and cheerful about it, like some irritating chimaera made up of you and Sir Robert combined."

"*Real ghosts?*" Edwin's mind refused to move past this point.

"Of course not." Billy brightened. "I suppose you'd find it interesting, if anyone would. It was an echo spell. We'd found out where it *looked* like the pieces of the contract were—don't ask me how, that part was terrifically dull—and that led us to a tiny, ancient church in some mining town in the Moors. Secret hiding places in the crypt and all. But it was empty." He paused, eyes skimming Edwin hopefully, as if for some sign that this was helping to make his case. "It took eight of us, in the end, to coordinate the echo spell reaching far enough back, and covering—God, *decades*, it was frightful. Took most of a week to pinpoint the right time. Even the strongest of us were shattered by the time we finally saw the girls taking the contract from the crypt."

"Girls?" Edwin said sharply.

"I know—not what you'd expect, is it? Girls. Four of them. Young and dressed to the nines *in 1855*, so of course we'd no idea if they'd even still be living today, but at least we knew we were looking for women. And the whole time the village was in hysterics about ghosts walking through the streets and appearing in their kitchens, because we couldn't keep proper hold of the *size*—getting the eight of us working strictly in concert on the time parameters was bad enough, and something about doing magic in that place was like trying to keep hold of a bar of wet soap. Ghosts! Some of us had to stay nearly *another* week to deal with the cleanup."

Another puzzle-piece spun and fitted into place. Triangulation, via ley lines, looking for the footprint of powerful objects, which had been resting in that church for—maybe even centuries. And which had created there a place of fossilised power, which took an echo illusion spell cast into the previous century and blew its spatial parameters as wide as an entire town.

Not ghosts in the active sense, then, but in the passive. Moving photographs of the true past, called briefly into being.

"And Reggie turned up investigating the reports of ghosts,

and insisted on involving himself when he learned what the contract could do," said Edwin slowly.

"We figured he might be useful." Billy shrugged. "The fact that he was there at all meant he had a knack for keeping his ear to the ground."

"And once he knew that you were looking for elderly women with an interest in old magics . . ."

"Yes—he ran off to wheedle the coin out of his aunt, and then was foolish enough to think that he could *lie* about it. He wanted to find the whole contract himself, *use* it himself. He thought that non-magicians could use it to turn themselves into something they're not."

"Can they?"

"No. Well. We're not certain."

He'd stopped trusting their intentions, Mrs. Sutton had said of Reggie. Was that it? Or had he truly been overtaken by personal ambition? Edwin wanted to believe the best of Reggie, but he clearly hadn't known him at all.

He said, "It sounds like you're not certain of a lot of things."

"It's a legend," said Billy, "that just happens to be real. The Last Contract is three items, and it can be used to draw power from every magician in Britain, and those bloody women stumbled across this fact and found the items in the church. But they couldn't work out the last step. They couldn't make it work. So clearly they gave up."

We didn't know, Flora Sutton had said. *When we did, we stopped.*

Conscience, not lack of ability. Edwin burned suddenly to read more of her diaries. She, like Billy, possessed a *we*. Billy's was whatever shadowy group of people Reggie had tangled himself up with and unwisely tried to hide things from; Billy was obviously being careful not to mention any names until he was sure he had Edwin on side.

Flora Sutton's *we* was another puzzle again.

Those bloody women.

Edwin tried to lift the lens of what he now knew and peer backwards through it at the events of the last two weeks. All right. He was being, albeit clumsily, recruited to a group of people in search of a way to increase the amount of power at their command. They thought he'd be tempted.

And God, God, he was. The idea had buried itself beneath his skin like ink. To do it the *right* way, of course, with full knowledge and consent, but ... to have *more*. To be able to combine his own techniques with a reservoir of power as deep as Charlie's, to build his experiments and set them loose, to push the bounds of known magic and to *create*. To discover. To be fully the thing that he was, and not a few stitched-together scraps.

Edwin looked at Billy Byatt—cheerful, apologetic Billy, who'd always seemed the least awful and the weakest-willed of Bel and Charlie's set, and who'd been simmering away with the same ink beneath his skin this whole time.

Edwin said, carefully, "Did you kill Reggie Gatling, Billy?"

"Me?" Billy made a face. "My dear chap. No."

And nobody else had left Penhallick in the days that Edwin and Robin were gone, so he couldn't have been their attacker at Sutton Cottage either.

"But you knew about it. You knew people were being killed."

Billy's mild eyes were wide with belief. "What's that saying about omelettes and eggs? This is *important*. There's something terrible coming, the Assembly thinks, and we're going to need all the power we can get. We can't suddenly increase the number of magicians in the country. But we can make some of us more useful."

Useful. The word was a sting. The thought of Robin crowded into Edwin's mind, where he'd been doing his best to keep it at bay. He was glad that Robin had bowed his way out of this dangerous mess. Even if the search for the contract had begun on the Assembly's word, it had clearly become something else, steered by hands that weren't squeamish about dirtying themselves. Not even the Assembly went around authorising murder.

"And there'll be plenty of magic to go around, once we can discover how the contract works," Billy went on. "It's something extraordinary. Something new. Don't you want to be part of it?"

That, too, had its own sting. It meant that Edwin, who'd always assumed he faded into the background when not being teased for general entertainment, had been observed and understood, at least on one level. It meant that this recruitment wasn't as clumsy as it appeared.

"If your lot wanted me on side," Edwin said, "why not just tell me all this at the start?"

"By the time I suggested you, we weren't sure if Gatling had told you already. Thought you might be working with him. And then you show up all chummy with his replacement, some chap nobody's ever heard of. I thought he was a pal that Gatling had pulled into it, who'd nabbed the job as an excuse to sniff around the office for wherever Gatling left the contract."

"He's not," said Edwin. "Robin doesn't matter in all of this. He's," and it tasted hotter and more painful than the drugged tea, "a paperwork error."

"We know that *now*," said Billy. "Frightful muddle, but what can you do. Some unmagical higher-up got wind that someone had abandoned their post, and they shoved Sir Robert in to replace him. We wouldn't have bothered with the curse if we'd known—that was to shake him up, make him happier to talk. Nobody expected him to have foresight. Or for you to drag him to Penhallick and not let him out from under your nose." He tapped the side of his forehead, playful. "Had to get creative, to get close to him. Thank goodness for Bel and her games."

That made no sense. Then it did. "You cast Dead Man's Legs," Edwin said. "In the lake. You were the only one who was close enough."

A breezy nod. "Worth a try. Thought it might scare him back to the city."

"He could have *died*," Edwin snarled.

"You said it yourself, he doesn't *matter*," said Billy. "Why do you care?"

Edwin tried to wrench back the calm that he'd been using to navigate his way through this conversation, but he couldn't. He'd slipped, his anger was out, and it wouldn't pack itself back into his chest. He bit his cheek and looked at the carpet, hands tight on the arms of the chair.

"*Oh*," said Billy, loaded with meaning. He was smirking when Edwin looked up. "I knew you leaned that way, but didn't realise you moved that fast. You really are easy for anyone who'll smile at you, aren't you?"

"Go to hell," said Edwin.

Billy had better luck collecting himself. His pleasant expression drew together like curtains. "All right. You two had your adventure—very brave and clever, running around solving riddles. But we have the rings now. And we're going to find the other pieces of the contract, and I think your knack for the fiddly theoretical bits of magic would be an asset to us. It's as simple as that. Come on board, and you'll have the power you've always wanted."

Edwin wasn't brave. He wasn't. He was tempted and tense and he was terrified of pain. But he'd found a line in himself, right where Billy's casual shrugs met the memory of Robin gasping on the lakeshore, and he wasn't going to cross it. It was a relief to know that the line was there. He would take the consequences.

He said, "Or . . . ?"

Billy stared at him for a long moment. The curtain by the cracked-open window moved gently in a draught, and the noise of the late London evening filtered into the silence.

"Honestly?" said Billy.

"Honestly. I won't lift a damn finger for you."

"Damn," said Billy with a sigh, and started to build a spell. "Now you've left me looking a right idiot, Win. I did tell them I'd be able to talk you round."

The spell taking shape was one to burn away memories, a soft and cheerful yellow like filtered sunlight. Lethe-mint was preferable to these spells for a reason: they were difficult and relied on absolute precision of clauses, and the potential for adverse consequences was high. There were maybe three magicians in London to whom Edwin would have entrusted his mind with this sort of spell, and Billy Byatt had neither the skill nor the power to appear on that list.

Despair soaked Edwin like spilled wine. He tried to burn the feel of Robin's mouth into his skin along with the scratches and bruises, wanting almost to cry at the idea that he would wake up having forgotten how it felt to be . . . smiled at, yes, and touched in ways that he craved, and thought to be fascinating. He *had* been easy. Robin had walked into the maze of him and solved him with no string required at all, and Edwin had been stupid enough to let that slip out of his hands.

"All right," said Robin's voice, terse and clear. "Stop."

The jerking-round of Billy's head was the only clue that Edwin hadn't hallucinated a speaking illusion of Robin Blyth through the force of his longing.

If it *was* an illusion, it was the strangest Edwin had ever seen. Emerging from the fading shimmer of a curtain-spell was a small group of people. It was Robin, along with an unfamiliar woman shaking the last sparks of the spell's banishment from her fingertips, and Adelaide Morrissey. Who was standing with her feet planted and a longbow in her hands, an arrow drawn back flush with her cheek, for all the world as though Edwin's parlour were an archery range.

The arrow was pointed at Billy.

Billy said, "What the devil . . ."

"Hullo, Byatt. This is, as someone once told me, a game of nerve," said Robin. "I suggest you don't move."

24

It turned out that having a truly strong magician on one's side made a lot of difference, when it came to quietly opening the locked door of a hotel suite and quietly tiptoeing, disguised behind a spell, through an entrance hall and into the parlour that Robin had seen in his vision.

Robin's two contributions to the adventure thus far had been baroneting Edwin's suite number out of the concierge, and managing *not* to step through the subtle shimmer of the spell and plant his fist in Billy Byatt's freckled face. He'd been all for charging in as soon as the door was open, but had been persuaded otherwise by Catherine Amrit Kaur's calm voice, laying out this plan. Robin felt rather silly; he'd worried Mrs. Kaur might be made incautious by emotion, given her history with Billy. She'd looked strained, and kept her hand on her sister's arm as they listened, but she'd been a model of patient caution.

Robin's emotions, as Billy talked about the contract, had been howling for caution to be thrown to the winds in favour of . . . well, punching.

"*Kitty?*" said Billy.

The yellow spell in Billy's hands sat quiescent, half-built, already dimming as his attention wavered. Edwin leaned over and shook Billy's wrist, dissipating it completely. Billy spared him only a quick, jerky glance before his eyes swung back to Kitty Kaur. He began to stand; Miss Morrissey said, "*Ah,*" warningly, and he froze.

Edwin looked like a poor reproduction of himself, tainted by disbelief. He'd been readying himself for something awful, Robin had *seen it happening,* and now here Robin was appearing out of nowhere. A magic trick. Robin managed a smile, giving Edwin something to latch on to, if he wanted it.

"Kitty," Billy said again, a bewildered plea. "What are you doing here?"

"And where did you find a *bow*?" Edwin asked.

"Transformed a broom," said Mrs. Kaur. She didn't seem inclined to answer Billy's query.

"I couldn't be much help there," said Miss Morrissey. "But I *did* get a ribbon at school for archery."

"Edwin," said Robin. "Are you all right?"

"Yes," said Edwin. Their gazes held. Robin had to bite his tongue against blurting out accusation and apology and admission, all at once. Edwin stood and began to cross the room.

Mrs. Kaur made a short, broken-off noise of warning, too late. As Edwin moved to step past him, Billy stood—grabbed him—Robin started forward to help, but came up short against Mrs. Kaur's urgent arm.

"Hold it there," said Billy.

Edwin held. Was held. The switch-knife pressed against his side was not large, but it winked deadly sharp in the light. Billy's other arm snaked around Edwin's chest, dragging Edwin back against himself.

"Edwin here knows that those of us without much magic have to rely on other things, from time to time," Billy said. "It helps to have something in reserve."

Edwin breathed shallowly and fast. Robin felt paralysed with the speed at which things had swung in their favour and back out of it. They could overpower him, certainly, but Billy had already shown he could move fast and believed in . . . broken eggs. Omelettes. Perhaps he didn't like the idea of getting blood on his own hands, but he was cornered and annoyed and there was nothing hesitant about his grip on the knife.

The tip of the arrow wavered as Miss Morrissey, too, considered her options. Robin was grateful that she'd had the sense not to release it when startled. Billy was shorter than Edwin; he'd be able to keep Edwin entirely between himself and the weapon, and Robin could only assume that a similar sort of constraint held for spells. Anything Mrs. Kaur cast, even if she could do it quickly enough, would affect Edwin as well.

"Put it down, Adelaide," said Billy.

She hissed her breath through her teeth, but let the string slacken. She bent and placed both bow and arrow at her feet.

Edwin held Robin's gaze again. He dropped his eyes to his own hands—which he'd moved to clasp in front of him—and back up. Robin's heart gave a pound.

"Kitty?" Robin inquired, turning to Mrs. Kaur as though he hadn't already heard the outline of their relationship on the way here. "Do you two know one another, then?"

Mrs. Kaur took up the thread immediately, tilting her elegant brown neck and touching the base of it, as if uncertain. Her eyes were liquid pools. Anyone who'd ever loved her would find it hard to look away from her at this moment.

At the edge of Robin's vision, Edwin's hands were pale flickers.

"We used to be close, yes," said Mrs. Kaur. "This isn't like you, Billy. You're a good man. Put the knife down and let's talk, shall we?"

Billy's lips pressed together. Edwin's breath hitched and Robin saw the tip of the knife move.

"A good man," said Billy. "I'd like to think so. But that wasn't enough for you. For your family."

"My parents and grandfather asked me for my cooperation," said Mrs. Kaur softly. "I made my choice. I'm happy with it."

"Happy? Marrying a man you were barely friends with at the time?" This argument had the weakly bitter note of leaves twice-steeped. "If you loved me enough, you'd have told them to go hang."

"Yes," she said.

The syllable hung there, simply.

Something shifted in Billy's posture that spoke to Robin's instincts from years of boxing. The man had moved past an inhibition of some kind. He was considering his move, and was close to making it.

Edwin's eyes were downcast. Edwin's fingers moved slowly, slowly, bare of string.

"What do you want us to do?" asked Robin. "You're the one with the knife. Make your demands, Byatt."

"I do wish you'd kept your noses out of this," Billy said, still addressing Mrs. Kaur. "You *can't* be allowed to remember. And you can't run back to your life and play pretend," spitting this at Robin, whose instincts were shouting even more loudly. "Even if I let you all walk out of here now, we'll find you tomorrow. Or the next day."

Edwin's cuff brushed against Billy's arm as he began to raise his hands.

"Stop. What are you doing?" Billy demanded.

"I'm reaching into my pocket," said Edwin. He was. Gold sparks danced between his fingers as they vanished. "You know there's nothing dangerous in there. You checked them yourself. Here."

And he moved: one hand closing over Billy's where it was pressed against his chest, a mockery of tenderness. The other— Robin couldn't see, was he holding something, passing it from his own hand to—

Thunder expanded in the room with a deafening crack. A flash of white light sent Robin flinching with a hand over his eyes. There were more sounds: a human choke, a ragged grunt of exhalation, a thud in two parts. All very fast. And then nothing.

When Robin blinked his vision back again, Edwin was bent over, leaning on the arm of a chair for support. On the floor was a small pile of prickly splinters and ash, as though a half-burned conker casing had somehow rolled out of the fire. The empty tea set had been knocked to the ground as well, the cup split into three wet shards.

Sprawled next to this minor pile of wreckage was Billy Byatt. There was a pattern like lightning, like the veins of a leaf, charred in black in the centre of his palm, over the mound of his wrist, and disappearing beneath his cuff.

Billy stared at the ceiling. He looked mildly startled.

He did not move, no matter how long Robin gazed at him.

Mrs. Kaur made a harsh sound of surprise and knelt down. Her fingers hovered, then sought a pulse beneath the chin. "Billy?"

"Oh hell," said Edwin, and his knees buckled.

One moment Robin was standing near the window; the next moment, without any time or distance seeming to register in between, he was at Edwin's side, supporting him, Edwin clinging to him for balance.

"I'm all right," said Edwin. "He didn't—Robin, I'm all right." He righted himself, chin lifted and eyes everywhere but the body on the floor.

But when Robin released him and began to pull away, Edwin's grip on his arms tightened, a wordless refusal. Something inside Robin collapsed. He pulled Edwin closer, wrapping his arms all the way around him. Edwin alive and warm, and not stabbed, or memory-wiped, or anything else that might have happened. Robin rested his temple against Edwin's for a long moment. The Morrissey sisters could think whatever they wished. Hell, they'd already heard Billy's question—*Why do you care?*—and seen the answer that was Edwin's lack of answering.

Edwin pressed his face into Robin's shoulder and took a breath deep as a sail snatching a breeze, expanding in Robin's arms. Then he disentangled himself.

"Thank you," he said. "For coming. How did you—where did you—"

Robin smiled. "I had help."

"Mr. Courcey," said Miss Morrissey, "what did you *do* to him?"

Edwin prodded the splinter-pile with his shoe. "I cast a splitting charm on an imbued oak-heart, with a clause for release of power. I closed his hand around it. I didn't know quite what—I thought it would. Distract him." Edwin looked almost grey. He rubbed at his forehead and left a smear of ash. "There was a lot more power stored in there than I thought."

"Bloody sodding hell," said Miss Morrissey. "Er, sorry."

"And there was me," said Edwin savagely, "sitting there going on about how we're the ones who *aren't* murdering people."

"Bugger that," said Robin. "Sorry."

"I think," said Mrs. Kaur, "that we can extend to one another some diplomatic immunity as regards the use of foul language. Given the circumstances."

"Right," said Robin. "*Bugger* that, Edwin." Edwin gave a small explosive sound that was halfway to a laugh. Robin went on, "He had a knife to your ribs, and he was working his way up to using it. You acted before he did. You didn't mean to—you didn't mean him to die, but he did. It's over." He bit back *and I'm glad*.

"And I have a dead body in my parlour," said Edwin. "A body with friends. *Family*."

"His family are in Bath," said Mrs. Kaur. She, too, had gone washed-out and uncertain, but there was an emotion more complicated than grief in the way she looked at Billy now. "I'll go back to the Barrel. I used to work for the Coopers; the night shift all know me. I'll explain. They'll send someone along."

"You can't," said Edwin.

"I beg your pardon?"

"You heard him. Anyone who knows about what they're trying to do, about the contract, can't be allowed to remember. Or *live*, I'd guess, if they're trying to contain the damage. You used to work for the Coopers, ma'am? Do you want to tell me you'd bet all of our lives on there not being a single person in that office who's mixed up in this plot, somehow?"

They exchanged a look that Robin didn't understand. It felt like trying to guess the shape of an animal having seen only the ears; it was related to Edwin's reluctance to go to either the Coopers or the Assembly for help, at any point in this disaster. Robin pushed his questions down to join all the others. They would, he sincerely hoped, have time for them later.

"No. Damnation," said Mrs. Kaur. "Then what do you suggest we do?"

They all looked at the corpse of Billy Byatt. The switch-knife was lying half-concealed by his body; Robin bent to retrieve it. Edwin's gaze clung to the blade like fearful glue, so Robin folded it hastily and pocketed it, getting it out of sight.

"Can you make him disappear?" Robin asked. "*Not* turn up having been dragged from the river in three days, I mean." He felt rotten for asking such a thing of a woman who'd cared for the man at one time. But he didn't see many other options.

"Not tonight I can't," she said, sharp. "I'm not a bottomless well, and that curtain-spell took effort." She added grudgingly, "Tomorrow. I'll come back. You'll have to keep the staff out of your rooms for a while, Courcey."

Edwin nodded.

"And when his friends start asking about him?" said Miss Morrissey.

"I've an idea," said Robin, thinking of Billy at the Penhallick dinner table. *Not my girl any longer.* Mrs. Kaur's rejection of him was public knowledge, which had clearly rankled as much as anything else. "He came to you, Mrs. Kaur. He visited you at your office, this evening. You argued. You didn't realise how upset he still was, about everything that had happened between you."

"This idea had better not be heading in the direction of framing my sister for murder," said Miss Morrissey.

"No. He told you he couldn't stand to be in London any

longer, where it was so difficult to forget you," said Robin, searching Kitty Kaur's face. "He said he needed to get away from everything, and everyone."

"Suicide?" said Edwin.

"I was thinking more an impulsive trip to the Continent, or the Americas," said Robin, startled. "Do you think people are more likely to assume he did away with himself?"

"I'd believe either," said Mrs. Kaur. "That's . . ." She swallowed. "Clever. Yes. I can sell that, when the questions start. But *you two* are coming to tea sometime in the next few days—you as well, Adelaide—and you're going to fill me in on everything. I don't keep secrets without cause."

"We can do that," said Robin.

The Morrissey sisters left together. They didn't show any sign of expecting Robin to leave with them, which was as well. Robin had no intention of going anywhere.

Edwin tidied the broken crockery and swept up the ashes, and Robin dragged Billy's corpse into a corner, where at least they wouldn't have to trip over him on the way through the parlour. Edwin didn't have a trunk large enough to bundle him into, unfortunately.

"I'll ring down for some extra blankets to drape over him, in case any of the Cavendish servants manage to blunder in," said Edwin. "And some dinner. Billy ate all my bread." He leaned against the frame connecting parlour to entrance hall, creating a striking and exhausted geometry of his own angles against those of his setting. His eyes made circuits then landed, skittish, on Robin's face. "How long were you lurking by the window, then? How much did you hear?"

"Something about the contract allowing magicians to take power from other magicians." Robin came and stood close enough to touch, but didn't. "A lot of nonsense about how they expected you to cave if they dangled the idea in front of you, as though you weren't twice the man Billy Byatt is. As though you were *nothing* without enough magic to fell a bull."

"It could have worked." Edwin reached out a deliberate hand and touched Robin's wrist with one finger. Robin, slow and daring, tangled their fingers together. Edwin let him do it. "A month ago it might have worked."

"You're hardly nothing," said Robin. "You made me see the future."

"I think we've established that wasn't me," said Edwin. "We don't know if it was even—*them*. I think it was latent. Triggered."

Robin smiled at him. "I wasn't talking about the visions."

The vulnerable line of Edwin's mouth wavered in confusion, then deepened at one side. His grip on Robin's hand tightened.

"Robin," he began, and was interrupted by the rap of knuckles on the door. They dropped hands at once. Whoever was on the other side didn't wait for a reply before trying the door handle.

"That's efficient," said Robin. "Hold on, you didn't ring yet—oh."

Walter Courcey stood in the doorway, coat folded over his arm. Recognition took Robin an awkward moment; he'd only seen the eldest Courcey sibling at the start of all this, at that single dinner before Walter and Clifford Courcey took themselves back to London. All three of them—Robin, Edwin, and Walter—seemed just as startled as one another to have found themselves in this situation, even though there was nothing remarkable about any of it.

Apart from the corpse in the next room, Robin reminded himself with a mental kick.

He mustered his best manners, the ones that could deflect awkwardness like a neat clip to the off-stump.

"Evening, Courcey. You'll be here to see Edwin, then," he said. "We were thinking of dining at my club, would you care to—"

"I don't think that's why he's here, Robin," said Edwin in a voice Robin hadn't heard before.

And then Robin, too, saw the glint of metal: the two rings, side by side on Walter's smallest finger, merry and silver against the black of his coat.

25

Walter closed the door behind him. His nonplussed expression was different to Edwin's. Not as closed-down; not the desperate, iced-over defences of someone who'd learned early that there was no protecting yourself from some things. Walter's expression was a calculation.

"Byatt didn't mention that he'd dragged the foreseer along," he said. "Believe it or not, I'm very pleased to meet you again, Blyth. I'm sorry it couldn't be under better circumstances."

"What would *better* be, exactly?" said Robin through his teeth.

"To begin with," said Walter, lifting the hand with the rings on it, "there wouldn't be a missing piece to this, and I wouldn't have had to come knocking on the door of my brother's ridiculous insistence on living apart from his family."

He stepped towards them. Robin sensed Edwin's minute flinching-back, and decided not to complicate things; he took a few steps back into the parlour, pulling Edwin with him, rather than make Walter have to physically shove past them.

"What do you mean, a missing piece?" Edwin sounded bloodless and dull.

"An object of power wants to be whole," said Walter. "Not that I should have to explain this to *you*. Brought together, the simplest of rectifications should have transformed it back into the coin. The rings failed to transform. The old bitch kept part of it *back*."

A sneer carved itself around Walter's nose. At the sight of

it Robin knew, though wasn't sure how he knew, that it was
Walter in front of whom Flora Sutton killed herself to frustrate
his efforts; Walter who would have tortured information out
of her otherwise.

Walter who pushed his own brother into the maze and left
him there to die.

"There's nothing else," said Edwin, but with a thread of uncertainty. How would they know, after all? Edwin had taken
one ring and gone off in search of its twin. Who was to say that
there wasn't a third?

"I—" said Walter, and at that moment caught sight of Billy's
body. His eyes widened. It took him a moment to speak. "Well,
well. So you're not entirely the limp piece of cabbage you seem
to be, Win. Or was this your handiwork, Sir Robert?"

"Byatt tried to be clever," said Robin. "It didn't suit him."

A smile that rose no higher than the mouth appeared and
then disappeared on Walter's face. Where Billy had been tense
enough to snap, Walter's posture was entirely relaxed. This was
the poise of a man who knew himself to be the biggest threat in
the room, and knew his own capabilities; who'd left his inhibi-
tions behind long ago, buried them beneath the floorboards as
a boy. Or perhaps never had any to begin with.

"Then let's not mess about with cleverness," he said. "Tell
me where the rest of the coin is, Edwin, or I'll break every
finger on both your hands."

Edwin's shoulders had curled in as if to make himself
smaller. At the threat his hands clenched together. Walter's
smile, as he watched his brother's reaction, was much more
genuine now.

"I told you, you *have* all of it," Edwin said.

"Stop it," said Robin, stepping half in front of Edwin.
"There's no need for any of this."

"I am practical, Sir Robert," said Walter. "Direct action pro-
duces results."

"That's rot," said Robin. "I think you just enjoy fear, and

you know you've managed to tangle Edwin up so much that all you have to do is tug on his edges and he'll produce it for you."

Walter's nostrils flared. "I am also not a fool. And neither, it seems, was Mrs. Sutton. This section of the contract is still missing a piece. Enough of this faffing about." He raised his hands, casual as a master swordsman would raise a blade. Behind his shoulder, Robin sensed Edwin go still. "Blyth. As you seem so keen to deflect me from my brother, you're more than welcome to take the punishment in his place."

"Go fuck yourself, Courcey."

A thin smile in response, and Walter began. He cradled with none of Edwin's painstaking care and none of Charlie's casual sloppiness. His fingers moved quick and sharp, and the spell was a dart, far too fast to defend against. It felt like a sharpened stick jabbed sickeningly through Robin's front, stirring his guts in an agonising roil. When he collapsed and spat bile onto Edwin's floor he was surprised not to see blood.

Part of him managed to think, with a red-tinged dispassion: *It's not nearly as bad as the curse was by the end.*

"*Stop,*" yelled Edwin. "Walt. Stop. Stop."

The tide went out on Robin's crippling nausea. He pushed himself to knees, then feet. He knew how to get up again. He could do that.

"I don't know where it is," said Edwin, "but I know where Flora Sutton would have kept it, if she didn't hide it in the maze with the other pieces."

"And if it was in the maze?" said Walter.

"Then the whole stupid mess died with Reggie, and you're no worse off than you were yesterday," said Edwin.

Walter narrowed his eyes, staring Edwin down. They were like strange shadows of each other: Walter a little taller, a lot broader, but with the same fine features looking almost too delicate for the rest of him. The same blue eyes. Robin was full of admiration for Edwin, who was ice-carved and rigid but holding himself strong, in the face of that stare and the weight of their history. If Edwin meant what Robin thought he meant, then even if he was guessing, he'd at least thought of something that would buy them time. And move them onto a kind of home turf.

"Tell me," said Walter. "I'll take this one with me," with a tilt of his head towards Robin, "and if you send me on a wild goose chase, well." His smile was nauseating as the spell had been. "He doesn't need the use of his legs to tell the future."

"I have to show you," said Edwin. "You need me to get into the room."

Robin could see this deteriorating into mistrust and yet more useless attempts to coerce information through pain. He said, "Is there such a thing as a truth-spell?"

Both Courceys looked at him.

"Seems to me it'd save us some time and argument," he added.

"No," said Walter shortly, but Edwin said, "Ye . . . es. Of a sort."

The next few minutes went over Robin's head entirely. Edwin claimed he'd seen a theoretical mention of a way that two other spells could be combined to make it difficult for someone to lie, and something something bind negation something. Walter refused to believe him; Edwin fetched a book, looking more stubborn than ever now that they'd moved into an area of his own strength. Walter, after studying the page thrust in front of his face, grudgingly agreed that it might work in principle but looked very imprecise.

"I know," said Edwin. There was a strange moment of accord between the Courceys, like two violins played at random meeting briefly on the same note.

"Er," said Robin. "I wasn't suggesting anything *experimental*." Sense smacked him around the face and he added, before Edwin could do anything absurd and martyrish like volunteer himself to be put under a truth compulsion by his hideous bully of an older brother, "But I'll give it a try."

"Edwin," said Walter. "Cradle it."

Edwin looked startled. Walter said, "I've seen the notation; I'll know if you're doing something else. And I hope you don't expect me to stand here with my hands occupied and let you get the hop on me."

Relief trickled through Robin. He trusted Edwin to do this far more than he'd have trusted Walter.

"Billy took my string," said Edwin. "I—wait." He cast a look at the body, and went to retrieve a different loop of string from a drawer of the desk tucked beneath the window.

The truth-spell was the mauve of building storms, and felt like inhaling in a steam room.

"Blyth," said Walter, impatient. "Did Reggie Gatling remove a third piece from the maze?"

"I've no idea," said Robin promptly.

A sigh. "What room is my brother referring to? Why does he need to be present?"

"The Rose Study. It's behind a mirror in the parlour at Sutton Cottage." He threw an apologetic glance at Edwin, but it wasn't as though Walter's question had been ambiguous. "Only a Sutton heir can open it."

"Sutton *heir*?" Walter demanded. "Explain."

Robin could feel it now, the way the spell crept in hot tendrils around the cavities of his mouth, waiting to catch him in an outright untruth. Sailing uncomfortably close to omission was as much as he could manage. He explained that Edwin had made a pledge with the Sutton estate to get them out of the maze. He was delighted to realise that the spell enjoyed him being forthright and effusive—and it was easier to distract them all with irrelevancies than glide around the fact that Edwin was directing them back to a deeply magical house that was bound to his blood—so Robin went into some detail about exactly what he thought of Walter bloody Courcey's character, appearance, and habit of attempted murder via shrubbery.

Edwin's eyes widened. He hadn't made that connection yet, Robin saw at once.

Walter looked half-angry, half-amused. "Enough. Do you agree that's where the old woman would have hidden it? Yes or no."

"Yes," said Robin, who actually believed that if Flora Sutton had been clever, she'd have been buried with it. But if she *had* hidden it, it was obvious to the blindest fool that a secret study opening only to your touch was the place to choose.

"Very well," said Walter. "Then that's where we'll go."

Rain stroked the train windows and melted the view into a blur of greens, browns, and greys. It was a cold and miserable September Saturday in comparison to the previous one, when Robin and Edwin had taken almost exactly this journey to Cambridgeshire.

There were several glaring distances between the circumstances, of course. Not least of which was the presence of Edwin's brother, wrapped in a red muffler and with his hands visible on his knees.

The previous night had been tense and unbalancing. Walt hadn't trusted them out of his sight—Edwin had a feeling that it was only Walt's *practicality,* and the prospect of falling asleep within an enclosed space that also contained Robin's fists, that had stopped him rushing out and demanding they arrange an overnight coach. Instead Walt had overseen Robin sending a message to the Blyth townhouse that he wouldn't be home for a day or so, and requesting a bag of his belongings be sent back with the messenger. After all, Robin had pointed out in flinty tones, he would hardly be paying a visit to a friend without at least a change of clothes.

Then Walt had paid for a room at the Cavendish and sealed Robin inside it with a charm, done the same to Edwin in his bedroom, and probably slept the peaceful sleep of the undeserving on Edwin's sofa.

Edwin had barely slept a wink. He was exhausted this morning, feeling as grey and washed-out as the world outside, trying to make his thoughts arrange themselves into a plan. Part of him was entirely unconvinced they'd find anything in the study at all. And the larger question was whether Edwin had done the right thing; whether he should have simply kept on insisting his ignorance rather than reaching desperately for a possibility and hoisting it like a white flag.

He closed his eyes against the memory of Robin falling to his knees and retching. No. He was always going to give Walt something, because Walt didn't stop until he had the result he wanted.

Edwin should have been surprised when his door opened to reveal Walt with the rings on his finger. He hadn't been, somehow. All the pieces put together felt like a logical progression, a statement argued perfectly from precedent. If asked to imagine a person capable of what had been done in the name of the Last Contract, and who valued magical power above all things . . . the shape of it would have been, indeed, very like Edwin's elder brother.

"The curse on Robin," Edwin said, breaking the silence in the compartment for the first time. "What *was* it? Where did it come from? I didn't recognise it at all."

"And yet you managed to lift it, nuisance that you are," said Walt. "It wasn't my invention. I've no hand for runes. A neat little thing, though, wouldn't you say? Pain at diminishing intervals, with a tracking clause layered in."

"Neat," said Robin, drenched in sarcasm. "Indeed."

"*Whose* invention, then?" Edwin batted aside the small glow of satisfaction. He'd been right about the tracking.

Walt's eyes glinted. "Our leader," he said. "Of a sort. Don't think you'll get any more than that."

Walt would only deign to follow a man who outstripped

him in pure power, and there weren't a great many of those. Edwin thought wistfully of the truth-spell he'd managed the previous day. But Walt had watched him dress, watched him pack; he had no string to hand, and even if he did, he'd hardly be able to build something that complex without Walt noticing and stopping him. Walt wasn't Billy.

Edwin's heart gave a queer hiccup as though an echo-spell were trying to take place within his ribs, showing him a past that might have been. Edwin hadn't been recruited early to this conspiracy, despite being cleverer and more desperate and far more primed to swallow the hook of promised power than Reggie Gatling. Now he knew why. *Walt wasn't Billy.* Billy was the one who had, belatedly, suggested Edwin as suitable.

It would never, not in the full length of his effortless life, have occurred to Walt that his younger brother might be worth anything at all.

Perhaps Edwin should be glad of that, bitter pill that it was. If these people had come to him before the murders, before anything had gone wrong—if they'd sold the quest for the Last Contract to him in the right intellectual light, it could have been so easy for Edwin to become what Reggie became.

Would he have clung, pathetically grateful, to the chance to finally *be on Walt's side,* and thereby break their old and exhausting pattern of hurt and response?

Would he have stood by and watched a curse of pain laid on Sir Robert Blyth and told himself, dispassionate, that it was a means to a worthwhile end?

Edwin didn't know. He felt dunked in cool and unclean water.

"*I* have a question," said Robin to Walt. "Did you tell Billy Byatt to kill me? Once you realised at dinner, the first night, that I didn't know anything about the contract?" He'd donned the mild, pleasant expression that Edwin could now recognise as Robin's version of armour.

Walt raised his eyebrows. "Kill you at *Penhallick*?"

"Of course not," said Edwin.

"What?" said Robin.

"Guest-right," said Edwin. "Having a guest die on pledged land makes the land . . . unsettled. And Walt visits Penhallick a lot oftener than I do."

"Easy enough to wait until you got back to London," said Walt. "And thank goodness we kept you alive, hm? Foresight's a rare thing for us to have stumbled across." He was eyeing Robin with satisfaction, as Bel eyed people and objects she wished to collect, though without even a spark of Bel's tempering merriment.

Edwin pressed his leg against Robin's, as much of a warning and comforting touch as he would allow himself. Simply existing in the same space as Robin felt like holding a flame close to a fuse. Apart from the moment of relief in the aftermath of Billy's death, they'd not been given time to settle anything; the fight that they'd parted with still hung over them, fragile as glass. And Edwin was a ghastly bubble of fear that Walt, too, would see what Billy had seen. Would realise that he didn't need truth-spells or curses or anything of the sort to make Edwin do whatever he wanted, so long as Robin was there to be hurt.

The rest of the journey was quiet.

The closest stop to Sutton Cottage was in a large enough town that they easily found a hackney coach to take them to the estate itself. The driver was eager to tell them how they'd all wondered if the house was going to close to tourists after the old lady had passed, not that anyone ever saw her, famous recluse she'd been, God rest her soul, and had they been there before? They had? What did they think of the hedge maze?

Edwin had forgotten the estate warding entirely until Walter began to stir, frowning. "I don't like the feel of this," Walt said. "You two are—deceiving me, somehow. The coin won't be here."

"This'll pass," said Edwin wearily. "Hold tight, Walt."

"Think of England," put in Robin, not at all pleasantly.

Walter showed no intention of holding tight. By the time they turned onto the long driveway he was half-standing, jabbing his finger in Edwin's face. "Turn around. You bloody little pest, tell him to *turn this around*."

Edwin's heart shoved cold water through his veins. He wanted to hide. "Walt—"

"Courcey," snapped Robin, actually grabbing at Walt's arm.

"*Stop!*" Walt shouted, all the force of his personality behind it, and the carriage settled to a halt.

Edwin managed not to choke on the irony of it all. He *didn't* want them to keep going. He didn't want Walter to have anything he wanted. And yet, he did.

The stronger the magician, the stronger the warding, and now Walter had no tracking spell to trump the wards. Edwin didn't think they'd manage to drag Walt over the elm-tree boundary with haste, as Robin and the Daimler had managed to drag Edwin.

Edwin opened the door of the coach and stepped onto the road. He walked past the line of elms and felt the moment when the estate awoke to him, the air suddenly fresher and more alive in his lungs. *I'm sorry,* he thought, miserable. *I'm sorry, I'm sorry.*

"This is my brother, Walter Courcey." He couldn't manage the words *he is welcome*. "I am inviting him onto these lands."

26

The staff of Sutton Cottage were startled to see Robin and Edwin again, so much sooner than Edwin had told them to expect him, but there was a glint of pleasure in Mrs. Greengage's eye even as she over-apologised for the likely quality of dinner with the superbly passive-aggressive air of the expert.

Walt looked critically around the house. Edwin was afraid he'd demand a tour, but single-mindedness won out, and all three of them headed to the parlour as their bags were carried upstairs. Walt's brow furrowed at the empty chair in which Flora Sutton had died. Edwin knew that look. Walt was looking for a triumph that would overwrite the failure he'd last experienced here.

Edwin, last into the room, touched the doorframe and again felt the ache of apology in his fingertips. If London was normal and Penhallick was a dull itch, then Sutton was like discovering that one had been breathing shallowly one's entire life; that there was an extra inch of rib cage to be filled. It was new, it was still uncertain, but it *welcomed* him. Edwin felt vertiginous with it. Walt's presence meant he managed not to show it on his face; he'd learned before he graduated into long trousers not to show either of his siblings the things that he valued, if he could possibly help it.

"Show me this secret study," said Walt.

Edwin had left the rose pendant in a shadow box hanging on the parlour wall between two enormous floral embroidery samplers. The box was in the shape of a tree, with the trunk a series of stacked small windows. Edwin pulled the rose from the lowest of these, touched it to the mirror's frame, and watched the glass dissolve.

The Rose Study was exceedingly cramped for three grown men, especially when one of them had shoulders like Robin's. Walt called up a light and tethered it to the empty glass bowl on the desk, an old-fashioned style of guidekeeper. In the glow of it, mingling mellowly with the spill of daylight in from the parlour, Edwin looked around at the neatly shelved books and the polished floorboards, which suddenly seemed vulnerable; ready to be torn up. He remembered the destructive mess that he'd walked into in Reggie's office—Robin's office—the day after Robin was cursed. Walt would be methodical, but no less destructive.

"Where do we start?" Robin asked. "You *did* say you can't do a spell to search for it, didn't you?" Perhaps he was thinking about the wrecked office as well. It really was a shame that the objects were muffled against detection, because inability to define parameters—

"Hold on," said Edwin. He dragged pieces of thoughts around like a Latin sentence, until all the parts made tentative sense. "We don't have to search for the contract in particular, or anything magical at all. We're in a small space and we're searching for silver."

"Fossicking," said Walter.

"Yes," said Edwin. He sat at the desk and located in a drawer some pencils and a pile of writing paper. A floral scent wafted into the air as he lifted the paper onto the desk. Attar of roses. Flora Sutton had sat at this desk and written a letter to her great-nephew after he'd left her estate with two rings in his pocket. After she'd trusted to family and a secret-bind to keep the contract safe, when she knew danger would be closing in on her soon. She'd trusted in the wrong things.

Edwin wrote down a line of notation, tapped the pencil against his chin, put it down to move his fingers and remind himself how the blazes one defined *silver* in a cradle, and wrote another line.

"Fossicking?" Robin asked.

"If you can define something, you can find it," Edwin said. "There's a story about a magician who took himself to California, convinced he'd be able to make his fortune using it to find gold. It *does* work, but only if you're very close already, and only if the amount of gold is large enough."

"Did he make his fortune?"

"Killed in a fight over land boundaries. Or fell down a pit. Or did in fact strike it rich, and then changed his name and married an heiress in Boston. It's a rather apocryphal story." Edwin frowned at his work.

"We're not here to be lectured," said Walt.

Edwin defined the diameter of the fossicking spell to just beyond the walls of the study—they could always expand it to search the whole house later, if they felt like spending hours checking the teaspoons and candlesticks—and pushed the completed spell across the desk to Walt, who skimmed it and gave another nod, then pulled Edwin's cradling string from a pocket of his waistcoat and tossed it across the desk.

"Go on," said Walt. He still intended to keep his hands free and his own power untouched.

Building the spell here in the heart of Sutton was easy, easy. It was that extra inch of space, that friendliness to the air, the sense of molecules bending themselves to comply. The spell was one of those that was more palpable than visible, a cool throb between Edwin's palms like water lifted from a lake and made spherical enough to dash in someone's face—another favourite trick of magical children during careless summers.

Tossed wide, the spell splashed through him, then tossed itself back in pinprick form.

"Anything?" said Walt.

"Something." Edwin stood and followed the pinpricks, which became sharper and sharper without ever registering as pain. *By the pricking of my thumbs,* he thought, and narrowly avoided laughing.

His thumbs tugged him first to the silver pen-stand on the desk and then to one of the drawers, where he unearthed a handsome letter opener that looked part of a set with the stand. He turned a slow circle in the centre of the room. Robin politely crammed himself beside the desk to give him space. There was only one more signal, one insistent tug, and it came from the bookshelf, where there was nothing visibly metallic at all.

Edwin exhaled. He hadn't been *sure.* But he'd seen the intense kinship in Flora Sutton's eyes, beneath a personality stronger than his would ever be. He'd felt the brand of her hands on his cheeks, and even now her house breathed around him. She'd hidden her magical ability from the world, she'd hidden the beauty of what she could do by warding away any magician who came close to her lands, and she'd hidden her part of the contract in the centre of a labyrinth. And kept part of it back from even her own great-nephew.

She hadn't trusted a single one of them. Her mind had been a hedge of its own, thick with suspicion, comfortable in dark corners. She wouldn't be the sort to toss something in with her jewellery-box, or hide it plain sight on someone's finger. It took Reggie to think of that.

Edwin stepped closer to the bookshelf, eyes skipping along the spines of the top row, and then stopped.

What are you doing? he asked himself, furious. *Flora Sutton died to keep this hidden, and you've led Walt right back to it.*

It was like being mesmerised by one of Belinda's damned arrows. It was like breaking out of that same mesmerism. Thoughts flooded him from every direction, his mind making a frantic grab for information that it could turn into the right answer, the right choice.

He thought: I don't have to tell Walt anything.

He thought: Walt will tear this house apart if he thinks

there's the slightest chance it could be hidden in the walls. *Mine to tend and mine to mend.* Did I mean that pledge or not?

He thought: *Every living magician in Britain.*

He thought: I showed him that damned truth-spell myself, and any minute now he's going to remember it exists.

Edwin forced the churning flood to settle, and pulled his decision clear.

"This is it," he said.

The book was a thick dictionary of spells from the previous century, rough at the edges, soft over the spine with age. Opened at the midpoint, the book fell open like a muscle relaxing. Two hemicircles of space had been carved, one in each side; the angling of the pages made them uneven, with papery sloping sides. It was obvious that when the book was closed, this empty space was a single sphere too perfect to be anything but a spell-made hiding place for the final piece.

It was another ring. This one had a place where the flat band poked out on either side, as though someone had sketched a setting for a gem and never bothered to fill it. Placed between the other two with their triangular notches, together they would be a single ring—flat, thick. Whole.

Edwin went to touch it, felt the tension of Walt behind him, and smoothed his finger over a random entry in the text instead. *Mingling, see also Commingling. A framework for charms with the basic intent of combining two substances.*

Walt reached over his shoulder and picked up the ring like a penny on the street. "Let's have some proper light." He led them back out to the parlour, where it was brighter, even though the rain had followed them from London, then slid the other two rings from his finger and arranged them on a wooden display plinth that held a ceramic vase. The rings formed a perfect stack as Walt placed them atop one another. He glanced at Edwin and then at Robin: *You're not what I'd have preferred as an audience,* the look said, *but you'll do.*

The spell Walt cast was not a mingling, or even a commingling. It was, as he'd said, a rectification. The sort of spell that would repair a dropped plate, if you cared enough for the plate to put the energy into making it whole again.

Edwin found he was holding his breath.

There was no flash of light. Nothing impressive. The seams between the rings became fainter and vanished, and then the stack of them simply collapsed, in a puddling-out of the silver, and then there were no rings at all: just the coin, stamped with the crude outline of a crown.

"It's real," Robin said. It was exactly what Edwin had been thinking, right down to the edge of bafflement.

"You thought it was just a story?" said Walt. He plucked up the coin and slipped it into a small velvet pouch he'd pulled from somewhere, and thence into his inner pocket. Only the light of triumph at the corners of his eyes spoke to his satisfaction at what he'd just steered into completion.

Edwin thought of Robin in the Penhallick library, a week and a hundred years ago. *Magic is just a story.*

"A lot of stories *aren't* true," said Edwin. "And plenty of them aren't an object you can touch."

"And yet even the untrue ones are powerful," said Walt.

Robin snorted. "That's not very practical of you."

"On the contrary," said Walt, relaxed in victory. "Stories are why anyone does anything. Byatt was living in a story about love denied. Reginald Gatling, idiot that he was, was the hero of a story about the first non-magician to somehow give himself magic. And you, Sir Robert, standing there so *angry* at me. You think this is a story about the plucky boy standing up against the evil magicians. You think, somehow, that you've still got a chance of taking this back from me, because that's how it *should* end." His smile was friendly. "It's not. And you don't."

"Thirst for power," said Edwin. "That's old enough to be dull, Walt."

"Pure foresight isn't the only way to glimpse the future," said Walt unexpectedly. "Only the clearest. You want to know the story? *There's something coming.* We don't know what, or when, but we need to learn to use all the power we have. The search for the Last Contract is a project with the backing of the Assembly. This is a story about the magicians of this land coming into the fullness of our birthright, as we were always meant to."

Something coming. Billy Byatt had said it too. Edwin looked at Walt's thrown-back head and heard the certainty in his voice, solid enough to carve into bricks and build with. He was right about the strength of stories. Walter Courcey—firstborn, favoured, never second-guessing himself for a moment in his life—had never seen anyone around him as anything but a supporting figure. A tool.

Edwin thought of the paper man he'd created in the library and set waving in an echo of Robin's movements. The danger of the situation crashed back over him, drawing every muscle tight with fear. The sheer thrill of discovery had kept it at bay when watching the coin take shape. He'd half forgotten that they were here under duress, with no guarantee of safe exit.

"You're still on the side of the murderers," Edwin said. "Does the Assembly know how much blood has been shed in the name of this *project*?"

"I might point out that you're the one with a dead body in your rooms."

Not for much longer, Edwin thought grimly. Kitty Kaur would have turned up back at the Cavendish by now, and she didn't seem one to let a locked door get in her way. He'd written her an explanatory note during the sleepless night confined in his own room, and left it tucked under a brush on his dresser with a scribble of a cat on the fold.

Walt laughed at whatever his expression was. "Really, Win, that peevishness of yours has never been attractive. You should be careful. Another few years of it and you'll be going down the same road as Mother."

It was perfectly, exactly Walt: a whiplash of hurt both casual and precise, delivered for no other purpose than because he'd glimpsed a piece of unmarked skin and wanted to raise a welt. Edwin's fear transmuted into a helplessness that rang through him like a plucked string finding resonances that reached back two decades, a sudden surge, an unstoppable tide. It passed the boundaries of his skin. It burned his feet, and his feet must have spoken to the floor, because there was a sudden crack of wood. One of the floorboards on which Walt was standing slammed upwards as though an elephant had stepped on the other end.

Walt staggered, and fell to the floor.

It was as though Robin had been poised for the opportunity. He took two huge strides and was almost upon Walt, one hand already drawing back for a blow. Walter kicked out, keeping Robin away from his hands, which were moving swiftly. Edwin wanted to help, but he didn't think he could; he'd only managed to hurt Billy because he'd had time to come up with a plan, and anything he'd just transmitted to the house had been entirely by accident.

The spell Walt was cradling flared into life—a white whip of power, snaking wildly out and around a chair leg. Walt jerked his hand. The chair flung itself across the room and right into Robin—Edwin threw his arms out, uselessly—who toppled off Walt and went sprawling with a grunt. Something that Robin had been holding flew out of his hand and dropped onto the rug with a thud. It was Billy Byatt's switch-knife, folded open.

Edwin's stomach lurched. Robin could have fallen *onto* it.

Walt was back on his feet now. He shook himself like a cat, rubbed at one shoulder, and then let his arms fall loose. Edwin saw his eyes land on the knife and narrow. In the sudden quiet, Robin also stood, darting looks at the knife the whole time.

It felt as though the next move anyone made would smash the air like glass.

"Very well," said Walt. "You've had your try. Are you finished now? You really *should* have believed me when I told you how this ends." He looked around the room. "So the house does like you, Win. It's an impressive place, Sutton. That maze, now—extraordinary. And that cunning little study. I'm sure it has plenty of other secrets, and I do hate to waste any kind of power. Please believe I would feel *very* bad about burning it all to the ground."

Edwin didn't know if what he was feeling was his own molten fury or if the house really had enough sentience to have understood Walt's words. Either way, he was shaken by the force of his desire to—to throw Walt over his shoulder, if that was what it took, and march him to the edge of the estate and throw him over it once more. But Walt had never been one of those bullies who just made noise. He truly meant every one of his threats. He followed them through.

Edwin took a deep, deep breath, and tried to hold this sensation at the boundary of his skin and not let it any further. "What now?" he asked.

Walt turned to Robin.

"Don't tell me," said Robin. "You want to take my memories."

"Take? No, indeed. I want to offer you a job."

"Ha-ha," said Robin, flat.

"Forget the contract. That's got nothing to do with this. Think of that as—a hobby. A passion project. I work for the Magical Assembly, and I know they would be delighted to have you working in an official capacity at the Barrel. It's almost unheard-of, for a non-magician. But you're far too good a catch to be passed up."

"No, thank you."

"Let me rephrase," said Walt. "*You* are the most valuable thing in this place. Possibly in the entire country. We need you; we'll have you. And it's just another branch of the civil service, you know, in its way. You could do good work there."

"What makes you think I'd go along with anything you want?" said Robin.

"Curiosity. And money, of course." Robin's face shifted. Walt smiled. "I've been looking into you, Sir Robert Blyth, since the day my brother brought you to Penhallick. I know you have family relying on you." A gleam of meaning in his eyes. "Be reasonable, Blyth. *Think.* Don't let your emotions ruin the future. I'm sure you want life to be happy and healthy and long, for that *enterprising* young sister of yours."

The last sentence fell like stones into water. Robin went very still.

"You wouldn't," said Robin.

"Threaten someone's loved ones?" Walt spread his hands, irony painting his smile.

"Mm. I suppose you would." Robin bent down, a seemingly absent motion, to retrieve the knife where he'd dropped it. He straightened again with it clutched in his hand.

Walt sighed. "Do I need to point out—"

Edwin was having trouble watching both of them at once. Instinct kept his eyes tied to Walt, as the more likely threat, but Walt cut himself off abruptly and his eyes widened. Edwin followed his gaze. Robin had pressed the tip of the knife to the soft tuck of his own jaw, over the pulse.

"Put out your hands and keep them apart, Courcey," Robin said. "I think I can push faster than you can twiddle."

"What are you doing, Blyth?" But Walt did splay his hands. He did keep them apart.

"Touch my sister and I'll kill myself," said Robin. Edwin's breath seized and he bit the inside of his mouth. All he wanted was to wrench the knife away. "She won't be any good to you as leverage if there's nothing on the other end of the lever."

A long pause. "Now, that, I don't think *you* would," said Walt.

"That's because you don't know him," said Edwin.

Robin smiled, humourless. "Yes. To protect someone I love? You don't know me at all." His fingers tightened. Edwin felt himself make a soft, noiseless sound of denial; saw Walt's hand twitch in an equally urgent motion.

Then they were all still again. Now a thin trickle of blood ran down Robin's neck where the knife's tip had just, *just* pierced the skin. Edwin felt the push of his own pulse like knuckles, like fingers tucked there to raise the face to be kissed.

Walt hissed a curse. "This is pointless. You have no defences. I could let you go today and then put a compulsion on you next week, to preserve your own life above all things."

"And I could take it off again," said Edwin. Robin spared him a look of pale, blazing gratitude.

"I'm not trying to out-bluff you," said Robin to Walt. "I know you've got us outclassed. I just want you to *listen*. Here's the deal: take the coin and leave us be, and we'll return the favour. I don't care about this sodding contract—it's caused me nothing but trouble. Leave my sister alone, leave Edwin alone, and I'll liaise with your bloody Assembly about my visions." Another hollow smile twitched at his mouth. "That's supposed to be my job, after all. To liaise. I'll tell you what I see, and you people can do whatever you want with that. The visions don't seem any godly use to me."

An answering smile began to find its way back onto Walt's face. He didn't like that Robin was setting terms. But it was the misery, the defeat in Robin's shoulders, that decided it, Edwin thought. Walt liked to win as much as Bel did. He just played nastier games.

"How eager you are to bargain for the safety of others, Sir Robert," said Walt. "But I can be fair. Cooperate, *fully*, and you may remain at liberty as well. Take one single step in a direction I don't like, and I'll keep you shut up nice and safe and convenient in a room somewhere. My little brother here tries *very* hard, but I'm sure you've realised he can protect you about as effectively as a damp paper bag."

After a long moment, Robin nodded, and lowered the knife.

"I'll take that, if you don't mind," Walt said, arch.

Robin held the knife out handle-first; Walt took it from him and shook Robin's hand, brief and businesslike, then stepped back. He patted his pocket as if to reassure himself that the coin was still there.

Edwin's nails dug hard into his palms to stop himself from screaming. Of course Robin, stupid bloody selfless moron Robin, would bargain for everyone else's safety and not his own.

"Leave, Walt," said Edwin. "You have everything you want. Just as you always do."

Walt made a tutting sound, but did start towards the door that led back into the hallway. He gave Edwin a considering look as he drew level with him. "I'm a man of my word. Once we leave this room, I won't lay a finger on you. But this is too important a matter to leave loose ends flapping around London where they might trip me up, and I'm afraid I don't trust *you* to keep your inquisitive nose out of this, Win. Not enough to leave without taking . . . precautions."

Edwin's mouth was forming the question when Walt's hand closed around his arm, Walt's grip was wrenching him forward and down, until Edwin was half-crouched, half-knelt, his hand splayed on the closest low table. He saw the shape of his hand distinct against a crocheted lace doily. A cry rasped uselessly in his throat as memory swamped him. He was ten years old and at school and someone was holding him down and Walt was stepping on his fingers, leaning harder and harder, waiting for Edwin's begging to go shrill before he relented. He was twenty-five years old and standing in his Cavendish rooms, yesterday, hearing Walt say, *I'll break every finger on both your hands.*

He saw a flash of light on metal. The knife. Walt had the knife.

Oh God, Edwin thought, and then his fear exploded past his skin like flour tossed onto a flame.

It felt like the resonant tide of emotion that had flipped the floorboard, only more so. His vision went red and then black and his whole body jerked as though the ground were erupting in chunks beneath his feet. The weight of Walt's grasp was abruptly gone from his wrist, and he heard a cry that might have been Walt himself, and Robin shouting something, and a tearing, crunching, slithering sound, and then—quite distinct, the last note in a symphony—the *ching* of a glass vase falling to the floor and shattering.

Edwin was trembling. The whole *room* was trembling. It subsided, slowly, as he stood.

His brother Walter stood with his back pressed up against one of the ivy-carved wooden panels. But the ivy was no longer a carving: the ivy was *moving,* was solid, had formed writhing loops of dark woody vines that held Walt's legs in place and pinned his arms wide on either side of his body.

Edwin's hand was at his mouth. He almost couldn't hear anything over the ringing of disbelief and his own pulse in his ears, but Robin was speaking.

"It—came right out of the wall," Robin said, strained and odd. "I've not seen anything move that fast. It dragged him off you."

Walt was half-stunned, but he was recovering. Even as Edwin watched, his brother shook the glazed look off his face and wrenched with a snarl at his constraints, then froze when the wooden loops tightened like the coils of a snake. The snarl gave way to an expression that it took Edwin a nonsensical amount of time to recognise as *fear.* Walt met Edwin's eyes, and neither of them spoke.

I should be enjoying this, Edwin thought. It was a mirror-version of the past, days after endless days when Walter had Edwin exactly where he wanted him. This moment here: the pause in which to savour the first spark of true fear. And the moment after that, where both participants settled into the knowledge of exactly whose hands held the power in the room.

Edwin thought about the Goblin's Bridle, and about hedge-vines grabbing at his ankles. He watched Walt's fear rising and mingling with an impotent fury; watched Walt's mouth open and then close again, as entitlement came up hard against pragmatism and all the possible words cancelled one another out.

Watched his older brother seeing him, for the very first time, as an equal.

"You probably shouldn't have threatened to burn my house down," said Edwin. "I don't think it liked that."

"I'm going to get the coin from his pocket," said Robin.

"Wait," said Edwin.

"Edwin—"

"*Wait.*"

Robin frowned, but waited. Edwin thrust his exhaustion aside and thought faster and more carefully than he'd thought all day, forcing himself to see the whole pattern. Yes, they could take the coin now. But Walt followed through: he would bring every resource he had to bear on taking back the thing he wanted, unless Edwin—what? Wiped his brother's memory? Even if Edwin could muster enough power to do it properly, there were other people involved in this. They'd simply fill Walt in on what he'd forgotten, and then—again—Walter would come after them, bent on revenge. What did Edwin want from this situation? What was he trying to win for them?

Freedom. Safety. And a chance.

"It's only one piece," Edwin said. "One of three. It's useless without the others."

"You can't be serious," Robin said. "Edwin, you *have* him, you can—"

"What can I do?" Edwin said sharply. "Kill him?"

Robin blanched. Walt sucked in his breath. Then, unbelievably, shook it out in a laugh. "You wouldn't," Walt said.

"I could," Edwin said. It would be easy. He could slow Walt's heart, beat by beat until it stopped, and thereby lift the curse that had been Walt's presence in the whole quarter-century of his life. But it would be deliberate, it would be cool-blooded and cruel, and Edwin had already identified his own uncrossable line. "I could. But I think I'm going to hold you to your word, instead."

Mrs. Sutton had demanded it of Reggie, hadn't she? *He put blood into the swearing.* Yes. There was more than one sort of blood-pledge in the world. This one was very old, and very exact, and could only be broken by death.

"No," Walt began when he saw what Edwin was doing. Edwin raised his head and Walt stopped.

"My vote is for killing you, Courcey," Robin snapped. "Whatever Edwin wants, we're going to do it."

It took nearly ten minutes. The cradle did not require a great deal of magic to build, as it was powered largely by the blood of the participants, but it was complex. Robin located the knife, which had spun beneath a chair when the ivy took hold of Walt. By then the spell was ready and waiting, glowing a deep orange in Edwin's hands.

"I, Edwin John Courcey, am overseeing this oath," said Edwin, and outlined the terms. That Walt would not cause—directly or indirectly—any harm, of any kind, to come to Robin, to Maud Blyth or any other member of Robin's household, or to Edwin himself. That in exchange Walt would leave here with Flora Sutton's coin, and that Robin would liaise with the Magical Assembly and give truthful report of the contents of his visions.

Edwin paused. "Do you consent to these terms?"

Robin shot him a look, eyes widening slightly. He'd heard the missing piece, then. Had Walt? Edwin raised his eyebrows in warning.

"I consent," said Robin.

Walt, after another two heartbeats, voiced his grudging agreement. A cut on Walt's hand as he spoke his full name; a cut on Robin's. Blood from each of them dripped into the cradle, where it disappeared in flurries of white sparks, and that was that: Walter Clifford Courcey of Penhallick and Sir Robert

Harold Blyth, fourth baronet of Thornley Hill, were bound in oath by blood. Robin gasped and clutched at his bleeding hand as the magic took.

"We're done," said Edwin. He touched one of the ivy loops. Usually he'd have been tense enough to snap, standing this close to Walt, but his fear had washed out of him. He'd never outgrow it entirely—he'd grown up with it woven into his nerves, a spell cast on a sapling—but he also didn't think it would ever return to the same extent. "Thank you," he said to Sutton Cottage. "Let him go."

Walt's nerves held old patterns too. He lifted a furious hand to Edwin as soon as the ivy released him, but it was the hand with the cut on it, and it spasmed into a useless fist. *No harm.*

"So you've found yourself some power after all," Walt spat. He steadied himself on the back of an armchair—Edwin thought that was rather brave of him, all things considered—and massaged his wrist. "A power that you won't have if you're anywhere but this estate. Much good may it do you."

"Walt, you still have what you want," Edwin pointed out. "You have what you came here for in the first place."

For a very long time, he thought, he would remember the look that came over Walt's face when Walt realised that he *had* won this battle—for his cause, for his passion project—but had lost every scrap of his leverage over Robin, and also lost his ability to threaten Edwin. Ever again. It was a look that meant Walt was seeing something shatter, and what was shattering was the *story.* The story about the relationship between the Courcey brothers, a story that Walt had built and Edwin had always believed he had no choice but to inhabit. Now it was in pieces.

Edwin thought of the oak-heart: an explosion, and charred splinters on the floor. He put his shoulders back, met his brother's eye, and did not smile.

"This is my brother, Walter Courcey," said Edwin. "I am revoking his guest-right. He is not welcome on these lands, and I would like him to remove himself from my property. *Now.*"

Sutton was an estate that understood warding; more than that, it understood Edwin. And vice versa. Edwin felt it in the soles of his feet, in the whites of his eyes, as the boundary's warding swept inwards across lawns and hills and ponds and paths, seeking, until it found the target of Edwin's displeasure and took him in its grip.

Walt's face went greenish and he stumbled for the door. Edwin felt his brother's frantic footfalls as Walter shoved his way through the house and out onto the long drive, like fingers tapped on his own skin. He was aware of the servants exclaiming as Walt continued to run, away from the cottage and towards the boundary. He was aware of the golden net of strange, wild spellwork that ran through the roots of trees and spiderwebbed its way across autumn-sleepy rosebushes, through beds of peonies and primroses and asters and violets.

Beneath that, impossibly, he could feel the throb of the ley lines that crossed as they ran through this place and away: south to north, east to west, tugging with their vast tidal strength at the spark of magic in Edwin's core.

His body fell to its knees. He barely noticed.

Hello, Edwin thought. *My name is Edwin John Courcey, and I am determined to do this right.*

This wasn't just an ease of magic and of breathing. This was something ancient and unmapped, the land reminding him that blood-pledge was the oldest contract played out small—power for responsibility, *to tend and to mend.* Edwin breathed through it, dragging his awareness in from the trees and the hedge-roots, nearly gasping with relief as it shrank and sharpened to only the house itself. Even that was overwhelming for a few long moments: he was the joins of the wooden furniture, he was the skitter of mouse-feet in the gaps between walls, he was mirrors and clocks and dried herbs hung in the rafters and the charms for safety laid around every fireplace.

"Edwin," Robin was saying.

Edwin dragged it all in until the tendrils of connection were only here in the parlour—and then it was all inside his chest, his throat, the whole world burning there as though if he opened his mouth it would all come pouring out like sunlight—

And then it was just him and Robin, kneeling on the floor.

Robin's face was close to Edwin's and he looked worried. He was gripping Edwin's fingers in his own, hard enough to be painful.

"Robin," Edwin said. Coughed. "May I have my hands back?"

Robin gave him his hands back. Robin gave a grin of open affection and pure relief that brought the sunlight back into Edwin's mouth for a fleeting moment.

"Are you all right?" Robin asked.

"I don't know what I am," said Edwin. "But yes. I'm all right." In the spirit of enquiry, he sat back on his heels and tried to identify what he was feeling.

Somewhat to his shock, he decided it was joy.

27

Robin's hand had mostly stopped bleeding, but one of the kitchen maids was summoned anyway. She cast a ticklish charm, which left the cut looking two days old; Robin supposed a knack for that sort of thing would be useful in her line of work. Edwin was telling Mrs. Greengage the housekeeper why Walter's bag needed to be brought back down again and sent to London. The explanation was along the lines of the one he'd given to Sutton Cottage itself. *My brother. Not welcome here.*

Mrs. Greengage had only appeared, with a stately knock, in the wake of Walter's hasty departure. Unlikely as it seemed, the disturbance in the house had been contained to the parlour alone; Robin should have realised it from the fact that no servants came running to see what the fuss was about when the room shook and the ivy moved. Now the ivy panel looked innocent and flat like all the others.

"May I ask if you and Sir Robert are still intending to stay overnight?" Mrs. Greengage asked.

They were. They would appreciate the chance to wash up, and possibly to rest before a late luncheon. No, they would not require assistance to dress. Robin hid a brief smile in his collar at the new notes of authority that filled Edwin's voice.

Mrs. Greengage looked relieved at the prospect of not having to produce an impromptu valet from among the footmen. The housekeeper was thin and capable, with creases at her eyes as she looked at Edwin, who was toying fondly with the trim of his chair.

"I'd say it's likely the house will show you to your rooms, sir," she said. "Sir Robert, we've put your bag in the next room down."

She was right. The house showed them the way. Sutton Cottage was large enough that light poorly penetrated the interior corridors of the largest wings, and old enough that the darkness of the wood and stone rendered it shadowy, deep, and cool. The way needed to be lit and warmed, and lit and warmed it was, by clusters of candles in glass lantern-shields. Whenever Edwin hesitated at the foot of a stair or the end of a hallway, a cluster would flare briefly brighter in invitation, guiding them on.

"You're going to have a terrific chandler's bill, with this lot," murmured Robin.

Edwin's face lit in turn with a smile, even as he reached out a hand to the nearest wall as though to protect it from Robin's teasing. He'd been doing that—small touches, odd smiles— since he'd fallen to his knees in the grasp of whatever power of this magical estate had sent Walter packing. There were subtler changes too. That authority in his voice. A straighter angle of his shoulders.

They certainly weren't being stashed in a guest wing this time. The suite Edwin was led to had gold damask wall coverings and comprised at least three rooms joined by doors. There was a bedroom with an imposing four-poster dominating the middle, and an adjoining dressing room, but the bulk of the suite was the large, friendly space that combined study and sitting room. A series of sofas surrounded a pale round table that looked like marble; the centre of it was a chessboard, black stone inset amongst the white. There was a writing desk and chair, a winged armchair adorned with cushions, and a sideboard with a row of full decanters and a tray of crystal glasses. The silk walls were otherwise bare, with faint squares showing the gaps where pictures had been; politely awaiting the imposition of a new occupier's taste. It was a man's haven of a room and Robin wanted to wrap himself in it like a blanket.

He directed his comments to the ceiling. "You do realise he's only going to haul bookshelves in here and crowd everything else out."

"I shan't need to," said Edwin. "I have entire rooms for books. I have. A house's worth." The sentence veered, unsteady with disbelief.

"So you do." Robin hesitated, but the question had been niggling at him. "Edwin, if Sutton Cottage could do *that* to Walter—for you—why wouldn't it have done the same for Mrs. Sutton, when he was here before?"

"I've been thinking about that—about how it felt when it happened. I can only suppose . . ." Edwin rubbed at his face. He looked tired, as though he'd lived a week in the few hours they'd been here. "Mrs. Sutton realised the same thing that I did. That Walt's group, whomever they are, knew she still had something they wanted, even if it was just information and not the contract itself. She knew that Walt was only the beginning. The house doesn't *think*. It responds to what's felt, and what's wanted. I wanted Walt not to slice my fingers off." A brief, humourless smile. "Flora Sutton wanted to take her secrets to the grave, as the best way to keep them safe. And so she did."

"What a cheery thought," said Robin, shaken.

"Indeed." Edwin went to the sideboard and poured them both drinks. Robin didn't give a fig for the hour of the day; alcoholic fortification seemed suddenly like the perfect idea.

"A toast," said Edwin. "To the most valuable thing in the country."

Robin touched the tiny self-inflicted cut on his neck, which he hadn't bothered to point out to the kitchen maid. A frisson of awareness, more sexual than painful, echoed the soft burn of spirits in his throat.

"Walter showed his hand there, didn't he?" he said.

"Walt gets the things he wants," said Edwin. "He's never had to pretend he doesn't want them. He wouldn't know how."

Something about that cracked Robin's heart into pieces and rectified it with the next beat. "It's odd to think that if his lot hadn't killed Gatling, I'd never have come into contact with magic at all, and the foresight would never have—woken up."

Edwin blinked. "And I'd never have inherited Sutton."

"He got what he wanted." Robin smiled. "And rather a lot that he never bargained for. It's going to be extremely satisfying to ruin his plans." He chased that declaration with the rest of his drink, all in one gulp, then set the glass down.

"Yes." Edwin's piecemeal smile appeared in response. "When do you think he's going to realise that you *didn't* actually promise to return the favour when it comes to non-interference?"

"Hopefully not for a long time. That was a dashed clever thing you did, leaving it out of the oath. How did you know you could slip it past him?"

And it had slipped past: the fact that Robin and Edwin were still perfectly free, by the terms that Edwin had defined, to do their best to sabotage Walt's efforts. To find the rest of the contract themselves. Walt had gained a coin, a blood-oath, and a pair of determined enemies that he couldn't lay a finger on.

"I didn't," Edwin said. "But he was off-balance enough that it seemed worth trying."

Robin shook his head. "Someone should have told him to pay attention to his contracts, before he consented to—" He didn't get further; Edwin was laughing, quiet and helpless, the action like a new form of light that brought out his pigments, and Robin couldn't remember anymore why he wasn't holding Edwin in his arms. It seemed urgent enough to interrupt himself over.

Edwin was still laughing when Robin kissed him. It turned at once into a sharp inhalation; an equally sharp press of fingers at Robin's neck, keeping him close. Edwin's mouth opening to his. It had the same urgency, the same carmine edge of exultation and not-being-dead, that had flooded Robin's veins when they escaped from the maze. Robin kissed him, kissed him, drank him in like water.

They parted only when Edwin sloshed spirits onto Robin's back, from the glass he hadn't been given a chance to put down. He hastily took it to the sideboard to join Robin's.

"We're going to do this," said Robin. Best to have things laid out clear. He unbuttoned his damp waistcoat and Edwin's eyes followed his hands. "We're going to find out exactly what Walter and his chums are up to, and we're going to find the other parts of the contract."

Edwin swiped his hair back, a hectic motion. His lips were reddened. Robin found the sight maddening. "Rather optimistic of you, I'd say."

"They don't know that I have any control over the visions at all—oh, I'm starting to feel my way there, I think," Robin said, to forestall Edwin's questions. He tossed his waistcoat aside. "They *also* don't know that Miss Morrissey and her sister are aware of what's afoot. Only Byatt knew that. So, there. They're not the only ones with allies."

Edwin's hands were on Robin's chest now, making a delightful exploration of the gap between two shirt buttons. Robin allowed himself a brief, searing moment of entirely selfish gratitude that Edwin's fingers had come through that ordeal intact.

"And Walt doesn't know that Flora Sutton kept research diaries," said Edwin.

Robin groaned. "I suggest a daring stealth adventure, and you have to ruin it by telling me it's going to involve *books*."

"A great many books." Edwin's smile was a tease. "Flora Sutton did magic one-handed, and soaked Sutton in spells I've never seen. I don't think she knew how to practice within the normal rules at all. And—I have her books. I have her land." He directed the smile around the room. "I don't know if I can learn to do what she did, but I'm going to try."

"I think you can probably do anything you set your mind to."

A flush of pleasure stole into Edwin's cheeks, but he said, "I can't stop wondering what might have happened if I'd set it to—the wrong thing. I told you, a month ago Billy's offer might have worked on me. We could have been on opposite sides of this."

"Oh, nonsense," said Robin. "Never would have happened."

"But I—"

"You sat there knowing you were in terrible danger, you were offered all the magic you could want, and you still refused. You were magnificent."

The flush deepened. Robin wanted to make a leather-bound book of his belief and hand it to Edwin, make him read it over and over until Edwin could look in a mirror and see something of what Robin saw.

"I'll have to shape up and pull my weight as well," Robin added. "Get the foresight under control." He glanced at the scab on his hand. "I wonder how this oath of yours defines *truthful report*. I could always try giving the Assembly exhaustive details of some visions and simply leaving others out—that worked for the truth-spell. And especially if I'm to learn to steer it—"

"Robin," Edwin cut in. "Robin, *I don't care about the bloody foresight.*"

Robin stared at him. Edwin dropped his hands from Robin's chest and his colour deepened further. "I mean to say—I do care, but—even if you never had another vision, I'd still want you on my side." Edwin looked so earnest, so determined to have Robin believe in *his* own worth. Every last drop of the anger that Robin had been hoarding against Edwin, for his behaviour at Penhallick, vanished like blood in a cradle.

He grinned. "I'm also a fair hand in a fistfight, it's true."

"Robin—"

"I know what you meant." Robin leaned closer and dropped

a single careful kiss on Edwin's mouth. Edwin made a half-conscious noise of complaint, when Robin pulled away, that was nearly as potent as the blue nerve-magic. "Of course I'm on your side. You complicated my life," Robin said warmly. "You woke me up. You're incredibly brave. You're not kind, but you *care*, deeply. And I think you know how much I want you, in whatever way I can have you."

Edwin reached towards Robin's face and stopped, fingers curling back on themselves. He had the expression of someone who'd hit a stone in their path and was rolling up their sleeves to move it so that the journey could continue.

"I owe you an apology. At Penhallick, I was so afraid, I didn't—I couldn't bring myself to take the next step, even when you were standing there telling me how much it meant to you. To want this. To want . . ."

"You," said Robin. Every time it was easier. It was carving its own groove in his mouth. "I want you."

Edwin closed his eyes. "You could still hurt me," he said. "But I do think you'd somehow manage to tear your own arm off before you did it on purpose." His tone walked a tightrope between disapproval and wonder. "And I'm sick to death of being afraid, and I want *you*. Enough to risk it. More than enough. You make me feel like something—extraordinary."

The things Robin wanted to say thickened in his throat. He put his hands to Edwin's jawline and felt a patch of roughness there where Edwin's morning shave had been less than impeccable; small wonder, given he'd probably had to do it with Walter watching. Edwin swallowed before opening his eyes, and his gaze was naked, somehow, far more naked than a simple disrobing. His hair was a forest of shadows touched with candlelit gold.

Of course I'm on your side, Robin thought numbly. *I'm yours.*

"I want to touch you," he said. "I want to take off everything you're wearing and—just touch you."

Edwin swallowed again. His eyes tightened and Robin thought about the way Edwin had acted when they'd been intimate before now; the way he'd been generous with his actions, with bestowing pleasure, but kept his own pleasure in reserve. Or rushed it to completion before it could be properly observed. The care, the hunger, the drawing-back, the *fear*—how hadn't Robin seen it? *You could still hurt me.* Edwin, who'd learned to hide the things he wanted so completely that he almost didn't let himself want them at all.

Edwin said, "You can. Touch me."

Robin undressed him: waistcoat, necktie, shirt, undershirt. He bent his head to kiss the slope of each shoulder as it was bared to the light, and felt the fine shivers. He rubbed his thumb up and down the gentle undulation of rib cage. He was careful. He wanted to be worthy of the way Edwin was lowering himself into trust like water on the verge of over-hot.

"Stop *stopping,*" said Edwin, with a waspish edge. He claimed Robin's mouth and there was a scrape of teeth to the kiss. Robin grinned and returned it with one that was softer and hotter, punishingly gentle. When Edwin pulled away he was breathing hard; he took a few steps back, raked Robin with his eyes, and said, "Your turn."

Robin hastened to comply. He winced through the discomfort of freeing oneself from one's trousers and drawers when both blood and cock had been stirred into impatient excitement, gave himself a surreptitious stroke, kicked away the last stitch of clothing, and turned to face Edwin.

He hadn't thought he'd feel self-conscious. He'd been undressed amongst other fellows hundreds of times, for sport, and several of his casual encounters while at university had been sufficiently leisurely to involve undressing and the use of a bed. And he'd been naked in front of Edwin before, for goodness' sake.

Even so. It felt different: larger and smaller, more profound and more intimate. Edwin's gaze travelled across his body and reached his face, where it stuck. Edwin had removed his trousers, though he was still in his linen drawers. The effect of Edwin's erection, the flush of it only just visible where it strained against the delicate fabric, was glorious.

"What is it?" said Robin. "What are you thinking?"

Edwin's precise chess-master voice said, "I'm thinking about anticipation. Imagination. I am—wondering if reality can ever truly match them."

"Not for safety," Robin said. Because that was what this was about, wasn't it? "I wouldn't do a thing you don't want, Edwin. I swear it."

"I know." Edwin went to the sideboard and retrieved his drink, which he'd only sipped at. He said, eyes once again intent on Robin, "I need to tell you this now because I know myself, and I know once we get started I may be—unfocused."

"Unfocused?"

"Incoherent," said Edwin, little more than a breath.

Most of Robin's self-control turned to hot air in his lungs, desperate to escape. Edwin threw back the drink, an elegant motion that made light play on his bare collarbones. He set the glass down. "I want you to fuck me," he said. "I want to feel like I can't get away from it. I want everything you have to give." He looked surprised to still be whole once the words were out.

Robin said, mildly strangled, "I told you that you were brave."

"Well?"

"Well—oh. Yes. *Yes.*"

The bed was unnecessarily large. Robin could nearly have lain sideways on it and had an inch to spare at both head and feet.

It was the perfect size, as it turned out, for laying Edwin Courcey out like a feast and tracing every perfect angle of him, every prominence at ankle or elbow or hip bone that begged to be touched.

And by God, did the man's body beg. He was the most sensitive partner Robin had ever had. Some men had spots beneath their jaws that drove them wild, or reacted as though a tickle behind the knees was a caress of the prick. For the most part Robin had discovered these by accident, and enjoyed bringing someone pleasure once he knew they were there, but he'd seldom had the chance to use the knowledge during a second encounter.

Edwin seemed composed entirely of sensitive spots. He shivered when touched. His breath hitched. He made soft, broken noises of enjoyment when Robin finally allowed himself to take each of Edwin's fingers into his mouth, one by one, and suck hungrily on them with pulses of his tongue. It was as though someone had taken a patch of skin that was finely attuned to the drag of fingertips or the teasing brush of lips, and stretched it out thin so that it could cover someone whole. Like bookbinding, Robin thought in a rush of dizzy fondness. Like he could brush his fingers down Edwin's spine—so he reached out and did it, one finger dancing down over knob after knob—and hope that he would splay open and reveal his secrets.

"Come here," Edwin murmured, and tugged Robin closer, turning onto his side so that he could drape a leg across Robin's and push into the side of Robin's hip, the thickening length of him dragging against Robin's skin. He tangled his hand in Robin's hair and used it to command a tilt of Robin's head so that he could nestle his face where Robin's neck splayed out into shoulder.

Robin reached across their bodies and filled his hand with the curve of Edwin's arse, just enjoying the feel of it, as Edwin rocked gently. His own nose was tickled by Edwin's silky hair. When the hardness of Edwin's cock became urgent, Robin pulled away so that there was distance between them once more. Edwin let him do it; he was clumsier now, his movements less defined.

Robin thought about what Edwin had done during the first time they'd been together, when Edwin had draped himself over Robin's shoulder and brought him to climax, then insisted on it fast and hard for himself. He wondered if it was too much of a leap to assume that Edwin's stubborn self-protectiveness had made him ask for the opposite of what he truly needed, and decided it wasn't.

Best, though, to ask.

"Edwin. Do you want me to—draw it out? If I can?"

Edwin shuddered, a fine motion visible only at this close distance. "Yes," he said, rough as sandpaper. "Yes."

Robin moved down the bed, shifting himself around so that he had easy access to Edwin's cock. Edwin made a noise in the back of his throat, mutely demanding, but when Robin put his hands on Edwin's thighs to settle himself between them, they were tense. Edwin was still. His stomach heaved with his breath. He was visibly fighting, torn between want and wariness, and Robin ached for him. This was a time to be absolutely sure, for both of them.

Robin stroked his thumb in the crease at the top of Edwin's leg, soothing over the tendons, savouring the softness of the skin there. Slowing down like this, he was aware of the heaviness of his own cock, full and needy between his legs. Edwin's cock was straining, glistening at the tip.

Robin caught Edwin's eye and said, deliberately, "May I use my mouth on you?"

A choked sound. "Yes. Anything. Please."

"You're the one who warned me about the danger of open contracts."

"*Robin*."

"Edwin," said Robin earnestly, "I really think you need to *understand* this before you *consent* to it—"

Edwin leaned back on the pillow and laughed, that glorious silver laugh like water on rocks. His foot nudged Robin in the ribs, and Robin sucked in a breath—that was a sore spot he hadn't realised was there, probably from where the chair had crashed into him earlier—but didn't once consider pulling away.

"All right," said Edwin. "Consider me warned." He lifted himself onto elbows, looking down his body at Robin with humour that bled at the edges to wariness, and then melted altogether into an expression that took Robin's breath away. "Thank you," Edwin said, very soft. And let his thighs settle apart, slackening into the relaxed welcome that had been missing before.

Robin, satisfied, bent his head to taste him. He'd been anticipating this for so long that his mouth was watering. Even so, it took a little while for him to reaccustom himself to the sensations: the shape and weight of a cock on his tongue, the strain of his jaw, the salty taste of fine skin.

When he took a full half of Edwin's length into his mouth and sucked hard, he realised that Edwin hadn't been exaggerating at all with the word *incoherent*. Edwin seemed to be trying to rip up handfuls of the bedclothes like weeds. The sounds he made now were just as sweet, just as responsive—but bewildered, nearly edged with pain. A symphony of breathy vocal pants and whines as his hips tried to rise.

Robin pulled back enough to focus, and recognised in a crash of heat and wonder the vision he'd had that very first night. Edwin a painting of pleasure, laid out on pale sheets. Edwin's face, the obscene *O* of his mouth—the agonised and beautiful line of his neck, like a tortured saint. Looking at him made Robin feel *reverent*.

He could see why Edwin would be afraid of this. Of bringing it into the light and sharing it with someone. Robin wanted Edwin not to regret his decision for a moment. They'd been through so much, had so much threatened and taken so much hurt. Edwin deserved all the pleasure that Robin could give him, and more.

He'd forgotten; he was meant to be drawing it out. Robin

abandoned suction and kept to soft, wet movements: circles of his tongue, openmouthed kisses just beneath the head. Teasing dips of his tongue into the slit, which made Edwin's legs shake. Robin pulled back entirely, light-headed with his own want. He knelt up, wiping his mouth with the back of his hand.

"I'm trying like hell to take it slow, I really am," he said. "But if you do still want me to fuck you, I don't feel you should credit me with more restraint than I actually have."

Edwin looked questioningly at him, brow furrowed.

"I'll be going off untouched in another few minutes if I have to keep watching you, and then I'll be no use at all," Robin clarified.

A smile glimmered through the wreck of Edwin's features. "In my bag," he said, waving a hand in that direction.

No hair oil this time, but a jar of petroleum jelly—"For chapped lips," Edwin explained, as though Robin honestly gave a damn at that point.

More of those pained noises emerged from Edwin's mouth as Robin carefully stretched him, slicked him, generous with the clear jelly. Robin had to stop and breathe when Edwin was clenched hot around his fingers. He had to drop shaky kisses on Edwin's stomach, on the line of blond hair leading down from the navel. He felt nearly overwhelmed with responsibility, with tenderness, with Edwin having walked open-eyed into this room and placed his most vulnerable self in Robin's hands.

He helped Edwin bend his legs, knees splayed wide and lifted back enough to allow Robin access. He took himself in hand. Lined up. And pushed, biting down on his own lip, feeling the immediate throb of pleasure as he worked past the initial resistance. He stopped, just like that, just the head of himself stretching Edwin open. It was torture. It was incredible.

"All right?" he said, a breath.

"All right."

Robin kissed him again, a soft promise of a bite that dragged

Edwin's lip between his own. Leaning down changed the angle and sank him in further. He remembered what Edwin had said about wanting to feel like he couldn't get away, and guided Edwin's arms up one at a time to lie just beneath the corners of the pillow. He laid his own hands over Edwin's wrists, testing the pressure.

"Is this—shall I—?"

Edwin nodded. His eyes were dark as dusk and he looked drunk. Effortfully, Robin held himself still. He was aware of his size in comparison to Edwin's, aware of the muscles of his arms and chest and legs. He had a near-delirious moment of knowing how this must feel from Edwin's perspective: being both absolutely trapped and absolutely secure.

Then Edwin lifted his head and kissed Robin, very light, finding Robin's mouth and landing a little off-centre. Warmth like summer noon flooded through Robin and he chased the kiss down to the pillow, his cock sinking further into Edwin, inch by inch. He was greedy; he took every sound of Edwin's into his own mouth, a kiss that demanded all of Edwin's attention.

Then he was all the way in, the two of them flush together. Robin drew out, perhaps halfway. He shoved in again at once, harder than he'd meant to, and Edwin gave a shout that was nearly a sob. And everything began to blur.

Who needed magic for this? Pleasure shot through Robin as though painted on his skin at every point of contact; as though something older and more guttural than magic was struck, tinder to flint, by his hands at Edwin's wrists, by the sudden and wonderful clench of Edwin's legs lifting to wrap around his back, driving him further in. All of these mingled with the sensation of fucking, liquid heat winding tight in his groin whenever he sank into the slicked grip of Edwin's body.

Sweat ran into Robin's eyes and stung them. He wouldn't have closed them for the world. Edwin was unravelling fully beneath him, thrust after brutal thrust. Edwin's fair head tossed back and forth in snaps. Edwin's own sweat gathered in the dip of his throat as he made short, ragged gasps that became ever more frantic, and which seemed to find their way directly to Robin's cock.

Robin had wanted to hold out, to wring Edwin's orgasm from him first, but his own came in a rush that couldn't be stopped, like fire from Edwin's hands engulfing dry thorns, hotter and wilder than anything had been before. Robin gasped, and sucked in a breath that nearly hurt, as his body brimmed with fading pleasure.

"Robin," Edwin was saying, broken and writhing beneath him, *"Robin."*

Robin wrenched his wits back together. He wanted to see this happen. He released one wrist, wrapped his hand around Edwin's cock and stroked once, twice, three times, rocking his hips with the same rhythm—and Edwin's eyes flew open, startled and blue and sure.

He was surprisingly quiet when he came, as though all the noise had been wrung out of him already. In the jubilant flare of the candlelight he was the loveliest thing Robin had ever seen.

EPILOGUE

"Good morning, Edwin."

"Good morning, Adelaide. Is he in?" Edwin inquired, as though the door into the Office of Special Domestic Affairs and Complaints weren't flung wide open, and as though he couldn't hear the sound of Robin's boot thumping against the leg of the desk.

They were still professionals, after all.

"Don't be daft," said Adelaide Morrissey, who had an alarming tendency to treat one like a childhood intimate as soon as one agreed to be on first-name terms. Robin had said she treated them like siblings; Edwin had argued that Robin was coming from a position of possessing an unfairly superior example of a sibling.

Robin had made a face and accused Edwin, amiably, of playing the lawyer just because *his* brother was a murdering sadist.

"Edwin!" Robin called now. "Is that you? It's past nine, you're late."

Edwin hung up his coat and hat, and came into the office, Adelaide on his heels. Robin was seated on the desk. He'd recently passed out of the mourning period, which meant they were all being treated to Robin's startling—and yet absolutely unsurprising—fondness for colour. In a building full of civil servants whose ventures out of the usual black-and-white office attire were constrained to the occasional necktie in respectable shades of olive and navy, Robin was the man wearing a maroon waistcoat with gold buttons. He looked as bright and warm as ever. Edwin nearly tripped on the edge of the rug, simply enjoying the sight of him, and enjoying even more the tiny kernel of possession inside him that split and sent out a green shoot of happiness. *Mine. This one's mine.*

"I lost track of time at breakfast. I was reading," said Edwin.

Adelaide mimed genteel shock. Robin grinned. "The diaries again? Any leads on the cup and the knife?"

"It'd be going a lot faster if she hadn't insisted on using code names for everything, as though she were some sort of intelligence agent engaged in high-level treason," said Edwin ruefully. "Even in her private diaries. Not that I'm surprised."

Edwin was learning that Flora Sutton had been as busy and brilliant as she was untrusting and suspicious. In the previous century, when women were even less likely to be taught anything in the way of systematic magic, she and three of her friends had formed a kind of ladies' club and simply . . . done it themselves. They'd looked into the land as a source of magic, and thus into the story of the Last Contract, and spent years tracking the items to a medieval church in a small town in Yorkshire. And then years more trying to erase that fact, because they'd realised what could be done with the contract by those without scruples.

"Speaking of magical items." Robin pulled a shilling from his pocket and held it out. "My very own pass token for the Barrel."

"You had another meeting? How did this one go?"

Robin shrugged. "I gave them enough excruciating details about that vision of a horse race that I nearly bored *myself* to death. That chap Knox they've roped in as my handler looked rather glad to see the back of me, by the end of it." Robin's visions had become much less frequent since he'd begun to learn the trick of allowing them in at will. He still only had the barest amount of control over what he would see. They were working on it, as on so many things.

"I saw that blond woman again," Robin added. "I'm thinking

of giving her a name, for reference—how do we feel about Harriet? She was on a ship. One of those big ocean liners. Just as Lord Hawthorn was, the first time I saw him."

Edwin had been on a ferry exactly once in his life and had *felt* the shade of green he'd turned. "I'm not convinced that any boats are in my future," he said. "And I'd prefer if Hawthorn wasn't either."

Robin smiled. "I'll tell you at once if I ever see myself punching him, how's that?"

"Could you pretend you *did* see that, and describe it for me in excruciating detail?"

"Could you instead set the violent fantasies aside until morning tea?" said Adelaide. "And ditto for any imminent lectures on liminality, thank you, Edwin. They're easier to digest when delivered with biscuits."

Liminal spaces were the basis of Flora Sutton's system of magical practice, and Edwin was still teasing out the extent to which she and her friends had learned it in pieces or developed it themselves. Life and death. Night and day—oh, that too had been in that silly poem all along. *The gifts of the dawn*. Seasons and solstices. It was all highly agricultural. Edwin was having to develop a keen interest in gardening to follow along with her notes.

And Edwin had thought, at one time, that there was nobody in England doing truly original work.

Two days ago, Edwin had sat in the rose garden at Sutton Cottage and called up an echo-illusion of Flora Sutton carefully cutting a bloom with scissors. It wasn't her true spirit; only a memory imprinted on the air. She couldn't hear Edwin, when he pledged himself to avenge her and Reggie the only way he knew how: to continue her work with the old magics, and to find her contemporaries and warn them. To do his best to ensure that nobody would use the contract as she'd feared it might be used.

He could only hope that her land, which was now Edwin's land, and in whose thriving green lawn he'd buried his fingers as the image of the woman faded, had both heard and felt the strength of his intent. Mrs. Sutton had lived her last hour with the guilt of sending Reggie to his death. That guilt, along with the burgeoning kinship she'd felt with Edwin's magic, was what had been enough at the moment of her death to tip Sutton over into accepting Edwin as her heir, and thereby save *his* life. Edwin was sure of this without being able to say why. He could only assume it had been written on the blank spaces of him, somehow, in the incoherent moment when he banished Walt; when he *was* the Sutton lands, and the house.

It wasn't up to Edwin to decide if he was worthy. He had been chosen, and he would fight to live up to it. Chosen twice over, in fact; his heart lightened again as he met Robin's affectionate smile.

"I did have something to show you," he said, trying for offhand.

He came and leaned against the desk next to where Robin sat. He breathed deeply and bent his will to the thought of what he wanted to achieve. One hand position. And then another. The transition was important; he'd discovered that after weeks of stubborn experimentation and muscle cramps.

Edwin hadn't realised how rigidly his mind had grown around certain structures until he'd begun, painstakingly, to deconstruct them. Performing magic with single-handed gesture was like learning a new language from scratch—more, it was like building a new alphabet yourself because none existed that would suit. It felt like grinding away at a piece of sandstone, slow and wearying and deeply satisfying.

Robin gave an encouraging whoop. "There! I can see it!"

There. In proper daylight it would have been barely visible, but here in this poorly lit office the tiny white light made Edwin's fingers look ghostly.

"A none too marvellous light," said Edwin dryly. "For my next trick, I shall fly to the top of Nelson's Column, and bring the lions to life."

Adelaide tucked a pencil behind her ear and came closer to look. "It's still something. Good job."

Edwin watched the pale glow in his palm, unfelt but undeniable. Despite his sarcasm he was fiercely, wonderfully proud, even if that feeling was new enough that he was still making space inside himself for it.

Walt had been right: Edwin was safest on Sutton grounds, but he'd inherited far more than power and property. He wasn't going to skulk there within the warding like a fox in a hole. Not when there was so much to be done. He thought about all of the books yet unread, and the blond woman, and Lord Hawthorn, and the danger of setting themselves up against a group of powerful figures who included Edwin's brother.

He leaned sideways and encountered Robin's shoulder, firm and warm against his.

"It's a good start," he said. "Let's see if I can get it any brighter."

And he paused, in the space between inhalation and exhalation, and invited magic in.

ACKNOWLEDGMENTS

It's long been a suspicion of mine that you can tell a debut novel by the length of the acknowledgments, and I've no intention of diverging from tradition. Buckle in.

Firstly, a book about the responsibility we owe to the places we live would be incomplete without the acknowledgment that I wrote most of these words on unceded Ngunnawal country, where the traditional owners have been the land's caretakers for many thousands of years.

And now for all the thanks.

To Alex and Macey, my co-conspirators and fellow serpents. Everyone should have writer friends, I have a tendency to say, cheerfully and sagely and with deceptive ease. What I mean, every time, is: find someone who'll support you and laugh with you and share the journey with you, the way you two have for me. I have now used up my allotment of sincerity for the decade and you can expect nothing from me but irony and dry insults until 2030.

To Magali Ferare, for devouring each chapter as it was written. To Emily Tesh, for caring so hard about these boys. To Kelsey, Becca Fraimow, Marina Berlin, and Iona Datt Sharma for their invaluable comments on various drafts. To Sam Hawke and Leife Shallcross for sitting on my couch and letting me make them cocktails. To Jenn Lyons for keeping me motivated and laughing, even when it was my turn to hold the self-pity stick.

To the people of Fox Literary: Isabel Kaufman, Ari Brezina,

and my indomitable agent, Diana Fox, who never stopped believing in this story and who told me to stop sending characters into sex scenes with severe injuries. Sorry. I'd say I don't intend to do it again, but we all know it would be a lie.

To the team at Tordotcom Publishing: my incredible editor, Ruoxi Chen, who fought for this book and made it better, and everyone else who made it happen, including but not limited to Irene Gallo, Caro Perny, and Renata Sweeney.

At Tor UK, I have to thank the fabulous Bella Pagan, Georgia Summers, Becky Lushey, and the enthusiastic Black Crow PR team. I'm so glad the book found a home with you too.

Especial thanks to Will Staehle for that stunning, grabs-you-and-won't-let-go cover design. And to the late Misters Morris and de Morgan, to say nothing of Singer Sargent and Turner and Rennie Macintosh and every other artist whose visuals found their way into this book. I'd like to apologise to Wightwick Manor for nicking so many of its design elements—Penhallick, the Cambridgeshire house with the Cornish name, was heavily inspired by this wonderful National Trust property in the West Midlands. If you're in the area, I highly recommend a visit.

To the coven of booksellers who read and championed this book even before it had things like "a cover" or "physical form," and to everyone who's blogged, tweeted, 'grammed, 'tubed, or 'tokked about it: I'm in awe, and thank you.

To all the writers who came before me and created the stories that were my building blocks, the books that held me together and made me strive to do better. A fond and grateful toast to the memories of Terry Pratchett, Diana Wynne Jones, Georgette Heyer, Joan Aiken, P. G. Wodehouse, Dorothy Dunnett, and Dorothy L. Sayers. And to my contemporaries in SFF, who are making the genre wider and deeper and richer and weirder and queerer: I'm thrilled and honoured to be working at the same time as you, in the same spaces as you.

To Cosmas, who I hope reads this one day: you were the

warp to my weft at a time when the fabric of me was forming, and I know I wouldn't have made it to this point without our friendship.

To my siblings, for growing up wrapped in fantasy books along with me and sharing my exact sense of humour, and to my parents for being wonderful, loving, supportive people who are nothing whatsoever like any of the parents in this book. (And a special shout-out to my mother, who was the first person to tell me that she couldn't put this book down, and who forgave me for making her read the sexy bits.)

And finally, I owe thanks to everyone who watched me learn to write, live and in technicolour on the internet, and whose comments and fellowship kept me going through the long years while I built my toolkit. Fandom, this one's for you. Keep talking about the things that interest you; don't let anyone teach you otherwise.

ABOUT THE AUTHOR

FREYA MARSKE is one of the cohosts of *Be the Serpent,* a Hugo Award–nominated podcast about SFF, fandom, and literary tropes. Her work has appeared in *Analog Science Fiction and Fact* and been short-listed for Best Fantasy Short Story in the Aurealis Awards. She lives in Australia.

freyamarske.com